K.B. Wood

The Prodigal's Foole

A Novel of the Arcana Chronicles

PfoxChase Publishing

PfoxChase, a division of Pfoxmoor Publishing
4972 Lowhill Church Road
New Tripoli, PA 18066 USA

www.pfoxmoorpublishing.com
www.pfoxchase.com

The Prodigal's Foole

Copyright ©2011 by R.B. Wood

Print ISBN: 978-1-936827-33-6
Digital ISBN (PDF): 978-1-936827-34-3
Digital ISBN (EPUB): 978-1-936827-35-0

Cover by R.B. Wood and Sessha Batto

This is a work of fiction. Names, characters, places and incidents either are the product of the authors' imaginations or are used fictitiously and any resemblance to actual persons, living or dead, business establishments, events or locales is entirely coincidental.

All rights reserved. No part of this book may be used or reproduced or transmitted in any form or by any means, electronic or mechanical, including photocopying, recording, or by any information storage and retrieval system, without written permission from the copyright owner except in the case of brief quotations embodied in critical articles and reviews.

First PfoxChase electronic publication: October 2011
First PfoxChase print publication: October 2011

Published in the United States of America with international distribution.

Dedication

For my muse, partner and love of my life, Tina,
who stands by my side no matter what.

For my mother and father who taught me everything with love.

And for my children who retaught me how to dream

Acknowledgements

I blame Neil Gaiman.

Well, not *just* Mr. Gaiman. There's Arthur Conan Doyle, Mark Twain, J. R. R. Tolkien, Jim Butcher, J. K. Rowling, Alan Moore, H. G. Wells, Jules Verne, James Morrow and many, many others.

Dreamers. Storytellers.

They all had a hand in this obsession of mine to write.
A fellow author and dear friend of mine, Sean Develin, recently said to me: "The beauty of middle age is that we now actually *finish* what we start." Both he and Chris Davis—old comrades for many years—started me down a writing path back in the eighties. We'd develop grand ideas, fantastic dialogs, and build whole worlds.
And then we'd drink some beer and the conversations would drift off to other topics.
Since then, Sean has become a writer and a consultant. Chris develops live shows for his stint as 'The Renaissance Man.' And I built a career in the technology world.
Fast forward to 2007, when my children, whom I always spun tales for when they were little, both said to me "Dad, you should write your stories down." My partner agreed. And thus, the Arcana Chronicles, and *The Prodigal's Foole* were born.
Writing in the 21st century is very different than when I dabbled with crafting stories when I was younger. Social media didn't exist back then. Neither did ebooks nor the number of Indie Publishers that have embraced the new mediums of publishing that exist today. It's a whole new world and the possibilities are exciting.

Which leads me to the surprising fact that it still took a lot of people to get my book published.

My "alpha" readers—family for the most part (my partner, mother and sister) all made comments for the very first draft of the book. My cousins did a read through of the second draft, joined by my beta readers (and WONDERFUL friends) Leah Petersen, Eden Baylee, Deb Moses, K. A. Storm, J. D. Robinson, Karen Smith, Matthew Munson, Tesse Conte, Kate Danley and Emmett Spain. Most are authors I "met" through Twitter.

There was the 50-page critique I won via an online auction done superbly (and encouragingly) by Amy Boggs, an agent for The Donald Maass Agency in New York. And editing by C. A Marshall.

But the most amazing set of editing and comments came from my brother, Charles Wood. They say you should never let family edit your manuscript. "They" never met my brother. Nor have "they" met his wicked-sharp red pen.

Of course there is also the creative director for Pfoxchase, Diane Nelson, whose eye for detail and ability to make me laugh while ripping a scene to shreds is unique in my experience.

I'm sure I've left out folks—but you know who you are and you know how absent-minded I can be.

With that all said, I sincerely hope you enjoy what follows.

R. B. Wood
OCTOBER 2011

Chapter One

Present Day

The old lady next to me in the window seat died somewhere over the Atlantic. I know because she told me.

"Symon Bryson."

The husky voice surprised me. I hadn't spoken to anyone either at Dublin airport or on the flight. I first looked to my right the see the well-built, mustached man sleeping next to me. By the number of empty little bottles of vodka on his tray table, I guessed that his sleep wasn't due to exhaustion.

"Symon Bryson. Look at me."

I turned slowly to look at the old lady. She was staring at me through milky-white eyes, smiling.

"Who are you?" I asked cautiously.

Most people would freak out if a corpse suddenly reanimated and wanted to have a nice chat with them. Not me.

I'd seen worse.

"Who I am matters not," croaked the old woman.

"Yoda?" I asked. No one in the supernatural world of Heaven and Hell—the Shadow-world—gets pop culture references. It's a sad commentary on the priorities of the Shadow-world.

"I have a warning for you. Fortunately this body died so I could use it to speak with you."

"Oh goodie," I said, sighing. "Lay it on me then."

"Your return to Boston at this time is not happenstance."

"Look, dead lady," I snarled, pulling a scrap of paper from my pocket. "I'm going to see the Monsignor, find out what this telegram he sent is all about, and get the hell back to Dublin as soon as humanly possible. Who the hell sends a telegram in this day and age anyway?"

"You must not give in to your powers, Symon," the creepy dead lady hissed. "You are the strongest Practitioner of this age. But you are undisciplined and dangerous."

"I don't plan on using any magic," I said.

"You never plan it, Symon. That is your biggest problem. Let me show you what you could be."

With that, she put a cold, dead hand on my arm and the vision began.

****

"Get the fuck off this plane! Now!"

"Sir, the captain has not turned off the 'fasten seat belt' sign. Please sit down and calm yourself," a flight attendant firmly stated, voice slightly raised.

"You heard me," I shouted, ignoring the flight attendant. "Out. Now."

The old woman was trembling, her soft, baggy eyes welling up with tears.

"Captain, we have a problem with one of the passengers," the attendant announced into the cabin intercom. "I need some help in the main cabin."

"Hey, buddy," the bearded man in the aisle seat slurred, "Why don't you leave the old lady alone? C'mon, I'll buy you a drink."

The drunk was nothing. A flick of my hand and he flew from his seat, pinned to the roof of the cabin.

People screamed, I ignored the sounds of terror. Passengers beneath the man scrambled to get out from under him.

"I know who you are, old woman. Last chance to get off this plane or I'll throw you out." We'd all die if I couldn't rid the aircraft of what I *knew* to be a creature of Hell.

"Sir! Sit down!" the flight attendant shouted, finally losing her cool. Her colleague approached from the rear of the aircraft, taser in hand. The plane banked sharply. The pilot turned the aircraft around.

The old lady looked up at me and smiled.

"Go ahead, Symon Bryson," she hissed in an unearthly voice. "Use your power. Do it."

Flame shot from my hand and engulfed the old woman. She laughed as the heat melted her seat and blackened her window. She laughed harder when the side of the plane blew out.

Wind howled around me at the immediate decompression and oxygen masks dropped in front of the screaming and terrified passengers. The plane lurched and groaned as a second piece of the fuselage broke away.

I ignored it all. If I could send the demon back to Hell, I could save the innocents.

Anyone not strapped in was sucked out of the aircraft, tossed out like a rag doll while I stood in the center of the wreckage pouring even more fire into the cackling cronc.

Aer Lingus flight 332 rolled over and began its twenty-thousand-foot death spiral, and all I could hear was the old woman's laughter.

"Remember this lesson, Symon…"

****

I awoke from the vision with a start as my flight touched down on the runway. I was drenched in a cold sweat and my hands hurt from grasping the armrests of my center seat. The window seat where the old woman had been was empty.

The overhead speakers cracked, "Aer Lingus would like to welcome you to Boston's Logan Airport. We enjoyed flying with you and hope you enjoy your stay."

"I'm not staying," I muttered.

I have too much power and I don't know how to use it. With great power comes a great capacity to fuck things up, I thought.

No shit. That's why I left a decade ago. Dozens of innocents had their lives snuffed out by one overly arrogant, out-of-control prick. The vision wasn't very different from every dream I'd had since. A decade of guilt and self-loathing changes a man.

After what seemed an eternity, we stopped at the gate with a jolt. Before the little light and bell went off, I unbuckled myself and stepped over my drunken, bearded row mate to get into the aisle as quickly as I could. *The faster I get off the damn plane the faster I can get back on a return flight.*

I grabbed my bag from the overhead bin and pushed my way to the front muttering "Sorry," without really meaning it. The door opened onto the jet-way and I could immediately feel the damp, chilly air that was typical of early spring in New England. Between the weather and my nightmares, my mood couldn't have been worse. I walked up the ramp into the airport terminal with the horrifying vision playing over and over in my head.

I exited the ramp with a start. It was a madhouse. There were a lot more people than I'd expected milling about. Then I remembered with a groan. Tomorrow was the Boston Marathon. The crowds added to the black cloud over my head.

I moved with the rest of the herd downstairs to customs and eventually made it to baggage claim. I saw lovers reuniting. Tired children complaining. Businessmen flicking open their cell phones. Voyeurism is a bit of a hobby of mine. It distracts me from my darker thoughts.

I waited and watched people for about ten minutes in baggage claim until the buzzer sounded and the carousel jerked to life. Still indulging my voyeuristic tendencies, I didn't notice when a smallish man bent over to grab my worn leather bag until his hand brushed mine on the straps.

"Sorry mate," I muttered. "That's..." I broke off as I looked at the man and met a pair of twinkling blue eyes, my bag momentarily forgotten. The smile on his face was broad and friendly but was nothing compared to my widening grin. "Peter!" I exclaimed. Bag momentarily forgotten, I practically picked the small man up in a bear hug that was enthusiastically returned.

Father Peter Fine had lost some hair since I'd seen him last, grown a bit in the middle as well. But his vestments fit him as if they were tailored and the mischievous twinkle in his eyes was as bright as I'd remembered.

"Symon Bryson. You look like hell." We released each other, silly grins still plastered on our faces. "You are a sight for sore eyes, my son. I wish the Monsignor were here to see you for himself."

I hadn't expected to be picked up. The plan was to jump into a cab and head straight to the old parish in Cambridge. I was going to use the trip to steel myself for the uncomfortable reunion with Monsignor Charles DuBarry. After all, it was the telegram about my estranged mentor crumpled in my pocket that was the sole reason I'd returned to Boston. Despite the fact that Peter had appeared unexpectedly, the sight of my old friend had a welcome calming effect. He's always had a knack for that, and he knew it. I expected that's why he'd come to fetch me.

As we released each other from the emotional—but very manly—display of affection, I took a closer look at Father Fine, and was shocked. Of course he had aged, hadn't we all? But he also looked exhausted, more so than I'd ever seen him back in the day. His eyes looked sunken and were surrounded by layers of shadow. The twinkle I'd seen in them a moment ago was replaced by a pulsating, nervous tick. There was a grayish tinge to his skin and he had a deep worry line over his brow. Peter was normally one of those people who lived the philosophy that the glass was always half full and that God would provide the second half in due course. Now I got the feeling that the metaphoric glass had been broken.

"I got your telegram," I said, "and despite the urge to bin the bloody thing, I jumped on the first flight I could get. What's going on?"

"Not here, Sy," Peter replied in a low voice. "I have a car waiting for us."

Peter hadn't called me "Sy" since I'd been a kid. Disturbing images swirled in my head as we waited in uncomfortable silence for my bag to make its way back around to us on the carousel. A million and one questions occurred to me all at once. The cryptic telegram had hinted at trouble and had concerned me enough to actually drop everything and fly back to my old home. Peter's appearance and mysterious lack of information downright scared me. A long time ago a group of us had been specially trained to fight the power of Hell. We'd been right on the front lines in a fight that made the conflicts currently in the news look like a schoolyard brawl. It had been a cluster fuck of gargantuan proportions that had broken us—broken me. Now things from nightmares I'd spent a decade trying to forget crept out of hiding and into the forefront of my brain.

Together we made our way through the crush of the crowd toward the exit. Outside the terminal there was a large, black, four-door sedan idling at the curb. A well-dressed brute of a man stood by the car.

Bald and with the build of a professional wrestler, he saw Peter and me and parted the sea of people streaming out of the airport with ease. The large man reminded of Mongo from *Blazing Saddles*, albeit a hairless version of that bull-riding, horse-punching character. Mongo looked me up and down once and gave a little "harrumph." If he knew what I could do when I got pissed off, he might not have dismissed me out-of-hand. Of course when I saw him open the back door for Peter and me with a hand the size of a dinner plate, I wasn't so sure I'd win that fight.

"Sy, this is Mr. Flint," Peter gestured at the large man.

Flint nodded to me once. Heading for the driver's side of our ride, he held up one of those massive meat hooks, and with surprising delicacy released the trunk lid. I heard a slight 'pop' and the trunk flew open. He stepped aside for me to toss my bag in, leaving me to slam the trunk lid closed a little harder then I'd intended.

Peter jumped in first, still clutching my other bag.

"Be careful with that, Peter! There are things in there that shouldn't be jostled," I said.

I followed Peter into the back of the Town Car, watching Flint warily as he squeezed himself into the driver's seat. His jacket opened slightly and I caught a glimpse of Sig or a Glock in a shoulder holster. Holy crap. This was no rent-a-cop. Peter had a bodyguard.

Flint gestured toward the smoking area, steeped in shadows near where Peter and I had exited. From behind one of the massive cement columns that held up the terminal overhang, a man quickly approached the car. It was the bearded drunk from the plane, looking very alert and very sober. I whirled toward my friend, suddenly furious.

"What the hell, Peter?" I practically spat. "That's the guy who was sitting next to me on the goddamn plane. Did you have me *followed*? Who are these goons? And what the bloody hell is going on?"

"Bear with me, Sy," hissed Peter, his jaw tensed with stress. "Close the door. I'll tell you what I can."

I hesitated for a second as I considered going back into the airport and immediately booking a seat on the next flight back to Dublin. I looked at Peter and, still fuming, slammed the door closed. I had to control my anger. Bad things happened when I got angry.

The vision of the cackling crone taunted me. *Go ahead, Symon Bryson, use your power. Do it.*

The bearded man jumped into the passenger seat next to Flint.

"Mr. Kowalski, is everything in order?" Peter asked the newcomer.

"Padre," said the smaller man, turning toward us and nodding at Peter. "All clear. We are good to go. Mr. Bryson wasn't followed."

"Except by you," I shot back at him. Kowalski glanced at me once and turned back around, motioning Flint to get moving. Although the steering wheel looked like a toy in his massive hands, the big man had a surprisingly delicate touch as he slid our ride from the curb and into the airport traffic.

"Okay," I turned to Peter, "spill it." But Peter shushed me yet again and closed the dividing window between the back passenger compartment and the men sitting up front. Once we were in motion and the privacy panel in place, Peter sat back and relaxed.

"I'm sorry, Sy. According to Charles, this," he pointed at the men in front of us, "is a necessary precaution."

Peter looked at me. "It really is good to see you again, Symon."

"It's really good to see you too, but I want some answers," I fumed. "I'm only here because I got a telegram saying that Charles was in trouble and I needed to get to Boston, pronto. So please explain to me why I shouldn't have Frick and Frack up there turn the car around and take me straight back to the terminal."

"Charles hasn't been himself lately," Peter said distractedly. "Something is happening and it's big, but he won't tell me what it is. He just told me to send telegrams and to arrange for heavy security."

"Heavy security for ... wait. Telegrams? How many did he ask you to send?" acid churned in the pit of my stomach as I was sure I knew the answer already.

"A few," Peter wouldn't meet my gaze. He ticked off fingers on his hand. "I contacted Aaron, Eden, Eve, Bill and..."

"Janice," we said together.

Crap. The old man got himself into something, all right. And now I was going to be dragged into it too, with one crazy old pastor and five people I'd rather not see again, ever, thank you very much. Especially Janice. Double crap.

"Peter," I growled, my frayed nerves making it come out a little harsher than I meant. "Why in God's name would Charles want the six of us back together? He knows how we all feel about each other. And after what happened at Plum Island, we all swore off Charles' damn crusade once and for all. Hell," I added, "I'm not sure he didn't *cause* the mess we got ourselves into in the first place."

"Never say that again!" Peter growled, eyes flaring. "Charles would *never* have caused it!"

The priest closed his eyes for a moment and took a deep breath. When he finally opened them, I could see he was close to tears. The ice on my heart melted a little.

"I don't know what's going on with the Monsignor, Symon." Peter said softly, his worry lines deepening. "I really don't. But what I *do* know is that, whatever it is, it's bad enough that he had me send for all of you and hire extra security," he nodded forward at Flint and Kowalski. "Out of his own pocket."

Jesus. Whatever trouble the old man was in was extremely bad. Now I'm not implying Charles was cheap. He'd raised the others and me, after all. And we never wanted for food or any necessity. But if you looked up the word *frugal* in the dictionary there would be a great big picture of Monsignor Charles DuBarry looking down at you. So when I tell you for him to shell out his own money for top security, it meant there was serious trouble—and not the kind his parish could help out with. As images of past horrors danced around in my head, the car moved swiftly onto Storrow Drive. I was worried. I guess I should have mentioned it before, but the Monsignor had a unique way of fighting evil. He used magic. Not the "bunny out of the hat" type. He was an honest-to-God sorcerer. The good kind, of course. And since I'm in a confessional sort of mood, I should also mention that I'm one too. Charles was my teacher, and he had taught a group of hand-picked students how to wield magic like in the stories I'd heard as a kid. But I'd left that world ten years ago because I wasn't prepared to deal with the consequences. I wondered how painful it would be if I just jumped out of the car right now.

But the Monsignor always could take care of himself. He was literally a warrior of God in the fight against evil. Charles had a powerful belief in God and the Church. He also had what was considered by the Catholic Oligarchy to be a "Holy Gift." The Vatican, of course, officially frowned on such things. But Charles' work—and for a while it was the work of his charges, myself included—was necessary to keep the balance. If Charles had taken the chance we'd respond to a call and come back to him, that meant one of two things—either the Monsignor had lost some of his game and desperately needed us, or he wanted to have a reunion party. I was pretty sure there weren't any party hats in my future.

Peter and I sat in silence for a few moments. I tried to imagine the sort of trouble that Charles couldn't handle by himself and shuddered. Why bodyguards? And, to be honest, I wasn't sure how these heavily armed goons would be able to protect us from a demon's curse with mere bullets.

I couldn't believe I was about to get pulled back into a world I'd deliberately turned my back on. After we had gotten our asses handed to us on Plum Island ten years ago, the group broke up. It wasn't a cowardice thing, honest. We all believed that what we were doing had gotten to a point where the pain and suffering we were causing outweighed any good we might do. People had died by my own hands and we'd had enough. Obviously Charles and Peter had continued the work without us.

I looked over at Peter. Worry lines creased his forehead. No doubt he was concerned about his long-time friend and mentor. I forced myself to focus on what potential horror had caused Charles to reach out to his ex-pupils. And—I'm not ashamed to admit it—a part of me thought about how I could get my sorry ass extracted from whatever this situation was, and back into my nice warm flat in Dublin as soon as possible.

Our car crossed the Longfellow Bridge into Cambridge. A Red Line train clacked past us, heading back into Boston and I watched it longingly as it travelled away from the apparent danger we were heading toward. We drove past hotels, businesses, and large laboratories owned mostly by MIT and moved into an older, more residential neighborhood. The roads were narrower here, and Flint slowed down accordingly. I noticed that he and Kowalski were looking in their mirrors more frequently. The smaller man in particular was checking the view out of each window so quickly that I thought he might give himself whiplash. We were in my old neighborhood now and the brownstones were close together, clustered in a way that made our bodyguards obviously nervous.

Night had fallen and despite the car's heater, there was a biting cold to the air. I'd like to say that the chill was due to the early spring weather in New England, but I never was good at self-denial.

Something about the play of lights in the homes on either side of the street, aided perhaps by my imagination, seemed to taunt me with a tapestry of horrors from my past. As I continued to stare out the window, brooding, I slowly realized the lights were no longer just a steady yellowish glow from the brownstones, but strobing blue and red as well. The rhythmic flashing seemed to be coming from someplace in front of us. Our escorts had noticed it too and the car slowed down to a crawl. Kowalski tapped on the glass dividing us, and Peter lowered the privacy partition.

"Sir, I think there are emergency vehicles up ahead. Want us to go around?"

"No, that's okay Mr. Kowalski," said Peter. "St. Ignatius is right around the corner. Park the car here and we'll pop out and see what the trouble is."

Flint pulled the car toward the curb as I looked around. I was so lost in my own thoughts that I hadn't noticed we were only one block away from the familiar church and dormitories that had once been my home. The four of us got out of the sedan, our two bodyguards with their hands in their jackets. With Flint in front and Kowalski behind us, Peter and I made our way to the end of the street. The flashing lights grew brighter and the source became apparent as we rounded the corner. Half-a-dozen patrol cars sat blocking the road, engines running, and doors open. They had cordoned off both ends of the street, dissuading any road traffic that might want to enter. Or leave. And right in the middle of the roadblock sat our destination—St. Ignatius.

Peter paused. "Gentlemen, perhaps you could be good enough to go and retrieve Symon's bag and make your way back to the church discreetly while we see what the authorities want."

"I don't think that's a good idea, Father," Flint commented, shaking his head.

"Nonetheless, Mr. Flint, I insist. Your presence might lead to questions, whereas an old priest accompanying a poor young man with a soul in need of saving might be easier to explain away."

"Hey!" I protested.

The two men nodded, and with a smirk moved behind us. Peter started toward the commotion, quickening his pace as he went. I jogged to catch up.

I'm back in town for thirty minutes and the cops are already involved. Even for me, that's a record.

Chapter Two

Our two bodyguards melted away into the night leaving Peter and me to check with the local cops.

I caught up to Peter and together we made our way toward the church, spotting a cluster of three patrolmen near the main entrance. As we got closer, I could see that the large oak doors that led directly into the sanctuary had been damaged, with one hanging at a strange angle off one hinge and the other missing altogether. There is nothing easy about kicking in two fourteen-foot-high, five-hundred-pound doors. Trust me. I tried to do that very thing many years ago. My foot still hurts every time it's about to rain.

Peter called out calmly, "Good evening, officers. I'm Father Fine. What seems to be the problem?"

Oh, I don't know, Peter, I thought loudly. *Something large and strong beat down the freakin' front doors of the church.*

One of the cops, a guy with sergeant stripes on his shoulder, muttered something to the other two and they chuckled softly. The hairs on the back of my neck bristled. What was so funny about a vandalized church, bub? I kept my mouth shut. The sergeant made his way down the steps toward us. He was wearing one of those fake smiles that showed everything but mirth. My hands clenched into fists.

"Good evening, Father," he said with a silky, accusing voice that made me want to hit him. He thumbed behind him at the damaged entranceway. "A few of the neighbors called in a disturbance. We responded a few minutes ago and discovered the mess with the doors and were waiting for permission to enter from our commanding officer. The detective went in alone as no one from the church responded to our calls." The cop paused. "Father." As if adding the title made his sarcastic tone acceptable.

The cop was fortyish, a big guy—six feet or so as he looked down his nose at Peter. He had the graying temples and slight paunch of a man that used to work out, but had gone to seed as he approached middle age. He looked quizzically at Peter. "Mind telling me why no one seems to be here? And while you're at it, mind telling me where *you've* been and who your companion is?" I could hear the camel howl in pain as the final straw broke its back.

Now I know I'm a bit disrespectful. And I haven't been the best Catholic in a very long time. And Peter is particularly fun to take the piss out of, as they say in my current home city of Dublin. And, did I mention I have a real issue with disrespectful, piss-taking authority figures?

So that's when my brain heard my mouth say, "We've been at the Policeman's Charity Ball. We're raising money to buy you a pair."

The next thing my brain registered was pain as the middle-aged sergeant—who, without missing a beat—spun me around, pinned my arms to my back, and slammed my face down on the hood of one of the patrol cars. I guess I need to work on my delivery.

As I was playing astronomy by watching the stars dance across my vision and tried to catch a bit of drool that was about to fall out of my mouth, Peter continued the conversation as if I hadn't just been jacked onto the hood of a police cruiser.

"Well, Sergeant," he said calmly. "I was coming back from the airport, having picked up my guest—whom you currently have pinned to your car. The Monsignor is inside. I'm not sure why he hasn't..."

That's when I heard another voice, one I hadn't heard in a long time. One that made my head ache even more than it already did.

"That's enough, Sergeant," called a calm, almost bored voice. "I'll take it from here. Please go round up the rest of the men and tell them to pack it in. I want reports on my desk by morning."

"Yessir," muttered the officer behind me. He tightened his grip a bit more. A numbing sensation spread from my shoulders to my fingertips.

"You can let Mr. Bryson up, Sergeant," said that same, maddening, calm voice again. "I think I can handle him."

I stood up slowly, rubbing my jaw and trying—but failing—to nonchalantly wipe a bit of spittle from my lip. I was slightly surprised to see that my head hadn't left a dent in the hood of the patrol car. My back creaked as I stood. I waited a moment and, realizing the man wasn't going to just go away as I had hoped, I turned to stare at him.

He was tall, taller than I had remembered, and rail thin. Clean-shaven with a short, slightly spiked haircut, the officer—no, detective I corrected myself as I saw the color of the badge—was dressed in a gray two-piece suit with the gold shield clipped to his jacket pocket. He shifted a pair of Benjamin Franklin specs up the bridge of his nose absent-mindedly. He'd been doing that since age seven.

"Hey," I said, meeting his steady gaze.

"Hey," he replied. We stood in silence for a moment.

"Congrats on making detective," I said, looking him in the eyes. Aaron North, my best friend from childhood, my right-hand man as a young adult and now a complete authoritative bastard—and I mean that literally as well as figuratively—stood with his hands on his hips looking me over with that prissy 'I don't approve' look. Hated that. Broke his nose when we were thirteen for that same look.

"Symon, I didn't think you'd actually come. I heard you were doing missionary work in Ireland. Running a pub and minor cons being God's work and all. How the mighty have fallen." That damnable calm voice again.

Prick.

"I see you are still playing Cops 'n Robbers," I sneered, turning toward him. "But now you have the cheap suit to go with it."

Peter, probably sensing that things might be heading rapidly down a rabbit hole, leaned into me and whispered loud enough for Aaron to hear, "Symon, you've been here for less than an hour. Please don't get yourself arrested your first night in town."

I laughed. I couldn't help myself. Peter had the exact same look on his face now as when he'd caught Aaron and me trying to sneak back into our dormitory at four in the morning having spent an evening with Harvard co-eds. We'd been fourteen at the time.

Aaron laughed, too, and I could see some of the tension leaving his face. It didn't mean we were all right, mind you. It just meant we weren't going to beat the hell out of each other. Just yet.

"Aaron, what's happening here? I've only been gone for a couple of hours to bring Symon back from the airport. And where is the Monsignor?" Peter asked.

"Father," Aaron said, shifting back to a more formal tone, "We received a call that St. Ignatius was being vandalized. But by the time we got here, the person or persons responsible were gone. We found the main doors to the sanctuary knocked almost completely off their hinges, and I found some minor damage inside. We haven't seen the Monsignor. In fact, we haven't seen anyone associated with the church until you walked up. I was about to search the place when you and Symon arrived."

We headed up the stairs and walked together through the ruined threshold of the Sanctuary. Something was here. Peter was looking around with a curious expression, but Aaron was looking at me. A chill went up my spine as soon as we entered. I shivered.

Immediately to my right in the narthex was the baptistery, a cold marble basin that I must've passed a million times in my youth. The nave, made up of countless oaken pews—always polished lovingly by Peter's own hands—reflected via countless layers of wax the chaotic flickering from dozens of prayer candles. A strange shadow, like liquid tar, moving from behind the altar across the apse made me shiver. It might have been my eyes playing tricks on me, but I knew deep in my bones that something was very wrong.

"You felt it too, then," Aaron whispered. There was something dirty surrounding us, something ancient. There was a stagnant, musty feel to the air and the stench of sulfur and decay. I may have been out of the game for a while, but once trained in the arts, you can't miss signs of demonic magic. Whatever had desecrated the church was still there.

"Aaron," I said, still looking around. The choir loft, maybe? "Make sure your people are out of the area. Now."

As calm as could be, Aaron slowly unclipped is two-way from his belt. "This is Detective North. All units head back to the precinct." Acknowledgements could be heard from the little speaker on the radio. I could hear the sound of cars pulling away through the gaping hole that had once been an ornate oaken doorway. The three of us didn't move.

Peter, Aaron, and I continued to search the church, barely breathing as if any movement would draw attention to us. Light seeped in from the few streetlamps outside the church and the flickering glow of candles inside made the shadows dance and move.

"I have him," A scratchy, deep, and utterly foul-sounding voice whispered.

All three of us jumped back, me crashing into Aaron. Mirthless laughter rang throughout the sanctuary. Whatever it was sounded like it was standing next to me, whispering in my ear like some sort of demented lover.

"He left himself open to me and he is mine." There was a sound like the flapping of large, leathery wings and then nothing. The smell began to dissipate.

"Jesus Christ!" Aaron exclaimed. "What the hell was that?"

It was all happening too fast. I'd given up this life a decade ago, yet less than two hours after getting off a plane, I was already knee-deep in the bloody supernatural.

Charles had been in trouble. So much so, that he'd had Peter contact the only people he could trust that would help him despite the years of estrangement. Something evil had entered a church, which, by the rules of the demon Shadow-world I'd been involved in most of my adolescence and early adulthood, should have been impossible.

There was an audible series of echoing clicks, and the church lit up in all its glory. Peter had thankfully found the lights and flipped them on. Aaron hadn't left my side and I noticed he'd drawn his automatic. I blinked in the sudden light and began to survey the church in detail.

With the evil sensation gone, I could focus on our surroundings. Other than the front doors, nothing in the sanctuary looked out of place or disturbed. In fact, most of the interior hadn't changed since I'd last stepped inside. But something was bugging me. It took me a jet-lagged moment, and then it hit me. I'd never seen the place quite so empty before. Usually at any time of the day or night, there were both parishioners and church staff inside.

Aaron turned to me and said, "Stay here Symon. I'm going to take a look around."

"Like hell," I responded. No way he was going anywhere by himself, gun or no gun. We made our way toward the altar down the center aisle. As Aaron genuflected and made the sign of the cross, I glanced around to see where Peter had gone.

I looked over to Aaron, about to ask him if he'd seen our priest friend, when Peter's voice, a half an octave higher than normal, rang out.

"Boys! come back here. There is something you need to see."

His voice came from our right and Aaron and I went behind the altar through the door that leads to the choir room and the church offices.

We hurried down the corridor and saw that the door at the end of the hall was open. Charles' study. We both got to the doorway at the same time and I slowed down long enough to let Aaron go through first. He was the one with the gun, after all.

Peter was standing there, speechless and I could immediately see why. The room had been torn apart. Not a single piece of furniture was left intact. Inscribed in what looked like blood on the walls, ceiling and floor were symbols that were unintelligible to me. But instinct told me that whatever had taunted us in the church probably had written the cryptic letters and symbols. There were a lot of them. And a lot of blood (if that's indeed what it was) had been used.

Peter said quietly, "What, in all that is holy, does it mean?"

I looked again at all the foul writing. "Well, I'm no expert, Peter, but I'm guessing it means Charles has been taken. The Monsignor's gone."

Chapter Three

After a quick search of the remaining areas of the church and dormitories, we found nothing else out of place. We also found no sign of Charles. The three of us consulted quickly, and Peter asked Aaron to hold off reporting Charles' disappearance until we could gather a bit more information. Aaron had been, as you can imagine, completely against this but I shouted him down. I'm guessing the phrase 'kidnaping by demonic servant of Hell' wouldn't have looked too good in his report. Besides, even rusty, Peter and Aaron were better equipped to investigate Charles' disappearance than the police. Aaron excused himself curtly and stepped away to make a few calls. Peter went to make arrangements to have the doors repaired and to have parishioners who might turn up shepherded to the Anglican Church down the street for the time being.

This left me alone to contemplate the symbols in the ruined study. Runes and ancient languages had been a mandatory part of my studies when I'd been a student here, but it had never been one of my strongest subjects. I was just thinking about going to find an old grimoire or text on the stuff when Flint and Kowalski seemingly materialized out of nowhere right next to me.

Kowalski looked around the room with an appraising eye. After a minute he said "Sumerian ... written in Manon marks or Kolbryn? What do you think Flint?"

"Dunno," the big man grunted. "I called it in. She should be here in a bit. Wants us to take pictures and told me to tell you, Bryson, not to disturb anything." Kowalski nodded and reached into his jacket pocket and pulled out a miniature digital camera. It looked expensive.

"Mr. Bryson," barked Flint, "Could I ask you to step back please? You're contaminating the scene."

I couldn't believe this. Charles was missing, St. Ignatius had been breached, and here I had found my way into the cast of a witty forensics drama.

"Who the hell are you guys?" I asked.

The flash on the camera went off as Kowalski started documenting the study. Without missing a beat from his work, Kowalski said, "Private security." And just like that I was dismissed.

I grudgingly moved out of the way as the two men continued to work the room quickly and methodically. I really wanted to know who these guys were and why they seemed to have the run of the place. And to be honest, I was annoyed at being treated like a petulant child by these goons. I rubbed my right temple. Great, now my headache was getting worse. Peter seemed to trust these guys, but for all I knew, Kowalski and Flint might be involved in Charles' abduction.

I watched for a few more minutes, when I heard footsteps coming down the hall. I looked up and Peter was there, notebook and cordless phone in hand, looking as worried and tired as I felt. I glanced at my watch, and it took me two tries before I could see the hands properly. Damn headache. It was a quarter to midnight.

"Symon, I need you in the sanctuary. There are a few people there who've just arrived and they want to talk to you." Before I could ask, he continued. "No, they aren't the police. Aaron is still here, but he hasn't called it in as of yet." Peter turned on his heel and went back down the hall, dialing the phone as he went. With a glance back at Charles' study, I followed.

There was a small group of people near the front pews, speaking in low voices with Aaron. Despite the years, I recognized them immediately. One was a very tall, thin, black man wearing a priest's frock. His hair had started to recede a bit and he was sporting a thin moustache and goatee. I hadn't known that Bill had joined the priesthood. He was chatting with a blonde woman dressed in what looked like a very expensive business suit, complete with a short yet tasteful skirt. Eden Engel looked like the epitome of the modern business executive, from her five hundred dollar haircut to her matching shoes and handbag from Gucci. I stopped when I noticed the third person that I'd initially thought was sitting in a pew behind Eden. But now I saw she was actually in a wheelchair. Eve Engel had been identical to her sister in every way, but the resemblance was no longer as uncanny as it had once been. I knew that she had been affected by the disaster at Plum Island more than any of us, but the past decade had been harder on her. I was shocked to see her condition. What happened to Eve was one of many reasons I'd left. One of many things I blamed Charles for.

I honestly didn't know how my old friends would react to seeing me. Maybe it was a combination of the long flight and exhaustion, but at the moment I didn't care as much as I had thought I would during the flight over. I left this place ten years ago and chose to break my connection to these people. But Charles and I had some unfinished business to attend to once the current trouble sorted. That was the real reason for getting on the damn plane in the first place. But that had to wait until he was found.

Based on what I'd seen tonight, I understood why Charles had wanted to put the band back together. The Monsignor had been snatched from Holy ground and that was supposed to be impossible. The only way I could think to find him and get the hell back to Ireland was to work with my old team. Which included Aaron, Bill and the twins. Also, unfortunately, Janice. I wasn't looking forward to that.

So I took a deep breath, held it for a moment, and then let it out counting to ten as I did so. *Suck it up Symon*, I thought. You need these people. And besides, Janice doesn't seem to be here.

Aaron and Eden were engaged in a very low, yet animated conversation when I entered the sanctuary. Bill was standing silently by their side. Eve seemed to be sleeping quietly in her chair. All of this, of course, stopped as I, too distracted by my own thoughts, snagged a foot in one of the tall, free-standing candelabras near the altar. With a loud crash that probably echoed for a week, the ornate candle and metal stand tumbled to the floor.

"Schmuck," I muttered to myself.

Aaron and Eden stopped talking and turned to look at me. Bill stood there with one eyebrow raised like Mr. Spock in *Star Trek*, arms folded, giving me a very Peter-esque look. Must be taught in Priest school. Eve stirred, but settled back down.

"Nice one, Sy," Aaron said in that voice of his. "I like the entrance. Subtle and with all the grace of..."

"Oh shut up, Aaron. When did you become such a pompous ass?" That was Eden. Tonight, she was my hero. Eden came over and hugged me, something I wasn't even remotely expecting. I hugged her back. It had been a long night.

"Awful news about Charles. I know he'd be glad you came." It was a strange comment with the circumstances being what they were. I filed it away as something I could think about later.

"I didn't know Eve was in a wheelchair," I said in a whisper. "What happened?"

Eden's facial expression turned icy. "Eve was never right after Plum Island," she said, her voice breaking a little. "I thought she'd turned a corner, but she's gotten really bad in the last few months. She doesn't have any lucid moments anymore—it's almost like she's in a constant dream-state. It's frightening, Symon."

I looked over at her twin. It looked as though she were sleeping peacefully in her wheelchair. I knew better, of course. Eve was an empath. A damn strong one, too. If what Eden had told me was true, Eve was trapped in her own personal Hell, and it broke my heart to see her in such a state. At this point Bill had come to stand by Eden, putting his hand on her shoulder to comfort her.

Without looking at me he said, "Symon, it's good to see you again. Eden, there isn't a lot of time."

Eden swatted away a tear as if it were some annoying, minor pest and pulled herself together. "Of course you are right, Father. I'll go look at the Monsignor's study."

Eden, apparently, was the expert the two creepy security guards were waiting for. I should have guessed that since the study of ancient languages and symbols had been one of subjects she excelled at when we were growing up. It wasn't a field of study that many kids majored in. And just for fun, she'd gotten degrees in biology and chemistry as well. She was unbelievably smart, as smart as Eve had been intuitive. Eden left us and headed toward the back, pausing to show her respect to the altar and the figure of Christ depicted hanging on the cross—suspended on the wall. When I was younger, I'd thought that the image looked a little sad. Now, it seemed to be mocking me. I looked away.

I watched her go, mixed emotions all fighting for dominance in my mind. I turned to look back at Eve when Bill clasped my arm.

"Sy, we've all missed you. Charles the most, I'm sure of it. He'd be very glad to see you've come to help."

"When did you get ordained, Bill?" I asked, changing the subject.

"A few years ago," he answered dismissively, then continued back on topic. "I already spoke to Aaron. What's your take on what's going on?"

I went through everything that had happened since I stepped off the plane at Logan: Peter and the security guards, what I noticed about the damaged church, the feelings and smells ... the voice we'd heard.

"It took some very evil and powerful magic to get into the church," Bill mused. "Something must have invited the creature in, either accidently or on purpose, I don't know."

I agreed with him. We started to discuss possibilities when Aaron came up to us.

"I need to get an APB out on Charles," he said, frustration coloring his every word. "I can get the airports and train stations closed and coverage of all the highways within the hour."

I laughed. I probably shouldn't have, but I did anyway.

"What, Aaron," I mocked, sounding much harsher then I'd meant to, "you think the demon grabbed Charles, called a cab, then put him on a flight to Bermuda? For God's sake..."

"I don't see the great Symon Bryson doing anything to find him," he spat back. "We can handle this. Why don't you go back to Ireland and hide? It's what you're good at."

"Son of a *bitch*." I moved to hit him, but Bill grabbed me.

"Stop it. Both of you. This is the worst thing that could happen now. We'll never find Charles if the two of you are at each other's throats!"

Aaron and I pretended not to hear him. We continued to hurl insults at one another and I could feel the hairs raise on the back of my neck. The pews around us begin to vibrate as my anger grew. I was losing control. Ten years was a long time to keep emotions bottled up and I was approaching my breaking point. I could feel my power coming to the surface...

Go ahead, Symon Bryson. Use your power. Do it.

All of a sudden the pain in my head exploded. Stars danced across my vision. I put my hands to my temples but the pounding wouldn't stop. I staggered and grabbed the edge of the nearest pew to keep my balance.

That's when Eve screamed.

Chapter Four

When I came to my senses, I found myself lying in a large antique bed. I blinked my eyes a few times, trying to remember where I was, why my head hurt so much, and what the hell pub I'd been in. I noticed a beautiful crucifix hanging next to the single window in the room, and that's when I figured out I wasn't in my Dublin flat.

I sat up quickly. The pounding in my head told me I probably shouldn't have done that.

"Ow." I put my hand to my temple. "Damn it!" I closed my eyes and that seemed to help a bit.

"You probably shouldn't do that. Sitting up quickly and all," a woman's voice said softly, although the quiet words echoed deafeningly in my head.

Janice.

A short grunt was all I could manage by way of reply.

"I'm going to turn on the light, Symon. Cover your eyes or it will hurt. A lot."

I did as I was told and I heard a soft click. Slowly, I removed my hands from my face. A heartbeat later I opened my eyes. There was still pain, but it had receded to a manageable dull ache. My eyes adjusted to the light and I could see Janice clearly for the first time. She was sitting in a high-backed chair, curled under a blanket. On her lap was a book with one of those miniature lights attached to it. Good Lord, she looked even more beautiful than I remembered—her jet-black hair and bright blue eyes reflecting her mixed Narragansett Indian and German heritage.

"Before you ask, you've been out for about six hours. Charles is still gone. I got here about three hours ago. The bright orb you can see rising outside the window is indeed the sun. Eden has been up translating the runes in Charles' study all night and should have something for us soon. And it's good to see you." Janice had ticked off a finger for each fact as she'd listed them.

I looked at her for a moment.

"Thanks, but what I was going to ask was 'Where am I?'"

"Oh," Janice muttered, a little taken aback. "You're in Charles' bedroom." I looked away, staring at the sun as it slowly came up, backlighting making the taller buildings over the river in Boston look almost ... magical. I could tell she was pouting at my feigned indifference. She has great lips for pouting.

"Okay, then." I said, adjusting the pillows behind me so I could sit up properly. "Next question. What happened to me?"

"Hm." Janice was still pouting. "Eve had a nightmare," she snapped, a bit clipped and matter-of-factly.

"Okay..." I drew out the 'kay' part. "That still doesn't explain why I'm lying in a bed..." I lifted the sheets a little and looked down. "...naked."

"I forgot," Janice said standing. "You left right after Plum Island." I couldn't mistake the bitterness I heard in her voice. "Eve's magical strength is ... *was* emotion-based. Charles taught her the discipline to filter out all the emotions that constantly bleed out from people. But her brain was severely damaged, and the mental filters she had learned to use to block out feelings of those around her were stripped away."

"I know that," I snarled a bit crossly. "I was there, remember?"

"No, Symon," Janice said shaking her head and beginning to pace. "You weren't. You only saw the beginning. You saw her collapse. You saw the seizure. She was never the same after that. About a year ago it finally got to the point where she couldn't function anymore. Eve needed full time care and Eden provided it."

"That part I didn't know."

"You were so wrapped up in blaming Charles for what happened, disavowing magic altogether and throwing a temper tantrum of biblical proportions..."

Janice was getting a full head of steam. I just couldn't take that this morning.

"Stop," I said, and she actually fell silent. I think that surprised me more than anything. "Look, I know you want to have a go at me. And I probably deserve it. But can we postpone this argument for a little while? Please?"

She pursed those stunning lips again. "Sure." Janice actually looked a little relieved.

"Now, instead of using all smart and confusing words as Eden does just to piss me off, can you explain to me what happened to Eve and why it flattened me?"

Janice took a moment to answer. I could see her internal struggle to put aside things she obviously wanted to get off her chest. Trust me when I tell you she is a very passionate woman in every way and that emotional control is difficult for her. Especially in front of me.

"Let me put it this way. Imagine that you are the little Dutch boy with his finger in the dyke holding back the water on the other side. Occasionally, you take your finger out of the hole to fill your cup for a drink, but you are able to stop the leak anytime you want. Now imagine being that same boy standing in the same spot when the dyke just vanishes. What would happen?"

I thought about that a bit. When we'd gotten the hell off Plum Island, Aaron and I had carried Eve. She had been unconscious at the time. Shortly after we had her back in Cambridge under care, Charles and I had ... words. I was gone a few hours after that. Regret welled up in my chest and threatened to overwhelm me.

"You'd drown," I answered Janice quietly.

"Yes," she said simply, her pacing stopping just long enough to look at me. I met her gaze, waiting. There was a lot of pain there, and a lot of disappointment. She turned away and the pacing started again. "As near as we've ever been able to figure it out, Eve's filters never came back. Her brain is completely overwhelmed by thoughts and emotions bombarding her from complete strangers twenty-four hours a day. The doctors called it a 'constant waking dream state' because they didn't know any better."

"Eve knocked me unconscious with some sort of emotional attack, then."

Janice nodded. "She doesn't know when she does it. It seems people with whom Eve had a close bond, a connection, if you will, feel it when the overload in her mind becomes too much. Usually when she's having some sort of nightmare. We've all been learning to deal with it over the years. Obviously with you living in Europe, the distance was great enough for you not to notice it."

I couldn't miss the return of bitterness in Janice's voice. She was blaming me for leaving when things got bad. Leaving the rest of my group to clean up the mess we'd made. Charles had made, I reminded myself. This was his fault. Somehow, the deflection didn't make me feel any better.

The thought of Charles brought me back to our present predicament. After ten long years he'd sent the word out to his former star pupils, which meant that whatever he needed us for was probably as bad as, or worse than Plum Island. We'd been younger then of course, but we were at the top of our game when it came to raw magical power. And we'd still gotten our asses handed to us. I needed answers, and finding Charles was the only way to do that. It was also the only way to make peace with my past.

Janice had remained quiet during my musings, arms folded, her back slightly turned toward me. "What are you going to do, Symon?" she asked.

"I'm going to find Charles," I responded. "And get some damn answers."

"Good." Janice's shoulders relaxed slightly. "Then come downstairs. Everyone is here and we need to hear what Eden has found out so far." She walked to the door and opened it. "Oh, and to answer your last question, you smelled like you'd been traveling all day. You needed a bath." And with that she closed the door.

****

My bag had thoughtfully been placed in Charles' bedroom for me sometime the night before and I quickly jumped into the shower, shaved and dressed. I found my way downstairs to the kitchen, and the smell of eggs, bacon, and strong coffee made my stomach growl. All I'd eaten the day before was airline food and I found myself suddenly ravenous.

The kitchen of St. Ignatius was large and very old. It was built to be able to feed hundreds of parishioners and the students who boarded there. The appliances were all new, state-of-the-art, industrial stainless steel. But everything else seemed exactly as it had been when it was built nearly a hundred years ago, certainly the same as I'd remembered it from my school days. There was a scarred and worn butcher-block table sitting off to one side, a place for the staff to eat during busier times. The well-worn table was covered in yellow legal pad pages, empty coffee mugs, and discarded pizza boxes. Eden, Janice and Bill were sitting over the notes, and Aaron was on his cell phone standing in the opposite corner. Peter was trying to clean up the debris from last night, while balancing a very large platter filled with enough breakfast goodies to feed an army.

"Hold on, let me get that," I said to Peter. With a look of gratitude, he handed over the platter.

"Morning, Symon," Bill said, and both Janice and Eden looked up. "Coffee is on. Come sit. We've made some progress since last night. How's your head?"

It hurt like hell, but I wasn't going to tell him that.

"I'm fine."

Janice looked at me, opened her mouth to say something, and then quickly covered it with her hand, hiding what I strongly suspected was a smirk.

I flashed her a dirty look, then turned to Eden asking, "How's Eve?"

"Resting," Eden sighed. "She'll be out for a while. Her nurse gave her a pretty strong sedative."

I nodded, pulled up a chair, and started to dole out large portions of hot breakfast to everyone. Janice got up and handed me a fresh mug filled with piping hot caffeinated goodness. Aaron finished his call and joined us at the table. If Charles and Eve had been here as well, this would have been like old times.

"Fill me in. What's going on?" I said, feeling the coffee work its magic.

"Well, the boys were partially correct last night," Eden began. The symbols in Charles' study were written in blood, human blood. They're a form of Germanic rune with ancient Babylonian scattered throughout. And the language is very chaotic as well. There is no flow or rhythm to it, making a full translation difficult." Eden paused for a moment. "There is also a name mentioned over and over: Belial."

"Who's he?" I asked.

Bill shook his head. "Read your Bible, Symon. The Bible calls Belial one of the crowned Princes of Hell. Fortunately, we have more detailed information. We'll have a better idea what we're up against in a little while."

"So where is this progress you've mentioned?"

"Oh that!" exclaimed Eden, sitting up a bit straighter in her chair and getting a familiar "I know something you don't" gleam in her eye.

"Well, it looks like this Belial was conjured up right here." She tapped on the table to indicate St. Ignatius itself. "So that's pretty good news."

I choked on my eggs. "How is someone conjuring up a Monsignor-stealing demon in the middle of a church a good thing?"

Janice pulled a couple of the yellow pad pages off the table. "Well, since we haven't heard of this guy outside of the Bible reference, and knowing how demons inflate their own importance, Belial is more than likely a minor player. Which means he can't go far from where he entered our world or his physical body would just stop working."

"Possibly," I said, a piece of bacon that had made it half way from the plate to my mouth momentarily forgotten. "But what if his only job was to deliver Charles to a stronger, more powerful creature? Higher demons can roam the Earth for centuries. Go anywhere they please in any plane of existence."

I was struggling to remember what I had learned from Charles. The Shadow-world exists in the same space as Earth. It's slightly out of phase, resonating at a slightly different frequency than what we call normal space. Which means there is a world of chaos just slightly out of step with our own. Some call it Hades. Some call it the Underworld. We Catholics call it Hell. One of the reasons Charles' belief was so strong is that he knew Hell existed. Therefore if Hell existed, as he always affirmed, God must exist.

"I don't think so," said Eden lightly tapping her spoon on her coffee mug with a rhythmic *tink, tink, tink* that brought my focus back to the conversation. "The runes name this Belial numerous times. He seems to be the one conjured here specifically."

"I'm still waiting to hear how this gets us anywhere," I said, annoyance creeping into my voice, "and how this helps us find Charles."

Aaron answered. "While you were sleeping, I made some calls. Not to the precinct," he hurried to add at my questioning glance. "I have eyes and ears all over the place in the Boston area. I put the word out and got a hit this morning. Something strange was going on in Dorchester last night around the same time Charles went missing."

Aaron looked over at Peter who had just come back into the kitchen from a trash run. The old priest had always busied himself with menial tasks when he was worried. "If you guys would've let me call this in, I could've gotten a few units in the area to scope it out."

"I spoke with the Archdiocese this morning, Aaron, and they approve of keeping the authorities out of this for the time being." Peter went over to a closet and pulled out an ancient-looking broom. "Monsignor DuBarry's work was a little unorthodox. The Cardinal himself strongly suggested that we continue to use the private security we retained for, as he put it, 'information surrounding this incident could be grossly misinterpreted if shared with the general population and might cause serious issues for the Church.' I'll send Mr. Kowalski to accompany you to Dorchester, Aaron. He'll have access to backup should you need it."

I nodded at Peter. "Eden, Bill," I said leaning in toward them. "Can you get us a bit more on this Belial? And can you confirm he's the only one involved? I think we need a little more information before Aaron and company go in, guns blazing."

"I'm ninety percent sure I'm right, Sy. Bill and I will keep at it." Turning to Peter, she asked, "Father, may Eve and I impose upon your hospitality a little longer? I could really use Charles' library."

"Of course, my dear." Peter said. "I'll need to stay and coordinate the repairs on the church; however, I can help with your research if you wish."

Janice, having barely touched her food, stood up. "I'll need to head home to get my kit, then. If we are really all going to do this, I'll need my stuff. I left in a hurry last night."

We all stopped at Janice's words. I couldn't believe we were all so quick to head back into the lion's den. By the concerned look on everyone's faces, I was pretty sure they were thinking along the same lines.

I broke the awkward silence. "It's a one-off. We find Charles and get him back safely, then go back to our own lives." There was a chorus of nodding heads and the group began to split up.

"Janice," said Peter, "have Mr. Flint drive you. He's quite good and, as the Marathon is taking place this morning, he'll get you up to Maine and back in no time. Safely."

Janice thanked Peter and kissed him on the cheek. "Oh," Peter said, "take Symon with you. He doesn't seem to have anything else to do today. The two of you can chat all the way to Maine and back."

I spit coffee out of my mouth like an old vaudevillian. Peter's attempt at ... whatever he was attempting ... aside, the last thing I wanted right now was to be trapped in a car with my ex-girlfriend. I noticed Aaron glaring at me as he left the kitchen and thought again. Oh, yeah, that was the *next* to last thing: the actual last thing was to be trapped in a car with my ex-girlfriend who also happened to be Aaron's ex-wife.

Swell.

Chapter Five

Flint had the car waiting for us when Janice and I left the church. It was still very early but a construction crew was already hard at work on the entrance doors, a testament to Peter's pull with the local unions. We got in the vehicle and Flint pulled away from the curb. Today was Marathon Monday. Traffic from Cambridge through Boston would be murder, even at this early hour. Flint nimbly took a round-about way through Cambridge and then Lexington to get on the highway, thus avoiding most of the roadway crazies. Janice and I didn't try to make small talk. We both sat in the back of the big car, staring out our respective windows, lost in thought.

Circumstances had put us all back into the game. I wasn't happy about it, but I couldn't think of a way out of it. I'd been sitting on the plane yesterday, scripting in my mind exactly what I needed to say to Charles face-to-face, and that was supposed to have been that. The trip was meant to purge myself of all the bullshit that'd been rattling around in my head for a decade. Hell, I should have been winging my way back to Ireland this very morning, the slate finally wiped clean. Instead, I was sitting in a car stuck right back in the middle of Charles' game. And to top it all off, sitting next to me was the only woman I ever loved and who was still pissed as hell at me. Never mind that she went off and married my best friend.

We were about halfway through the bit of New Hampshire we needed to cut through before entering into Maine, when Janice suddenly sat up and spoke, breaking my current bout of feeling sorry for myself.

"We're being followed."

"No way," said Flint. "I've been watching the mirrors since we left. I would have picked up on it."

"You sure?" I asked her.

Janice just looked at me.

"Right. Flint, if the lady says we're being followed, then you'd better believe it."

The car smoothly accelerated until we were going nearly a hundred miles an hour. I turned to glance out the back window, but couldn't see anyone trying to keep pace. I looked at Janice questioningly.

"Helicopter," She declared. "West of us. Flying below the tree level."

"Well, since lead foot up there," I pointed at Flint, "is trying to break the sound barrier in a Lincoln, it's a good bet they know we're on to them. And since there's really only one reason for us to be heading this way, they probably have someone at your place too."

Janice's eyes went slightly out of focus for a minute. Her body went very still, like she'd turned to stone. Finally she let out a small sigh.

"There is an unknown car about a mile south of my place. It's the only way in, so they picked a good spot to wait." There was a strange, almost dream-like quality to Janice's words.

Flint got on his cell phone immediately and relayed our situation to whoever was on the other end of the line. I asked to borrow it and called Peter. Janice and I leaned in toward the phone so we could both hear through the tiny speaker. The good Father picked up on one ring.

"St. Ignatius," he answered.

"Peter, it's Symon. Janice says we are being followed and that there are already unfriendlies at her place. I'm assuming Aaron hasn't had us followed by the men in blue?"

"He gave me his word, Symon."

"Ok. Then we have a problem. Someone must have picked us up after we left the church. That means Aaron's probably got a tail too."

"I'll let him know right away. Please be careful, Symon," Peter paused, then added, "We still don't know exactly with whom we are dealing. I'll ask Eden to whip up a little extra protection and I'll bring in more security. Maybe you should consider coming back here."

Janice shook her head no.

"No can do," I said, sounding vastly more confident then I felt. "We'll be okay. Just let Aaron know and get us some backup."

"Will do. Be careful."

The line went dead.

I hit the 'off' button on Flint's phone and tossed it back to him. He caught it with one hand without taking his eyes of the road.

I looked at Janice. "Peter's got a point. Any chance you can do without your stuff at the house? I'd prefer not to confront these guys directly, at least not until we know who they are."

With a slow, sensuous smile, Janice purred, "You worry too much. Not all of us took a magical sabbatical. And yes, I need my gear, so we go." Peering into the front seat, she raised her voice over the roar of the engine. "That okay with you, Mr. Flint?"

The big man looked in the rear view mirror at her and grinned. "I've been baby-sitting religious folk for a couple of weeks now, ma'am. I could use a little workout."

I was trapped in a speeding car with a couple of lunatics.

****

Somehow, we didn't pass a single speed trap or police cruiser during the rest of our trek through New Hampshire. We slowed to about ninety as we went through the state tollbooth crossing the border into Maine. During the wild ride, I'd occasionally catch a glimpse of our pursuers. Not long enough to identify them, of course. But just long enough that I could confirm their existence and that they weren't going to leave us alone. They were playing a game of cat and mouse and it was beginning to piss me off.

We hadn't been idle during our ride. We discussed a plan to reverse the "cat" and "mouse" roles. We figured they knew we were on to them based on Speedy Gonzales' lead foot and had probably called ahead to the team waiting near Janice's home. We were counting on the fact that the bad guys were sure we didn't know about the second team. The helicopter baddies' lack of action beyond the game of peek-a-boo suggested their tactic was to drive us toward the second group on the lonely road leading up to Janice's place and then either kidnap or kill us. No fuss, no muss. So that's where we'd turn the tables. Flint had arranged for a reception at the other end by his company men. It would be set in motion at the same time we encountered the guys in the chopper. Risky as hell, but Janice and Flint were comfortable the bases were covered. I wasn't so sure.

The car cruised through suburban secondary roads, then off onto a gravelly back road a little south of Ogunquit where Janice lived. We were about to make our move when the helicopter goons sprang their own trap. Painted in cliché black, the chopper had gotten ahead of us, popping up over a slight ridge about two hundred yards off to the left. It was the kind featured in 'Apocalypse Now' and I swear I could hear Wagner playing in the background.

Flint jerked the wheel hard to the right, then to the left. Although the gravel road we were on was only about a lane and a half wide, he was able to move the car around just enough that the helicopter shot past us, bullets ricocheting all around the vehicle. Did I forget to mention the huge honking machine gun hanging off the side of the helicopter? I love the smell of napalm in the morning.

"Get down, both of you!" shouted Flint as the car slid sideways and began to fishtail on the gravel. The car clipped a big tree and Janice and I were thrown around like ragdolls as the big Lincoln spun around from the impact. We bounced off, around, and through a few more trees of varying thickness, finally crunching to a stop facing the exact opposite way we had come. We ended up embedded in a cluster of silver maple trees. The engine made a horrible grating noise then died. A billowing cloud of white smoke poured from under the hood.

Other than banging my shoulder against the car door as we'd been playing smash-up derby, I seemed to be ok. I checked on Janice, who had been thrown to the floor of the car. Her eyes were closed and there was a trickle of blood from her mouth. I could see nothing obviously broken and her pulse was strong, but I needed to get her out of the damn wreck to be sure. She groaned and tried to move.

"Flint, we have to get Janice out!" I shouted, trying to untangle myself enough to get a car door opened.

"Bryson," choked a voice. It was Flint. "That chopper is coming back. Pull down the back seat and get me that plastic case about the size of a toolbox. Do it quick: my arm is broken and I'm close to going into shock."

I could hear the *chop chop chop* of the returning helicopter's blades. I had suspected that the car was armor-plated when I had first got in it at the airport. But there would be no way it would hold up against the heavy machine gun mounted on that chopper. All three of us would be dead if I didn't move fast.

I pulled down my side of the back seat. Thank God the case Flint mentioned was still there as the trunk had popped open in the crash. I grabbed the case and yanked it out.

"I got it Flint! Now what?"

No answer.

"Shit!" The sound of the chopper's blades had become loud and steady. The bastards were hovering right in front of us. The steam from the radiator was beginning to swirl from the turbulence caused by the beating rotors. But there was no machine gun fire. What were they waiting for? They had us dead to rights.

"Open the case, you idiot," Flint gasped.

He wasn't as dead as I thought. I opened the plastic case and saw what looked like...

"It's a shoulder-fired rocket launcher," the big man coughed. "It's easy to use. Slide it apart to expand, twist to lock. Break the safety tab, point and shoot."

As I looked at the weapon wondering if I could actually fire the thing the sound of the helicopter suddenly moved off, providing an opportunity. I followed Flint's instructions, but hesitated before I removed the safety. I decided to leave it intact for the moment. The last thing I wanted to do was to accidently blow us all up.

My view out of the car was again obscured by the steam from under the hood as the air disturbance caused by the chopper faded when the machine moved off. I figured they were maneuvering for a better kill-shot. Maybe they were waiting for us to get out so they could just pick us off. I needed a plan.

I figured that crawling through the trunk would offer me the best chance of surprising them when they came back. I started to scramble out of the car when Flint coughed. He croaked out "Bryson, there is a red arrow labeled 'Point toward Target.' Make sure that's the end you point at them, okay?"

Right. Shooting the wrong way would be really embarrassing and I certainly didn't want that on my tombstone.

I climbed out of the trunk, ripped the safety tab off and pointed the tube back down the road. But the chopper wasn't there.

"Where the hell..."

I could still hear the damn thing, but now it had moved off to my right. I frantically swept the top of the trees looking for the helicopter when it rose into view. But there was something very wrong. The flying machine had popped up at a crazy angle, facing away from us and listing at about forty-five degrees. The chopper made a lazy semi-circle in mid-air so I could see inside. It looked like the machine gun wasn't manned anymore. I could also see the pilot, and he seemed to be struggling, swinging his arms wildly as if he was having some sort of fit.

Never let it be said I couldn't take advantage of a situation. I pointed the rocket launcher at the chopper (yes, the red arrow was pointed AT the bad guys). I was about to pull the trigger, when the helicopter flipped on its side. It hung there for a second, and two things shot out of the open hatch where the machine gun had been mounted. Then the machine fell to earth like a stone.

The explosions you see in movies when things crash are cool-looking, no doubt. But in real life these events are a little less dramatic. There was a loud crunching sound as the chopper crashed into the trees across the road. I heard a high-pitched whine from the engines, then nothing. Just a cloud of dirt spreading out from the crash site to indicate anything happened at all.

I just stood there dumbfounded for a moment, and then lowered the unused weapon. I heard a scraping noise from the ruined car and saw Janice climbing out of the passenger side rear door she'd just kicked open.

Two large hawks landed on the roof of the car next to Janice. She reached up and lightly ruffled the feathers behind each of the bird's necks.

"Thanks guys. I owe you."

The birds took off silently and disappeared into the trees.

"See?" She said smiling at me. "Piece of cake."

"Let's get Flint out of the car. We still have another group to deal with down the road. How long have you been able to talk to birds?"

"Oh, you ain't seen the half of it sweetie-pie."

I bet.

Chapter Six

Janice and I pulled Flint out of the car. Fortunately, the big man was able to move under his own power. Janice rigged a makeshift splint for his broken arm. While we were patching him up, Flint spent the time sitting on an old tree stump and talking on the phone with his office. The three goons that had been subdued outside of Janice's home were being held there until Flint's people could arrange to send a car back down the road to get us. I started to walk toward the wreckage of the helicopter when Janice grabbed my arm.

"Don't. There were three of them in there and they're all dead. You don't want to see."

I took her word for it. Flint had settled himself to the ground with his back leaning against the remains of our car, and I plunked myself down next to him.

"How's the arm?" I asked by way of small talk.

The big man grunted, "I'll live."

"I would imagine the cops will be arriving shortly. It's not every day a helicopter gets shot down in Maine."

Flint pointed at the now disabled rocket launcher lying on the ground.

"I think the little lady had more to do with taking out that chopper, Bryson. Seems to me you didn't get to shoot anything."

I nodded. "True enough. Still, I'm surprised that I don't hear any sirens." I held my hand to my ear in an exaggerated way. "Nope. Nothing. Why is that, Flint?"

"I dunno, Bryson. Why don't you ask your witch-friend?" Flint snarled.

I poked his broken arm.

"See, here's what I think," I said, continuing on and ignoring the man's grunt of discomfort. I would have screamed like a little girl.

"I think whoever you guys are, you've got your fingers in a lot of pies. I'll bet the cops won't come out here because they've been told not to." I poked him again. I was really tired of being jerked around, and Flint with his little buddy Kowalski had been doing that since this whole thing started.

"Damn it Bryson, don't do that! I swear I'll…"

"You'll what, Mongo? Tell on me? Who are you working for!" I stuck my face right in his.

"Sy," a soft voice chided behind me. "Back off. Let's figure out who just tried to kill us and who has Charles. Flint and his men are just trying to help."

"I'm not sure they are," I replied, coming to my feet and turning to Janice. "What if they are playing both sides of the fence? Isn't that what you mercenaries do?" I glared down at Flint. "Play both sides so you can milk every penny you can from everyone?"

Flint said nothing. I'm not the nicest guy in the world. A part of me took some pleasure in the fact that the big man's complexion had noticeably paled. He was in a lot of pain and for the moment I was okay with that. Maybe I could get a few answers.

"What proof do you have that he's up to something nefarious?" Janice now stood between us.

"Listen to her, Bryson," Flint said through gritted teeth. "She's pretty smart. Besides, you and the witch ain't paying me so you only get to hear what I'm told I can tell you. No more, no less."

I contemplated poking Flint's broken arm again when Janice stopped me.

"Look Sy, we all thought that…"

Just then a car, identical to the one we'd wrecked, came around a bend in the road and crunched to a halt in front of us.

"We're not done with this, Flint," I snarled at the wounded man. "We're gonna sit down for a nice chat."

He gave me a look and struggled to his feet. A woman, about five-foot-ten with long red hair, got out of the car.

"Problem, Flint?" She asked looking back and forth between the two of us.

"Nah, Crystal. Just a fractured arm. Mr. Bryson and I were just," he hesitated a moment, "chatting. Let's go."

We got into the car, Flint up front and Janice and I in the back. The redhead—Crystal—turned the car around and we shot toward Janice's home.

We sat in silence for the minute or two it took to reach the location where the ambush had been laid for us. There were three men dressed in dark suits holding sub-machine guns pointed lazily at a white Hummer that looked the worse for wear. Most of the windows had been smashed and one door was lying on the ground in front of the behemoth.

Our car pulled up and we all got out. Once I'd cleared the front of the big SUV, I could see three disheveled figures sitting on the ground, their hands tie-wrapped in front of them. They were dressed in identical fatigues, all albinos completely hairless from the neck up. They looked up at me with unblinking eyes. Their pupils were as black as the darkest night. I'd seen this before.

"Oh hell," I said coming to such a quick stop that Janice banged into me and almost fell. "Channelers."

Channelers once were people, but now they're just residences—more like crack houses—for demons. Demons prey on the wretched and weak. People whose lives have become so desperate that they look for any way out possible. That's when somebody makes an offer, it's accepted, and then a soul is claimed early, leaving an alive, but far from living, shell. After taking control, the biology of these former human beings changes. The most obvious signs of which are complete hair loss, the skin losing all its pigment and those soul-less black eyes.

I walked over and picked one of them up by the scruff of the neck and slammed him into the Hummer. "I want to speak to your Master. Now."

The creature just looked at me, unblinking, with no emotion whatsoever on its waxen face. I noticed that the channeler in my grasp had deep ragged cuts on its face, but, of course, there was no blood. Another side effect of total demonic control.

I stared at it for a few more seconds, then, in Latin said, *"Speak to me!"*

The creature smiled. Actually, all three of them smiled at the same time.

"Symon Bryson. How good it is to finally meet you," spoke the three mouths.

I could smell the foul breath of the one I held up against the Hummer. It reeked of rot and decay. It was speaking with a voice identical to the one Aaron, Peter, and I had heard the night in St. Ignatius when Charles had gone missing. It was very freakin' creepy, and I'd be lying if I told you that my bladder didn't suddenly feel very full.

"You are the reason I have my gift," it—they—continued. "But if you are thinking of taking him back, on this point, I fear we must disagree."

"Belial, I'm coming for Charles. And I'm coming for you."

"We shall see, Symon Bryson. I felt it was good manners to say 'thank you.' But I have business to attend to, and time grows short. And I grow bored. Goodbye, Symon Bryson."

And with that, all three of the channelers disintegrated before our eyes, decaying in seconds. In an instant, I found myself holding the remains of a human shoulder and neck. The rest of the creature's skeleton had collapsed in a fetid heap.

"Jesus Christ!" I shouted and jumped back about three feet. I tried to shake the rotted bits out of my hands and off my body, but it was no use. I was covered in corpse.

There were two big Lincolns outside of Janice's place. Crystal opted to stay in order to drive us back to Cambridge while the rest of Flint's team piled into the second vehicle. The big man gave me a look that would have killed a lesser animal before allowing himself to be helped into the car. Once they'd gotten themselves sorted, Janice, Crystal, and I made our way toward a beautiful Cape-style home.

The outside of the place was decorated in Native American woodcarvings. Wind chimes jangled lightly in the late morning breeze. Trees and plants, many on the verge of full bloom, surrounded the little cottage and I couldn't catch a hint of any other houses in the area.

"I'll just be a second, Sy. Wait here." Janice looked at me and wrinkled her nose. "You can hose yourself off...over there by the vegetable garden," she said, then disappeared through the front door. I blinked for a moment, then, catching a whiff of human decay, I made my way over to a garden hose she'd indicated near a patch of newly tilled earth.

My shirt was a goner, so I stripped it off, turned on the water and began to clean myself as best as I could without soaking the rest of my clothing.

Crystal was watching me, and, to avoid that sort of silence and scrutiny I'd always been uncomfortable with, I decided to take a different tack and go on the offensive.

"You guys did good back there. Channelers are tough ... they can't die so guns and such don't work as well on them. How did you do it?"

She looked at me for a second or two, eyes lingering on my bare chest, then she turned away.

"We didn't have to do much. When we arrived, the Hummer was already under attack."

"What—damn!" I had turned to look at her and had proceeded to douse my crotch with cold water from the hose. Soaking wet, I slogged over to the spigot and turned off the water. At least the dead person smell was gone.

"You were saying?" I asked, turning back to Crystal.

"Two of the biggest black bears I'd ever seen had ripped the Hummer apart and were dragging out those ... things. The animals ran off when we pulled up," she finished.

Janice again. She was practically knocked unconscious in a car wreck and had still managed to take out three channelers in the chopper and three up the road at her home. Pretty damn impressive. Her Native American heritage had always played a role in what Janice could do. Her magic was tied to the animals and natural surroundings, especially here at her home—the focal point of her power. But what she did to the channelers was beyond anything I'd ever seen her do before. I mean, yes, she certainly had an affinity for animals and they tended to like her as well, like the time we were attacked by a group of Rottweilers and she was able to calm the animals down to the point where they actually fell asleep. But today...

"Mr. Bryson? Are you okay?" Crystal inquired. Apparently I had stopped mid-stride. I can't chew gum and walk at the same time either.

"Yeah," I said. "Just wet."

A towel hit me in the back of the head.

"Dry yourself off rocket-boy and let's head back south." Janice had come out of her house, a large gym bag over her shoulder. She tossed a tee-shirt at me as she passed by.

I toweled off, threw on the shirt, and followed the two women to the car.

****

The trip back started off uneventfully. I tried to make conversation by asking Janice about Aaron and what had happened between them. Perhaps that wasn't one of my better ideas as she flatly refused to talk about it, so instead I decided to call Peter (using Crystal's cell) and brought him up to speed on the morning's events. He told me that Aaron's lead had turned out to be nothing more than teenagers, beer, and black lights. And that it seemed we were the only ones followed. I told Peter we'd be back in about an hour and hung up the phone.

"Aaron's lead was a dead end," I said to Janice, leaning back in the seat with the soft squishing sound of wet jeans on leather upholstery. "We'll be back in Cambridge in a bit. Want to tell me what was so important in your house that we needed to get in a car crash, shot at by a helicopter gunship, and ambushed by some demonic zombies?" I thought the question was pretty suave myself.

"Well, you didn't have to come, you know. Peter only suggested that you go along for the ride," she said sounding rather hurt. She made a face I'd seen many times before. Pouty lips. I do love that look on her.

"Yeah, well you're one of the few people I trust at the moment." I lied, crossing my arms and mustering up a look of indignation. "I really have no idea who Flint, Kowalski, or the others work for. Just that Charles hired them out of his own pocket. I really wasn't going to let you go all the way to Maine and back with someone I didn't trust."

"Did Peter tell you that?" Janice smiled. "Bless him! He's so cute when he's lying to protect Charles' dignity."

"What?" I was astounded. "Peter did what?"

"*Lied*, Symon. Charles didn't hire security. They were put at his disposal. Free of charge, I might add."

Okay. That sounded more like Charles.

"Why?"

"Because he didn't have us anymore and he's getting old. Charles never stopped fighting evil, Symon. He felt it was his calling, even more so than the Church." She gave me a sad look. There was something else she wasn't telling me.

"You kept practicing magic," I commented. We'd made a pact ten years ago and I was beginning to think I was the only one who kept my word.

"When you left, Charles was heartbroken," she replied. "He never tried to find another group of kids with our talents, never taught again. Some of us even offered to come back to help him. But he refused." She sighed heavily. "So we found another way to help."

"Who's we?" I asked.

Just then the cell phone I'd left on the seat between us rang. Janice looked at me, then away. The phone rang a second, then a third time. I picked it up on the fourth ring.

"What," I answered curtly.

"Symon, it's Peter. We have a problem."

"What's wrong?"

"The word's out. They know Monsignor's DuBarry's missing." Peter sounded distraught.

"Who's they?"

"The Press. There must be ten news vans outside the church and about three-dozen reporters staked out at all the entrances. Get back here as fast as you can."

"Shit. Okay, Peter. Will do," I replied.

"Don't swear. See you soon." The line clicked off.

I tossed the phone to the floor. This would complicate things.

"What is it?" Janice asked.

"Crystal, step on it will you? We need to get back to St. Ignatius as soon as possible." I turned to Janice as the powerful motor revved and the Lincoln picked up speed. "Our super-secret mission to rescue Charles just got a lot less super-secret. The press has the story and St. Ignatius is now under siege."

"How the hell did they find out?" Janice asked.

How indeed. It didn't make sense for our demon abductor to get the news out. Scrutiny was the last thing minions of Hell wanted. The less the mortal world knew about them, the better. Publicity also made the security company's job a lot harder. I doubt they'd want to make it tougher and expend more resources. Who would benefit from...

"Son. Of. A. Bitch," I enunciated through a clenched jaw. I knew who let the cat out of the bag.

Aaron.

Chapter Seven

There were press and cameras everywhere in front of St. Ignatius. Crystal brought the car down an alleyway two blocks away to let Janice and me out. Back in our teenage days, Aaron and I had devised many ways to sneak back into the church, so I was confident we could slip in unnoticed by the press.

I helped Janice over a chain link fence with her 'bag of tricks' and we trotted behind a gas station and through a gap in the dilapidated wooden fence surrounding the back of the churchyard. We entered through the fire door, whose lock I knew intimately, into the old girls' dormitory. Don't ask.

We closed the rusty metal door behind us with a clang. Turning, we saw a small man sitting with a flashlight.

"About time. I was beginning to worry."

The press I could fool. Peter, on the other hand, used to catch Aaron and me every time. We never did figure out how he knew when and where we'd try to sneak back in.

"What's happening?" I asked, pretending to be nonchalant about his presence.

"Walk with me and I'll explain on the way."

We walked through the deserted dorm and through the small but well-cared-for garden quad area. Peter brought us up to speed.

"Aaron and Mr. Kowalski couldn't find anything in Dorchester. They've been back for a couple of hours. Eden found out who this Belial is. I'll let her explain, but I don't think you'll like it, Symon." He glanced over his shoulder at me. "The press has been outside for about an hour. Apparently they got a tip this morning that a Monsignor was missing, presumed kidnapped. It's all speculation on their part and the Diocese is about to release a statement. The Cardinal is here and he's pretty upset."

We entered the back office area. Peter continued, "The Cardinal is in the main church office. I'd like you to come see him with me Symon, if that's okay."

"Let me go and see if I can help Eden," stated Janice. "She still in the kitchen?"

"Charles' study," Peter said, looking a bit relieved. "Thank you, Janice."

She nodded at him, gave us both a little smile, and went back down the hall.

"Where's Aaron?" I asked.

"He and Bill are in the kitchen working on trying a different divination incantation. Nothing has worked so far but they think they might be more successful now for some reason. Why?"

"Go see the Cardinal, Peter. I'll be in with you in a sec."

The old priest gave me a quizzical look, and then shrugged saying, "Okay, but Cardinal Maguire is not a patient man. Don't be long, Symon."

I watched him head in the opposite direction that Janice had gone, and made my way to the kitchen. Bill and Aaron were sitting at the old butcher-block table poring over notes. There was a stack of very old books scattered both on the table and the floor. I cleared my throat and they both looked up.

"Symon!" Bill exclaimed, standing. "Thank God you and Janice are okay, Peter told us about your trip. Come, sit and tell us everything."

"Bill, could you excuse Aaron and me for a moment? We need to talk."

A look of concern furrowed his brow. "I'm not sure that's a good idea." He looked from Aaron to me, and back to Aaron once more.

"Please, Bill. Just for a moment."

"It's okay," Aaron said, standing. He put his hand on Bill's shoulder. "We need to clear the air anyway, and I'd rather do it now as I have to head back to the station shortly."

Bill looked at me one last time and then left the kitchen without a word.

"We're alone now, Symon. What..." But he never finished the sentence. I caught him in the mouth with a right cross. He crashed back into the table and landed in a sitting position on the floor. Blood trickled from a split lip.

He blinked drunkenly a few times, then wiped his mouth. "Feel better?" he asked.

"Why!?" I shouted.

"Why, what?" he asked calmly, just looking up at me. "Why didn't I come with you ten years ago? Why did I marry and divorce Janice? You'll need to be a bit more specific."

"Why did you call the goddamn press?"

"Symon, you're still acting like you're twelve. You need to grow up. I called the press because we need their help. Even if nothing is confirmed, the rumor of Charles' disappearance will bring hundreds of tips into the department. We'll be able to tell what's bogus and what sounds more like a lead." He got to his feet and grabbed a napkin from the table to hold against his still bleeding lip. "In case you haven't noticed, Charles has been gone almost twenty-four hours now. The best chance of success in any kidnapping, demonic or otherwise, is if we get to the victim in the first day. And we've got almost nothing to go on at the moment." Aaron pulled the napkin from his mouth and crossed over to the fridge. He dumped an ice tray in the sink, grabbed a couple of cubes and placed them on his now swollen mouth.

I felt like an ass. There was nothing he mentioned that I didn't know already. I sat down heavily onto one of the chairs at the table.

"The Cardinal is pissed," I stated simply.

"Screw him. This isn't a game. We need all the help we can get, and by any means necessary." Aaron came over and sat next to me. "Nice punch, by the way."

I looked at him. "I didn't want any part of this, you know."

He sighed heavily. "I know. But it's time to put your big-boy pants on. *We* need you to grow up. You were always Charles' favorite, and one of the reasons for that is he saw you as a natural leader." Aaron stood, the chair scraping loudly behind him. "It's time for you to lead, otherwise we'll get nowhere and Charles will likely die." He held out his hand.

I looked at him for a moment and finally remembered why he had been my best friend. I shook his hand. It was a temporary truce until I could figure out what the hell was going on.

"There's other stuff we need to chat about," he said, letting go of me. "But that will have to wait until we have a bottle of Jack Daniels on hand."

"Agreed," I responded. "I've been summoned to go see the Cardinal. You and Bill might have something?"

"We'll let you know in about an hour."

"Good enough."

****

Cardinal Maguire was a big man. Not fat, although he had his fair share of late-middle-age paunch. But he looked like the type of man you might see protecting a major pop star or bouncing at a high-end club in the Back Bay. I'd met the Cardinal only once before. I knew him to be smart, calculating, and someone who didn't take crap from anybody. The one meeting I'd had years ago with him hadn't gone well.

The Cardinal has been head of the Boston Archdiocese for thirty years and there were rumors that the last couple of Popes had needed his blessing before becoming Pontiff. He had never wanted the top job himself, of course. He preferred less of the limelight and more of the power. His influence and insight were the reasons the Vatican put him in charge of the more 'esoteric' activities of the Church.

When I walked into the church office, His Eminence and Peter were watching the local news over tea and pastries. The female talking head on the screen was broadcasting live from just outside St. Ignatius.

"...Archdiocese has promised a statement on these strange and disturbing rumors. Back to you, Doug."

A second reporter appeared on the screen. "Thanks, Brenda. As soon as there is an update, we'll go back to Brenda Sung, broadcasting live from St. Ignatius in Cambridge. In other news, European officials are reporting that an explosion in the early morning hours rocked a..."

The TV clicked off and Peter jumped up from his chair.

"Symon! You know Cardinal Maguire, of course."

The Cardinal was dressed in his full choir regalia: red cassock, a rochet trimmed with lace, red mozetta, and pectoral cross on a cord. The only addition to the traditional garb was a silver ring with a black stone on his right hand.

"Your Eminence. A pleasure to see you again." I held out my hand.

He didn't take it. Instead he took another sip of his tea. Peter still stood, a smile frozen on his face. I continued to hold my hand out. *Uncomfortable* didn't even begin to describe it.

"Sit down, Bryson," he rumbled. "We need to discuss the mess Monsignor DuBarry has caused and how I'll be expecting you to clean it up."

I sat. My hand still hurt from the last person I'd hit today.

"With all due respect Cardinal Maguire…" I began in my best suck-up tone of voice.

"Save it, son. I don't like you and I know how you feel about me." He put his tea down very delicately for a man with hands the size of trashcan lids. He fixed me with a stare that was unreadable, but made me nervous nonetheless.

"How did the press find out about Charles' disappearance? I gave strict orders about this."

I couldn't help myself. "Actually, Your Eminence, you gave orders regarding the local authorities. I don't believe the news media came up."

Peter made a small noise that sounded suspiciously like a whimper. Both the Cardinal and I ignored him.

"So you admit this is your doing?" he very quietly asked. I'd seen him take this tack with Charles in the past. The fuse was lit. The angry explosion inevitable.

"I admit nothing, Your Eminence." Maybe a little verbal genuflecting would be appropriate here. "I apologize for the unintended flippancy of my remark. I don't know how the media found out about Charles." Lying to a Cardinal. Peter will make me do about a thousand Hail Marys.

"Damn your apology, boy!" he roared, his face turning a mottled red color. "You and your band of misfits have cocked this up good. I want you to expunge this demon that Peter told me about and find Charles quickly and quietly, or there will be hell to pay." He stood up and I did as well. Mister Respect, that's me. Peter apparently had been frozen in a standing position since I'd come into the room.

"The Archdiocese will issue a statement that Monsignor DuBarry has taken ill suddenly and is being cared for by the best doctors the Vatican has to offer and reports of an abduction are completely false. We will ask for everyone's prayers for a speedy recovery." He glared at Peter, then at me. "Father Fine, Mr. Bryson, I expect you both to corroborate this if asked?"

We both nodded.

"Good." The Cardinal held his hand out to Peter and the priest kissed the larger man's ring. "Bryson," Cardinal Maguire grunted, turning to me. "Get the Monsignor back in one piece." He stormed out of the office, slamming the door behind him.

I gave a low whistle.

"Did he really call us a band of misfits?" I asked Peter. "Jinkies, Scoob, isn't that one step below 'meddling kids?'"

"You think you're funny, Symon, but this is serious," Peter replied. "Without his support, not only would Charles' life be put even further at risk, but the work the Monsignor has done to fight the darkness for so many years would be wasted."

One of Charles' many repeating themes he preached was that evil was everywhere. I've seen it firsthand. It permeates spaces and individuals and things on levels that most ordinary people could never comprehend. Many of the old stories, myths, legends, and yes, even the scariest portions of the Old Testament, are based on truth. Every day the Shadow-world tries to encroach into our own. According to Charles, only those of us born with magic in our souls can protect the world from falling permanently into the abyss. It's why he spent most of his adult life searching for and training us. He was building an army. So when Peter said 'without the Church's support it would all be for naught,' I knew we were in trouble.

"Let's go see what the others have," I said, and we left the office to check in with the rest of the misfits.

****

"Eden, is there any way to make what you are about to tell us simple and quick?" I asked. Janice, Peter and I were sitting on the floor outside the open door of Charles' study. The study itself was brightly lit with heavy-duty lights, despite the afternoon sun. The contents of the study had all been catalogued and removed, leaving only the demonic writing on the walls.

"I could, Symon," she uttered tartly, "but I'd need crayons, sprinkles and construction paper that I could glue macaroni to. Now shut up."

I did something unusual then. I actually kept my mouth shut.

"Belial is known in many different religions. It's got about a dozen alternate names, such as Meterbuchas or Belu. In one of the Dead Sea scrolls, Belial is mentioned as the leader of *The Sons of Darkness*." She referred to some notes, crumbled up the page, and tossed it to the side.

"This demon might be a little nastier than I thought. In fact, in one reference I actually found it to be listed as, and I quote, *the father of Lucifer himself and the angel that convinced Satan to wage a rebellion in Heaven.*"

"Satan's *father?*" I exclaimed. "I guess you and I have a different definition of 'a little nastier.'"

"I'll get to that, Symon," an exasperated Eden said. "Only five more minutes. And then you can have a cookie. Seriously, the background is important, okay?"

I made a zipping motion across my mouth.

"As we know most of these guys like to make themselves out to be bigger and badder than they really are, thus all the different stories and legends about them. A demonic version of penis envy, if you ask me.

"It was Eve who held the key to which direction I needed to look. After her attack last night, she spent a couple of hours saying one phrase over and over. *You'll find it in the mines of old, the mines of gold. Holding the key.*"

"*Clavis Salomonis!*" Janice exclaimed. "The Key of Solomon!"

"Exactly," Eden answered, nodding vigorously.

"Ok," I said, confused. "What's this key?"

"It's a book, dummy. Did you ever pay attention in class? A grimoire: a book of demonology, spells and stuff." Janice had a 'tut-tut' sort of look on her face.

"Yes," Eden chimed in, "but more specifically the lesser key called the Goetia."

"The seventy-two demons Solomon locked away!" exclaimed Peter.

"So," I said trying to sound as smart as everyone else. "How did this Gatticka…"

"Goetia," corrected Janice.

"Whatever," I said. "How did it describe Belial?"

"As a demon of lies and guilt," Eden answered. "That's how it got to Charles in the first place."

"How do you know that?" I asked.

"Because I've finished translating the room," Eden explained. "It seems Charles was being consumed by guilt—and his guilt along with his abilities, as well as his position in the Church, made him a target. His guilt made him extremely vulnerable."

"Guilt about what?"

"You, Symon. His feelings of guilt are about you."

Chapter Eight

If Eden had told me the day before that Charles was beset by guilt over me, I would have felt some sort of vindication. Today was a different day, however. The news dropped like a bombshell and all I felt was a hollow, empty space, as if my guts had been ripped out of my body. I could feel all of them—Janice, Peter, and Eden—just staring at me. I think they were waiting for some sort of explanation, but all I had were suspicions.

"That's ... strange," I muttered, deciding to keep my darkest thoughts about Charles to myself for the moment. "Are you sure about your translation, Eden?"

I knew better, of course. She wouldn't have voiced it if she had any doubts about her work.

"I'm positive, Sy," she said, shaking her head. "Any ideas?"

Plenty. Could have been Plum Island. Could have been information about our collective families, but that would have manifested itself as remorse concerning all of us. Why me specifically?

"Not yet," I replied. I couldn't look at Janice. I couldn't look at any of them. "Let me have a think about it and I'll get back to you."

"Knowing the focus of Charles' guilt might finally give us a way to find him," Aaron commented as he and Bill came down the hall. "Bill and I haven't been too successful coming up with a good tracking spell yet."

"Jesus, Aaron. What happened to your mouth?" asked Janice.

I looked up at him to see Aaron staring unblinkingly at me. Our gazes hovered for a second, and a slight smile played across his swollen mouth. "I bit my lip," he lied. I bit mine too and kept quiet.

"What were you saying about tracking the Monsignor?" asked Peter. Thoughts of the former Mr. and Mrs. Aaron North would have to wait.

"Belial seems to have extended some sort of veil around the surrounding area," said Bill. "We've confirmed that Charles is within twenty-five miles of here, but that could be in any direction. Since Symon is the focus of the guilt that allowed Charles to be taken in the first place..."

I stood up, my legs tingling from sitting on the floor for so long. "What do you need?" I asked.

"We need you to think, Sy," said Aaron. "Why did Charles feel so much guilt? Something that ties you to that, so we can bind it with the incantation Bill and I have worked out."

"Time is paramount," stated Eden. "Belial will extend Charles' life to curry favor with the other overlords of Hell. He'll want to display and torture a man of the cloth in front of them to add to his power and reputation."

"I'd better get cracking, then." I said, heading down the hall. "I'll let you know what I come up with."

****

Peter had insisted I stay at St. Ignatius in Charles' apartment. I was uncomfortable with the arrangements, but the school dormitories had been closed and unused for years and the only remaining guest accommodations were taken up by Eden, Eve, and Eve's nurse.

I moved over to the bed, grabbing my old leather travel bag. I tossed the case on the worn, patch-work quilt draped over the bed, and opened it. The bag was filled with the remaining items I originally planned on throwing in Charles' face when I saw him. Boy, that plan changed.

Anger had motivated my return to the States. Now I was knee deep into things I'd been avoiding for years. I mean, c'mon. Who wants to get shot at, deal with a demon, and get covered in the remains of a zombie all in one day? If I were honest—truly honest—I was beginning to think I enjoyed being back in Charles' world.

And that thought terrified me.

Plum Island had taken the wind out of my sails. I hadn't been ready for the real scope of Charles' life-long battle against evil. Theoretically, I had known how bad it could get. But when it came to really seeing what evil was capable of, I froze. And when it was too late, I overreacted. The rules of the game changed that day, and I decided that I didn't want to play anymore, so I took my ball and went home. And I never looked back.

For ten years I never even cast a spell to light a candle. I pretended my gift was nonexistent. I lived a half-life of sorts. Moving from day to day, seeing what scam I could pull or who I could get into bed. If I was truly going to find Charles and go after the bad guy, I was going to have to be better prepared than I was a decade ago. I was going to have to take a crash course in being a practitioner again in the next couple of hours. Oh, and while I was doing that, I was going to have to find something that represents Charles' guilt. No pressure.

I was sifting through my bag, covering a glass orb, when there was a light knock at the door.

"Come on in," I replied.

I expected to see Janice at the door. To my utter surprise, Aaron sauntered into the room.

"How's the lip?" Yeah, okay that was a dick-ish thing to ask, but I was still miffed at his end-run with the press.

"Shut up," Aaron lisped through still swollen lips. He reached into a paper bag he was holding and produced two plastic cups and a small bottle of Jack Daniels. "I thought we should come up with a plan. You know. For a change."

"Aren't you supposed to be on duty?" I asked while taking the bottle from him and opening it.

"Personal leave of absence," he answered, shrugging his shoulders. He didn't offer any more information, so I didn't ask.

I poured a generous portion in the two cups and handed one back to Aaron. We looked at each other, than drank, shooter style.

I'd been drinking pints for years. It'd been a while since I'd had some Jack—bad memories.

I coughed as the Tennessee whiskey seared my throat.

Aaron laughed.

"The big man never changes," he said, shaking his head with a wry smile. Aaron grabbed the chair from in front of the antique roll-top desk Charles loved. The old Monsignor always was fastidious about separating Church duties from his personal business. Aaron's smile faded as he placed the chair next to me and sat down. "Why does Charles feel guilty?" he asked simply.

I hesitated a moment. I had developed suspicions and probably embellished them over the years. I figured Aaron had most likely pieced it together by now. Maybe it had taken him longer to put it all together, but he was pretty smart when not blinded by religious influences of his youth.

"Could be a few things," I uttered slowly. "He was a priest during Vietnam..."

"Symon," said Aaron, looking at me steadily. "Why is he guilty about something to do with *you*?"

"There were things about my parents Charles knew and never told me." I avoided his question, standing up and looking around for the bottle. "There were also the wicked-long hours of beatings I took under Charles' direct tutelage."

"It's the same story for all of us," Aaron replied shaking his head. "This is specific to you Symon. Think."

I had thought about it. For ten years.

"He knew, Aaron." I poured myself a second drink.

"Knew *what*?" asked Aaron.

It was incredible. Aaron had either become the best actor this side of Marlon Brando, or he had never figured it out. All these years I'd assumed I was the only one kept in the dark during the mission. And that they had all betrayed our friendship ... betrayed *me*. I'd hated them all for it—Aaron, Janice, and especially Charles.

"Charles knew what we would find on Plum Island." It was amazing to hear myself say these words out loud. The last time I had uttered that phrase, I'd shouted it much louder and had spiced it up with expletives. Right into Monsignor Charles DuBarry's face.

"No," said Aaron. "He couldn't have. He would have prepared us better..." He looked like someone had punched him. I mean other than me.

The shock in Aaron's voice was genuine and it infuriated me. It was so freakin' obvious after the Plum Island fiasco. That's when I had confronted Charles and the son of a bitch had admitted it, in a calm, almost unfeeling voice. I couldn't *believe* Aaron hadn't figured it out after ten long years.

"It was a test!" I shouted at him. "A goddamn fill-in-the-little-circles-with-a-number-two-pencil test!"

Aaron sat in stunned silence.

"You never guessed that, Mister Detective, no?" I mocked. Floods of images were coming to the surface, helped by the Jack. "Not even an inkling? He wanted to see how we would do when confronted with a real nightmare. He wanted to gauge our performance. Plum Island was an experiment!"

"I..." he started, then gulped. "I thought we failed him. That's why we all went our separate ways. I thought what happened to Eve was God's punishment for failing our duty... I blamed *you*, Symon. I didn't know!"

I laughed, but there was nothing but ironic cruelty in the sound. "So did everyone else. Hell, even *I* blamed me, at least partially. I figured you all knew. But there *has* to be something more to this whole thing other than just a test..." but I stopped talking. Something Aaron had said...

"What?" asked Aaron, his voice cracking a little.

"What did you say? Just before?" An idea had started to blossom.

"I said that I thought Eve was God's punishment..."

Interrupting him, I said, "That's what I thought. So explain this to me, Detective North. If Eve was the person most damaged—most traumatized—by what happened on Plum Island, why is it *me* Charles feels the most guilt over?"

"I ... don't know," Aaron admitted.

"Me neither," I replied. "But I'll bet Eve does. Let's go ask her."

****

Aaron and I left Charles' room and headed back down the stairs. The suite Peter had arranged for Eden, Eve, and the fulltime nurse was on the first floor on the opposite side of the kitchen, down a hallway past the pantry. The series of rooms were always kept ready for high profile guests and visitors to St. Ignatius who might arrive with little or no notice. During my tenure as a student, I'd never seen it used, but keeping it ready at all times was one of Peter's pet obsessions.

We passed through the kitchen. Peter was cooking again, and the smell of roast leg of lamb and garlic was positively amazing.

"Boys, can't fight evil on an empty stomach!" he said. "Symon, have you found something that we can use to find Charles?"

"Later, Peter," I waved my hand dismissively. "Eve in the suite?"

"Yes. Eden is with her as well. I'll get them for you."

"Thanks, but we'll go see her ourselves," Aaron said.

"Smells great, Peter." I patted the little man on the back as Aaron and I walked by him. I felt a little bad that we left him wearing an apron and spluttering about privacy. On the other hand, lamb tasted awful if it was overcooked. I was sure he'd thank me later.

Aaron and I continued out the side door and into a brightly lit hallway. There was only one door, other than the kitchen, so we walked over and opened it.

"It's polite to knock."

Eden was standing in the little kitchen off to the right. She had one of those health drinks in her hand. You know, the ones where you take any fruit, plant, or green thing and throw it in a blender.

"So, what can I do for you two?" Eden asked. "Have you figured out something we could use for Bill's tracking spell?"

"Where's Eve?" I asked.

"She's in the den, resting. Why?"

"We need to speak with her," Aaron said.

"Impossible," replied Eden, shaking her head. "She hasn't had any lucid moments for months. What's wrong?"

"Please, Eden." The alcohol must really be affecting my brain because it almost sounded like I was pleading. "Let me try."

She thought for a moment. "Okay, Sy. But please don't agitate her. The seizures get worse when she's upset."

We walked through an archway and opened up a set of French doors into a large common room area. I stopped in amazement.

There were a dozen people and loads of electronic equipment set up in the den. Five computer systems were up and running, and there were people typing away on keyboards. Two people were chatting on cell phones. I was even more surprised to see Kowalski sitting at one of the machines engaged in what looked like some sort of videoconference. In the far corner of the room was a hospital bed. Eve lay in it, seemingly asleep. A wire harness was connected to her head, and the harness, in turn, looked like it was connected to at least one of the computer systems.

"What the hell, Eden?" I asked angrily.

"These people work for me, Sy. Eve is well taken care of. You can go talk to her, but don't touch her, ok?"

"Flint, Kowalski and that chick I met at Janice's place … they're *your* people?" I asked, still a bit confused.

"Yes," she replied. "I own the company they work for. I made some money in biotech, Symon. You should have studied more." A smile threatened to break out on her face. "I'll explain later. Go see Eve. And when you get nothing, then we'll talk."

I looked at Eden as she turned away to join Kowalski's conference. Holy crap. I thought everyone got out of the business after Plum Island. It looked like some folks just expanded their involvement. Ten years. For ten years I turned my back on...

"C'mon, Symon," Aaron said, grabbing my arm and interrupting my jump into the abyss of self-pity. "Let's see if we can get through to Eve."

We went over to the hospital bed where Eve lay, but I hesitated. Her hair was meticulously combed and her skin glowed as if she'd just had a spa treatment for comatose beauty queens. It was a little creepy.

"She's well taken care of," Aaron echoed Eden's comment.

"Eve," I whispered.

She didn't wake. She didn't really move. The only sign she was even alive was the slow movement of her chest as it rose and fell with each breath.

I grabbed the nearest chair and pulled it close to Eve. My chest suddenly felt very heavy as I imagined Eden sitting in this chair for hours, combing her sister's hair and holding her hand. I looked down and saw Eve's hand outside of her blanket. Again, her skin looked well pampered. Her nails had recently been manicured. I thought about Eve being in this state for ten years, and my eyes filled with tears. How was I going to be able to communicate with her?

"Oh, Eve," I said, as I reached down and touched her hand.

And all hell broke loose.

Chapter Nine

I was standing next to a hospital bed in what may have once been the same suite where Eden had set up her command center. I say *may have been*, because the room looked like a bomb had hit it. The ceiling was gone and the walls were in shambles. Debris littered the floor. The hospital bed was the only thing that was pristine. It looked freshly made and very empty.

A hot wind blew up around me and I closed my eyes against the onslaught of sand and other small particles that whipped across my face.

"Be still," I heard a voice say.

The wind died immediately and I opened my eyes.

Eve.

Her blonde hair was pulled back in a ponytail. She was dressed in jeans and a man's sweatshirt, a size too big for her. Her sister Eden had always been the fashionable one. Eve was the tomboy twin—comfortable in oversized clothes and jeans. Just one of the boys.

"Hello, Symon!" she squeaked gleefully. She skipped over some shattered stone on the floor and hugged me. "Thank you for coming to visit me! Nobody comes to see me anymore." She frowned. "Well, almost nobody."

"Eve, where am I? What happened to St. Ignatius?" I asked.

"Oh, it's still there," she said, her voice very cheerful. She twirled away from me. The chill I felt had nothing to do with the temperature.

"Then where am I, Eve?" I asked firmly.

"Oh, don't be so cranky, Symon," she laughed in what would have been a delightful manner under different circumstances. "St. Ignatius is fine. This," she gestured all around us, "is a different St. Ignatius. Needs a little work, don't you agree?" She tittered again.

Okay. So I'm either locked in her mind, or I've been transported somewhere. Neither option provided me with a cozy feeling, as it seemed my only companion was a crazy person.

"Oooo. Be careful, Symon!" She began that little dance again. "I can hear your thoughts!"

Shit.

"Shit," she giggled. "Peter would be very mad at you for swearing, Symon."

"He would indeed," I agreed, trying to keep my mind clear. "Eve, I have to ask you something and I need your help. Can you help me?"

"Maybe," she teased, still dancing around the ruined church.

"Good," I said in what I hoped was an encouraging voice. "Do you have any idea why Charles has feelings of guilt ... especially about me?"

"You know," she answered and began humming to herself.

"Because of the Plum Island thing?" I inquired. She was making me very nervous and I had no idea how she would react to anything I said, particularly about the incident that put her in this condition.

Eve stopped dancing right in front of me and looked at me with her eyes wide. She started to rock back and forth in place, humming all the while.

"Eve, please. I'm trying to help Charles. I need something that will help me find him."

"Only a fool can help find the great Monsignor," she said, looking at me. "And you're a fool, Symon Bryson!" she giggled again. "Hey!" Eve added, "do you want to play with me?"

"Eve..." I started to say.

"Oh," she muttered, suddenly looking distraught. "No time for playing. You have to go now. Eden is really mad."

"Eve, I can stay a little longer..." I really needed to get answers.

"No!" She screamed. But the voice wasn't hers, it sounded deeper and menacing. She pointed at me. "You are going to get me in trouble, Symon! You have to go *now*!" Eve's face began to change, her skin became broken and cracked—almost charred. Her teeth yellowed and her eyes—the whites and the irises of her eyes—had become a deep glossy black.

Eve's limbs had become misshapen and her body contorted out of proportion. It was almost simian in appearance. The hideous caricature of Eve hobbled over to me and grabbed me by the shoulders. I tried to run, but my own body stopped taking any commands from my brain. I was completely paralyzed, frozen in abject terror.

The Eve-thing hissed at me and put its face no more than an inch in front of mine. I couldn't even shut my eyes as its mouth—which had grown very large yellow fangs—opened wide.

"Symon, you are the key. And I give you a gift for coming to see me," the hissing thing that used to be Eve said. A large purple tongue came out of its mouth and licked my cheek. A strange sensation filled my body. A combination of the sort of warmth you feel under a comfortable blanket during a winter's night and the nausea you feel after a night of heavy drinking.

"I wasn't the one who should've been stuck between worlds, Symon," the creature hissed softly, seductively, into my ear. "Come back and visit soon, and tell Eden I hate manicures."

****

I was suddenly back in St. Ignatius—the *real* St. Ignatius and was thrown violently away from a hospital bed—where Eve lay still unconscious—crashing into a combination of chairs, people, and equipment.

There were three things I noticed as my senses returned: One—the acrid smell of burnt electronics. Two—the sounds of a lot of people shouting and a fire alarm ringing loudly. And three—the fact that I was covered in what I figured was my own vomit.

Someone picked me off the ground. Apparently I'd fallen. I guess touch wasn't one of the senses that had come back yet.

"Jesus Christ, Symon! What the hell did you do?" Aaron hoisted me to my feet. My legs were shaky, but at least I could move them again.

"Hey, Aaron," I asked drunkenly. "How is your day going so far?"

"You stupid son of a bitch," yelled Eden as she came over to me. She was disheveled and had a small cut over her eye. "What did I tell you? I specifically told you not to touch her!"

"My bad," I mumbled. I raised my hand and said a bit louder, "*Mea culpa* everyone! That was all me."

"What happened?" Aaron asked. I described my encounter with Eve as best as I could, but like a dream, the details were fading quickly.

I was feeling stronger and able to stand on my own by the time I finished bringing Aaron and Eden up to speed.

I fixed a stare on Eden who looked like she might water-board me on the spot. "Eden, can we go someplace and talk? I'd really like to understand what happened to me, and we," I pointed at Aaron, "have a few more questions for you."

Eve had been right. Eden was furious. But she turned from both Aaron and me and headed back toward the bedrooms. "Follow me," she commanded.

I noticed Eve's nurse was already by her side but the unconscious twin seemed no worse for wear, unlike the rest of us. The memory of the creature she had become was the only vivid one I retained from our brief encounter. I shuddered.

Aaron and I followed Eden and I could hear the sounds of fire extinguishers and cursing—the latter of which seemed to be directed at me.

We entered the first bedroom on the left, a large well-appointed space decorated tastefully in a colonial New England motif. Eden closed the door. She turned to both of us, arms folded expectantly.

Aaron and I looked at each other and I said, "Peter is gonna be pissed when he's seen what I did to his guest suite." The impact of spanning dimensions and seeing Eve's demonic form had left me numb and shaking. Jesus Christ, what had been done to Eve?

"You could have killed her, Symon!" shouted Eden. Her face—well the parts not covered with soot from burnt electronics—drained of all color.

"I'm fine, thanks," I said, irritably. I was getting tired of being jerked around and kept in the dark. Eden's harsh countenance softened. "There's a lot I guess I should've told you guys. I'm sorry."

"Why don't we start with how you and Eve knew Plum Island was a test?" I asked matter-of-factly as I looked around the room for a towel. The combination of Jack Daniels and bile really didn't make a good Eau de Parfum.

"How? Oh God. That's what got Charles in trouble?" Eden said.

"Yep. I pretty much had that figured out from the moment you finished the translation," I explained. "It's coming up with something to add to the tracking incantation that I'm struggling with."

Eden sat at the foot of the bed. "We found out by accident, Symon. I hope you believe that."

"I don't. But go on," I prodded, finally finding a very nice expensive-feeling towel of Eden's and using it to wipe the yuck off myself.

"Charles caught me and Janice eavesdropping on a conversation he was having with Eve, discussing the Plum Island operation. He explained to us how important it was not to tell anyone else and swore us to silence. You don't break a promise to a priest."

"But why keep it from the rest of us?" Aaron asked a bit harsher than I suspected he meant to. I could tell he was still crushed over learning about Charles holding back critical information. The fact that Eden and Janice knew as well didn't surprise me, but I bet it hurt him. Welcome to the club, my old friend. You're ten years too late.

"He needed to see how we would react and if we could improvise. He knew the poor souls were gone already," Eden said. "I think he wanted to drive home the fact that you two couldn't always be cowboys running in with guns blazing." Eden pointed at us. "Plum Island was supposed to be an easy lesson, not the horror show it became. I don't think he expected everything that happened."

"I think that it was fairly obvious that Charles was surprised, Eden. Especially based on the woeful lack of preparation we were given for that mission. I figured that out ten years ago," I said, tossing the now filthy towel in her sink. I could really be a bastard when I felt like someone was screwing with me. "Why does Charles feel guilt having to do with me and Plum Island when your sister was completely ruined by the experience?"

"Because she and Charles had an arrangement. Had it for years," she said miserably. Tears welled in her eyes. "As a sensitive and an empath, Eve could get closer to the Shadow-world than any one of us, including Charles, ever could. Charles wanted her to become a spy with one leg in our world and one leg in Hell. They just needed a catalyst to get Eve to cross over at will, and at Plum Island they found it. Now you've seen the result of constant exposure. Eve has gone completely insane."

"Why would Charles want Eve catatonic and trapped in her own mind?" Aaron asked.

"After Eve's seizures stopped, and soon after you'd left, Symon," she began, "my sister found that she could jump back and forth between our reality and the Shadow-world with ease. She loved the danger and Charles received good information he could act on, even though most of us didn't work with him anymore. Eve became his primary source of intelligence and a major weapon for him."

"But something changed," I prompted.

Eden nodded. "About a year ago, Eve started to spend more and more time in Hell. Her body here began to fail and Eve's personality changed. She became less lucid and spoke to us in a dream-like state."

"So Charles realized his weapon was about to backfire and sent up the mayday flares via telegram. Peter knew something was up. He as much as told me he sent letters to everyone, but you and Eve already were involved." The half-truths began to unravel.

"It's not Peter's fault, Symon," she said. "He was under strict orders. If it helps at all, he spent an hour in confession over it."

I'd given up believing a long time ago, so the fact that Peter was in confession didn't necessarily mean anything to me. But I know it meant something to him. Besides, I'd seen Charles put Peter between a rock and a hard place before, so I couldn't be too hard on the priest.

"Eden," Aaron asked quietly, "is there anything we can do for Eve?"

"I have people working on it," she answered, wiping a tear away from her cheek. "But I need Charles. I think he's the only one who might be able to find a way to bring her back. And now that we are all together again, there might be some hope. The fact that you were able to go to Eve is a huge step, Symon." Eden looked at me. "But we need Charles. Not just because it would probably be a good thing to wrestle a Monsignor back from a demon. He got her into this and I'm hoping, if you're willing, that with all of our help, Charles can save her."

I nodded. I'd seen what Eve was becoming. She was my friend once, and I was going to have to help her. So much for just getting Charles back and going back to nice, safe Dublin. "Yeah, we're in, Eden. But we still have a problem. I don't know what I can use to make Bill's spell work."

Aaron started to pace. "You told us that Eve said only a fool could find Charles and that you were the fool, correct?"

"And that I was the key." I nodded in agreement. "I was thinking that maybe the old rosary Charles gave me might work. Or that pendent I got when..."

"Wait!" Aaron exclaimed, cutting me off. "I think it's more basic than that. You, yourself are the key." He stopped pacing for a moment. "It couldn't be that simple, could it?"

"What?" Eden and I asked together.

"I think *you* really are the key," Aaron said. "Eve told you exactly what we needed to find Charles. Well, as exact as Eve could be."

I got the sinking feeling I knew what was needed to make Bill's spell work. I started to get queasy again.

"Tell me, Symon," Aaron muttered slowly. "Does the sight of your own blood still make you sick?"

My stomach lurched a little.

Yes. Yes it does.

Chapter Ten

I nipped up to the private bathroom off of Charles' bedroom and grabbed a quick shower to wash off the day's accumulated filth. The hot water felt good, easing knots in my muscles from two days of nonstop insanity. Showers always gave me time to think. Thinking was something I wish I'd indulged in a bit more ten years ago.

The fact that Belial had seen an opportunity to grab a senior religious man was not a surprise. Demons are opportunistic creatures. What I couldn't figure out was why the attacks continued. Why was an attempt made on Janice in broad daylight, for example? Sure, the Maine woods she called home were rural enough. But it was a coordinated effort that crossed many miles. I was missing something important, but for the life of me I couldn't guess at what it was.

My musings conducted under the jets of the shower were interrupted by a soft knock at my bathroom door. As I turned off the water, the door opened.

"I brought you some food," Janice said with a smile as I dove for a towel. "The rest of the animals downstairs would have finished it all off before you got dressed."

"Uh, thanks," I mumbled, wrapping the towel around my waist. Janice may have been the only woman I had ever been comfortable being naked around, but that was a long time ago.

"Bill is about ready for us. We are in the old gym. Eat something and we'll see you downstairs in a few minutes."

And just like that she was gone.

****

I threw on a fresh pair of jeans and a long-sleeved tee-shirt, gobbled down the dinner Janice had brought me, and headed downstairs; on the way grabbing something I haven't used in years.

The old gym brought back memories. We'd all trained there. It's where we were taught basic martial arts, as well as combat magic. Dread filled me as I walked into the large, oak-paneled cavern, not just because I was about to lose some of my blood, but also because being in my old training ground reminded me of how much I wasn't prepared for what we were about to do.

Bill had set up a series of folding tables in the gym almost in the center of the old basketball court. The circle drawn in the middle marked off more than just the spot for tip-off.

Charles had inlaid the parquet floor with a circle of pure silver, covered during games and other functions that the old gym had been used for back when there were students of both the magical and non-magical kind roaming the campus. The circle was the first basic component of any incantation or spell where a practitioner wanted to either focus magic for fine detail or to keep a spell active for a longer period of time with minimal effort. A circle could be any size, but it needed to be made of pure metal. Silver works the best for some reason I don't remember, but was probably explained to me some time in the past.

When we turned eighteen, Charles had given us each a small silver circle attached to a pure silver chain. That is what I had grabbed before leaving Charles' bedroom. It was ironic that the little circle I now wore around my neck was what I was going to throw in Charles' face before heading back to Dublin. Now I was going to use it to help find him.

I approached Bill's table and saw that it was covered in ingredients, books, and glass beakers. A dozen candles were laid out on the tables. They'd burned almost to the nubs, and there was a really interesting smell that couldn't wholly be attributed to decades of smelly, sweaty teenagers doing calisthenics.

"How's it going?" I asked Bill, my voice echoing in the empty space.

He jumped a little. "Hey, Sy," he said recovering quickly. "I didn't hear you come in. Where is everyone else?"

As if they'd read the script, the doors opened behind me, and Janice, Eden, Aaron, and Peter entered the gym.

"...Kowalski's team is outside waiting on orders, so we should be set to go, Aaron," Eden was saying as she came into the gym. "These guys know how to handle themselves. The cops don't."

"Maybe," Aaron grunted. "But I'd be happier if I could call in a SWAT team."

"And probably get a lot of cops and Charles killed?" said Janice, shaking her head. "Are you out of your mind?"

"You don't know that, Janice!" snarled Aaron. "The department..."

"The point is moot anyway," interrupted Peter. "You know what the Cardinal said, and his influence with the local government makes involving the police a non-starter. It's up to us and," he glanced guiltily at me, "Eden's security force to get Charles back." I guess Eden had let Peter know the cat was out of the bag.

"Then we'd better find out where he is so we can go and get him," I said. "Bill, how are we going to do this?" I asked him in a loud voice that hopefully didn't betray my concern that I was probably going to barf again when they took some of my blood. Bill lifted a legal pad off the table.

"It's been a while since I've done this stuff," he apologized, "so I'm going to have to refer to my notes. Sorry about that, Symon."

I nodded my head, "S' okay Bill. It's been a while for a lot of us. What do you want me to do?"

"Okay. Symon, I'm going to need you to be in the circle," Bill explained. "Please make sure you aren't touching the edge."

"I remember, Bill," I said, trying to be encouraging.

"You won't need to strip, but you will need a solid connection to the Earth," he continued as if lecturing a class, "so take off your boots and socks, please."

I removed them and stepped into the circle. I could feel, rather than hear a subsonic hum as soon as I had crossed over the silver boundary. My feet snapped to the floor inside the circle like two magnets when they get too close to each other. I was "plugged in," for lack of a better term.

"Good, Symon," praised Bill, his voice slightly distant. "I'm going to pass two things to you. First, a bowl containing the potion Aaron and I made." Careful not to touch the silver circle, he handed me an old wooden bowl. Inside was a substance that looked more like a greenish-yellow paste than the watery potions I'd been used to when learning the craft. It smelled like a combination of lilac and rotting meat.

"Next," said Bill, more hesitantly, "a knife." Again, being careful, he passed me a five-inch sharp silver knife. As soon as I touched the pure silver of the handle, I could feel a static charge connect the knife, through me, to the earth.

I watched as Aaron crossed to the tables and picked up a folded piece of paper. "This is a map Bill and I have treated with silver dust," he explained. Gently, he opened the map and placed it in front of me, outside the circle.

"Symon," said Bill, "you'll need to cut yourself and place three drops of blood in the bowl, and three more on the circle. No more, no less and in that order."

Everyone, I saw, was looking nervous as hell. But maybe it was me projecting.

"Anything else?" I asked.

"Yeah," replied Aaron," you'll feel a bit lightheaded as the spell begins to work. You'll need to eat all of the paste, then focus on the map." He knelt down by the silver-crusted piece of paper. "Focus is the key. Your mind will want to do other things, take you to different places. But stay sharp and concentrate and you should be fine." It didn't sound like he believed that last part.

A lot of times when you see people taking a blood-oath of some sort in the movies, you see them slice the palm of their hand to get at the blood. In the very next scene, you see these macho people wielding a sword or a gun or doing something that requires the use of their hands. I've sliced my palm before. I couldn't lift anything or move my hand properly for a week.

So I took the knife, thought about Charles, took a deep breath and stuck the tip into the little finger on my left hand. I won't tell you it didn't hurt, because it did. I won't tell you that my stomach didn't lurch at the sight of my own blood, 'cause that happened too. But I did as I was told. Three drops in the bowl and three on the circle.

The effect was immediate. I felt like one of those bobble-head dashboard dolls, with my noggin joggling crazily over cobblestones. I looked around and saw my friends outside the nice warm circle I was standing in and couldn't figure out why they weren't with me.

"Hey guys!" I slurred. I had to enunciate carefully because my mouth wasn't working right. Not that I cared. "Whatcha doin' way over there?"

"Concentrate, Symon!" yelled Aaron. Why was he yelling?

"Grumpy bastard," I complained. "You not getting laid these days, mate?"

"Symon, shut up and take the potion!" Aaron spat.

I looked down and saw a bowl in my hands. Right ... focus. I dipped my hand into the bowl and felt a squishy substance. I pulled a large glob of it out. 'Weird' I thought, but I ate Bill's concoction. It tasted bloody awful, but my mind, acting like a tiny drill sergeant screaming at me to eat, began to clear. Mechanically, I kept dipping my hand in and eating until the bowl was empty.

I closed my eyes. Warmth rose from my belly, and I used that feeling to hold onto the moment. I forced myself to concentrate on my old mentor.

"Charles," I said through gritted teeth, "where are you?"

In my mind I saw myself suddenly perched over St. Ignatius. I was drifting there, about a hundred feet over the steeple. I could see a couple of large black SUVs idling outside the front entrance. Must be Kowalski. I thought about waving to him.

"Focus, Symon!"

That was Janice's voice. My beautiful Janice. Oh, how I missed her. Focus. I needed to focus.

I continued to hover dreamily over the church when a large, black raven flew past me. I watched it circle me once, flapping madly until it settled into a hover in front of me.

"Focus, Symon," the raven croaked.

I blinked once. My mind finally cleared as if someone had thrown a switch. "Charles," I said again. "Focus on Charles."

Now my body zoomed straight up and away from St. Ignatius until I could see across the Charles River and into downtown Boston. I flew toward the southeast. Cars and lights moved below me and I could see little trails and flairs as they slithered along the highway. I followed the nighttime commuters out of downtown Boston until I descended into a dark and foreboding area made up of cheap row homes, boarded up businesses and an old brick church with an overgrown graveyard. As I got closer I saw that the steeple of the church was charred and in a state of advanced decay. The roof had two massive holes, obviously where flames had once broken through. The old building's stained glass windows were smashed and all the ground floor openings were sealed with plywood. Somehow I knew there was something in that dilapidated building. I decided to look.

I dropped in through one the larger of the two holes in the roof and hovered near the burned out trusses. The smell of charred wood and stagnant water was overwhelming. What I was looking for was, I knew, near the altar.

Drifting down slowly, I neared my goal. New smells suddenly assaulted my nose. Bodily smells. Sweat and urine along with the unmistakable odor of human desperation; they mixed with the pungent smell of brimstone and permeated the air around me. I could see the faint outline of a man, tied to rubble that had been stacked into a makeshift altar. Even though I could barely see in the dim light, I knew I had found him. Expecting the worst, the reality still left me gasping in horror.

"Symon?"

The voice was barely recognizable. It sounded weak and old. But there was an echo of a remembered timbre...

"Symon, I can sense you, but cannot see you. Are you there, my son? Symon? Listen to me please..."

I opened my mouth to speak when a second, raspier-sounding voice, filled with evil, shouted something in a tongue I didn't recognize and my vision faded abruptly.

****

I stumbled and fell, breaking the bond between the earth and the magic that the silver circle in the gym had enhanced. I landed on my knees and, placing my face in my hands, I shook uncontrollably. Janice was suddenly at my side. She held me and kept me from collapsing completely.

"Symon, it's okay..." Janice stuttered to a halt, her face pinched, reflecting that she knew full well it wasn't okay. It might never be fucking okay.

"Charles is dying!" My voice broke a bit. "That bastard Belial has him strapped to some abomination of an altar!"

Aaron came over to us. He was looking at the map that he'd originally laid out in front of the circle.

"You did good, Sy," he said tentatively. "Better then we'd hoped."

"Do you know where he is?" I asked. "All I saw was a burned out church..."

"Holy Name on Blue Hill Avenue," responded Aaron holding up the map. There was a little tower made of silver dust adorning a section of it. "There was a massive fire three years ago and the church has been sitting dormant and condemned ever since."

Blue Hill Avenue is in one of the seedier areas of Boston. A neighborhood traumatized by crime and filled with frightened, desperate people. The demon picked a good spot to hide Charles. It could draw power from the despair that permeated the streets.

I could still see the image of Charles lying bare on the rubble. It had been almost twenty-four hours since the Monsignor had been taken. Which meant he'd been tortured by that demon for twenty-four hours. My gut told me Charles wouldn't survive the twenty-fifth.

With my anger at my old mentor all but gone, a new emotion had grown to take its place. Revenge. I was taught that using magic for personal reasons was strictly forbidden. A tingling sensation came from my belly. Power—my power—was stirring. My head screamed, "Stop! Think! There is a logical solution to every problem!"

Go ahead, Symon Bryson. Use your power. Do it.

The book of Romans says: *"Do not take revenge, my friends, but leave room for God's wrath, for it is written: It is mine to avenge; I will repay, says the Lord."* Wise words. The battle between thoughtful logic and emotion-fueled revenge was short-lived.

Revenge won.

I stood, gently pushing Janice away from me.

"First, let's get my boots," I growled. "Then, we save Charles."

Chapter Eleven

We all exited St. Ignatius together. As in my vision, two massive black SUVs were idling at the curbside waiting for us as per Eden's request. Kowalski and Crystal were leaning on the first vehicle having a quiet conversation. They both looked up as we approached.

"What's the plan, Ms. Engle?" Crystal asked Eden.

Eden looked at me.

"I guess walking in there and blasting everything that isn't Charles into little pieces won't work," I said to her.

Eden smiled a bit. "Probably not."

"Okay then," I turned to Janice. "You appeared to me as a raven in my vision," I said slowly, an idea forming. "Up at your place you mentioned I 'hadn't seen anything yet,' correct?"

"Yes," she replied simply.

"Janice, speaking to animals is one thing. I'm guessing you can actually transform *into* an animal."

"Legend has it that the women who became shamans of my tribe could," she answered coyly.

"I'll take that as a yes," I said. "How small of an animal can you become?" I asked. "Can you, say, transform into a moth?"

Janice shook her head. "Mammals and birds only. The raven you saw in your vision is about the smallest I can become."

"That will do," I nodded, a plan beginning to gel.

"What do you have in mind?" asked Aaron.

I told them.

"You're insane!" exclaimed Eden. "But I like it. Kowalski?"

70

"It could work," the man answered, stroking his beard thoughtfully. "We'll need backup from the company, and we'll need to keep the authorities away for a while..." He looked at Aaron questioningly.

"It's dark now so the law-abiding citizens in that neighborhood tend to stay shut up in their homes," mused the detective. "Might be some gang activity, though. I'd be happier if we could get the Boston PD involved."

"No," I replied. "It's got to be just us. Belial has proven itself to be a nasty customer and who knows what else it has waiting for us. Both Charles and the demon sensed my presence so it's been warned."

"We should get going, then," said Peter. "It will take us twenty minutes or so to get there. Belial could move Charles by then."

"Kowalski, can you make arrangements en route?" I asked.

"Yeah," he answered. "And Crystal and I brought a few toys with us. They're in the back of the trucks."

I thought about Flint's rocket launcher and smiled.

****

Janice had excused herself to transform as I had requested. She said she would be able to communicate with us when she arrived at the abandoned church and I took her at her word. Kowalski and Crystal got us into the pair of SUVs—myself, Aaron, and Eden in the lead car with Kowalski. Peter, Bill and Crystal following close behind as we raced through Cambridge at a seriously unsafe speed.

Kowalski signed off his cell phone as we made a wild turn onto Memorial Drive that, I was pretty sure, caused a great deal of consternation among the drivers who were now behind us. I could tell by the horns blaring and the screeching of tires.

While Kowalski had been arranging for more of his people to meet us on Blue Hill Avenue, Eden gave us a rundown on the toys Kowalski had mentioned.

"Sub-dermal microphones attach to your throat with a bit of spirit gum. The ear pieces fit into your ear canal like a low-profile hearing aid," she said, handing Aaron and I each a small box. "In the back are army prototype auto assault shotguns with a twenty round drum. The military are currently testing them in Afghanistan."

"Holy crap, Eden. How much money do you have?" I asked, not being able to help myself.

"Enough," she said. "The recoil of the guns is muted by a sophisticated dampening system so they shouldn't have a kick." She continued down her laundry list of items, which included spare drums for the military issue shotguns, flash grenades and Kevlar vests.

"Could have used this stuff on Plum Island," I said, struggling into my vest as Kowalski passed a line of cars by swerving into the breakdown lane.

"I know," Eden said. "That's why we have it now. We'll never be caught unprepared again."

"Never again," Aaron and I responded together.

Kowalski finally turned onto Blue Hill Avenue and shut off the SUV's lights.

"There's a cemetery just before we reach the churchyard," I said. "It's overgrown and should give us some cover."

"Symon."

Aaron and I turned to each other at the same time and asked "What?"

"It's me, you idiots," the voice said. "It's Janice."

"How do you stick a sub-dermal mike to a bird?" I asked Eden.

"You don't," she snapped.

"Listen up, guys," said Janice's voice. "Charles is still in the church. It looks like he's still breathing although he's definitely unconscious. Belial is there too, but I sensed rather than saw him."

"Any other baddies around?" I asked hopefully.

"Yes," Janice's disembodied voice answered. There are about twenty bikers drinking in the parking lot on the opposite side of the church from your present location."

"Bikers aren't necessarily bad, Janice," said Aaron. Apparently Janice was broadcasting to all of us.

"Yeah, well I'm pretty sure these bikers have been dead for a while, so I'm guessing, since their rotting corpses are milling about, that there might be some evil afoot," Janice cawed a bit nastily.

"Leather-clad channelers," I commented. "Fantastic. Stay away from them, Janice. I know how you like undead bad-boys."

"Enough, people," Eden said. "Janice, were you able to follow up on the first part of Symon's plan?"

"Yes." Janice's voice had calmed down a bit. "But it's really close to Charles. You'll have to get right up to him, Symon."

"Backup is here," called Kowalski. I looked out the back window and saw that two more large black SUV's without lights had pulled in behind Peter and Bill's vehicle.

"Janice," I said, "we need you to keep one birdie eye on Charles and the other birdie eye on those goons in the parking lot. Can you do that?"

"No problem," her voice replied in my head. "I'll be ready for phase two of your plan when you need me. What's the signal?"

"You'll know it when you see it," I said.

We got out of our truck and saw that Peter, Bill, and Crystal had already donned their vests and had their weapons at the ready.

"Two priests wearing Kevlar and brandishing shotguns," I said. "Not something you see at Sunday Mass."

"Onward Christian Soldiers is one of my favorite hymns," replied Bill with a wry smile. He cocked his gun. "I'm thinking the Lord will be okay with us kicking a little Satanic booty tonight."

"Amen," said Peter.

There were close to twenty of us gathered around, awaiting final instructions. They were all looking at me, and I have to say I was beginning to have second thoughts. It'd been a long time since we'd done anything like this together. But at least, back then, I trusted everyone. Now, I wasn't so sure who to trust. I wasn't sure I could even trust myself.

But I had to try.

"Um..." I started. I wonder if Patton had ever come up with such a clever opening. "Right. We'll go through the cemetery. Aaron and I have to make it into the church or this whole party is for nothing. I'm sure Belial is expecting us so keep sharp. The goal is to get Charles and get out in one piece. We need you to cover us so we can do our thing. Questions?"

"Yes," said Bill. "Peter and I are coming with you. I guess that's not really a question."

"Actually, I was thinking about that," I answered Bill, putting my hand on his shoulder. "I need you two to do something that only men of the cloth can sort out. I mean besides blowing the shit out of a few of Hell's minions with large caliber weaponry. Can you hang back here for a bit?"

I explained what I had in mind. It took a minute or two for it to sink in but they both finally and reluctantly agreed.

"That's it. Eden?" I finished.

"Radio check: One. Two," she said. "Everyone set?"
There were a series of affirmatives.
"Move out."

****

We spread out and moved in teams toward the old overgrown cemetery. If there had ever been a fence around the deceased, it had long since decayed and fallen away. We entered their final resting place and began to weave in between broken headstones and over scrub brush and long unattended grass. With the exception of the rustling sound we made as we moved through the overgrowth, it was eerily silent.

The cemetery grounds were on an uphill slope heading toward the old church and we climbed it steadily in silence. We got about halfway through the bone yard when I heard a buzzing in my ear. I thought it was the earpiece Eden had given me and tapped it with my fingers.

The sound grew in volume. It was like the buzzing of a cicada in late summer, only deeper. A shiver ran up and down my spine as I realized the sound was not from some faulty equipment in my ear, but coming from all around us.

"Look sharp," I heard Kowalski say. "We're not alone."

Okay, hindsight being twenty-twenty and all, I guess I shouldn't have tromped everyone through a creepy graveyard.

Suddenly I heard a series of loud reports off to my left. Panicked voices flooded my receiver.

"What is that?"

"Shoot the damn thing!"

"Dammit they have some sort of wooden hatchets. Davis is down."

The brush moved in front of me and a series of red eyes glowed between gaps in the underbrush.

Aaron fired his shotgun into the brush. "Here they come!" he yelled.

"Janice," I whispered quickly, "Get it to him now."

"Do you need my help?" Her voice said in my head.

"Stay with Charles!" I shouted loudly as a creature about four feet tall shot out from behind a tombstone on my right. I had enough time to see dark green skin, red eyes, a flash of yellowish fangs and a raised wooden weapon before I turned and blew the thing in half. I'd never done more then read about skratta—demonic goblins—before. They were nasty buggers.

"Stay calm, people!" I shouted as I blasted another one that was about to jump Aaron. "Peter, Bill. Any time you're ready as long as it's now!"

I'd seen Peter do a bit of fancy magic once. He'd explained that men of the church with the gift could do things that some of us less holy folk couldn't pull off. Through my earpiece I heard both him and Bill begin chanting in Latin. A euphoric feeling came over me as I heard the words. I knew the gist of what the two priests were incanting, it was both beautiful and sad at the same time.

High-pitched squealing surrounded us and I took the opportunity to blast another one of the creatures. The few advancing on Aaron and me stopped dead in their tracks, hands over their bat-like ears. From the sounds of the guns going off around me everyone had noticed that our attackers had become ... distracted.

The gunfire ceased soon after.

"Thanks, guys. If it weren't for the celibacy thing I'd have become a priest just so you could've taught me that."

There was no response.

"Bill? Peter?"

Nothing.

"Kowalski, take the wounded and a few of your guys back to the trucks. Make sure the priests are okay."

"On my way."

"The rest of you, let's get going. We need to get to the church now."

"Symon, the channelers are on the move," warned Janice telepathically.

"Heads up, we've got company," I said into my microphone.

Aaron and I quickly crossed the last stretch of the cemetery, clearing the last of the tombstones at the same time as Eden and a dozen or so of her men. The Church was about fifty yards further up the slope.

"Almost there!" I said. "Run for it!"

We all sprinted over trash and weeds up toward the front entrance of the ruined building. We had almost made it to the steps when the channelers appeared.

"You and Aaron go get Charles!" screamed Eden. "We'll hold them off and come get you!"

"Eden..."

"*Go*, Symon!"

The sound of heavy weaponry clattered to life, heavy-gauge rounds blasting dirt and debris all around us as Aaron and I made the final dash up the steps. A bullet ricocheted near me and I flinched as pieces of shattered brick pelted my face, but I kept moving.

We made it into the remains of a large burnt-out sanctuary. It looked exactly as it did in my vision and, if anything, the smell of burned wood was even stronger than it had been in my potion-induced visit.

My eyes took a second or two to adjust to the dim light. I could see the rubble-pile-cum-altar and a figure tied to it. Charles.

There was also a figure standing over him. It was vaguely humanoid, with a large pronounced beak for a nose, glowing eyes and bat-like wings folded against its back. It had what looked like a human torso covered with a white collared shirt that glowed in the dim light. It was also wearing dark colored pants that were ripped at the bottom to accommodate its large clawed feet.

"Symon Bryson," Belial sneered, that scratchy voice unmistakable. "And I see you brought a guest. How nice."

I lifted the shotgun to blow the demon's head off. It raised an eyebrow at me. "Tut tut, Symon Bryson. 'Do not be quickly provoked in your spirit, for anger resides in the lap of fools,' as it says in your book of Ecclesiastes." Belial slowly raised up one hand that held a wicked-looking curved blade. The demon smiled and it held up its second hand. Black feathers were flying in all directions as a struggling raven tried to free itself from the demon's grasp.

Shit.

"Now be a good boy, Symon Bryson, and drop your toy. Your friend, too. Come to Belial and I will let you say goodbye to the old man before I sacrifice him to my Lord and Master."

We dropped our weapons and approached the demon and the prone form of Charles. The Monsignor's skin was a sickly gray and bled from a series of wounds. I was livid, but tried to control my emotions. I still had an ace in the hole that might help get all of us out of this mess, as long as Janice had done what I'd asked and I stayed calm. The plan was still...

"That's a good boy," Belial scratched. "Let us discuss too, Symon Bryson, why you thought an Indian witch disguised as a bird could deliver a small silver ring to your man of God. Did you think my presence in this world could be severed so easily?"

Double shit.

Chapter Twelve

The plywood acting as doors to the burned out church banged open behind Aaron and me. The zombie biker gang entered the building dragging with them Eden, Peter and Bill, along with a half dozen bruised and bleeding members of Eden's team. They were trussed up and were all tossed to their knees beside us. We were royally screwed.

"See, Symon Bryson," said Belial triumphantly, "you and your friends are no match for us." Janice, still in the form of a raven, let out a low squawk of pain as the demon squeezed her even tighter. "But I am not without sympathy for your pathetic situation. I have an offer for you that just might let your friends live another day."

Demons are chaotic creatures. You never know what they will do. Their agendas are always complicated, and their goals change on a whim. However, there was one constant I'd discovered during the few encounters I'd had with them. They love to tell anyone who will listen how powerful and almighty they are. If I could just keep this jackass talking, I might be able to figure a way out of this mess.

I looked over at Aaron and saw him nod slightly at me. Along with Janice clutched in one claw-like hand, I saw that the demon also held the little silver circle that she was meant to place with Charles to sever Belial's connection to earth. Despite the creature's massive ego, I noticed it was very careful to hold the magical item by the strap as far away from its skin as possible. That gave me a bit of an idea. Now I just had to play for time.

"Belial," I said in my most humble-sounding voice, "you have the Monsignor. Apparently you wanted me here as well. You have achieved what you wanted so I see no reason not to let the rest of these people go." Blood from a cut in my forehead caused by the flying debris trickled into my eyes and I wiped it away.

"Oh no, Symon Bryson," it replied in that scratchy voice. "Although my initial task was to corrupt your Man of God, opportunity has provided me with the bonus of his star pupils. It will be amusing to kill the rest of the teacher's pets in front of the old man. However, I have a counter-proposal."

This should be good, I thought.

"Give to me voluntarily some of your blood and I shall consider the request regarding your friends," Belial snarled.

"Of course!" I said. "If the Monsignor was fully corrupted, you would have been able to deliver his soul to hell. You need my blood to complete the journey with Charles."

It nodded and smiled. "Very good, Symon Bryson. The old man is strong. Stronger than I anticipated. But now that you're here it does not matter. Do you agree to my offer?"

"Um, let me think for a moment," I replied. If Belial had my blood, he'd disappear with Charles into Hell and I'd never be able to get him back. "The answer's no."

"Then you have sealed the fate of your friends." It kicked the unmoving form of Charles and I winced. "Wake up, Monsignor Charles DuBarry," Belial said. "You have visitors and I want you to see them before they die."

Charles groaned a little and in the dim light I could barely make out his eyes fluttering open. The old man tried to sit up but his bindings held him firmly to the rubble. Charles moved his head drunkenly around. His head stopped moving as his eyes met mine. A look of panic came across his face.

"Symon, no," Charles croaked, his voice barely a whisper.

"Yes, Charles DuBarry!" said Belial, regaining some of its swagger. "See? Your favorite students have come to see you! But you and I have business elsewhere, so I am afraid taking time to inflict pain and suffering on them is not possible. Take heart, Charles DuBarry! Their deaths will be quick."

As Belial continued to wax on about our impending doom, I saw a little red light appear on the demon's chest. Then a second. And a third. I looked around and more little red dots on the channelers. A few of them started to swipe at them as if they were bugs. I looked at Eden, down on her knees near me, and she smiled as she mouthed silently, "Backup plan."

"Duck!" I screamed as I dropped to the ground yanking Aaron with me.

Belial and the channelers all screamed with one voice as Eden's snipers let loose multiple rounds of heavy gage ammunition, red laser sites targeting the biker meat-puppets methodically. Belial fell off the makeshift pile of rubble it had been using as its podium; dropping both Janice and my silver circle in the process. The leather-clad channelers fell away from their prisoners all still screaming in one furious voice as bits and pieces of them were shot off.

Shards of stone and wood blasted all around me. Unintelligible screams, both from the living and the undead, echoed off the old church walls. A piece of the makeshift altar exploded in front of me when an armor-piercing round struck the corner. I fell to my knees, sharp debris shredding my pants and drawing even more blood. If Belial hadn't killed the Monsignor and Janice by now, it was likely friendly fire would, as the shots fired into the church became more erratic with the rising debris cloud. I scrambled over to where Belial had fallen looking for both Janice and my one chance of finishing this right now.

"Get to Charles!" I shouted in desperation toward Aaron.

The Monsignor moved feebly. He tried to speak, but his words were drowned out by noise of battle surrounding us. A quick glance told me that Eden and her people, despite being bound and already roughed up, were systematically kicking the crap out of the bullet-ridden channelers.

I reached where I thought Belial had fallen, neither finding my silver circle nor a raven, when I heard a deafening growl. Bloodied and spurting a foul-smelling black liquid, I saw the demon crouched on all fours, wings now extended high above its back, but it wasn't moving a muscle.

Honestly, guns really can't do much to a demon. Its life force was still safely tucked away in the Shadow-world of Hell. Certainly a significant amount of damage to Belial's earthly body could cause it enough pain to annoy it, or even in extreme cases break its soul connection, sending it back to its home realm. But Belial wasn't doing a stone gargoyle impression because of the damage Eden's snipers had caused.

Belial was not moving because there was a large, really pissed-off magical white wolf growling about three inches from the demon's face. I really have to be nicer to Janice in the future.

"Hold Belial there!" I shouted at Janice and began a frantic search for my blessed silver circle. "Hang on, Charles ... hang on." I muttered, as I saw Aaron struggling with the binders on Charles. The Monsignor had gone limp and I feared the worst.

I could hear the muffled *phwip, phwip*, of bullets as they flew into the church from the snipers posted outside and a hiss of laughter came from Belial. "So much to learn, Symon Bryson. You think this shape-changing shaman bitch can hold me? Let me teach you about Hell's power, young magician."

There was a blur of movement and a yelp of pain as the Janice-wolf was hurled into a fire-damaged column. The charred timbers buckled from the impact. With a large crack, the column broke and tumbled to the old stone floor of the church, bringing pieces of the remaining ceiling with it. The wreckage obscured my view of Belial and anyone else for that matter. The sniper fire stopped as the potential for collateral damage increased exponentially with the amount of dust kicked up.

I dove for cover to my left as slate tiles and burnt wood continued to tumble from above. I ended up closer to Aaron, who had thrown his body over Charles to protect him from the collapsing ceiling. As I avoided the rain of roofing materials, a glint caught my eye. My silver circle was hanging on a piece of broken timber not more than half a foot from the makeshift altar Belial had built. Coughing from the dust, I struggled to reach my necklace. I reached out to grab it but I was thrown into the pile of rubble Charles had been tied to.

Black, tar-like liquid dripped on me as I struggled to breathe. The bleeding demon was standing over me, having just kicked me as if going for the longest field goal in history. I was sure Belial had cracked a couple of ribs and the pain was excruciating.

"I am forbidden to spill your blood, Symon Bryson," Belial hissed. "But there are no instructions regarding the use of blunt force. I will take pleasure..."

The creature stopped mid-sentence and began sniffing the air. It looked down at me with a sneer, teeth coated with its slick oily black blood that dribbled down its evil face.

"Blood," the creature said. "Your blood, Symon Bryson. I might be forbidden to spill your blood, but using it, having not caused the injury..." It reached down and placed a slimy claw on my scalp, brushing the cut roughly.

"Thank you, Symon Bryson. You are the key to my glorious return with my prize!" Its claw, smeared with my blood, drew back. Belial laughed as he reached out for Charles. I was the catalyst for Charles' guilt. With my blood, the creature could return to Hell with Charles in tow. His fate would be sealed and the Monsignor would be lost forever. And it would be my fault.

Ignoring the pain, I rolled to my side, hand scrambling in the debris. "Oh, you can go," I shouted, "but not with Charles!"

I'd grabbed up my silver circle and slammed it on Belial's calf in one smooth motion.

The creature let out a real scream this time and the surviving channelers scattered throughout the ruined building echoed it. Lightning accompanied by the loud crack of thunder flashed and boomed inside the church. The static electricity made the hair all over my body stand straight up. A wind kicked up, and grit, wood, and bits of broken masonry began to swirl around the sanctuary, bouncing off everything and everyone. A reddish fog streamed from Belial's mouth and enveloped the demon. It lingered for a second, and then it, the wind, the whole storm was gone. The silence would have been deafening, if I didn't have a ringing in my ears from the thunder.

The lifeless embodiment of Belial collapsed to the ground.

Wheezing and clutching my side, I crawled over to where Aaron still lay sprawled protectively over Charles. I picked myself up, room spinning, and collapsed near the beaten form of my old mentor and my best friend.

"It's gone," I croaked.

"Good," said Aaron, lifting himself off of Charles while checking the old man's pulse. "Weak but steady. We need a MedEvac."

"It will be here in two," Eden responded as she limped toward us. "We made a mess of things tonight."

"We got Charles back," I snapped, hoisting myself to my feet. "Aaron, help me get him down from this." I worked to untie the unconscious man.

Aaron picked up a sharp piece of masonry and cut through Charles' bonds. He came over to my side to help me as my hands were shaking and I couldn't get the knots undone. We gently lifted the broken man to the ground.

"God, look at this," said Aaron, his voice a hoarse whisper. I could now see in detail what I'd glanced at earlier. Hundreds of tiny cuts, all oozing blood, covered the monsignor's body. His skin was clammy and cold to the touch. His breathing came in little gasps.

"Somebody get me a coat and some water. Nobody outside of us sees him like this," I said, as the tears I had been holding back since I first saw Charles in my magic-induced vision streamed down my cheeks.

More of Eden's team came toward us, having extracted themselves from under pieces of masonry and roofing materials. They were all walking wounded, with injuries that spanned from bruises to broken bones.

There was a loud crash and we all turned wildly to its source. Flint and a few others stormed into the church. They all held military-grade sniper rifles—Sig SSG-3000's maybe—at the ready.

The whirring blades of the MedEvac helicopter Eden had summoned sounded through the open space once occupied by the roof. I could hear sirens drawing closer to the church.

It wasn't until a moment later when a gentle hand touched my shoulder that I realized I'd been cradling Charles, wrapped in an overcoat donated by Flint. "Back away, Symon," Janice said quietly. "I can help him."

Sirens wailed in the distance.

****

"Yeah, we screwed up," I said, looking at Janice after the officials had taken our statements. There was a nasty cut on her cheek and one of her eyes was swollen shut. "But we got Charles back. It all worked out."

The helicopter that landed right in the middle of Blue Hills Avenue was long gone at this point. Charles would be at Mass General by now. The rest of Eden's crew had been attended to and only two had been injured seriously enough to be hospitalized. I shifted uncomfortably at the bandages holding my bruised ribs in place.

We'd been lucky.

"We're in serious trouble, Symon. It's only because of Eden that we haven't been locked up yet. There're gonna be consequences."

Eden had apparently used her connections to bring the Feds in to take control of our battle aftermath. Prior to that, Boston PD and the SWAT team had been ready to shoot us all. Aaron had held them at bay while Eden's political machine worked its own sort of magic.

Both Bill and Peter had been summoned back to St. Ignatius, where I suspected a very angry Cardinal was waiting for them. Aaron had been called back to his Cambridge precinct after his shouting match with Boston's finest. Eden and her team were working on 'cleanup' with the Feds. That left Janice, a driver from Eden's firm I hadn't met before, and me. Well, okay there were still two companies of the Boston Fire Department giving us dirty looks as they hosed down the remains of the abandoned church.

Consequences, Janice said. Charles was alive. The rest we could handle.

I looked at Janice. "Screw the consequences. You do what you need to in order to get the job done. We did that. We saved Charles' soul. End of story."

Boy, was I wrong.

Chapter Thirteen

Ten Years Ago

The train arrived in New London, Connecticut, late one rainy fall afternoon. Monsignor DuBarry hopped off as soon as the train jolted to a stop. The rest of us moved rather slowly, having been tasked with carrying heavy backpacks that Peter had provisioned for us this trip. The Monsignor had taken the opportunity of a long train ride to educate us about all the little nuances of the New England rail system. Aaron and I had a bet whether or not our verbose mentor would be giving us a pop quiz on the way back.

"Let's go everyone!" the Monsignor's voice boomed over the crowd. All around us, people turned in alarm and a toddler in a stroller burst into tears.

"Nice one," complimented Bill quietly to Aaron and me. "Now he's making small children cry." We snickered, but stopped at a sharp look from Janice. All three of us, Aaron, Bill, and I, saluted her mockingly. Janice, still in a mood, gave us a disapproving stare.

Aaron, Bill, Eve and I had been chatting excitedly about our first real mission away from the Church. Charles finally thought we were ready. Although there weren't many details, we hadn't cared. Years of training and minor demonic skirmishes were about to pay off. But Eden and Janice hadn't seemed nearly as excited, preferring to be off on their own, engaged in private conversation.

"Monsignor," asked Bill, "why are we in Connecticut?"

"This is but a way point, William," the Monsignor answered. "We're going on a bit of an expedition for our first mission. New London just happens to be our next departure point." Other passengers quickly dispersed from the station until all that remained were the seven of us.

The cool autumn evening had turned colder and the steady misting rain that had dogged us since Boston was now accompanied by a sea breeze that made the train platform roof all but useless. But it didn't matter. The excitement ahead would keep me warm. At least I hoped it would, as I *may* have left my heavy jacket back at St. Ignatius in the rush to leave.

"Why are we waiting?" I asked through chattering teeth.

"Patience, Symon. It's a virtue you could use a little more of," chided the Monsignor as he put on his signature black fedora, his only acknowledgement of the inclement weather.

A few minutes later, a pair of headlights cut the evening mist as a white van pulled into the station drop-off area. Simple black letters identified it as a bus belonging to the United Methodist Church Choral Society.

A heavyset, matronly woman with graying curly hair rolled down the driver's side window. Charles always called in favors allowing him to travel as cheaply as possible. The train ride had been an extravagance on his part. I wondered what favor this woman owed Charles.

"Evening, Father Charles. I see you brought your brood with you," the woman said, surveying both us and our copious amount of gear. "Planning a camping trip?"

"Always a pleasure, Sarah," Charles said. "Everyone in the van, please."

Bill slid open the door and we loaded our gear into the van. He and Aaron were still discussing the possibilities of our mission, about which we'd been told exactly nothing. I was just happy to get off the chilly, wet platform and into the heated, rain-free van. Eden and Janice moved themselves to the bench seat in the back and with silent, scary looks warned us away from joining them. We knew what that meant, so Bill, Aaron and I squeezed into the middle seats with Eve. Aaron and I, of course, had to make a joke about Bill's girlfriend, Jasmine, getting jealous. Eve laughed.

The Monsignor got into the front passenger seat and slammed the door behind him. I closed the sliding door, no easy feat with four of us clamoring for space on the one seat.

"Where to, Charles?" asked Sarah.

"Fort Trumbull State Park. We have a boat to catch."

Aaron and I looked at each other. Chill and rain forgotten, we both had the same thought. Now this was getting interesting.

****

The ride to the park probably took only fifteen minutes. I say "probably" because the Monsignor's apparent past life as a tour guide manifested itself again:

"Our current destination, Fort Trumbull, had a major ribbon-cutting ceremony a few months ago and will open to the general public early next year," said our teacher, launching into another lecture. "It was originally built at the start of the Revolutionary War. Governor Trumbull himself ordered it finished to protect the seat of government in Connecticut from a British incursion via the mouth of the Thames."

I rolled my eyes and Eve kicked me.

"More recently, it was the Coast Guard Academy and then it became the Merchant Marine Academy just before the outbreak of World War II. In the fifties the Naval Underwater Sound Laboratory took it over and it remained a research facility until the mid-nineties. I happen to know the curator, and he has generously offered to let us use the docks here."

We pulled up to the gates and there was a man dressed in a trench coat holding an umbrella, waiting for us.

The woman—Sarah—rolled down her window. "Evening, Jacob."

"Sarah. Father Charles," the man nodded. "You're all set, Monsignor. The *Katie Mae* will be here shortly. She'll pull in front of the *Eagle*."

"Bless you, Jacob. Much appreciated," said Charles, tipping the brim of his hat.

Jacob snorted. "Did I have a choice?"

"No," answered Charles.

"There you go then. Safe trip, Monsignor."

The enigmatic conversation apparently over, Sarah rolled up the window and proceeded into the park. After a few turns on the winding road, the docks finally came into view. Even in the evening gloom, a gleaming white three-masted ship shone like a beacon through the mist.

"The USCG *Eagle*," said Charles quietly. "One of only two remaining sailing vessels still commissioned in the U.S."

Charles pointed at the ship. "That's our stop, Sarah. Appreciate the lift."

"Sure," she said. "When will you be back so I can pick you up?"

"I'll ring if I need you," replied Charles mysteriously. "Everyone out, please."

We all hopped out of the van and thanked Sarah for the lift. With a jaunty wave, she drove off. The drizzle of earlier had now become a steady downpour and, unlike at the station, there wasn't even an overhang to protect us.

It wasn't long before we all heard the deep chugging of powerful diesel motors approaching the dock area. A large fishing vessel, without running lights, appeared suddenly out of the gloom and slid expertly into position in front of the tall ship. Deck hands jumped off the boat and made fast to the cleats spaced along the pier.

Bill leaned toward Aaron and me. "Isn't that like the boat we saw in that George Clooney movie this past summer?" he asked. I looked at him and saw that his skin had turned a bit gray.

"Ladies and gentlemen, I give you the *Katie Mae*," Charles announced, sounding strangely proud of the ship. To me, it looked like a rust bucket in need of serious work.

"I'm surprised she's still floating," I said, forgetting how well sound travels over water.

"It's not a cruise ship, boy," answered a cranky Scottish burr. "But she'll get ye where ye need to be and back again. That I'll guarantee."

"Jack, is that you?" the Monsignor called up toward the direction of the voice.

"Aye, Padre, it's me. Why don't you bring your cheeky boys and girls on board and we'll get under way. Storm's a comin'."

With a bit of trepidation we hoisted our gear and made our way up the gangway and onto the main deck of the ship. A tall, thin man of medium build with a scruffy, full beard, equal parts salt and pepper, came over to us and grasped Charles' hand in welcome.

"Been a long time, Padre. Was glad to get your call."

"Captain Straw," said Charles warmly. The Monsignor turned to us. "Students, this is Captain Jack Straw. Don't let the burr fool you, he's an old friend from the Marine Corps. We served two tours together. You will treat him as you would a member of our order."

Greetings and introductions followed. Charles spoke rarely about his Vietnam days, and I looked forward to perhaps finding out a bit more about the Monsignor from the captain.

****

A couple of crewmen grabbed our gear and moved to stow it below deck. The Captain showed Charles and the rest of us to the crew mess as it was the only space on the ship for a large group to gather. It was about one-eighth the size of the kitchen back at St. Ignatius, and my stomach rumbled as I realized Peter would probably be cooking one of his marvelous meals right about now. Looking at a tray of ham sandwiches that had been left out for us, I was momentarily jealous of the 'normal' students back at the parish school enjoying a hot meal and the warmth of the dormitories.

"We'll have some peace in here, Padre, as the rest of the crew are loading a few additional items I asked the curator for. It'll be about fifteen minutes or so before we get under way."

"Can your first mate handle the departure?" asked Charles.

"Old Joel? Of course. Trained him m'self. Despite that, he's a good seaman."

The noise settled down as we all grabbed a sandwich and made ourselves as comfortable as possible in the cramped space. There was an air of excitement in the room as we all waited to finally hear the details of our first mission.

"So," the Monsignor began, "first let me say thank you to Jack for bringing his ship up here to assist us." Jack tipped his Greek fisherman's cap at Charles. "You should all know," he continued, "that Jack and I go way back. We've both seen things you can only imagine. He's one of us and you can speak freely in front of him. But as far as the rest of the crew is concerned, you are to remain silent. Do not engage in any sort of conversation with them for the duration of this mission. Understood?"

We nodded.

"You can do magic?" Eve blurted out.

"Aye, lass. Didn't know it until near the end of my second tour in 'Nam, though. Saved the Padre's arse that day."

"Jack," the Monsignor said, in what I recognized as a warning tone.

To our delight, the Captain ignored Charles and went on.

"A couple hundred thousand Viet Cong came across the border in the early spring of seventy-two. They thought we were done, see, because o' the political pressure and anti-war movement at home. They thought they could just walk in and take the whole of South Vietnam for themselves."

"...but they were wrong," Charles sighed in a way that intimated he may have heard Captain Straw tell this story before.

The Captain nodded. "They were wrong indeed. But that was later. Our squad got caught in Quang Tri city and had to dig in. We'd been poking around up North, investigating reports about a massive build up by the People's Army of Vietnam. The reports were right..."

"...but our radios were out," said Charles in a bored voice.

"...but our radios were out. We tried to hightail it back to command to let them know what was about to come down, but we didn't make it. We were holed up in this old bar at the south end of town when fifteen or twenty..."

"It was five."

"...of them came into the place with Kalashnikov's ready to go."

"Machine guns," I whispered to Janice. She elbowed me hard to the ribs. Sheesh, I was just trying to help.

Really into his story now, the Captain stood and paced as much as he could in the small space. "Charles was a dead duck. Right out in the open, his weapon nowhere to be seen. I tried to open fire on the bastards, but my gun jammed. The Padre was about to buy it and there was nothing I could do about it..."

"So you asked God for help," Charles said.

Nodding at the Monsignor, Jack went on, "I'm not proud of myself, but I begged the Lord Almighty for a weapon to smite the enemy." He paused. The ship moved slightly under our feet.

"What happened next?" Eve asked quietly.

"The Lord's a bit funny sometimes, young lady," replied the Captain. "He tends to give you what you need, not what you want. See, I wanted my damn gun to un-jam. What I got..."

"You had it all along," Charles said.

"What I got was this ... power. I was so desperate to protect Charles and the rest of my friends. I just wanted the enemy to die. Unless you actually have been to war and experience the closeness and affection for your brothers-in-arms..." Jack fell silent, lost in thought for a moment.

"Well, what happened next was beyond anything I'd ever experienced. Duty. Honor. Back then, these things really meant something to a soldier, and I could feel them clearer tha' I'd ever felt them before—coming from very depths of my soul. There was this bright blue-white flame and all of a sudden the North Vietnamese were dead. It felt like an eternity, but from the time my gun jammed until the enemy lay dead all around us couldn't have been more than a second or two. It was the Grace of God that saved us that day."

I'd seen raw power like that used before. Hell, we'd all seen Charles, Peter, and a few others do amazing things. But to use that power to kill; that was different altogether. I'd always known what we were being prepared for, but I guess I'd never really understood that killing might be a part of it. Sure we'd sent a demon or two back to the Shadow-world. But the realization finally hit me that we might have to take a few mortal lives as well. I shivered a little.

"Charles took me under his wing after that," Jack said. "Taught me how to control what I have. Use it when I need to. And never abuse it."

A look passed between the two men that I couldn't read. Sadness perhaps?

"I met others who could do what I ... what we ... can do. I learned why we had this gift and what the real war was. Vietnam was nothing compared to the battle for Earth itself."

Charles laid a hand on Jack's shoulder.

Jack cleared his throat. "Anyway, it's my understanding that's why you folk are with us today. Time for you to perform a little magic and continue the fight. After all, the Padre and I won't live forever!"

"We finished with the war stories, Jack?" the Monsignor asked softly.

The Captain looked at Charles for a moment, then smiled and shook his head. "For the moment, Padre. I reserve the right to impress your students with a story or two at my discretion throughout the course of this outing."

"Fair enough," Charles smiled too. "Now, there are a few things we need to cover before we get to our destination, so I..."

"Where *are* we going, Monsignor?" I interrupted.

The Monsignor looked at me and I expected another comment about patience. Instead, he said, "We're heading across the Sound to New York, Symon. A little place called Plum Island."

Chapter Fourteen

Present Day

"Screw the consequences," I'd said. What a jackass.

Janice and I arrived at St. Ignatius in one of Eden's armored Town Cars to a total circus.

Okay, there weren't clowns, or that guy who cleans up after the elephants, but the press was there in force.

I gritted my teeth. Janice knew what I was thinking.

"I don't think it was Aaron this time, Symon," she guessed. "The press monitor all the police and fire radio bands..."

"Yeah, but showing up in this black celebrity-style behemoth will put the spotlight on us really quick. Oh, and look by the doors to the sanctuary," I continued. "Bad suits, faux silk ties, price club trench coats: The Feds are here, too." I winced as I shifted in my seat. Damn broken ribs. "And I thought rescuing Charles was going to be the highlight of my day."

The car pulled up to the front steps and we were immediately surrounded by lights, cameras and, well ... action. One of the Feds muscled their way to the car and opened the door. He was a balding, middle-aged man with a darkish complexion and a pencil moustache. He opened the door with one hand, holding his ID above his head with the other. "Federal Agents! Let these people through, please!"

"Why are Federal Agents involved in Church vandalism?"

"Who are you and why are you here?"

"We have a source that says Charles DuBarry was kidnapped despite the Diocese press release. Any comment?"

"Does this limousine belong to the Church?"

Whenever I see the press gathering like vultures, whether it be on TV or now experienced personally, all I can see is Ricardo Montalban telling Chekov in *Star Trek II* that the parasite he's about to stick in his ear is 'not quite domesticated.' And that's when the screaming starts.

The agent grabbed Janice and me and we shoved our way through the crowd and entered the church.

"Thank you agent...?" Janice prompted.

"Sanchez." He pointed at his partner who'd followed us in. "That's Special Agent Vitale. We're…"

"FBI," I said. "We heard."

"Good," Sanchez said, "but I figured you knew that. What I was going to say is that we are from the New York Bureau."

"New York? What are you doing in Boston?"

"Cambridge," Vitale corrected.

"Whatever," I said. "What are you doing here?"

"Mr. Bryson," Sanchez began to explain, "my Associate Director has been keeping tabs on you."

Well, that was interesting. I'd gone from being blissfully anonymous in Dublin to being tracked by Eden's company and the Feds. I wondered if I had my own satellite.

"Your passport activity alerted the Associate Director to your arrival here and he sent us to request your presence in our Boston field office for a consultation," Vitale said.

"That can wait, boys," an annoyingly familiar booming voice behind me bleated. "Mr. Bryson, join me in the Monsignor's study, will you?"

"Of course, Your Eminence," I replied with the utmost and totally faked respect. "That's my cue, guys. Hang out for a while." That last bit was for Janice, but I was pretty sure the Feds would wait as well.

I followed Cardinal Maguire back to the study where Eden, Bill, and Peter were waiting.

"How's Charles?" I asked as the door closed behind me.

"Critical, but stable," answered Peter. "They've put him in a medically induced coma."

"What about your boys and girls, Eden?"

"Stitches, a few broken bones. They'll all live to fight another day," she replied.

I smiled. "They did good, Eden. They've obviously had some serious training. We should discuss how, exactly, they were allowed to receive said training when it's been forbidden by the Church to teach non-practitioners."

"Enough, Bryson," boomed Cardinal Maguire. "We have things of our own to discuss."

"Absolutely, Your Eminence," I said. "Let's start with who has my ticket back to Dublin?"

Silence followed. Cardinal Maguire just glared at me, the red and purple splotches dancing across his face. I thought the man was on the verge of either a stroke or heart attack. Peter looked away and Bill just stared disapprovingly at me. Eden, on the other hand, covered what I could swear was a smile with her hand.

"Ahem," Peter cleared his throat. "Well, Symon, it's a little more complicated now. We don't think..."

"We?" I asked. "Who's this ubiquitous 'we,' Peter?" I waited for an answer, not really expecting one. After a few seconds of uncomfortable silence, I finally said, "Look, I did what you asked. I got Charles back."

"And you screwed up again, Bryson."

"I don't mean to be rude, Eminence," but of course I did. "You never really defined how I was to get the Monsignor back. *"We,"* I said, emphasizing the pronoun, "did our job. I've barely slept in days, I'm tired, banged up, and have had it with this nonsense. I'm going home."

"Which is why I shut down this school years ago," the Cardinal said, turning to Peter. "I always told Charles that his young obnoxious cowboys could never accomplish what trained, disciplined members of the Church could accomplish. Once again, I'm proven right."

"Which, of course, is why you asked the *Dalton Gang* to save a trained and disciplined member of the Church." You know that imaginary line you shouldn't cross? Yep, it was behind me.

"Why you little..."

"Gentlemen, please," Eden pleaded. "The point is we've just been part of a significant and very public event. Putting aside the fact that the Monsignor was directly involved, this is the third such event in the last year."

Cardinal Maguire took a deep breath and glared at me one last time. "You're right, m'dear. Satan's minions have been openly encroaching into our world of late. It's getting harder and harder to keep the general population protected from the realities of the Shadow-world."

Peter let out a heavy sigh and sat down. "Chaos is winning," he muttered miserably.

"That's an accurate assessment, Father Fine," said His Eminence.

"Did Charles know this?" I asked.

Cardinal Maguire looked at me for a moment, his political game face now firmly back in place. "Yes, Bryson. He's the one who has been documenting the changes in the 'Great Game.' The Pope himself asked me to verify the Monsignor's reports."

This was not good. The 'Great Game' quite simply was what the Cardinal had called the balance between good and evil. The scales, if I was hearing this right, were now tipping dangerously. If Charles knew this, then that explained why he'd reached out to us and why Peter had noticed a change in the Monsignor's behavior. It also may explain why Eden's sister had gotten worse over the last few months.

"What additional incidents, Eminence?" asked Bill. The look on both his and Peter's faces was genuine shock at the Cardinal's revelation.

"There have been attacks on special Vatican representatives around the world. Father Papadopoulos in Athens was killed. Fathers Nwoso and Mensah along with their entire team are still missing from the parish in Addis Ababa."

"I thought we were the only ones," I interrupted.

"You were the only ones raised in this school and trained specifically for this war," replied Peter.

"Then the incident with Belial…" I started.

"Is the third such attack documented in the past year," said his Eminence. "But this time we might have an advantage."

"And that is?" I asked.

"We have a surviving witness, assuming Charles wakes up," said Eden.

Boy, did I miss my apartment in Dublin.

"Eden, when did your sister start … getting worse?" I asked.

"A few months ago … maybe eight or nine, come to think of it," she said thoughtfully.

"When was the first incident, Eminence?"

"As I said, almost a year ago. Last May."

I looked at Eden. The timeframes were awfully close. Not knowing how much Cardinal Maguire knew of Eve's condition, I kept my face as neutral as possible. I shifted a little and my ribs screamed at me for doing so. There was no way that Eve's current deterioration and the three attacks in the past year weren't related somehow. I knew what my next step was, but I'd have to speak with Eden first. Not in present company, of course.

"What now?" I asked.

"I leave in a couple of hours for Rome to consult the Vatican. I have asked Fathers Fine and Duncan to join me," said the Cardinal.

Great. We'd lose an advantage with both Peter and Bill gone.

"What do you want us to do, Eminence?" asked Eden.

"Use your resources to see if you can find a pattern in the most recent activities. I will have all our data on the incidents from the past year transferred to you from the Pontifical Swiss Guard by morning. Coordinate your activities with them."

"What about the Feds waiting in the sanctuary?" I asked. "They seem to be all over what's going on. How 'in the loop' are they?" I really hoped that Cardinal Maguire's vast influence could make them go away. But I couldn't be that lucky.

At this, Cardinal Maguire smiled. "With Detective North, our local law enforcement expert, handling the Monsignor's protection at the hospital and Ms. Engel working with my people, I'll leave the Federal Agents to your wit and charms, Bryson."

Boy, I didn't like that smile.

"I have no idea what's going on!" I protested.

"Exactly, Bryson," said the Cardinal. "You can't give them very much even though that mouth of yours runs constantly. And you can find out how much they do know. Oh, and we will provide you with an attorney for the duration of your conversation."

Uh-oh. "And why is that, Eminence?"

"Didn't I tell you? How inconsiderate of me," the Cardinal chortled. "They are here to bring you in for questioning. And since it seems to be an excellent opportunity to find out how involved the government is, I've agreed."

I'd noticed the Feds around Blue Hill Avenue, but it just hit me now just how quickly they had actually arrived on the scene.

"I would imagine they have a lot of questions about this evening. But why just me?" I asked the Cardinal. He reminded me of a fat toad who'd just eaten a particularly tasty bug. "These guys are from New York. What happened tonight is a local matter."

"Although I'm sure they are interested in what happened this evening, they're here to speak to you about something else, Bryson," said the Holy Fat Toad. "See, boy, Plum Island was a Federal Facility based in New York." My heart leapt into my throat as the Cardinal continued. "However, they are willing to wait until morning to speak to you. Consider it a small favor from me to you, so you can get some rest. Sleep well, Bryson."

Chapter Fifteen

Ten Years Ago

The *Katie Mae* chugged out of the mouth of the Thames into Long Island Sound while we sat in the mess waiting for our first field briefing. Jack's war story had left me raring to go and, in my mind anyway, ready for whatever evil awaited us.

Charles opened the backpack he'd carried with him; it hadn't been taken below with the rest of our gear.

"First things first," he said, pulling out a small thermal lunch box. "Eden has been good enough to prepare a little something, and I need you to all take one and pass the rest on. Jack, I'll need you to get your crew to take it as well."

We passed the lunch box around and when it got to me I took out a small vial that contained a bluish liquid.

"What is this, Monsignor?" I asked.

"It's an anti-sleeping potion," replied Eden. "It will last about twelve hours, give or take variables like body mass."

"Just knock it back, Symon," Charles said. "I'll explain in a moment."

I took the stopper out of the vial and did as I was told. The liquid had the consistency of a sticky cough syrup and tasted vaguely like coffee. I immediately felt more alert and my senses seemed to come alive.

Captain Straw excused himself for a moment once we had all taken the potion to go distribute the remaining vials amongst his crew. He told Charles, with a laugh, that he'd tell them it was a shot 'of the good stuff' to "protect them from the fall chill. After all, his men were always up for a wee drink or two."

Charles pulled a map out of his pack, making room at the small table to unfold it.

"Plum Island," he commented matter-of-factly. "It's a little piece of rubble about three miles long by a mile wide off the North Fork of Long Island. For a change, I won't bore you with the history of the island."

"Praise Jesus," Aaron muttered. I choked back a laugh.

With a dirty look at Aaron, Charles continued. "Except to say that in 1954, the United States Department of Agriculture established the Plum Island Animal Disease Control Center there."

"But you don't think it's just a lab," said Janice. It was the first time she'd spoken since we'd left Boston.

"I know it's not," confirmed Charles. "Central Intelligence runs the place. They took ownership of the island and its facilities last year. It's a restricted area and high-level clearance is needed to get anywhere near the place."

"How do we get on the island, then?" I asked.

Charles smiled. "Well, that's why Peter is back at St. Ignatius. He's providing a little cover for us while we sail the Seven Seas."

"A long-distance sleep incantation," said Eden.

"Precisely," said Charles. "He's putting everything to sleep on the island even as we speak."

"The potion we just drank will counteract Peter's spell," guessed Bill.

Charles nodded. "So we can get on and off the island without local interference. Eventually the CIA will send either the Navy or the Coast Guard to see why they haven't had any communications with the place, but we should be long gone by then."

The boat rocked a little and I had to grab Aaron's chair to keep from sliding off mine.

"I'm hoping the cloud cover will also keep the military satellites from catching us—or more specifically, being able to identify the *Katie Mae*. We certainly don't want interference from the government in our business, or trouble for Jack."

"What is our business there?" I asked. I really hated long introductions.

"Well, laddie," said Jack, banging through the mess door, "there have been a lot of strange sicknesses and disappearances reported by New Yorkers who live near the various ports that ships would sail from to supply the island. And some very strange tales from the sailors in the area as well."

"That it?" Bill asked. "It's New York. There's a lot of strange stuff there, including people who like the Yankees." Everyone laughed.

"Our mission," continued Charles, "is to infiltrate the facility and destroy the catalyst the government has been using to cause the various illnesses reported."

"So, the government is using the facility as a bio-weapon testing ground. Possibly on the local population," stated Bill.

"If that were the only thing going on there," said Charles, "why would we be involved?"

The room was very quiet.

"So, let me get this straight," I said. "We are going to sail up to a CIA-controlled island, land, waltz into a high security government building, destroy whatever demonic thing they've been playing with, and then wander away as if nothing happened. Won't that piss a few people off?" Eden's potion apparently also gave me the gift of unbridled sarcasm.

"Symon," admonished Janice. "This is the will of God and what we've been training for. He'll protect us."

"I have as much faith in God as anyone here," I shot back not quite truthfully. "But we are not the military. And we certainly haven't had the training for something this big." Turning to Jack and Charles I asked, "What about your military contacts? Your old war buddies? Wouldn't it be easier for them to get to whatever it is on the island?"

"Easier to get there, perhaps," said Charles. "Jack, Peter and I are the only three left who have the gift. And we will need magic to eradicate this thing once and for all."

"What *thing*?" I asked skeptically.

"Symon," said Eve, "we can do this. All of us, together. We have to." She looked pleadingly at the Monsignor who nodded.

"*Have to*?" I asked pointedly. "Why?"

"It is up to us to sort this out," answered the Monsignor quickly before I could question Eve any further. "Although we know the government is aware of our world, they normally have bowed to the Vatican's will on supernatural matters—even the Republicans. Cardinal Maguire and his predecessors have done a marvelous job convincing governments to keep the realities of our world from the mortal one. The consequences of the knowledge we have, spread among billions of people, would lead to chaos. And victory for the darkness."

"Classroom lectures aside, sir, it apparently hasn't kept the government from running a black-ops project using knowledge of the Shadow-world," said Aaron.

"Nope," answered Jack. "They're not the only ones either. But that's why we're here. With Peter casting his sleep incantation, we'll be able to get on and off the island fairly easily. We'll need to use magic to get into the building, find what we are looking for, and get rid of it."

"The Cardinal will handle any problem the government has," added Charles. "Symon, I know I've spent a lot of time telling you to look at the big picture. But in this instance, we need to focus just on the task at hand. We've planned for everything. Trust in me and trust in God."

I didn't like it. I was beginning to realize that our preparation for this mission was sorely lacking any real substance. And I could sense that there was something Charles wasn't telling me. It was just a gut instinct, but my guts usually knew the score before my brain did. I saw a lot of places where this mission could come apart. What if Peter's incantation failed? Plum Island was a hell of a long way from the church. I didn't even know a sleep incantation could be cast over long distances. The island was three square miles. How many people could Peter put to sleep all the way from St. Ignatius? And if what Charles and the captain said was true, and there was some sort of evil thing there, wouldn't there be wards and other magical security in place to protect whatever it is from exactly what we were sailing across the Long Island Sound to do? "We don't even know what they have," I said.

"True, Symon," replied Charles, "but there have been confirmed cases of bubonic plague and a lethal form of leprosy. These are not animal diseases, as the powers that be would have us believe."

"They have something," a thought forming. "Something that can control sickness. Something evil," I said, looking at Charles.

"They do indeed," said Charles.

"Wait," said Aaron. "How did we go from a few people getting sick straight to the government is playing with something evil?"

"We have a source," Captain Straw replied. "My source, in this case. Someone who was assigned to the facility in the eighties."

"The eighties? Why has it taken so long to take these guys down?" I asked.

"It took a long time to confirm the information," said Jack. "My source had proof but it burned up with him when his car exploded. Charles and I took years to dig up more."

"Oh God," muttered Janice.

"What do they have, Monsignor?" I pressed. "A talisman? Some artifact? They must have a wizard working for them to use it..."

"No, nothing so simple and easy to destroy. As far as we can tell, they captured it in Korea right as the armistice was being signed and it's very happy in its government job."

"Captured...?" I asked.

"A Marquis of Hell," said Jack. "Its name is Sabnock, builder and afflicter of disease. The US Government has its very own demon."

****

We left the ship's mess, on Charles' orders, to go and grab our packs. The *Katie Mae* would be arriving at Plum Island in about an hour, and we needed to make final preparations for the unknown. Eve knew something more than Charles had revealed. Of that, I was certain. Which meant our mission was some sort of test. Fine. If Charles wanted to throw us into the fire, I was ready for it.

'Final preparations' meant different things for different people. Bill, for example, would find a small corner in which to pray and meditate. The twins and Janice would spend time together drilling spells and discussing what magical items they'd need. Aaron and I did what we've always done to prepare. We'd get some exercise.

The cargo hold of the *Katie Mae* smelled god-awful, but was thankfully empty of its normal contents. Getting to the cargo hold in the first place had been an adventure in itself as the voyage had become rockier when the storms had intensified. The pitching and yawing of the ship would be an added challenge to our routine. We both said a prayer, asking for guidance and strength, then set up.

We'd agreed to a simple warm-up using a few *Aki Taiso* exercises, then ran through our self-defense and non-aggressive Aikido routines as actual Judo sparring in the metal ship's hold would probably cause serious injury. Neither one of us wanted to explain a broken leg to Charles before our first real mission.

We took our positions and began with *Nikyo Waza*.

With hands down, we laid the outside of our left hands in the palm of our right hand. We brought both hands up and both elbows down, thus stretching the left wrist, counting as we moved.

"*Ichi-ni-san-shi,*" we intoned together. Doing basic warm-ups like this calmed my mind.

"We should go see what Peter packed for us," Aaron said trying not to break rhythm. "Might be a good idea to know what we have."

"Well," I replied, "you and I have a change of clothes, rain gear, two knives, our little silver circles, a sawed-off shotgun and plenty of ammunition. Oh, and some of Peter's cold pot roast in pita bread. Loads of mustard." Aaron's arms dropped to his side as he glared at me.

Without missing a beat or interfering with the grace of my warm-up, I said, "What? I peeked. And I was hungry."

He got back into position and rejoined the routine. "We had pot roast, and you made me suffer through one of those ham sandwiches?" he asked irritably.

The *Katie Mae* seemed to rock in sync with our warm-up drills. "Yeah. I thought we could have a victory snack once we finished the mission, since Charles won't let us smoke cigars in front of everyone," I said.

"He just gets annoyed since he knows you pilfer his stash," Aaron said, finishing our reps for *Kotegaeshi Waza* and sliding into *Sankyo*. "What do the rest have?"

"We all have clothes and food," I said. "Bill has a series of potions. According to the labels, they help with locating things. Janice's bag contained a couple of Tupperwares filled with powders and animal parts. You know: feathers, snake skin, eye of newt," I quipped. "I never got a chance to look in Eden's and Eve's bags 'cause Peter caught me snooping and told me to get lost."

"So we're just the muscle then," said Aaron, not able to hide the disappointment in his voice. "I was wondering why Charles' briefing seemed to contain nothing useful. He must have spoken with the rest earlier."

We positioned ourselves for *Tekubi-Furi*. We performed in silence following the rhythm of the rolling ship. I was feeling uneasy with Aaron's observation. Charles had often told me that I was destined for great things. I always took that to mean that one day I would lead the team when we were ready. Maybe it was arrogant to think that way, but now Aaron and I seemed to have enforcer roles. I looked at my best friend and he didn't look as though he was having the doubts I was having. Black and white. State the facts and move on. That was Aaron.

"Doesn't it bother you that we're like the hired help?" I asked.

"Nope," he answered.

"It shouldn't bother you either," Charles' voice came from the ladder into the hold. "How is it the two of you always seem to find the least inviting places in which to work out?"

Charles came toward us. He was holding Aaron's and my packs. "It's time boys. The dock is in sight. It looks like Peter's incantation is holding, as our approach hasn't been challenged."

We took our packs from the Monsignor and started up the ladder.

"Symon," Charles said, stopping my assent. "You aren't the hired help. The rest have specific tasks designed to get us into the facility, hold the demon, and finally banish it back to Hell."

"And Aaron and I are there for what, backup?"

Charles chuckled. "Of course not. You two are the best by far at both offensive and defensive spell-casting. The rest have to *think* before using a spell. You two cast instinctively. Your reaction times are the fastest I've ever seen." Charles slapped his large hand on my shoulder.

"Boys," he said, "you're not back-up. You are the Marines in this scenario. You have the training you need. You will get us safely on and off of the island and handle whatever it is Jack and I may not have of thought of. You two are our aces in the hole."

With that, Charles climbed the ladder and was gone from sight.

Aaron and I just looked at each other and blinked.

"We're aces. Huh. And here I was feeling sorry for myself," Aaron said.

"Yeah, well you can be the ace of clubs. I'll be the ace of diamonds," I replied.

"Why is that?"

"Because you can go club this Sabnock guy back to his hell-hole."

Aaron snorted. "And why are you the ace of diamonds?"

"Because diamonds are a girl's best friend, pal of mine. Let's get topside."

We laughed together as we climbed up and out for our first mission.

Chapter Sixteen

Present Day

I practically stumbled upstairs to Charles' bedroom. My body was ready for bed. Unfortunately, my brain was not on the same page as my body, and it insisted on spinning away at top speed.

Just as I was about to open the door to the Monsignor's suite, I heard voices coming from the other side. I listened, but the sounds were low and I couldn't make out any words. Apparently the adrenaline was still running through my system from Charles' rescue and was controlling my actions, as I burst into the room with all the grace of a spastic rhinoceros.

Bill and Aaron just looked at me.

"Sorry," I mumbled. "Heard voices."

"You should probably see someone about that," commented Aaron.

Both he and Bill hadn't changed their clothes from our rescue mission earlier this evening. The space smelled like a locker room, but, since I hadn't changed either, I wasn't one to complain. They had grabbed a couple of chairs from somewhere and were sitting there obviously waiting for me. I thought I'd start off by throwing them a curve ball.

"Feds are downstairs and want to chat with me. Know anything about that?"

Bill shook his head, while Aaron replied, "No, but I saw them combing the derelict church on Blue Hill Avenue before I left with Boston's finest to be debriefed. Good thing all that was left of Belial and his channelers was ash and piles of goo. I'd love to see a copy of their forensics report."

"How is Charles, really?" I asked, moving to sit on the bed. Bill handed me a paper cup. There was quite a bit of Jack Daniels in it. Oh well. So much for sleep tonight.

"Not good," said Bill. "The next twenty-four hours will be touch and go."

"We got him out, Sy," said Aaron. "The rest is up to the doctors, Charles, and God."

"Amen," replied Bill.

I sipped my Tennessee whiskey and remained silent for a few moments. Finally, Bill spoke up.

"We were just discussing the last few days..." he started.

"Oh?" I asked. "Something interesting happen to you two? I've been bored to tears."

"Look, Symon," Aaron's face flushed and his voice raised a couple of notches as he began to stand.

"Don't start you two," chided Bill. "You," he said pointing at Aaron, "sit down. And you," he said pointing at me, "stop with the bullshit."

"Wow, are priests allowed to..."

"Symon, I swear to God if you don't shut up, I will stick my foot so far up your ass you'll feel it for a year."

Aaron and I burst out laughing. That was Peter's phrase from when we were living here and he would use it on us at least once a week. Bill scowled for a moment, then started to laugh as well. It felt really good to laugh—despite the pain in my ribs—after what we'd been through. It didn't make things less serious, mind you. Just ... manageable.

A few moments later we were drying our eyes and finally settled down.

"What the hell is going on?" I asked.

"We were hoping you knew," said Aaron. "Bill was filling me in on what the Cardinal said about other Church teams being attacked."

"I've never heard about anything like this," said Bill. "While Cardinal Maguire and Peter speak with the Church leadership, I'm planning on poking around the Vatican archives to see if there is any precedent for the number of attacks on Vatican practitioners. I'll see if I can find out anything more on the missing teams as well. There are a few Scripture references to 'demons on Earth,' but they are, for the most part, allegory." He paused for a moment.

"And?" I asked.

"As a part of the Book of Revelation," Bill finished.

"Awesome," said Aaron. "Should we start looking for Gog and Magog?"

Bill looked at him seriously. "I honestly don't know yet, Aaron. But I'll tell you this much, Cardinal Maguire is nervous. When have you known him to seek council from the Vatican? Usually it's the other way around."

I thought about that for a little while, and Bill was right. Everything I'd seen and heard while eavesdropping on conversations between Charles and Peter when I was younger, pointed to Cardinal Maguire running the show for the Church from the shadows.

Just to add fuel to the fire, I said, "The Feds who want to talk to me are from New York. They want to chat about Plum Island."

From the lack of shock on Aaron's face, it was obvious that Bill had told him already.

"It can't all be a coincidence," I concluded.

"We agree," nodded Aaron. "But *how* all the dots are connected is what we can't figure out."

"Yeah," I said. "We have been kept completely off balance for the last few days. Really there's been no time to think, just act."

"We think it's by design," stated Bill.

"What do you base that on?"

"Remember," replied Bill, "I've been living and studying here after all of you left ten years ago. I got my Masters in theology here and was ordained in this very church. I guess my point," he said, noticing the 'yeah, so' look on my face, "is for the last few months, things have been very strange."

"In what way?" asked Aaron.

"Charles has been barely here, for one," said Bill.

Before I could ask, Bill continued, "I have no idea where he's been. Eden reappeared from her corporate tower about six months ago. Her people have been in and out of the church. And Peter has been acting strange as well—more anxious than I'd ever seen him in the past."

"What does that have to do with us being kept off balance?" I asked, noticing my cup had somehow been drained of its contents. I held it out to Aaron for a refill.

"Well," replied Bill. "it's been crazy here, like I said. But in the last two weeks it's been worse. Much worse. And suddenly Aaron, you, and Janice all show up."

"We were asked to," said Aaron. "Charles was in trouble."

"He's never really needed our help before," I commented, enjoying the warmth and pain-numbing effect of the JD.

"He's getting old, Sy," Bill said.

"Yeah," I agreed. "aren't we all. But that's not the only reason."

Aaron nodded. "That's why Bill and I were waiting for you. We don't think so either. Our theory is that Charles was trying to get us back here to protect us."

"Makes sense," said Bill, jumping on the bandwagon. "I hadn't known about the other practitioners around the world being attacked."

I shifted on the bed a bit, my ribs only protesting a little.

"I didn't know there *were* other practitioners around the world," I tossed out, which was a bit of a lie. But they didn't need to know the details.

Aaron waved a hand dismissively at me. "The fact that there are other practitioners really isn't as important as the fact that they were attacked." He looked around the room and said, "I wish we had a chalkboard or something. I think better when I write stuff down."

"There are plenty of chalkboards in the old classrooms. They're locked up and haven't been used in years, but I'm sure we can get into one of them," Bill said.

"Let's go," I said, standing up. "You think better with chalkboards and I think better with Jack Daniels, so bring the bottle."

****

We made our way downstairs. The church was very active, between the Cardinal's entourage preparing for his trip and Eden's folks patrolling the hallways. Being quiet wasn't going to buy us anything, so we boldly walked through the sanctuary as if we owned the place. I almost tripped over some power tools left behind by the crews working on repairing the main doors. Every time I walked through the sanctuary, I fumbled or tripped. What was up with that?

We made our way to one of the old classrooms undisturbed, interestingly enough. The room we finally selected was the Filosi Lecture Hall—named after a long-dead donor. Like the gym we'd been in earlier, the room smelled of neglect.

We picked the room because the dim light coming in through the windows from the all-night gas station across Mass Avenue allowed us to see pretty well without having to look for circuit breakers or flashlights. Besides, with my luck I'd throw the wrong breaker and cause a fire somewhere.

Bill found some old chalk in the desk at the front of the room and tossed it over to Aaron. He and I slid into one of the seats and I couldn't help but feel a combination of nostalgia and dread. Nostalgia for all the 'growing up' I did in the school. Dread, as I remembered those bloody blue books we used for tests. It always amazed me the impact things in childhood could have on your adult life.

I poured a rather generous helping of whiskey into our three paper cups and Aaron took his to the front of the classroom.

"So," he began, "where are we?"

Fatigue forgotten, and with a combination of pain and JD to keep me awake, I jumped into it with both feet.

"Groups who practice magic and work for the Church have been attacked."

"The Monsignor is the only one who's survived, at least as far as we know," added Bill.

"And the Monsignor was the one who knew something big was going on," said a voice behind us. Peter had come into the room.

"If you boys insist on playing detective while drinking, you should put something in your stomachs." I noticed a big plate of cold sandwiches in Peter's hands. If only Priests could marry, I thought.

We spent the next half hour eating, drinking and laying out what we knew. Unfortunately, as the pieces were laid out on the board, it became obvious that we didn't have everything. The big missing link was between what had happened recently and Plum Island. The timely arrival of the Feds to discuss our little adventure was surely connected.

There was another piece floating around the back of my head, but my gut said not to talk about it in front of the two priests. Peter finally stated it was time for Bill and him to join the Cardinal so they could make their flight.

"Peter, you and Bill have a long flight tonight and a lot of work to do tomorrow. Aaron and I will clean up this mess."

Peter had never been a fool. He narrowed his eyes at me slightly, then nodded his head. "Thanks, Symon. Remember, the attorney will be here at eight sharp and I won't be here to come wake you."

The two men of the cloth left the classroom, and Aaron looked at me quizzically.

"Hold on a sec," I said and checked the door by which Peter and Bill had exited.

"If this is about Janice..." started Aaron defensively. "She only married me on the rebound from you. There's something I should've told..."

"What the hell are you on about?" I asked, interrupting.

"Well, I figured you'd still be pissed..." he stuttered.

"No ... we don't have time for that now," I said in disgust. "God, for a detective you are such a moron." Shaking my head, I continued, "I want to talk about Eden, Detective Idiot."

Aaron looked relieved. I'd heard about Janice and Aaron getting married through the grapevine years ago—and yeah, when I found out about it I was pissed off for a while. And I admit I was pretty happy when I'd heard about their divorce a few years after that. But the whole Aaron-Janice-Symon love triangle soap opera would have to wait for a more appropriate time.

"What do you know about Eden and her company?" I asked.

"Not much. Just what she's told us," replied Aaron, but he started to rub his chin and I could see he had his detective's thinking cap on again. "She worked for a small biotech firm for a few years and was responsible for some break-out drug that got gobbled up by one of the big pharmaceutical companies. She made a fortune."

"Mmm," I said. "What about the company she has now?"

"Private security firm. Has a couple of big contracts; does fairly well, I think." "Based on the hardware and personnel at her beck and call, I think 'fairly well' is an understatement, don't you?"

"Yeah, I do. I see where you are going. You think she's the one keeping us off balance."

"Point for Detective North," I said. "For example, how was she able to train a security force made up of 'normals' to deal with magic when it is strictly forbidden by the Church to involve non-practitioners in the first place?"

"Let me do some digging," said Aaron. "I have a few contacts that might provide us some answers. In the meantime, what are you going to do?"

"Me?" I replied draining the last bit of the JD, "I'm going to find out what the Feds really want."

Chapter Seventeen

Ten Years Ago

We got on the deck of the *Katie Mae* to find that the weather had significantly deteriorated from when we'd left New London. A steady wind was coming from the north and it lashed the rain at us almost horizontally. Aaron and I took time to arrange our equipment for easy access under our rain gear, which was no small feat considering that the roll of the ship was even more pronounced than it had been while we were in the hold.

Through the rain, I could see the slowly blinking beacon of a lighthouse located on the westernmost tip of a landmass I assumed was Plum Island. It was in front of us, slightly to the left. Or should I say port?

Charles raised his voice to be heard over the wind. "Jack will swing around the lighthouse and pull into Plum Gut Harbor. The inlet should help shield us from the worst of the storm."

The *Katie Mae* plowed through the rough seas and our raiding party was ready. The inlet indeed provided shelter, as the ship's roll calmed noticeably once we'd passed the breakwaters. The rain and wind, however, stayed constant.

"You okay, Bill?" I heard Aaron ask.

I looked over at Bill. The poor guy's skin was still a sickly whitish-gray color. Well, our raiding party was *mostly* ready.

"I hate boats," I barely heard him say through gritted teeth.

We slipped quickly through the harbor and I heard the engines roar as the Captain threw the ship into full reverse. We slowed and berthed smoothly along one of the piers. It was an impressive bit of piloting.

Deck hands appeared from nowhere and jumped onto the pier as the rest of the crew tossed heavy lines to them. Within a minute, the *Katie Mae* was moored. Other than those of us who had just come to the island, I didn't see another soul.

Captain Jack, in full Gorton's Fisherman regalia, joined us on deck. "Joel will keep the old girl ready for us, Padre," he said to Charles.

Bill, who was showing signs of life, mumbled, "The building is about a mile and a half from here. Are we supposed to hike in this?"

Eve walked by us with a big smile. "O ye of little faith. Follow me."

Aaron, Bill, and I followed her down the gangway hunching our shoulders against the rain. Eden, Janice and Charles followed close behind.

"Monsignor, is the Captain coming?" I shouted over my shoulder.

"He'll be along shortly. He's finishing up one last detail."

At that moment I felt a strange vibration on the gangway originating from the ship. I turned to look and practically dropped my backpack.

The *Katie Mae* was gone. The wooden ramp I was standing on had its lower side resting on the Plum Island pier; the other end slopped up and ... disappeared into nothing. Eden and Janice both walked into me.

"Ow!"

"Symon!"

"Where the hell did the ship go?" I asked, flabbergasted.

"You have a lot to learn yet, laddie," rang out the familiar Scottish burr from the empty space that used to contain a large fishing vessel. "Even in this gale, I don't want anyone happening by and seeing ol' *Mae* here. Not that I don't trust Peter's skill to keep 'em all sleeping, Charles."

Out of nothingness, the Captain appeared on the gangway next to the Monsignor. "Padre, I thought you said the young-uns were all trained up?"

"Damn, Symon," snapped Eden irritably, "it's a veil. You've done hundreds of them."

"I never hid anything as big as a seventy-five-foot boat before!" I exclaimed.

"It's always size with you boys," Eden said as she pushed on by. "I'm soaked. Let's move."

****

Captain Straw explained to us, as we hurried down the rain soaked pier, that he'd ordered his crew to stay on board the ship below decks to wait out the storm. The lack of movement topside would allow the veil to last a bit longer.

"Besides," he chuckled, "wouldn't want them to walk off the ship and get spooked when they saw that she'd vanished!"

We joined the rest of the group at the end of the docks and saw that there were men dressed in fatigues sleeping in the doorway of a guardhouse. Whatever Peter was doing, it was obviously working. Looking around, I could make out everyone but Eve. I was just about to ask if anyone had seen her, when a white Chevy Suburban, lights blazing and windshield wipers flapping madly, came around the guardhouse and stopped next to us. 'US GOVERNMENT' was stenciled in black letters on the front passenger door. Before we could react, the driver's side window rolled down.

"Bus is here!" shouted Eve jauntily. "Everyone in."

We packed ourselves in like sardines, and Eve took off down the road at break-neck speed toward the center of the island.

****

The Plum Island Animal Disease Center was a large, two-story, white brick building surrounded by a barbed wire fence. A solitary guardhouse, a twin to the one we'd just seen by the docks, marked the only entrance through the enclosure. I could see another couple of guards asleep inside. I heard Eden mutter a few words under her breath and the gate opened by itself. I really do love magic.

The few lights on the perimeter of the structure, in combination with the white paint on the bricks, made the building seem to glow with an eerie luminescence. I could see that all the windows had been bricked over, and there was a long ramp on one side leading to the second floor of the structure. Presumably it was a cattle walk. I guessed that very few animals made it back out again under their own power.

We pulled under a corrugated metal carport at the front entrance to the building and got out of the Suburban. Although the rain was still coming down in sheets, the wind had lessened, and the carport offered us some respite from the storm.

"Bill," said Charles, "if you wouldn't mind."

Bill nodded and knelt down with his backpack. He pulled out a few containers of powder and his own silver circle.

"It will take me a minute to set up," he replied.

"I'll help," said Janice, kneeling beside him, pulling her circle out.

"I'll go work on the alarm and the locks," said Eden, and she grabbed her pack and trotted to the large steel doors. Eve went with her.

"What about the cameras?" I asked.

"What about them?" asked Charles, looking at me expectantly.

"Right," I said. "Aaron, help me with the incantation?"

"Okay."

Aaron and I grasped hands and our own silver circles. I closed my eyes.

"*Caecus oculos quod deleo memoria...*" we chanted together. I could feel my silver circle beginning to heat up as power flowed through it.

"Not bad, Charles," I heard Jack say to the Monsignor.

"*...permissum vestri vox fluo per mihi...*" I could feel the hum of energy ready to be used. Aaron and I finished chanting and at the same time, released our stored power.

The camera mounted on the carport above our head exploded. Little pieces of burning metal dropped around Aaron and me and we let go of each other's hands.

"A little too much?" I asked. There was a loud 'thunk' as the entire camera mounting fell to the ground right in front of us.

"Got the job done," Aaron shrugged.

"See? I told you they are ready, albeit a tad too exuberant," Charles said to the Captain.

****

Eve and Eden came back under the carport with us.

"Alarm's off and the doors are all unlocked," Eden updated us. "Just so you two Bobbsey Twins know," she added, pointing a finger at Aaron and me, "I was magically connected to the electronics of the building and had every intention of shutting off the cameras and erasing the video tapes. You practically fried my panties off with that spell of yours."

"Thanks for that image," I said.

"Whatever," Eden shrugged.

"We're ready," Janice called out.

"Saved by the shaman," said Aaron.

Bill and Janice had arranged a gray powder circle on the ground. In the center was a large feather. There were two silver circles identical to the one I'd been given placed at opposite poles of the powdered circle. Janice looked over their construct once, then glanced up at Bill.

"On three, then. One. Two. Three!" They both touched their silver circles and an orange glow enveloped the feather. A beam of light emanated above them, and in mid-air an orange circle appeared that danced as if made with fire. But I could feel no heat coming from it.

Within this first circle a second circle then formed. Inside the smaller circle, lines connected and moved like they were being made by one of those old Etch-a-sketch things I had as a kid. A complex demonic glyph appeared that was intertwined with a pictorial of gears. It looked mechanical.

The glyph connected with an arrow that was in turn connected perpendicularly to a 'U' shape. The symbol began to rotate slowly.

"That's Sabnock's symbol all right," confirmed Jack. "Looks like our sources were right, Padre."

Bill, whose eyes were closed in concentration, said, "Yes. It's in a space below us. Three levels down."

Both he and Janice opened their eyes and the image faded away. The feather, I noticed, still glowed faintly. Janice picked it up.

"It will guide us there," she said in answer to my questioning look.

"Okay, kids, it's time," Charles said. "Take only what you need and leave the rest here."

Aaron and I immediately grabbed our shotguns from our bags and loaded them. I put additional shells in the pockets of my slicker. I grabbed the pot-roast pita sandwich and took a huge bite, stuffing the remainder back in my bag. Aaron gave me a disgusted look.

"What?" I asked innocently, spitting crumbs on him. He shook his head and walked away in silence.

I really didn't want my last meal, should it come to that, to be a freakin' ham sandwich.

We approached the twin metal doors that led into the research center. Aaron had taken point and had motioned for me to follow behind. Reaching the doors, Aaron put his hand on one of the handles and looked at me. Silently, we mouthed a count to three and he yanked the door open.

I swept the room with my eyes, shotgun at the ready. The lobby was brightly lit and typical of what you would expect to find in any government building. There were plain gray square tiles on the floor and the sheet-rocked walls were painted a yellowish color. Cheap black-and-white prints hung on the walls and a large wooden desk sat in front of two sets of steel elevator doors. There was one guard with his head on the desk sleeping his shift away, courtesy of Peter. Two other men dressed in camouflage were also asleep, each one on the floor in front of one of the elevators.

"Clear!" I shouted.

I moved into the lobby and off to the right. Aaron came in immediately behind me and stationed himself to the left. The rest of our party entered and took up defensive positions along each wall.

I heard a clattering sound from down the hall that made me practically jump out of my skin. I relaxed a bit when I realized that the sound came from the ruined casing of a security camera fried by Aaron and me. It was still smoldering.

"Which way, Janice?" I asked.

She held the glowing feather in an outstretched palm and closed her eyes. "There are stairs to the right of the elevators. Down three floors and through a set of fire doors," she whispered.

We started down the hallway, Aaron and I leading the way. Our footsteps echoed eerily off the tiles in the spartan lobby. As I passed them, I looked at the cheap pictures hanging on the walls. I hadn't realized what they were until I got closer look. They were all photos of people. Although not one picture I saw was from the same period of time based on the clothing they wore, they had one common element. The people in every photo were suffering from some sort of horrendous ailment.

The first picture was of a small African girl lying on a straw mattress. Her body was covered in lesions and there was an older woman holding a washcloth to the girl's forehead. The woman was weeping. The next picture was a sepia-tone affair from the Civil War. In it a man with a large moustache was lying fully naked on a cot. Something had eaten away half of his flesh to the point that muscle tissue and bone were showing. He was obviously very dead.

"Jesus," said Bill off to my left. "Look at these pictures. What the hell kind of place is this?" I passed a third picture of an old woman covered in boils sitting in a high-backed chair next to an old-fashioned television.

"The kind of place we're shutting down. Tonight," I snarled, my voice quivering with rage. These pictures were here for only one reason: to proudly display pain and death. Charles had always told us of the evil that existed, both demon-made and manmade. This was the first time I really understood what he had been talking about.

I couldn't take my eyes off the horror gallery as we made our way to the end of the lobby. There was a picture of another dead man, a soldier in what looked like a jungle; blood was streaming from his eyes, nose and ears. Another had a dead child that looked like its insides had come out of her (his?) mouth. Bile rose in my throat and I choked it back as best as I could. Vomiting on my first mission wouldn't go over so well. As my stomach settled back down I vowed to kill this Sabnock myself.

As we got to the guard desk at the end of the lobby, I saw the double doors to my right that apparently led to the lower levels as indicated by Janice's magical feather compass. I turned to give the all clear so we could head downstairs when I noticed movement out of the corner of my eye. The guard lying in front of the elevator closest to me had begun to move.

"Shit! They're waking up!" I shouted. I guessed Peter's incantation finally wore off.

But it wasn't that sort of groggy motion I'd expect from one waking up from a magically induced sleep. The guard sat straight up and stared at me with unblinking eyes. The one at the desk and the third by the other elevator all sat up at the same time and stared at us emotionlessly.

"Oh crap!" Aaron exclaimed. "I don't think they're awake at all."

"It's Sabnock. He's controlling them!" shouted Charles. But I'd known that before he'd said it. The skin on each of the three guards had begun to form red pustules that oozed.

"Take cover!" I screamed.

We all moved for the doors leading to the stairwell when the guards, in tandem, picked up their weapons and opened fire.

Chapter Eighteen

Present Day

I awoke with a start as the car that my FBI handlers and I were in entered the parking garage of the Hancock Building, Downtown Boston, early the next morning. Apparently four hours of sleep hadn't been enough. The agents, Sanchez and Vitale, were good enough to follow the Cardinal's 'request' and let me grab a few hours' sleep in the church. My Vatican-appointed attorney had arrived precisely at eight.

My attorney had barely uttered two words to me since I shook hands with him at St. Ignatius. Father Moore was a stooped and wizened old man with wispy Einstein hair. His eyes were sharp, though, and he had shaken my hand with a firm, sure grip.

"Hello," I'd said.

"Keep your mouth shut Bryson and I'll have you back in Cambridge for lunch," he'd snapped. How come all the old priests I know are a pain in the ass?

My eyes felt like someone had used sandpaper on them and my mouth tasted like I'd subsequently eaten the sandpaper. I reached over to grab one of the water bottles some thoughtful government hack had placed in the center console and winced. I'd forgotten about my ribs and the pain shocked my brain into high gear. Well, into a medium gear anyway.

I'd been so tired and sore that I hadn't had time to think about where I was going and what was going to happen to me. And other than a quick update on Charles' condition and a peck on the cheek from Janice, I hadn't had time to speak with anyone about what to expect either. Aaron was nowhere to be found when I'd left the church. I hoped that he was out getting information on Eden and her company.

I closed my eyes and rubbed my temples in a vain attempt to massage my hangover away. I was seriously lacking caffeine, patience, and answers.

Father Moore and I were escorted up to the twenty-third floor via a freight elevator. We were brought through a back fire door into a tastefully decorated office suite. Before I could really look around, we were hustled into a sparsely furnished, ten-by-ten foot room containing a table and four chairs. A large mirror dominated one wall.

"Are we filming an episode of *Law and Order*?" I asked. "Is it the one with Detective Benson? I always liked her."

"Quiet, Bryson," hissed Father Moore.

Sanchez smiled. A little. Honest.

Vitale said in a heavy Brooklyn accent, "I'll get the funny man a cup of coffee and let the Assistant Director know he's here. You want anything, Father?"

Moore waved his hand at the special agent and proceeded to sit down. He glared me into the chair next to him.

"Special Agent Sanchez, I would like to have a conversation with my client in private please."

Sanchez looked at the priest, measuring him up for a moment. "Certainly, Father." And he left the room.

"Father..." I said.

"A minute, Bryson," interupted Moore. "*Secretum, privatus.*"

There was a muffled, electronic squeal from behind the two-way mirror, then silence.

"The Patriot Act gives the Federal Government significant latitude in eavesdropping on private attorney-client conversations. Now, you were saying, Bryson?"

"Oh hell ... you are one too?" I asked.

"Of course. I've been with Cardinal Maguire for decades. He is a very politically savvy and talented man, but understanding the finer art of the law is why he has me. And for a man in his Holy position, an attorney versed in international law, such as myself, is necessary. As a practitioner, I am doubly valuable to him."

I snickered.

"What's so funny, young man?"

"I had this funny vision of your calling to the priesthood being delivered in triplicate."

"Hmph. Let's focus on your issue right now, not some juvenile fantasy."

"What exactly is my issue? There are no charges that I am aware of and as far as I can recall, I haven't been read my rights, so why are we here?" I was hoping for a little more than the Cardinal had been willing to give me.

Father Moore paused for a moment. "The US ambassador to the Vatican specifically asked for this meeting on behalf of the FBI and one Assistant Director Palmer. It's a meeting only. You have yet to be charged with anything," replied Moore.

"Then why did his Eminence tell me I was to be brought in for questioning regarding Plum Island?"

"I know Plum Island was brought up specifically by the Ambassador, but I believe it was to signal that the FBI has some knowledge of our activities. It was also a subtle way to threaten action should the request be denied."

"Yes, but why me…"

"The Cardinal has a marvelous sense of humor."

"Yes. He's a regular Bob Hope," I said. "Why didn't they bring anyone else in if they wanted to talk about that catastrophe? We were all there. And for that matter, why ten years later?"

"I see your brain is finally beginning to work, Bryson. Both are good questions. I suspect we'll find out when this Mr. Palmer joins us."

The door opened, and Sanchez, a bit red-faced, walked into the room with a small styrofoam cup filled with coffee.

"We'll be a couple of minutes, gentlemen. We've had some, uh, equipment problems," he said while handing me the steaming cup.

"Oh, no problem, Special Agent," said Father Moore lightly. Sanchez looked at him, eyes slightly squinted, but left without saying a word.

"Bryson, pay attention. The only reason the Cardinal agreed to this meeting at all was to find out what the government knows and why they are currently so interested in you. You are only here to provide me with the opportunity to assess the situation firsthand. I will do the talking. When you are asked a question, you will look for approval from me before answering. You will answer only the question asked and nothing more. Is that clear?"

"Yes, Father. Crystal." I replied, sipping my coffee.

"And keep the smart-ass comments to yourself. Is that also clear?"

"But my cynical and sarcastic side is part of my charm!" I protested.

"Bryson," said Father Moore, warningly.

"Yeah, okay," I relented. My body was finally waking up due to the caffeine infusion and I had a sudden urge to find a bathroom. Good thing I have a strong bladder as it looked like I was going to be sitting here for a while.

A few minutes later, the door to the interrogation room opened and Special Agents Sanchez and Vitale entered, followed by a tall man dressed in a well-tailored, dark blue, three-piece pinstriped suit. His red hair was short and neat and, with the exception of the dark bags under his eyes and pale pallor, he looked like a bank Vice President.

"Thank you, gentlemen. That will be all," he said. Sanchez and Vitale looked at each other, surprised, but hastened to follow orders and left the room.

Once the door closed, Father Moore said, "Assistant Director Palmer, I presume."

"Correct, Father. You are Mr. Bryson's legal representation in this matter?"

"I'm here to witness a discussion, if that's what you mean, Assistant Director."

"Interesting that the Vatican would supply a senior member of its legal staff for an average citizen, don't you think, Mr. Bryson?" said Palmer.

"Not really," I answered. "Legal representation is guaranteed upon baptism, Assistant Director. Didn't you know that?" I could feel the daggers Father Moore was shooting at me.

"Well," Palmer said as he sat down, placing a thick folder on the table. He opened it. "Since it looks like you haven't been to a church since you left Boston for Dublin a decade ago, I find Father Moore's presence interesting, nonetheless."

It was a really thick folder.

"Assistant Director, when the United States government shows a keen interest in one of our flock, of course the Vatican also takes an interest. Just like your government watches over US citizens abroad and protects them when threatened."

Palmer grunted but made no further comment and shuffled through a few papers in silence. Neither he nor Father Moore spoke further, both looking as calm and cool as could be. It was driving me crazy, of course, but I did my best to remain passive.

Finally, Palmer closed the file, sat back in his chair, and stared unblinkingly at me.

"Mr. Bryson. Let's talk about Plum Island, New York, shall we?"

There's never a bathroom around when you need one.

Chapter Nineteen

Ten Years Ago

A shotgun clattered to the floor and Aaron, hands outstretched, jumped in front of all of us. Machine gun fire echoed in the lobby and bullets ricocheted off the invisible shield my friend had constructed around us. He was covered in sweat.

"I can't hold this shield for long!" Aaron called out. "Symon, take these guys out!"

I raised my shotgun and hesitated a moment. Sure, I'd practiced shooting. I also practiced with knives and unarmed combat. But I'd never killed anyone, or *anything*, before.

"Symon!" screamed Aaron.

I fired.

The guard closest to me was thrown against the elevator doors, blood streaming from his chest. I aimed at the possessed man shooting at us from behind the desk and took him out as well. Two shots after that, all three men lay dead in pools of blood on the lobby floor.

Aaron let his arms drop and I could feel the release of energies that had surrounded us. He staggered a bit, but remained standing.

"About time," he said breathlessly, looking at me. "I couldn't hold that shield much longer. Thanks."

I looked at the carnage I'd caused and muttered, quietly, "Don't thank me, man."

The Monsignor and Captain Straw were suddenly at my side. Charles muttered a quiet prayer and made the sign of the cross. A blessing for the men I'd killed, I guess.

"Well done, Symon," praised Charles when he had finished. "I know how difficult that was."

I looked at my mentor. I held back the retort I so desperately wanted to hurl at him. My entire body felt empty and lifeless. How the hell could he understand what I felt?

Perhaps seeing the look on my face, Jack cleared his throat. "Whatever they used to contain the demon, it was obviously tied into the electrical locking system the girls disabled. We'll have to hurry."

"Yeah," I said bitterly, "let's get the job done and get out of here."

"Guys," called Eden, "take a look at this."

She was kneeling near one of the corpses I'd created. The last thing I wanted to do was to look at the remains of a man I'd killed. What if he had a family? Were there young children expecting daddy home tonight, only to have the news broken to them that "Daddy is in heaven now?"

I shuddered and shook my head. I did God's work, I reminded myself. Casualties were part of the risk in what we had been called to do.

I shook off distracting thoughts, determined to complete my mission, and joined the rest of the team gathered around Eden.

The first thing I noticed was the blood. A shotgun can do a lot of damage if used effectively. I'd used it effectively. Although there was a lot of blood and tissue sprayed around the body, the color was off. The pooled, congealing liquid was a blackish green.

The second thing I noticed was the face of the guard. The features were horribly twisted in death. No, that wasn't quite right. The guard's features had *changed*. The face, although still covered in the pustules that had formed when Sabnock had taken control of them, now appeared grotesque and pig-like.

"You belong to your father, the devil, and you want to carry out your father's desire. He was a murderer from the beginning, not holding to the truth, for there is no truth in him. When he lies, he speaks his native language, for he is a liar and the father of lies," said Charles, quoting from the Book of John.

"This complicates things," Jack said, pulling at his scraggly beard. "That sleeping incantation of Peter's, Padre—it doesn't look like it works on demons..." He gestured at the mess on the floor. "...or their minions. Perhaps we should pull the plug on this operation now. My source told me one demon, not a whole tribe o' them running around the island helter-skelter."

Charles put his hand in the pocket of his rain slicker and pulled out a handkerchief. Removing his black fedora, he wiped his brow. I knew he was re-thinking our mission.

"We're not pulling the plug," I said. "This little piggy went wee-wee-wee all the way back to hell. We know now that maybe there are more of these things here." I looked at the rest of my friends. Aaron nodded slightly.

"You saw those pictures. This place revels in pain and suffering. Disease is fun for them. I say we take them all down right now." I could see that Charles wasn't convinced and that he was still considering withdrawing.

"Monsignor, you said yourself that this place had been in operation since the fifties," I said. "Some of those pictures looked even older than that. Isn't it time we shut off the lights on this establishment permanently?"

"Yes," replied Eve. "We're here now. Let's finish what we set out to do." Charles looked at her and nodded his head.

"No!" shouted Eden. "Monsignor, please…!"

I'd never heard Eden sound so panicky before.

"The decision is made, lass," said Jack. "We press on."

We moved to the stairwell and I noticed Janice looking at me, eyes heavy with tears. Between Eden's outburst and Janice's raw emotion I had to wonder what they knew that I didn't. They understood that this had to be done—so why all the melodrama? I shook my head. I had to purge the evil from this damnable island, no matter what the cost. I knew Aaron and Bill were with me. And thankfully Eve seemed ready for action. I waited for further objections, but Eden and Janice nodded in silent agreement with Jack.

"We go, then," said Charles simply, his face unreadable.

We'd started toward the stairwell, when Bill pushed past me. Out of his backpack, he had taken a piece of large chalk. On the ground, in front of the doors, he drew a runic symbol I didn't recognize.

"It's for safe passage," he said. "To help us get back out when the time comes."

"Good thinking," I said.

I had a feeling that we'd need it.

****

We made our way down the stairwell to the lowest sub-basement level. The overhead lights were slowly fading on and off as if there were a continual brownout on this level. Almost simultaneously, we drew our flashlights from our respective backpacks. I switched mine on and it sent a steady stream of light down the hall from where we stood. I had to wonder if one of the spells we'd thrown around had wrecked the lighting down here or if it was something else entirely.

The hallway pretty much went the length of the building, which I guessed ran for two hundred feet or more. The bricked walls were high, maybe ten feet or so, and the hallway itself was almost the width of the lobby we'd just come from. The malfunctioning florescent lights were tossing strange shadows around us. That made it difficult to make out further details other than the fact that a series of recessed doors, as high and wide as the hallway, lined up uniformly on either side of us.

"It looks like the lab building at my college," said Eden. She'd recovered from her outburst and was all business again.

As my eyes became accustomed to the bizarre lighting and shadows, I noticed each door had a magnetic card lock and numeric keyboard access panel next to the doorframe.

"Eden, did you knock out those swipe-card thingies?" I asked.

"All part of the same spell. The rooms should be accessible," she replied.

That would make our search easier, but also may have released Sabnock into the facility. I looked over to Janice, who still held the enchanted feather in an out-stretched hand.

"It's still down here," she said, as if reading my thoughts, "but something is interfering with my spell. I can't tell which door it's behind."

"We'll split up," I heard myself say. Isn't that how the situation in all those slasher-movies goes pear-shaped? "Jack, you, Eve, Janice and I will take the right-hand side. The Monsignor, Aaron, Bill and Eden the left."

Charles and Jack seemed to be holding back, letting us take charge. Unless I missed it, they'd done nothing to help in the skirmish upstairs. Come to think of it, they hadn't done anything at all other than to get us onto this bloody island. If, as I suspected, this was one of Charles' tests, so be it. I'd show the Monsignor and his old war buddy that we were ready.

Aaron and I took the lead of our respective groups and began to open doors systematically. Eden had been right: the rooms I entered had been set up with lab tables. Beakers, flasks, microscopes, refrigerators and other equipment I didn't recognize filled the rooms. I could never remember; was it the Erlenmeyer that was the triangle-shaped flask? I shook my head. The acrid smell of burnt wiring must be fouling up the air-handling system, as the stagnant air was causing my mind to wander.

The refrigerators were filled with vials containing a clear liquid. Each vial was labeled with a number code. I looked at Eve.

"Serum of some sort," she answered my quizzical gaze. "But I'm only guessing. For all I know they could all contain samples of smallpox. This is Eden's area, but I would suggest being very careful."

I'd reached into the fridge with a thought of taking a few samples to look at. At Eve's words I quickly withdrew my hand and closed the door. I was feeling uneasy at the number of things we were discovering that weren't a part of our mission briefing.

Maybe we weren't ready.

I shook off that thought. "Let's check out the next room," I said.

I compared notes quickly with Aaron in the hallway to discover he and his group had found a similar lab setup. We both moved to our next set of rooms. The sub-basement remained very quiet but my feeling of foreboding only increased. True, we hadn't come across Sabnock, or any more of its minions yet. I hoped that meant that whatever protection the government had placed around him was more than electronic based, but my gut told me we weren't going to be that lucky.

We entered the next room and it was set up exactly as the first lab had been. However there was a faint acrid smell hanging in the air. It took me a moment to identify its source: a computer system sitting on the far end of a workbench that had probably been fried by one of our spells. I looked at the machine, wondering if the hard drive could be removed for further study back in Boston, when I noticed a series of shelves containing small floating animals. I pointed my flashlight at the containers.

"They look like pig fetuses," I said.

"No, laddie," replied Jack in a hushed whisper, "those are human fetuses."

My stomach lurched as I took a closer look. I got a whiff of formaldehyde as I put my face up to one of the beakers. Jack was right.

"My God," said Janice. "They are experimenting with humans."

"Didn't the pictures upstairs give it away?" I asked her. "Taking care of Sabnock won't stop this. We'll have to banish the demon and destroy the labs. Otherwise the government can continue to work on this stuff."

We left the second lab and I was thinking about the best ways to shut down the Plum Island facility permanently when Janice elbowed me hard in the ribs.

"Ow! What?"

She pointed across the hall. A glow, like that of a fire could be seen coming from the little window in the door of the lab Aaron and his group had gone into.

I grabbed Eve by the arm as she had started to make her way down the hall to the next lab door. I pointed in the direction of the flickering light.

The Captain was muttering under his breath, preparing a spell. Janice and Eve began to prep their own magic as I hefted the shotgun. The frosted glass made it difficult to see inside. Only the flickering light shone through. I looked behind me to my three compatriots. They all nodded. It was now or never, so I placed my hand slowly on the knob and opened the door.

Unlike what my team discovered, Aaron's second door had led, not to another lab, but to a very large room—perhaps stretching the remaining length of the hallway—and it was lined with spaces that resembled an office's cubicle layout. But instead of desks, there were beds in each partially walled compartment.

Aaron and his team were spread out, examining what looked like a large dormitory designed to house a large number of people.

He waved over to me. "It's all clear. There's no one in here but us."

I thought at first that maybe the place had been set up for onsite scientists and researchers. Developing new and horrible ways to kill people probably demanded a lot of overtime, after all. But if that were the case, where were they? If Peter's spell was still working, any occupants of these communal quarters should be here, asleep. Other than the demonic goons in the lobby, we hadn't seen a soul and it was beginning to worry me. I was about to ask Janice to cover the hallway when I heard a sharp intake of breath.

"Symon," called Janice, standing in front of one of the cubicles. "You need to see this."

I joined her at the nearest stall. It was sparsely furnished, housing only a small bed and a shabby nightstand. Although the bed was neatly made, the pillow and associated bedding seamed well worn, almost threadbare. I was about to make a snarky comment about the accommodations being better than back at home, when I noticed why Janice had called me over. Sitting on the nightstand was a stuffed teddy bear.

My heart jumped into my throat. I remembered our briefing, which seemed to have happened a year ago, onboard the *Katie Mae*. People had gone missing. And some of those people had been children.

I looked around the large space and guessed there were about fifty beds laid out in the cubicles. Fifty beds. I looked at Janice.

Aaron and the rest of the group came over toward us. He had a distressed look on his face.

"The room is empty," he said. "Where are they?"

I thought back to the lab across the hall with human fetuses floating in formaldehyde.

"There are forty-eight beds," said Bill quietly. "And there is a closet at the other end of the dorm that has additional mattresses and bedrails. So they could fit more if they wanted to. And Symon," he added more quietly still, "all the beds are really small."

I thought about the large 'cattle' ramp attached to the outside of the building that I'd noticed on the way in.

"They're experimenting on kids," Eve said, choking back tears.

We came here to destroy a demon. Now, we had a new mission. We needed to save the children.

Chapter Twenty

Present Day

"Plum Island, New York?" I asked, trying to think quickly. "I..."

Palmer slammed his hand down on the table, making us all jump. "While you think up a plausible lie," he said, "let me ask you another question. What do you know about demons?"

"Demons?" I asked Palmer. I was sure I only stammered a little. "Like, personal demons? Well mine involve Jack Daniels and Greek women..."

"Don't be stupid, Bryson. You are neither cute nor funny," snapped Palmer.

"Mr. Palmer, I'm advising my client to keep silent as of now and plan on using duct tape on him if necessary. Perhaps you would do me the favor of explaining your question and why you are asking it," said Father Moore, giving me a warning look.

"My question and a significant number of follow-ups may very well fall under the umbrella of national security. I'm advising your client to have an open and honest discussion with me right here and right now. Otherwise, Father, I can make things very difficult for him."

"I don't take kindly to threats, Mr. Palmer. My client came here of his own free will. If you expect any cooperation from us at all, I suggest we tone down the rhetoric," said Father Moore.

Obviously, Plum Island had been a government-run operation; however, I got the sense that Palmer was fishing for information. That means the government's right hand doesn't know what the left hand is doing—not surprising. And, come to think of it, why was an FBI Assistant Director doing first-round interrogations?

I took the opportunity to study Palmer while he and Father Moore glared at each other like two bulls after the same cow. The man was pale, sweating and hadn't shaved this morning. Dark circles under his eyes told me he hadn't slept. His suit was expensive, but it was rumpled and slightly unkempt as if he'd been wearing it for a couple of days.

My gut told me that Palmer's threats were as weak as the 'national security' excuse. This was personal for him somehow.

"Mr. Palmer," I said in what I hoped was my sincerest of tones, "I really have nothing to say to you or the FBI at this point."

"Look, Bryson," said Palmer running a hand through his hair. "For years we have been aware of exceedingly strange things that happen in the world around us. We have worked very hard, as I suspect the Vatican has, to keep knowledge of these events from the general public." Palmer reached into the folder and pulled out a printout of a grainy black-and-white photograph. It was a picture of a younger version of myself exiting a car. I knew where that picture had come from.

"Mr. Bryson, do you recognize the man in this picture?"

I sure did. But I said nothing, hoping to play out what was really bothering Palmer.

"No? It's you, Mr. Bryson. Do you know where this was taken?"

I kept silent, waiting.

"It's the only photograph we were able to retrieve from the security system located at a federal facility on Plum Island."

"As I mentioned to one of your agents earlier, technology sometimes lets you down, Mr. Palmer," commented Father Moore. "At best, what you have there is a very grainy photo of someone who may or may not slightly resemble my client. What is your point?"

"I believe this is a ten year old picture of you, Mr. Bryson. And some very strange things happened at this facility, don't you agree?"

Silence.

"You leave me no choice, Mr. Bryson. Under the Patriot Act I can hold a suspected terrorist for seventy-two hours. I hereby inform you that you have been identified as such and I am placing you under arrest."

"This is ridiculous!" declared Father Moore.

"Be that as it may, Father. I'm within my authority to hold Mr. Bryson. Perhaps a few days behind bars will make your client a little more open to discussion." Palmer motioned with his hand. Sanchez and Vitale entered the room.

"Process Mr. Bryson," snapped Palmer.

"Symon Bryson, stand up please," said Vitale. "You have the right to remain silent..."

****

I've gotta hand it to the two guys who processed me. They didn't knock into my bruised ribs once, not once. Not during fingerprinting, the mug shots, the strip-search; no, not even when they removed anything I might hang myself with. It was really quite considerate of them.

Then they put me in a closet, six-by-six, that housed a cot and (thankfully) a toilet. Palmer's "behind bars" comment was obviously just a figure of speech: there were no windows with bars—no bars and no window either—and the one door into my cell was a solid steel number with a small windowpane crisscrossed with alarm wire. Locked from the outside, of course.

I lay down on the cot, my mind spinning a million miles a minute. At least we got an answer to one of the Cardinal's questions. The government certainly knew something was up. Of course, the activity on Plum Island ten years ago made it clear to me that at least one branch of the government had significant knowledge of the Shadow-world. In typical big bureaucratic fashion, not all branches of the government knew everything. Maybe the FBI was trying to piece things together for themselves. It looked like the FBI and I were in the same boat.

Palmer gave up more information than I would have expected from someone at his level in the FBI. Hell, I'd gotten more from him than he had from me. My gut said that this was personal for him. I needed to find out what he was hiding without giving him much information in return. It was a tightrope that would end up landing me in a federal prison if I fell off.

With no wristwatch and no outside window to gage sunlight, I very quickly lost track of time. To be honest, I should have been scared out of my wits, but the isolation and the constant hum of florescent lighting were comforting somehow. And it gave me time to think.

Cardinal Maguire had said there had been three incidents over the past few months. Although Biblical history is rife with all sorts of demonic parables, modern history tends to lean toward less fanciful interpretations. I was beginning to think the colorful interpretations from thousands of years ago were more accurate.

I was pretty sure that Charles' captor, Belial, was a lesser demon, despite some of the titles and descriptions both Bill and Eden had uncovered. Yet it could move easily on Earth. Why, then, were we able to send the damn thing back to Hell so quickly despite my being so rusty at magic? Crossing over from the Shadow-world was supposed to be extremely difficult, with only the most powerful of demons able to do it for any length of time. Belial also had control of a helluva lot of channelers in our world for a creature that I figured was low on the demonic power scale. Either my assessment of Belial was wrong, or there was something else going on between the Shadow-world and Earth. Neither thought was comforting.

Which brought me back again to Eden. Too many questions surrounded my old friend. What was the company she was running and how were they connected to all this? How was she even allowed to pull together the team she had? Flint and Kowalski, when looking over the runes in Charles' study, displayed familiarity with ancient languages and symbols. And those guys had seemed to be just grunts for Eden's company. Yet they showed a great deal of knowledge—the type of knowledge that took years of training. Why had Eden created an army? She must've had the Cardinal's blessing somehow. Or at least Charles' okay. Peter, Bill, and Janice were involved with her somehow, too. How did they fit in?

And what about her twin? What really happened to Eve ten years ago? I knew it was connected, but how?

My head ached. My body hurt. I was hung over and had too many questions.

Apparently I'd closed my eyes for some deep contemplation, because the insertion of a key into the lock of my cell startled me awake.

The door opened, and my attorney, Father Moore, came into the room. He had a look on his face that you never want to see on an attorney representing you on terrorist charges.

"Bryson," he said, worry doubling the number of wrinkles on his face. "When did you come to Boston?"

"I grew up here," I replied. "Why?"

"No, you idiot. When did you arrive this trip?"

"Um ... a couple of days ago. The Sunday before the Marathon."

"When was the last time you saw a newspaper or listened to the news?"

"Probably a copy of the *Irish Times* at the airport," I said. "Why?"

Father Moore tossed a copy of the *Boston Globe* at me. "Page six."

I picked up the paper and flipped over to page six. There was a color photograph of fire brigade trucks and Irish Garda in front of a smoldering building. The headline read: "Terrorism suspected in Bombing of Apartment Complex. Six Dead. IRA Denies Responsibility."

I knew before I saw the address that it was the complex where my flat had been.

"Dublin, Ireland: A sixth person has died in what has now been confirmed to have been a bomb explosion in an apartment complex across from the historical Christ Church Cathedral, off the High Street in Dublin. The device went off at 4 AM local time and was confirmed to have been placed in a storage facility that housed a motorcycle or other two-wheeled vehicle. The explosion caused a partial collapse of the building..."

"Oh God..." was all I could muster.

"God had nothing to do with that, son," Father Moore spoke softly. "Director Palmer handed this to me. Needless to say, the second floor flat mentioned in the article was yours, although the name of the flat's owner hasn't been released yet to the general public."

I wasn't really paying attention to Father Moore. I scanned the newspaper article looking for a listing of who had died. I knew a lot of people in my building.

I didn't notice Father Moore sit down on the cot next to me.

"Symon," began Father Moore, in a soothing sort of voice, "there are things in motion here that I do not understand. And I have to tell you that Cardinal Maguire keeps me informed about *everything*. I realize you don't know me from Adam, but I need to know all that you do. And I need to know it now."

I looked up at him, putting the paper aside. I was a pretty good judge of character and I didn't trust this man, collar or no collar.

He was the Cardinal's lackey and a lawyer to boot. And, despite his soft, friendly tone, he was a calculating son of a bitch.

"I really don't know any more than I've already told you, Father." Is it a sin to lie to a complete bastard?

Father Moore's eyes went very cold, and he pursed his lips so tightly they turned white.

"This is much worse than the Cardinal and I feared," he snapped. "I don't think my services will be of any further assistance to you, Bryson. Good luck in prison."

And with that, Father Moore rose, took the one necessary stride over to my cell door and wrapped his knuckles once on the little glass window. The guard let him out and closed me back in.

I picked up the paper and read the rest of the article. The head of the Garda investigation didn't provide any details, stating that it was an 'ongoing, active case.' The rest of the article went on to say that Christ Church hadn't been damaged by the blast and that, along with the six dead, over thirty had been injured and that there was still one person missing.

I tossed the paper disgustedly into the corner of my cell. Someone, or something was systematically taking out members (or, in my case, former members) of the Church who had "special talents." Cardinal Maguire said the great game was changing. It looked to me as though a full-scale war had started and we weren't on the winning side. I needed to warn Janice and the rest of my old friends, no matter who they were working for. And the only way to do that was to get out of this bloody cell.

I got off the cot, went to the door of my cell and pounded on the glass.

"What, Bryson?" asked Sanchez, who was stationed outside.

"Tell Palmer I'm ready to talk."

Chapter Twenty-One

Ten Years Ago

We spent ten minutes devising a new plan. Charles and Jack remained strangely silent. In fact, with the exception of arranging transportation, the most senior mages with us had relegated themselves to bit players. I was pretty sure that we'd run into things the Monsignor and Jack hadn't expected. Even if this mission were a test, why then were they still just observing for the most part? I'd have to deal with that later.

"So we're all set," I said. "Eden, Eve, Jack, and Charles are to continue searching this floor for Sabnock. The rest of us will split up to search the rest of this building to see if we can find out if there are still victims here and, if so, where they might be." There was a series of nods around me. I used the word *victims* instead of *children* specifically so everyone didn't see me get physically ill all over the floor.

"Jack, can you contact your crew?" I asked. "With the weather being what it is, we'll need to figure out some way to get the children back to the boat."

"Aye, Symon," Jack's burr even more pronounced. "Joel is standing by. Just give me a moment."

I knew his crew didn't really understand their Captain's abilities. I also knew they weren't really supposed to know what was going on here on the island. Right then, I didn't give a crap about any of that as long as they could help us save the kids.

I couldn't get the image of that old teddy bear and the small child-sized cots out of my head. I shook my head vigorously to try and get rid of that thought. Dwelling on the children wouldn't help me save them.

"All right then," I said, looking at them all. "We'll split up and see if we can find the kids. If we haven't found them we'll move to the basement levels. We'll communicate via wind-talk. Clear?"

Wind-talk was a method of communication from one person to another that Janice had brought to us years ago. Her brand of magic was very old and handed down through her Narragansett shaman ancestors. She and her magic were tied to the elements of earth, air, water, and fire. She even had names for each element, as if they were all imaginary friends. It was cute in a creepy sort of way. As she told it, ancient medicine men used to use the wind to their advantage, to sway people to their way of thinking or to influence tribal elders. We discovered that we could project emotions as a way to pass information. Wind-talking also helped our grades until Peter caught us. Sometimes it was reliable, sometimes not. I was hoping that any major discovery would radiate out from the discoverer, calling us to him or her immediately.

Next time I'd make sure Peter packed walkie-talkies.

"Be careful," warned Charles, offering his first real piece of advice. "Sabnock may not be roaming the halls, but based on our encounter upstairs, his influence can be felt. Trust your instincts, not your senses."

"Right," I added. "What the Monsignor said. Janice, you and I will head back upstairs and start on the second floor. Aaron, you and Bill start in the basement level above where we are. We'll meet in the middle. Let's go to work."

I hoped we'd find the children safe somewhere in this laboratory gulag.

My gut told me otherwise.

My heart told me we had to try.

Janice and I went back to the stairwell to head to the second floor. Taking the steps two at a time, I stopped at the top to wait for Janice. She was huffing a little and giving me the type of look that would kill a lesser man.

"Sorry," I muttered. I didn't mean it.

"Jackass," she puffed.

I looked around on the wall and found a bank of light switches in the "off" position. Throwing caution to the wind ("recklessness" was an instinct after all), I flicked them all on. Since there hadn't been any juice flowing to these lights when we'd cast our spell earlier, I figured (hoped) they would work.

I had to blink my eyes a few times before I was fully adjusted to the light. We were in a massive open room stretching the full length and width of the building. Circular metal columns were set evenly throughout the space to provide support for the roof. At the far end of the room, large steel doors marked where the outside ramp connected to the second floor. Near the doors were two government-issue, gray metal desks with accompanying office chairs. Other than that, the room was empty.

"That makes searching this floor easier," I said and made my way to the desks. Based on our bare surroundings, I wasn't really expecting us to find anything useful. I was already thinking of moving to the next level.

On each desk there was a smattering of standard office supplies: pens, pencils, tape dispenser, staplers. There was nothing unusual.

I started searching through the drawers of the desks, but wasn't too surprised to find them as empty as this room.

"Symon, take a look at this." Janice was standing near to the double doors.

I joined her to find that she was holding a clipboard.

"It was hanging on a nail next to the doors," she explained.

Looking over her shoulder, I saw a list of names. Next to each name there was a date from two weeks before and a series of unlabeled columns with various check marks. The last column contained what looked like a series of numbers and letters similar to the ones we'd found on the vials in the labs downstairs.

"Looks like they were matching names to those vials we found in the labs," I said.

"Uh-huh," Janice grunted. "I wonder what the checkmarks mean?"

Janice flipped through the pages on the clipboard. "There're about ten pages on this. Assuming twenty-five names per page, that's two hundred and fifty people, give or take."

"There were beds for about fifty downstairs." I said.

"So either there are more dormitories…" started Janice.

"…or about two hundred people didn't need beds," I finished.

"The beds were small," mused Janice. "Maybe that was the children's wing. Adults might have been kept elsewhere."

"Assuming they really did test on adults as well," I shook my head. I was struggling with how we were going to get fifty kids a mile down the road to the boat in a driving rainstorm. "How the hell are we gonna get *two hundred* and fifty out of here?"

Janice recognized one of my rhetorical questions when she heard one and didn't reply, although I'd be lying if I said that a part of me didn't want her to offer up some sort of an answer.

"Okay" I continued, "I think we're done up here. Let's head down to the first ... what?"

Janice had a strange look on her face.

"Something's ... wrong," she whispered in a faraway voice.

I felt it then, too. A weird, bubbling sensation under my skin. Someone was trying to wind-talk.

"I think it's Aaron," I said.

"Symon, we'd better get downstairs."

We sprinted for the door.

****

Janice and I arrived at the first sub-basement level to find both Aaron and Bill sitting on the floor, heads in their hands.

"Oh, hello," Aaron slurred drunkenly when he heard us approach.

"What happened? Are you guys okay?" I wheezed out, having sprinted down the stairs.

Janice knelt down to check Bill.

"Symon, they're in shock," she said.

I checked Aaron and Bill over quickly. No blood, no bruises, no broken bones. However, both of my friends were cold to the touch, and Bill looked as sickly as he had back on the *Katie Mae*. Aaron was white as a sheet.

"What happened?" I asked again.

Bill answered this time. "Inside," he said simply, pointing vaguely in the direction of the double doors that opened to the sub-basement they were searching.

"Janice, stay with them and see if you can get them back on their feet. I'm going to take a quick look."

"Symon, I don't think that's a good idea," she said.

"Probably not. Use your wicked Indian ways and fix up Bill and Aaron, please. I'll be out in a minute."

I figured since both the guys weren't harmed physically, the danger beyond the doors was minimal. Mr. Justification. That's me.

Something horrific had reduced my friends to one step above blubbering messes. So I had one advantage they didn't have. I already knew that there was something terrible on the other side of the doors.

I took a deep breath and, bracing myself, pushed them open.

The floor was laid out very similarly to the lowest level of the building we'd explored. A long hallway running the length of the building, with a series of doors evenly spaced on either side. The only difference between this level and the one Sabnock supposedly resided on was a strong antiseptic smell. It reminded me of a hospital. Antiseptic tinged with the scent of death.

The first door to my right was locked. I mumbled a spell to try to jimmy the door and was surprised to receive a small shock when I touched it. It was the first indication—other than the demonic guards who tried to riddle us with bullets, of course—that there was magic being used here. The door was neither mechanically nor electrically sealed. Yet it didn't budge.

I guessed that Aaron and Bill hadn't been able to get into this room either, so I moved across the hall to the first door that had been on my left. It was unlocked, so I opened it carefully.

The room reflected the beam from my flashlight from multiple polished surfaces as I pointed it in and around the space. I moved in to get a better look and saw a lone stainless steel table in the center of the room. I flicked on the light switch mounted on the wall and saw what looked like an operating theatre. Above the table there was a set of heavy-duty floodlights. Stainless cabinets lined the walls, and there was a washing basin off to my right. The place was immaculately clean and sterile-looking. Creepy, yes. But there was nothing in here that would have caused Aaron and Bill's current state. I moved on.

A shiver went down my spine as I shut the lights off and closed the door. To say I had a bad feeling would be an understatement.

The door next to the operating room was a big wooden thing with a large pull handle instead of a doorknob. On the ground was a heavy-duty lock that looked partially melted. I bent down and touched it and could feel the slight tingle of static electricity surrounding what remained of the brass and chrome lock. Magic had been used to remove it. Aaron and Bill had been inside. I shuddered as my mind began to make up images of what I might find.

I grasped the handle and pulled it toward me. I heard a loud 'click' and the heavy door swung partially open. A wave of cold air rolled across me. I felt a slight sense of déjà vu. I'd worked in a dairy for a while when I was younger. They had a large refrigerated room in the back for storage of milk, cheese and meat. I swung the door wide open and jammed it in place with the melted lock I'd found.

I could see my breath as I entered the frozen storage. Hanging from hooks were a series of large black bags covered in frost. With a sinking feeling I walked to the first one and tugged open the slightly frozen zipper.

A pig's carcass hung inside, gutted from head to crotch.

"Holy shit," I muttered to myself, both a sense of relief and disgust washing over me. I checked a few other bags, and they all contained frozen, butchered livestock.

My teeth chattering, I closed up the bags and left the freezer. I slammed the door shut and reconnected the damaged lock back on as best as I could. After blowing out the electronics and the mess we'd made in the lobby I was pretty sure someone would guess that there had been visitors to the building, so I'm not exactly sure why I bothered to put the lock back. Maybe I'd watched too many zombie movies in my youth.

I moved back across the hall to try the next door and found it open as well. I hesitated for a fraction of a second; then opened it quickly. Inside was another operating room.

But this one wasn't empty.

An unmistakable odor of decay, feces, and urine tinged with the coppery scent of blood assaulted my nostrils. The smell of death.

There were four people in scrubs and masks lying on the floor in various positions in the room. It was too much to hope that they were just sleeping due to Peter's spell and that I had been mistaken about the smell.

The stench was overwhelming now, and I had to pull my shirt up over my nose and mouth to keep myself from vomiting.

Closest to me were two corpses that might have been two women. It was difficult to tell, as their flesh had been cut away from their bodies to the bone. Bodily fluids had leaked over the floor, and I slipped as I moved in closer to examine the carnage.

Two other bodies had slumped on either side of the operating table. I didn't need to look that closely to see that they were butchered in the same way as the first two corpses.

On the operating table, there was a fifth corpse strapped down. It, however, hadn't been eviscerated like the scrub-clad bodies on the floor. It was the body of a young girl, no more than ten or eleven.

No wonder Aaron and Bill had freaked.

I should have been horrified at the scene, but all I felt was a strange combination of sadness and anger.

I walked over to the corpse of the little girl. She had been very beautiful, with long red hair and pale, perfect skin. There were no incisions that I could see, so whatever had happened to the surgical team had obviously occurred before they could cut into the little girl.

Tears again welled up in my eyes.

"God," I whispered my prayer, "why hast Thou turned Thy back on this innocent soul?" After all my training and all my teachings about how the grace of God triumphed over all, I couldn't understand why a place like this was allowed to exist. "If Thee art truly all-powerful and all-knowing, why doth Thou allow such evil to exist?"

I looked down at the little girl. She looked almost peaceful lying on the cold, hard steel. I reached my hand down to brush a stray lock of her red hair from her face.

I jumped back about five feet as her eyes opened, showing only the milky whites, and she let out a low, menacing hiss.

Chapter Twenty-Two

Present Day

I guessed it had been about an hour since I'd made my request to speak with Assistant Director Palmer. Sanchez had gone off right away to fetch him.

But no one had come back.

I'd been pacing in the cell but finally flopped back onto the cot. Gingerly, of course. I began to think that making me wait was some sort of minor torture that Palmer was employing to break me. I placed the lumpy pillow my tax dollars had paid for behind my head and closed my eyes. I could play the waiting game too.

Finally, I heard the click of a lock and my cell door was opened. I stayed exactly where I was.

"Symon," said a voice. A very familiar feminine voice.

Eden.

I opened my eyes and just looked at her.

"I hear," she said with a smile, "that you have the cops looking into my affairs, Symon."

"One cop," I murmured. There was no sense in verbally sparring with her at this point. "And he's one of us. Of course that depends on your definition of 'us,' Eden. How you operate doesn't sit well with me. I asked Aaron to get some answers."

"Well, Sy," she sat down on the cot next to me, "why don't you just ask me yourself?"

"Because you haven't been straight with me since I got to Boston, Eden," I answered. Her eyes flickered downward for a moment, then she looked directly into mine.

"What do you want to know, Symon?" Eden asked.

"Where am I right now?" I asked.

"You're in the Hancock Building"

"Yeah, the tallest building in Boston. I noticed that as I came in," I said nonchalantly. "I was brought in the back way, up a freight elevator, and through the back door of an office complex that looks far too pricey for government hacks."

"Is that so?" she asked.

"If you want me to trust you, Eden, don't play goddamn games," I replied.

She sighed. "This is my corporate headquarters."

"I figured as much. Why do you have interrogation rooms and an FBI presence?"

"The government is a large portion of my contract work. The FBI is a valuable customer. There are interrogation rooms here to limit exposure of magic to general law enforcement. Palmer and his team are my contacts."

"What about the CIA?" I asked.

"No. They ... have no interest in my company's services."

"And my apartment in Dublin?"

"That was news to me, Symon. It was probably the same folks who removed the teams in Greece and Ethiopia," she said. "Since you were in Boston, we had no one looking at things across the pond."

"You were the one who had me followed from Dublin, then. Not Charles." I knew this already, of course. But I wasn't ready to let Eden in on my suspicions.

Eden nodded.

"I've had you under surveillance for a while."

I bristled at that. "Why?" I asked.

"With teams from the Church disappearing, it was only a matter of time before they came after us."

"Who are 'they'?"

"I don't know. None of us do for sure," and before I could ask, "no one in my employ or any of my customers, I mean."

I thought about that for a bit. What Eden said fit with my suspicions. I decided to keep my own speculations to myself for the moment.

"Okay then," I said finally. "Now the big question: why am I here?"

"Mr. Palmer needed to meet with you. He has kept why very close to his chest. We are in my offices so I could control the situation."

"And Father Moore?"

Eden sighed. "The Cardinal doesn't trust you. Father Moore is here to protect the Church's interests. Not yours."

"I just pulled the Cardinal's big backside out of the fire by saving Charles!" I exploded.

"No, you saved Charles because he's the closest thing you have to a father. Maguire doesn't trust you because you *left*, Sy," said Eden, her tone was neutral but I could see her eyes flash with anger. "You're a wild card. There is nothing the Cardinal hates more than wild cards."

"I got the job done, Eden," I said, resentment building, "and after what Charles and the Church did to your sister, I'm surprised you have anything to do with either of them at all."

"What happened to Eve on Plum Island was her choice, Symon. Janice and I tried to convince her not to go through with the Monsignor's plan. But she wouldn't listen. She kept insisting that her empathic power was a gift from God and that she was chosen for the role."

"As his spy in the Shadow-world."

"Yes," Eden nodded. "Charles was convinced that Eve was the only one with the talent to be able to cross over to the other side and survive."

"I wouldn't call what Eve is doing right now surviving," I noted. "The Monsignor was wrong."

"Not at first," Eden said. "She's only been totally comatose for a year."

"Tell me everything."

Eden stood up and folded her arms.

"It's a long story," she sighed.

"I seem to have plenty of time," I said, gesturing around my tiny cell.

"The inhabitants of the Shadow-world want one thing," she began.

"Power," I spat.

"And all that comes with it. They use power to create the mayhem that they feed on. Complete power means total chaos."

"The mantra of the Fallen One, and why we were supposed to fight. I remember," I said. "When Charles taught us that, you cried for a week."

Eden smiled sadly

"I'm surprised you remembered that, Symon."

"What does this have to do with Eve?" I asked, trying to keep the information flowing.

"I'm getting there. Turn off your ADHD for a moment," she said. "The barrier that separates us from the Shadow-world is breaking down. Charles recognized this years ago."

"How?" I asked.

"Believe it or not, a prophesy. Remind me to get a copy of his doctoral thesis for you some day. As soon as the Vatican lets it out from under lock and key, that is."

"I never knew Charles had a doctorate," I said.

"Very few people do," Eden said. "Anyway, Charles sounded the alarms, but everyone in power turned a blind eye to him."

"Typical government," I said.

"Perhaps. Ever wonder why Charles taught non-Catholics to be Practitioners?"

"No," I really hadn't.

"Really, Symon? Janice is a Narragansett shaman. You two were lovers for years and in all that time did you ever see her take communion?" Eden gave me the same sort of look she used to give Aaron and me when we hadn't done our homework and asked to copy off of her.

"Um..." No. I really hadn't noticed.

"Charles taught non-Catholics because the rules of the game were changing," she said. "The Shadow-world was getting stronger and the balance was tipping in favor of chaos. Charles decided to create his own army from practitioners the Church had previously shunned. It didn't matter where the soldiers came from. He knew he could teach them without the restrictions and baggage of the Holy See."

"He was desperate," I said.

"In a way, yes," Eden agreed. "We were his first 'integrated class,' if you will. You were his pride and joy."

"And Eve?" I asked.

"Eve was supposed to bridge whatever rift had caused the imbalance between Earth and the Other Side. She was to be a savior, of sorts."

"Eden. What happened?"

She stopped pacing and looked at me, tears now running down her cheeks.

"Charles got his spy, but it was at a high cost. The rift opened wide. With the three recent attacks we think there is now a massive hole connecting our world directly to Hell."

"When did the tear happen?" I asked, although I was pretty sure I knew the answer.

"Ten years ago," Eden said quietly.

Chapter Twenty-Three

Ten Years Ago

I was thrown backwards as the possessed red-headed child looked at me and continued to hiss. My skin felt like it was beginning to boil. In a total panic, I started scratching at myself, trying to rip my flesh off to let the heat out.

Janice, and a recovered Bill and Aaron, burst into the room and practically slammed into me.

"Symon, you idiot!" Aaron screamed as he conjured another shield spell. As soon as it snapped in between us and the girl, the heat I'd felt was gone. I slumped to the ground in a bloody heap.

My attacker continued to hiss and thrash around, struggling to get out of her restraints on the operating table.

"Jesus Christ!" I exclaimed, scrambling backward. "She's alive?"

"I don't think she's alive in any human sense," said Aaron, struggling to maintain his shield.

Janice was suddenly at my side. "A few deep cuts, nothing serious. I can patch that up."

She muttered a quiet word and the bleeding stopped.

"Oh God," said Janice looking at corpses on the floor. "What happened?"

"She happened, if I had to guess," I said, getting to my feet.

"Okay, people," said Aaron. "We need to get out of here right now. You guys back out, and I'll drop the shield and follow. Hurry."

"No,"

"What the hell, Symon?" Aaron said. "I can't hold this shield forever."

"I said no, Aaron." I was over the initial shock and had regained some composure. And that change had given me an idea.

"Look, she's already calmed down," I said, pointing at the girl. "Janice, she's alive. I'm sure of it. Can you do what you did for me to calm her down?"

Janice looked frightened for a moment as she glanced over at the child.

Then she looked at me. She nodded. "I can try," she said.

"Drop the shield," I ordered.

"Holy crap, Symon..." Aaron began to protest.

"Do it," said Bill. "I think Symon's right, Aaron."

Aaron glanced over to Bill furiously for a moment then looked at me. He dropped his shield.

Nothing happened.

Janice went over to the girl and placed a hand gently on a small, pale shoulder. The child stopped trying to break her restraints and turned those creepy white eyes toward Janice. The little redhead was breathing heavily from the intensity of her fit.

"Shhhh," cooed Janice. "What's your name, sweetie?"

"What's she doing?" asked Aaron, reaching for Janice. I grabbed him.

"Shut up and watch," I said to Aaron. "If it doesn't work, be ready to pull Janice out of here."

"Sweetie," said Janice again, "we are here to help you. What's your name?"

"Winnie," responded a croaky, small voice. "I think ... my name is Winnie."

She started to cry. Janice began to remove her restraints.

"Yeah," Aaron said, "I think that's a bad idea, Janice."

"Shut up, Aaron. Symon, help me. The poor thing is traumatized."

When I hesitated, she said, "You're the one hell-bent on saving these children. Get over here."

She had a point. I'd never heard of a channeler or other demon-possessed creature that was susceptible to a calming spell. Nor had I ever heard of one who cried like the child was doing. She also referred to herself by name, indicating some sort of individual control. Granted, my experience was a bit limited here, but the little girl didn't seem to be acting.

Charles said go with our instincts. My instincts told me that this child was dangerous, but still a child. I decided to go with it for the moment. Besides, maybe this girl could lead us to the others.

I moved to the table and Bill and Aaron joined me. Tears streaked the child's cheeks. Her eyes were still completely milky white like a shark about to feast, but the expression on her face was unmistakable: fear.

Janice was singing a low, soft lullaby under her breath in a language I didn't recognize. It seemed to be working its magic on the child.

We slowly removed all the restraints. After the last restraint was released I stood there, unsure about what to do next.

That's when the little girl held her arms up to me and said "Up?"

My heart broke a little.

I looked at Janice who nodded her head. I reached down to the girl and hoisted her up. Holding her close, I quickly exited the room, instinctively shielding the child from the death and gore that littered the floor of the chamber. I dunno. Protecting her seemed to be the right thing to do.

Janice, Aaron, and Bill followed me and I turned to them.

"You guys okay?" I asked as everyone exited the chamber of horrors.

"Yeah," said Aaron. "The girl hit us with some sort of mental attack."

"Nightmares. Pain," Bill shook his head. "I grabbed Aaron and we barely got out of there."

"She must have done the same thing to the people we found in there," Aaron shuddered. "And they had access to surgical tools..."

"Enough," said Janice. "Tell us later," she inclined her head toward the girl.

"Well, from what I could see, the bodies belonged to adults: no children parts. So that's something," Aaron said, ignoring Janice.

"Jesus Christ, Aaron!" hissed Janice.

"Well, where are the rest of the kids, then?" I asked, cutting off further protest from Janice and looking furtively down the hallway.

The little girl, Winnie, raised her head off of my shoulder.

"Are you looking for my friends?" she asked in a tiny voice.

I gently put her down and got to my knees so we were at eye level.

"Yes, sweetie. Do you know where your friends are?" I asked in what I hoped was a soothing voice.

"I think so!" she said, her face brightening. "They are probably in the playroom with the kitty!"

"Kitty?" I asked.

"Honey," said Janice also squatting down, "can you show us to the playroom? We want to make sure your friends are okay."

"Uh-huh," Winnie nodded. She took my hand and started to walk toward the stairwell. "Do you want to play with me and my friends?"

"Of course we do," I answered quickly. "We want to play with all of them. Will they all be there?"

"Uh-huh," Winnie nodded again. "The doctors were all boring and stuff, so they'll be in the big room. The kitty gives us toys to play with. I like playing catch."

"How can she see through those creepy eyes to play catch?" Bill muttered. I was wondering something different. Winnie's eyes and behavior in the operating theater indicated she had been definitely touched by something demonic. However, she was seemingly in control of her own thoughts and actions. There was something different about this girl. Something strong. Maybe I was reading it wrong. There were plenty of evil people experimenting on human subjects here. Maybe one of those experiments caused what we'd seen with Winnie.

Of course it might all be a trap, too.

Winnie pulled me along, excited to show me to her friends. If we could find the rest of the children and get out of here, I'd call it a win. Even if we didn't get Sabnock this time around.

Janice had no such concerns as she confidently strolled up and took my other hand. Unlike Winnie's tiny hand, Janice's was warm and reassuring.

"C'mon boys," I called over my shoulder, "you heard Winnie. Let's go play."

****

Winnie led us back down to the third sub-basement level where Janice's magic had indicated Sabnock's presence. We walked straight down the long hallway and stopped at the solid brick wall at the end. I glanced over at Janice and her air of confidence had faded. Her brow was knit in uncertainty and she looked over to me in concern. My gut started to tingle again.

"Honey," she said to the little girl, "are you sure we are in the right place?"

"Oh yes!" she squeaked brightly. She paused for a moment, tilting her head a little. "Your friends are there too! We can all play together."

It took me a moment to realize that she was speaking about Charles, Jack and the twins. Wind-talking, the way Aaron had called to us, is very hit-or-miss; and I'd assumed that, since Janice and I were his closest friends, we were the only ones to hear Aaron's cry for help. I'd been confident that both Charles and Jack could hold their own against anything untoward they might come across. Eden and Eve were no slouches either when it came to welding magic. But now I wondered if they hadn't come to Aaron and Bill's aid, not because they didn't hear him, but because they couldn't.

"Get ready boys and girls," I murmured. "I think it's party time."

Winnie pointed at the gray brick wall and said, "Kitty lives in there!"

"How do we get in, sweetie?" Janice asked.

The child placed both her hands on the cold bricks. Immediately, a series of flame-orange glyphs appeared, one glyph per brick. A warm wind, like that of a nice summer's breeze blew gently across my face.

"Let's go!" screamed Winnie in delight, and yanked me right through the wall.

I stumbled as I crossed the magical threshold and found myself in a room lit by a magnificent bonfire in the center. The large chamber seemed to be lined with older stonework. The firelight was reflected upon the stones, damp with moisture from being buried so deep below the surface of the island, and I could see reflected in the center of each wet rock, a circle containing what looked like gear-shaped pictograms. Sabnock's sign. We were in the demon's lair.

Janice, Aaron, and Bill stumbled in behind me.

"Oh crap," said Bill. "I think we found what we've been looking for."

"Kitty!" Winnie called. "Where are you?"

A child-like voice responded, "Winnie! Have you brought new friends? Let us see!"

From the darkness beyond the bonfire, dozens of children came out of hiding. They seemed to range from a little younger than Winnie to pre-teen age. Boys and girls alike were all dressed in ragged dressing gowns and all had the strange absence of pupils that Winnie had.

The child let go of my hand and ran over to the boy that seemed to be at the head of the group.

"Oh, Donald! We have more friends! See? They've come to play with us like the others!"

"The others didn't want to play. They were like the doctors," droned the boy called Donald in a sickly monotone.

"Oh," said Winnie, sounding disappointed. "Are they dead too?"

"No," answered Donald, "we're saving them." The child pointed at us. "They have guns. It's just like he told us. They want to kill us like the doctors did."

"No, no, no!" said Winnie, looking at me. "They saved me! They all came to play with us!"

"Winnie," said Janice, "the others that are here are our friends, too. I'm sure they want to play. Where are they?"

Winnie turned to look at Janice, then back to the boy, Donald.

Silently, a few of the children disappeared again behind the bonfire. They returned a moment later with Charles, Jack, Eden, and Eve in tow. Eden seemed to be helping Eve to walk.

"Monsignor, is everyone okay?" asked Bill.

"Yes, William," said Charles, "we are all well. These children have treated us kindly." He smiled, looking at the young faces. None of them smiled back. The Monsignor was attempting to work his charm on the littlest possessed-ones, to no avail.

"What's wrong with Eve?" I asked. Charles shook his head; I took that to mean 'not now,' and let it drop.

I was sure that Charles, and I assumed Jack, could have easily gotten out of this jam. There were no physical bindings on any of them and I didn't get the sense that any magic was being used either as a restraint, or as a mind-altering mechanism. So I had to assume they had decided to wait and let the situation play out. I took a deep breath and willed myself to be patient. It was the only way we were going to get a shot at the demon and save these kids.

Eden sat Eve down gently next to Janice and the injured twin closed her eyes as if in pain. Janice and Eden exchanged glances. Both looked worried.

An uncomfortable silence followed. I knew we were in the right place to confront Sabnock, and I'd be lying if I told you I wasn't a little frightened about that. But other than the demon's apparent influence on the children, the creature was nowhere to be found.

Quietly, the remaining children encircled the bonfire. Only Donald and Winnie remained near us. Since the young girl seemed to be the only one not acting like a soulless channeler, I turned to her.

"Winnie," I said, trying to maintain the sort of calm voice children responded positively to. "Who are your..."

The bonfire suddenly exploded. Flames shot ten feet into the air and the color changed from a warm yellow to blood red, bathing the room in scarlet. The symbols on the worn stonework around the chamber began to glow with an inner light. After it blazed for a minute or so, the fire calmed back down to its previous size.

Standing in the middle of the flames was a powerfully built man, dressed in what looked like an ancient Roman centurion uniform that was as blood red as the fire had been. The crimson figure towered over us, its crested helmet nearly brushing the ceiling. I wasn't sure if I felt intimidated because of the rippling muscles and biceps, or the fact that he was armed with an honest-to-God short sword in his left hand and a long, lethal-looking spear in his right.

The centurion surveyed the children surrounding him, then slowly turned his gaze toward us. The demon placed its sword in the leather scabbard tied at his waist. He slammed the business end of the spear into the center of the fire sending up a shower of sparks.

Still looking at us, he slowly reached up and removed his helmet. The thing in the fire only had the *body* of a man. It had the head of a lion.

"Kitty!" exclaimed Winnie, clapping her hands.

Sabnock let out an earth-shattering roar.

Chapter Twenty-Four

Present Day

There was a knock on the cell door that interrupted my conversation with Eden. We both jumped.

"What!" I called, as if I owned the place and wasn't an incarcerated guest.

The door opened and Assistant Director Palmer entered the cell.

"Enough of this nonsense, Ms. Engel. I have questions I need answered by Mr. Bryson," he said. "Sanchez told me that you are ready to cooperate. Is that true, Bryson?"

"Back to the interrogation chamber of death?" I asked in the sweetest voice possible. I swear I thought Eden was going to slap me.

"No, this will do," he said. "Ms. Engel can stay, of course."

How nice of him.

"What is it you are looking for, Mr. Palmer? And what makes you think I can answer your questions?"

He looked at me for a moment in silence, studying my body language, looking for my tells. I used to do the same to new customers in my pub.

I threw on my best poker face.

"Demons. Plum Island. Tell me what happened."

"The FBI seems to be working very closely with Eden and her company. Why don't you ask her? She was there."

"I'm asking *you*, Mr. Bryson. Your name came up in conjunction with a recent investigation the Bureau is involved in, and I want—I need—your story."

"Look," I said, "I've been living in Europe for the last decade. My memory is foggy from time and Guinness. Ask me specific questions and I'll try and answer them."

"You read the article I gave to Father Moore?" he asked, changing tack.

"Yeah. Some terrorist blew up my apartment and killed a bunch of my neighbors," I said, my poker face slipping a bit.

"Want to get the guys who did it?"

Wow, he was good. Almost caught me in his trap.

"Isn't that the responsibility of the Irish *Gardaí*?" I asked.

"The Irish will never catch these murderers, Mr. Bryson," snorted Palmer. "They're professionals and know how to commit crimes across borders and not get caught."

"How do you know that, Assistant Director?" asked Eden.

"I'm happy to answer that, Ms. Engel," he said, "but I'm afraid it requires that Mr. Bryson provide me with a few answers first."

"I'll ask again," I said. "Why me?"

Palmer reached into his suit jacket pocket and pulled out a stack of photographs. He tossed one down.

"Do you recognize this?" It was a picture of a bedroom—a partially obscured white four-poster bed was off to the right. The walls might have been a pretty pink at one point, but they were smeared in bloody symbols. Very much like Charles' study looked a few nights ago. I kept my trap shut.

"No?" said Palmer, a bit desperately. "How about a closer look at some of the symbols?" He tossed down a few more photos. The symbols were similar to the ones I'd seen recently.

"Ancient runes really aren't my area of expertise."

He tossed down another picture. It was a close up of a symbol I did indeed recognize. It was a circle of blood surrounding what looked like gear-shaped pictograms inside it. A symbol that I hadn't seen in ten years, yet still had nightmares about.

"Sabnock," I muttered quietly.

"Is that its name? We found symbols like this all over the Plum Island site," said Palmer. "Since you seem to recognize them, you can help me with this case."

"What case?" I asked.

"A recent kidnapping," answered Palmer. His voice sounded strained, "The kidnapping of my daughter Elizabeth."

I *knew* there was something he was holding back.

"I'm sorry, Mr. Palmer, I really am. But I don't know how I can help the FBI."

The Assistant Director tossed down the last photograph he had in his hands. It was at a different angle and showed more bloody writing on the walls. This time the writing was in English:

Bring me Symon Bryson

"See, Mr. Bryson," Palmer's voice cracked with emotion, "you are the only one who can help me."

"Director," I said quietly. "I..."

"The picture of you from the security system at Plum Island sealed it." The man's words came in quick bursts. "You are the only one who can save her!"

"Director," said Eden, "my company can work with the FBI..."

"No!" the man practically shouted. "It has to be Bryson! He's saved her before!"

"What are you talking about?" I shouted at him, backing away from the FBI officer as far as my tiny cell would allow. "I don't know any Elizabeth..."

"That is my daughter's middle name," he said. "Since she became a teenager she insisted that her mother and I call her Elizabeth. She hated her given name. We named her after her grandmother on her mother's side: Winifred."

Palmer has red hair... Sabnock...

"Oh my God. Winnie!"

Chapter Twenty-Five

Ten Years Ago

I'd been preparing a pretty nasty spell since I'd seen the horrific photographs, tapping into my rage to give my magic an extra bit of push. But as I was about to unleash my power on Sabnock, Charles stopped me.

"Don't, Symon," he said quietly, grasping my arm. "We are in its lair. We'll get an opportunity. Be patient."

Emotions are a powerful force and can both enhance magic, and shut it off completely, depending on the wielder's state of mind. The sort of energy I was prepared to play with was significant and putting a lid on it was difficult, but somehow I managed to calm down.

"My children," lauded the lion-creature in a deep, echoing voice, "you have brought me presents! How thoughtful."

Winnie clapped and practically radiated pride. The rest of the children showed very little emotion.

"I must offer you thanks, Monsignor," continued Sabnock casting its yellow feline eyes at Charles. "Your arrival has broken the bindings placed around me and my prison here. I've been held too long in a state of near starvation."

"Don't you worry, beastie," growled Jack. "You've overstayed your welcome on our world and, God willing, you'll soon be back where you belong."

The creature laughed.

"You humans are so cute when you get holy. Your God doesn't care about you. He cares about rules and blind obedience. You are sheep to Him. We demons have a higher respect for the human race. Join with us. We can show you real power."

Charles started to speak rapidly in Latin and I could feel the energy building in the room. Sabnock waved its hand and the Monsignor fell suddenly silent. I saw something in Charles' eyes I'd never seen before. Fear.

Sabnock laughed again.

"I have been walking the Earth for millennia, Man of God. My power in this world has grown in the time I've spent here. Do you think a simple banishment from you would work? It took fifty men more powerful than you to contain me and place me in this cage which you have so thoughtfully unlocked."

Jack suddenly raised his hands, and screamed "*Exuro, Everto!*" A bright red, pulsating jet flew from his fingertips and slammed into the bonfire surrounding Sabnock. Energy splashed around the fire and dissipated harmlessly. The flames absorbed Jack's spell. Sabnock laughed again.

"You've become weak, mage," said the demon matter-of-factly. "How sad. Perhaps a demonstration is required."

In one rapid movement, Sabnock pulled its spear from the ground and pointed it at Jack. I moved to push him out of the way, expecting the creature to throw it. I bounced off an invisible force and landed in a sitting position, facing the old sea captain.

Jack was bathed in a greenish light, his mouth open in a silent scream. The light faded, and the Scottish warrior stood for a moment, then blood poured from everywhere. Jack fell to the ground, very dead.

"Hemorrhagic fever is one of my favorites," said Sabnock simply. "Makes a mess, though."

Other than a small whimper that came from Eve, the room was completely silent.

"I was there," boasted Sabnock, "when the Tartars laid siege to the double-ringed city of Kaffa. I whispered into their willing ears which putrid corpses of their own dead to launch from mangonels over the walls and spread the plague amongst their Genoese enemies. Thence the black pestilence crept by sea and land across the face of the earth, carried by flea, rat, human, and other vermin. Why, in Europe alone, five-and-twenty millions disgorged their lives in stinking corruption. I feasted for a year."

The creature continued to rattle off a list of its morbid accomplishments, but I'd stopped listening. The terror of the situation threatened to paralyze me and I was fighting to control myself using the techniques Charles had taught. I tried focus on organizing my observations since the appearance of the demon. Jack had been a mage for far longer than most of us had been alive, and he'd been put down as if he were no threat at all, so a direct assault would get more of us killed. Furthermore, the creature still stood in its bonfire, which seemed to offer it some sort of protection. So, how do we level the playing field a bit? I needed something to put out the...

Fire.

Water!

I looked around Sabnock's lair at the water glistening on those enchanted bricks with the light of the demon's sigil glowing from within.

The creature waxed on about the various plagues it had been a party to. Honestly, he could teach at St. Ignatius. It was that boring.

"Water," I said in a loud whisper in Janice's direction.

She blinked, obviously enthralled by the demon's lecture on the Tuskegee Airmen.

"What?" She whispered back.

"There's water on the walls," I said to her.

"What?" Janice said again, not really paying attention.

"There. Is. Water. On. The. Freaking. Walls." Good Lord, for a 'master of the elements' and a straight 'A' student, my dear Janice could be a bit dense at times.

She looked around for a moment.

"Oh," she said. "Oh!"

The brightness of the light bulb that finally lit over her head could be seen from space.

"Get behind me," I said. "I don't want Simba over there seeing what you are up to."

We shuffled silently to the point where I was blocking Sabnock's line of sight to Janice. The creature's monologue, I realized, was keeping the gaggle of kids enthralled. I hoped if I was right, and Janice was as good as I knew she was, we could make quick work of the monster in the flames and get the kids out in one piece. I looked at the sprawled form of Jack lying in a bloody pool. We'd need more than a little hope. Luck and maybe some divine intervention would be better.

Janice rifled through her backpack and I heard the slight 'pop' of a Tupperware container being opened behind me. To me it sounded like a gunshot and I winced, figuring the jig was up. No one seemed to have noticed though, and I heard Janice remove some ingredients for her spell from the plastic bowl.

"Hurry up," I said in a slightly hysterical hiss. I felt, rather than heard the spell charging. Air around me began to energize—and I realized too late that any other magic-sensitive would feel it too.

Including the Lion King, who immediately stopped its harangue.

In one motion, all the kids but Winnie turned toward us and let out a simultaneous low growl.

"Now would be a good time, Janice!" I said.

"*Contego!*" shouted Aaron, who had leapt out in front of me. It was a good thing he'd been paying attention to Janice and me instead of the creature's monologue, because the shield he'd thrown in front of us was hit almost immediately by the massive fireball Sabnock hurled at us. Aaron staggered backwards, almost banging into me, but the shield held.

Charles turned to Eve. "Prepare yourself, my dear. The time is near."

I had no time to muse on what Charles was talking about, as a second fireball hit Aaron's shield, knocking him to the ground. He remained motionless.

"Eden! I need your help here!" I shouted, as I prepared my own shield spell, knowing it would never be as strong as Aaron's. But Eden wasn't moving. She was just staring at her sister who had dropped to her knees in a pose of supplication.

"Eden! What the hell…"

Right then, Janice finished her spell. There was the sound of rushing water, and the moisture that I'd seen clinging to the inscribed stone walls streamed toward the center of the room.

There was a loud *hiss* and white steam surrounded Sabnock, obscuring him from view.

"Now, Eve," said Charles, his voice almost ringing throughout the chamber.

Like a sprinter running the hundred-yard dash, Eve was up from her kneeling position and racing into the cloud of steam.

"Kill them!" roared the lion-demon, its voice tinged with fear. There were screams from the center of the steam cloud, still too thick to see through.

The two screams grew into dozens as the possessed children, following their master's command, were on us like a pack of wolves.

Chapter Twenty-Six

Present Day

Assistant Director Palmer put his head in his hands. "You need to help me. You need to get my girl back."

"When was she taken?" asked Eden.

"Two days ago. She came home from college on a break. It was her eighteenth birthday."

I fixed my gaze on Palmer and took a deep breath.

"Director," I began. "Yes, you have a picture of me from Plum Island; yes, I know something of demons—"

I thought about a young, frightened girl.

"—and yes, I will help you find Winnie."

I thought Eden would be pissed at me. I was wrong. She just sat there with a smirk on her face.

However, I'd taken a gamble with the Assistant Director and I could see the pay-off in Palmer's eyes. He really wasn't looking to prosecute me. He was desperately looking for help to save his daughter.

In Palmer's case, help was in the form of a scruffy thirty-year-old bloke with a bit of a hangover. Beggars can't be choosers.

"Obviously, I need to get out of here first. Then I'll need to see what you have from the crime scene: a visit if it is still intact," I said.

Palmer hesitated for a second. Maybe my gamble hadn't paid off.

"Two conditions."

"Name them," I said.

"One: I need to see all the information from your Plum Island adventure," he said.

"It's mostly anecdotal, unless someone else took notes, but agreed."

Palmer nodded.

"And two: Sanchez, Vitale, and I will be with you every step of the way. They have worked with me for years on," he paused, "special cases for the FBI."

"Sure," I answered. "Just one more thing, then."

"What's that?"

"You are obviously Director Skinner in this scenario," I said, "But I still need an answer to which one of your two boys I call Mulder, and which one I call Scully."

****

We made a plan to head back to St. Ignatius to meet with the rest of the group I'd insisted on involving and to review the large file Assistant Director Palmer had provided me. The scene of the kidnapping was crawling with agents, so the photographs and reports now in my possession were all we had to go on.

Eden had offered the use of her offices. I politely declined. I wanted to be back at St. Ignatius where I felt more comfortable working on the case.

Palmer rode with Eden and me while his agents followed in the car behind us. She'd called Aaron at the precinct and Janice at the church to give them a quick update. Aaron promised to meet us there.

As soon as Eden hung up with Aaron, her cell rang. She looked at the caller ID, smiled and put the little handset on speaker.

"Eden! What in God's name did that little prick do?!" said a bombastic voice that made the speaker in the phone screech in protest.

"Hello, Eminence." I said. "How's the Pope?"

Cardinal Maguire apparently had served on a Navy ship when he was younger, judging from the salty and colorful language he used.

"Besides being anatomically impossible, that was rather harsh, Eminence," I said when he finally took a breath.

"Bryson, you little asshole. Who do you think you are, bringing non-practitioners into our affairs? Five hundred years ago I would have had you imprisoned. Hell, fifty years ago even."

"I believe that, Eminence. However, I have my reasons."

"Oh, and what are they?"

"One: the government already knows about magic to some extent. Take Plum Island as a perfect example of what happens when magic and the government get together to party," I said, ticking off fingers as I went. "Two: assisting the FBI with a very personal case will, quite frankly, do more to buy me out of a prison term then your lawyer ever could. Three: there is no way in hell that Plum Island, the second kidnapping of Assistant Palmer's daughter and the recent abduction of Charles are mere coincidence. And Four: your method of dealing with the Shadow-world is crap. I'm trying something new."

The Cardinal snarled something in Latin.

"Eminence, look at it this way. The more 'big brains' applied to this issue, the faster it will be resolved and the faster I go back to Ireland, never to be seen or heard from again."

Of course my home was a pile of rubble at the moment, but that was a moot point for this argument. Besides, things work out if you live right. At least that's what I've always told myself.

"Fair point," replied the Cardinal. "I'd love nothing more than for you to disappear into obscurity in the shortest amount of time possible. Limit the damage done by your big mouth and fix this situation and you can have your life back. What's the plan?"

"We will meet back at St. Ignatius and make sure everyone is up to speed, then map out next steps," said Eden giving me a look that said 'now would be a good time to shut up.'

"Good," replied the Cardinal. "We are coming back on a flight this evening. Bryson, don't do anything until I'm back, do you understand?"

"Sure," I said.

"Bryson!" shouted his Eminence.

"Don't do anything. I heard you," I said.

Eden's phone went dead.

"You really don't want to piss him off, Sy," warned Eden.

"Hey, he said 'don't do anything.' I'm not planning on doing 'anything,'" I said, shrugging my shoulders.

Something, on the other hand ... 'something' was very different from 'anything.' But the Cardinal didn't have to know that.

"Eden, where is your sister?" I asked.

"At home with the nurse," she said. "Why?"

"How difficult would it be to bring her to the church?" I asked, my mind churning a mile a minute.

"I know what you are planning, Symon, and I don't recommend it."

"Look," I said, "you told me that there is a rip that formed between our world and the Shadow-world and that it formed ten years ago, right?"

She nodded.

"And that the scales were now tipped in the demons' favor, right?" Again, she nodded.

"Well, it seems pretty obvious to me that Eve's the catalyst for this. She might know how to stop the demons from coming through. Hell, she might even know how to close the rift," I concluded. Take *that* Sherlock Holmes.

"Even if she would let you speak to her, I'm not sure you would get anything comprehensible," Eden said, sadness in her voice. "It's too risky."

"Yeah, but it's too risky not to, either. I promised Palmer we'd find his daughter. And I'd really like another shot at the demon who not only kidnapped her twice, but is also responsible for Eve's current state," I could see the gears turning in her head. "Look," I continued, "we were all able to come together to get Charles back and to send Belial back to Hell. Let's go for a second win."

She looked at me with one of the best poker faces I'd ever seen; then she made a call.

****

Twenty minutes later, we arrived back at St. Ignatius where both Janice and Aaron were waiting for us out front. The two cars pulled up and Eden and I got out, followed by the three G-men in the second car.

"I would've thought you'd be on your way to a federal pen by now," said Aaron, as he clapped me on the back.

"No golf for me, man," I replied. "We have more important things to do."

"Glad you're safe, Sy," said Janice giving me a quick hug. I tried to ignore the tingles her touch sent through my body and the smell of her hair. Really, I did.

I cleared my throat. "Uh, let's get inside and I'll make introductions and brief everyone."

Aaron stepped past me and held out his hand. "Assistant Director Palmer," he said.

"Nice to see you again, Detective," responded Palmer.

Now, I know local law enforcement and the Feds worked together a lot, but something bothered me in the familiarity between Aaron and Palmer.

I contemplated that as I pulled the door open and let everybody inside. Before closing the door behind me, I noticed a hawk that landed on the roof of Eden's Lincoln. "Stick around, bird," I muttered. "By the time we're done, I might need you to take down another helicopter or two."

We assembled in the kitchen area, which was, other than the open sanctuary or the musty old school portion of the campus, the largest space to accommodate everyone. Besides, the large refrigerators held some of Peter's leftovers, which, as my stomach reminded me, were a perfect hangover cure.

Janice helped me while I set up plates and doled out cold chicken and cheese for everyone. While we played house, I made introductions and briefed everyone on the situation with Palmer's daughter, Winnie. I brought Palmer and his men up to speed about our Plum Island disaster ten years ago, and on Charles' kidnapping. I also told them about my theory that they were all connected.

"So let me get this straight," said Aaron, in between mouthfuls of chicken. "Sabnock is back, has Winnie, and wants you? Okay, where do we drop you off to get the girl back?"

"I'm more curious," said Janice, with a warning look at Aaron, "as to why you think Winnie's plight and Belial's capture of Charles are related."

"Actually," I said, "Aaron's snarky delivery aside, he's pretty close. And it answers your question too, Janice."

"How do you figure, Bryson?" asked Palmer.

"Let's look at these situations. Based on the overwhelmingly consistent egomania that is rife in the demon world, Sabnock is looking for revenge. Belial's capture of Charles is what got me back here. Sabnock's kidnapping of Winnie is the next step in its plan. I don't believe in coincidences."

"Yes," agreed Palmer, "but it may have killed her, or eaten her soul or whatever by now."

"No, Director," I replied, "it hasn't. Because it wants me. Winnie is the bait. Sabnock won't do anything to her until it has me. At that point, it'll take Winnie too."

"Are you sure they're connected?" asked Janice.

"When we were attacked in Maine, Belial's channelers spoke in its voice, correct?"

"Yeah," said Janice. "But that's not a new trick. We've seen that before."

"True, but the attack by those channelers at your place in Maine wasn't an attack on you, love," I said.

Janice got it. "Belial, through its zombies, spoke only to *you*. They weren't interested in me at all."

"Correct," I said.

"Belial wants you too," added Palmer.

"Also correct," I agreed.

"Why?" asked Flint and Agent Sanchez at the same time.

"If it were just Sabnock, I'd say revenge. Belial's involvement means something else is going on. I don't know what, yet. But I'm the connection."

Eden's phone rang. She picked it up and listened for a couple of seconds, and then said, "Okay, Thanks. I'll be right there."

"Is it about Eve?" I asked.

"She'll have to wait," replied Eden.

"Why?" I asked.

"Because that was the hospital. Charles is awake and is asking for you."

Chapter Twenty-Seven

Ten Years Ago

Stop!"

The voice rang out, unearthly in its power, yet somehow familiar. The young channelers stopped their attack and turned to face the source of the command. Winnie began to cry.

The curtain of steam and smoke was thinning, and the pyre that had surrounded Sabnock now looked like a dying campfire. Floating over the smoldering embers was not an ancient warrior with the head of a lion, but Eve.

"Oh God," said Eden, her voice breaking. "You did it. Eve! No…! Oh God." Eden broke into sobs and Janice rushed over to her, glaring at Charles as she held the twin in her arms.

Eve hung in the air, swaying slowly back and forth. The clothes she had been wearing were little more than rags now, and her skin radiated a bright white light. Her eyes were sunken and were ringed with dark skin. She looked as though she had aged fifty years in an instant.

"I…" she croaked, then coughed. Blood trickled from the side of her mouth. "I don't have much time," she continued, looking directly at me while hovering above us all.

"Symon, when I'm gone, the children will go with me. Their souls are long gone. You must take the living off this island. I will be fine. Promise."

"Eve," I said, completely confused. "What…"

"No … time," she replied with difficulty. "Planned for a while now. It's up to you."

And Eve collapsed to the ground.

The possessed ones around us also fell, but unlike Eve who lay motionless but whole on the steaming embers, the bodies of the young channelers disintegrated quickly into nothing more than ash. With one exception.

Winnie was lying on the ground. Unconscious, but as whole as Eve.

The room was strangely silent for a moment. Aaron, who had been on the ground after Sabnock's second blast, got shakily to his feet.

"What the hell, Symon?" he asked.

"I'm not sure," I lied through my teeth. "We need to get out of here. Can you walk?"

"Yeah," he said. "Bill, help me with Eve." Bill had been standing silent and motionless since we'd arrived in Sabnock's lair. He shook his head as if coming out of a deep trance and followed Aaron over to where Eve lay.

Eden was holding on to Janice, the twin's face buried in her shoulder. Charles moved to the two women and Janice said, quite coldly, "Not now, Monsignor. Help someone else."

I had a horrible feeling in the pit of my stomach. I looked over to what was left of Jack again, then back at Charles. The temper Charles had been chastising me for since I first arrived at St. Ignatius was demanding to be let out. I swallowed it down and hoped that it would stay down until we got off this island.

I moved past the Monsignor and went over to Winnie. The young girl looked like she was asleep: her color was returning to something closer to normal and she was warm to the touch. It was as though she'd come back to life.

I gently picked her up and turned to find that Janice and Eden had let go of each other and had silently opened up the portal from Sabnock's lair back to the hallway of the Plum Island facility.

We made our way back to the lobby of the building, carrying our injured. Charles had insisted upon leaving Captain Jack Straw's body behind as bringing it with us might expose the crew of the *Katie Mae* and countless others to a disease best left on the island. Although I understood the order from the Monsignor, the callous way the old man had decided to leave his long-time friend behind only added to the suspicions and anger threatening to boil out of every pore of my body.

Hurrying through the lobby with those horrendous images of twisted victims didn't help my control any.

Outside, we found that the rain had slowed, but the wind still howled around us. We moved to the white Chevy Suburban still parked in the carport. Opening the back, we laid both Winnie and Eve gently inside. Eden climbed in with her sister and Janice followed to tend to the young girl. Bill jumped into the driver's seat and started up the engine of the monstrous SUV. The rest of the team silently opened the remaining doors to climb in. I didn't join them.

I turned and looked at the large white building, thinking about the evil performed within. Disease experimentation on children. Fetuses in jars, ready for further harvesting. Demonic entrapment for the sole purpose of devising new and horrific ways to extinguish life. Friends lost and lives ruined.

Once, when I was five years old and before I came into Charles' care, I'd gotten very angry. It was when I'd found my parents dead and the murderer still in the house. The magic let loose from my soul that day was horrible and swift. Charles had rescued me soon after and had taught me my first lesson about magic and the need to control my ability.

I'd learned that lesson well, and since that day had worked exceedingly hard never to let my feelings control my God-given power.

As I looked at the building, the heat from my soul grew. I could feel the controls and the filters I'd worked to perfect for so many years crumbling away; and I let them fall.

Somewhere in the back of my mind, it registered that Charles was screaming something at me. And I didn't care.

I basked in the seething emotion and power that was building up. I embraced it.

I said, simply, *"Aduro."*

The Plum Island facility exploded in a massive fireball.

****

We made it back to the Katie Mae. I have no memory of the drive: how Charles pulled me into the Suburban and we rocketed away before the entire carport vaporized with the rest of the lab and its outbuildings.

What I do remember is boarding the ship and watching a slightly dazed crew taking orders from Charles. I remember him telling us all to get below. After telling him to go screw himself, I wandered away from everyone to watch the glow from the fires my destruction had caused while the ship left the dock.

Once I could no longer see Plum Island, I went inside. Aaron was waiting for me.

"Charles wants to talk to you. He's in the ship's mess." He looked as though he wanted to say more, but I cut him off.

"Aaron, I've got nothing to say to him," I snarled. He looked scared. "Look, man," I sighed. "I'm not going to blow you up."

He gave me a strange look and then said, "Uh, okay. I wasn't sure."

At that point, I decided that maybe it *was* time for a chat with the Monsignor.

"Ya know what?" I said to Aaron, "I think I will go see Charles." And I walked away.

My best friend followed, keeping a good half dozen paces between us, as I made my way through the ship. I guess as a friend I should have said something soothing but I just didn't have it in me. I was bone-weary.

Charles was alone, writing in a little journal when I entered the mess. A moment later Aaron squeezed in as well. "I need to speak with Symon alone," the Monsignor said, not even looking up.

Aaron looked at me for a moment, a mixed bag of worry and fear dancing across his face. He hesitated, then backed out of the room, closing the door behind him.

Charles continued writing for a few more moments, then closed his little notebook and looked up at me.

"Sit down, Symon," he ordered.

"No thanks," I replied.

Charles frowned at that, but let it pass. Instead, he just leaned back in his chair with an air of forced relaxation. The wooden spindles creaked slightly.

"Not bad for a first mission," he said.

I looked at him incredulously. "Jesus Christ, how can you say that?" I finally sputtered.

"Losses are always a possibility when dealing with the pure evil I've trained you to face, Symon," Charles said softly. "You knew this going in."

"'Knew this going in?" I shot back. "My God, Monsignor ... your war buddy is dead, countless children's souls have been lost, and Eve and Winnie are hurt, God knows how badly."

"You defeated an evil that has been festering for decades, used in unspeakable ways by corrupt men with the specific intent of causing untold pain, suffering, and death. Jack knew the risks. He was one of God's soldiers. You must look at the big picture..."

"The big picture!" I shouted. "You and the goddamn *big picture*. Spare me that worn out speech!"

Charles paused for a moment, his expression unreadable. "Yes, Symon. The 'Big Picture' is what we and the others who have come before us have been working toward for millennia. Good must triumph over evil. It's as simple as that." He held up his hand to silence me before I could tell him where to stuff his *big picture*.

"You are a passionate young man. You always have been, but now is not the time to let your emotions override common sense," he said. "We will be pulling into the nearest port on Long Island shortly, where both Eve and the young girl will be airlifted to a hospital friendly to our cause. Put everything that has happened out of your mind for the moment. We have something more important to discuss."

"No," I said, making sure my disdain was obvious, "I don't think I'm interested in discussing anything with you right now."

"Symon!" Charles raised his voice, and I stopped with my back toward him half way to the mess door.

"Symon, please," Charles pleaded. "The Diocese and the Vatican will help us smooth over the entire Plum Island incident with the Government…we…"

I looked at my old teacher over my shoulder. "Yeah, you go do that." I left the mess without another word.

****

I went to the place I felt I was most likely to be left alone—the ships' hold. Only a few hours before, Aaron and I had sparred here, excitement about our first mission permeating every move, and now it was just a dark, fish-smelling cave where I could hide from the world, crouched in a little ball.

But I couldn't hide from myself.

Once I knew Eve and Winnie were safe, and once the rest of us were back at the parish, only then would I really be ready to finish my discussion with Charles. And it wasn't going to be pleasant.

I'd felt so high and mighty, sold from an early age on using the special gift I and my friends had, for the power of all that is good.

In God's name.

"Why couldn't You stop this?" I asked aloud. "Why did so many people have to suffer?" I stood and walked into the center of the hold with my arms outstretched, fists clenched in anger.

"If you are truly a God of light, why did you let so much pain happen when you could have stopped it in an instant?" I dropped to my knees and let the tears flow. It was all too much. I didn't want this. I didn't want any of it. I just wanted to crawl under a rock someplace and never come out.

I looked up and screamed, "*Quare vos relinquo qui es plurimus fidelis!*"

"*Forsaken* is a strong word, son," chided a quiet voice behind me.

I stood and spun around. "Who the hell are you?" I asked.

"Name's Joel—just Captain Straw's first mate, son."

"He's dead," I said miserably.

"I know. Life goes on," Joel said. "We are about to pull into port, and I came down to check that things were okay in the hold. I guess they ain't."

He walked closer to me, and in the dim light of the hold I could make out a man of about medium height with a dirty-gray, scraggily beard. He was wearing a heavy pea coat and a cap. He had a slight smile on his face that should have pissed me off, but instead had a calming effect. I looked away and down, running my hand in my hair sheepishly.

"It's no fun yelling at God when you have witnesses," I mumbled.

"You're a good man, Symon Bryson. That's why you were picked," the seaman said.

I looked up at him.

"You think Captain Straw was the only *talented* person on board? You have to learn to see things better than that, son. Might save your life someday." It was less a scolding and more just a statement of fact. That comforted me for some reason.

"Jack was dying, you know," said the first mate. "Pancreatic cancer. Nasty stuff, a lot of pain. He wanted to go out doing one more thing for our side."

I looked at the stranger closely. "And you helped him do that," I guessed.

"Smart boy. See? You can be taught," Joel laughed. It was a beautiful sound that, somehow, lessened the burden on my soul.

"But what about Eve? And Winnie? And the rest?" I asked quietly.

"You have to have faith that God protects the souls of the innocent. But also remember that free will cannot be interfered with. It's just the way things are. You know the story. The apple. Garden of Eden. That damned snake."

"I honestly don't know if I can do this," I said, finally giving voice to my insecurity.

"It's a difficult path you walk, Symon," the man nodded his head. "No doubt about that. But it's a worthy path, and there are so few people who can walk it in this day and age. It requires strength and passion, both of which you have in abundance."

I laughed. *"Passion will be my undoing*, Charles always says. He's like a large, African-American Yoda."

"Unfocused passion, maybe," said the man. "But to move forward you will need that passion."

"How can I move forward when all I can see is the pain around me?"

"Pain I can do something about," he replied, moving closer to me. "But you are at a crossroads. The direction you take now must be your own choice. But consider your choice carefully." He put his hands on my shoulders.

I saw a flash of images. Bright light, and beautiful wings. I realized I'd closed my eyes and when I'd opened them, the first mate was gone.

The pain holding me down wasn't gone completely, but it was more ... manageable. I could think clearly again. The conversation with the first mate was already fading, like a dream you remember clearly when you first wake up, but you forget it ever happened before you put the coffee on.

I saw my path clearly for the first time in my life. I knew I was going to make sure Winnie and Eve got to the hospital and then there would be the confrontation with Charles.

Tonight had been my first real taste of what evil could do in this world. I watched dozens of children, their souls already lost, disintegrate into nothingness. I watched a new friend sacrifice himself to protect us and an old friend sacrifice herself to save us.

Joel said it was my choice. Maybe it was cowardice on my part, but after all I'd seen that evening, I wouldn't be back. I was going to find some place as far away as possible, dig a hole there, and disappear.

After tonight, magic would no longer exist in my world.

Chapter Twenty-Eight

Present Day

"Magic doesn't exist!" exclaimed Palmer incredulously. The FBI insisted on escorting us to see Charles at the hospital, as I was still technically under arrest. I hate technicalities.

"It does, Mr. Palmer," I said, as we all got up to leave. I admit I was getting a great deal of pleasure from the shocked look on his face. "And the sooner you accept that fact, the better able you'll be to help both us and your daughter."

"Look," he grunted irritably, "I accept the fact that there may be some things I don't understand out there." He waved his hand to indicate the outside world. "But magic? I think I would have seen some evidence of that by now."

"You probably have," I said. "You just didn't understand the full scope of what you've seen. The general population tends to keep their heads buried in the sand when the extraordinary happens. Janice?"

I looked over my shoulder at her. She looked at me with an unreadable expression for a moment then, with a shrug, she transformed herself into her wolf form.

"Jesus Christ!" exclaimed Vitale as he, Sanchez and Palmer jumped back away from Janice-wolf by about five feet. Janice transformed back to her human form.

"Where do her clothes go when she changes?" stammered Sanchez.

"Hmm," I said thoughtfully. "Good question. I never thought to ask."

I remembered when Charles explained to me about magic the first time. I'd been a kid then, so accepting the fantastic had been a lot easier for me than it was for the adults whose world, up until the last hour, had been little more than donuts, bad coffee, brushing teeth, raising families, charity fundraisers and paperwork.

I closed my eyes for the ride into town. I still felt like shit, and my headache wasn't getting any better with the amount of things spinning in my brain.

Not the least of which was my upcoming reunion—or was it to be a confrontation—with Charles. I'd boarded a plane what seemed a lifetime ago specifically to tell the Monsignor to screw off and to leave me alone. Now ... well, I didn't have a clue about what I was going to say.

****

"How is he?"

We'd arrived at the hospital and been given a wide berth by anyone who was standing outside the hospital portico when multiple black cars and SUVs had roared up to the entrance. My question had been blurted out to the first person I saw near the Intensive Care Unit who looked like a doctor.

The doctor, a young man by the name of Hyuang, looked tired and a bit irritated by the number of people who had burst into the ICU. Eden, Aaron, Janice, the three FBI agents and I surrounded the doctor expectantly.

"Stable, but weak," replied the doctor. "Along with being severely dehydrated, the Monsignor sustained serious injuries. We have repaired most of his internal injuries; however, his spine is broken in three places, and it's doubtful he'll walk again. He's awake, but, please, no stress. You can have five minutes."

We made our way quickly down the hall, but didn't need to check room numbers, as a large, familiar man was sitting in a chair, obviously guarding one of the ICU suites. The man's arm was in a sling.

"Hi, Flint," I said. "How's the wing?"

"You're an asshole, Bryson."

"That seems to be the consensus, so I'll give you that one. We're going inside," I said.

He looked at Eden, who nodded her head. Flint shrugged, and went back to writing in his little notebook.

"Oh hey, Flint," I said, "has anyone else stopped by to see the Monsignor?"

He looked up at me with that I'm-going-to-kill-you-someday look. "Not a soul."

That meant we somehow beat Father Moore here. Assuming, of course, the hospital was his destination.

Eden, Aaron and Janice immediately entered the hospital room. I hesitated outside. Less than a week ago, I knew exactly what I was going to tell the Monsignor. I'd spent the ride to the hospital debating what to say now, and had come to the miserable conclusion that I had no idea what was going to come out of my mouth.

"Come in, Symon. No need to lurk in the hallway," said a weakened, low voice from inside the room.

I took a deep breath and entered.

Charles was partially propped up in his bed. He had an oxygen tube under his nose and an IV drip in his arm. The lower half of his body was braced with various winches and pulleys: some sort of traction torture device, I supposed.

Janice was holding the Monsignor's hand and sitting on the edge of the bed while Aaron and Eden maintained a respectful distance. All my old friends were looking at me with anticipation.

I know I'm a jerk sometimes, but my old mentor had just stepped back off Death's welcome mat, but was still on the porch. The last remnants of any anger I'd felt completely melted away.

"Hello, Monsignor," I said. "How are you doing?"

"I'm breathing, my boy, thanks to everyone here. That's a lot better than anyone thought, so I'll take it as a gift from God. I'd like a briefing please, and make it quick before that nurse comes back to adjust me, bathe me or replace my catheter."

Eden brought the Monsignor up to speed. As I listened to her outline what had gone on from when Charles had been kidnapped until this morning's events, my mind ran through questions that had been nagging at me. But I wasn't sure Charles would make it through the litany of bothersome thoughts.

When Eden finished, the room was silent. So quiet, that it shook me from my thoughts and back to where I was.

Charles' eyes were closed, and I almost thought he'd drifted off to sleep. Eden's briefing had been pretty boring compared to the actual live events.

Just as I motioned for everyone to leave, Charles said in his quiet baritone, "I'd like to speak with Symon alone for a few minutes. Please," he added.

The walls of the hospital room seemed to close in on me and I suddenly felt like I was back in that FBI holding cell. Everyone else filed out, and only Janice met my gaze before closing the door behind her. I was left alone with my old mentor.

"Symon, I'm so glad you're here. I've missed you, boy," the monsignor said with so much emotion that I was taken aback.

"Monsignor..." I began.

"Symon, they have me on some powerful drugs. I'm not sure how much longer I'll be lucid, so we need to save some of those burning questions I know you have. There is information you need before you jump head-long into a rescue mission."

Fair enough, I thought. We were on the same page at least.

"Eve..." whispered Charles.

"I spoke with her," I said quietly.

A pained expression came across his face.

"So you know. Everything."

"Not everything, but more than I did. And as you said, that is something we can discuss later. Right now, I need to rescue Palmer's daughter and close up the connection between our existence and the Shadow-world."

"Yes you do, but it's important for you to realize the whole thing is a trap. You'll have to be very careful," the Monsignor said.

Now I was confused. "What do you mean?" I asked.

"Symon, I find myself lying in this bed because I made a mistake ... a bad one..." The Monsignor stopped to cough. He winced in pain and closed his eyes for what seemed to be an eternity.

"Eve," I was hoping to prompt the Monsignor. His eyes fluttered open.

"Yes," he said, his voice sounding distant. "But it's bigger than that. You have no idea the danger you're in..." the Monsignor's voice faded away.

Bigger than condemning someone to live as a crazy person in two worlds? And I already knew I was in danger ... I mean if someone blows up your home and shoots at you from a helicopter, it doesn't usually count as a friendly 'how do you do,' does it?

I looked at the sleeping face of my mentor. I needed information desperately, but the Monsignor was obviously not in a position to tell me anything.

"He needs to rest now, Symon," said a voice from the shadows. I jumped about two feet out of my skin and whirled around. A man shuffled out of the corner. He had a scraggily beard, and was dressed in an old-fashioned pea-coat and Greek fisherman's cap. There was something familiar about him ... it took me a few seconds to remember.

"Joel, isn't it?" I asked tentatively. How did no one notice him standing there before?

The old man smiled.

"You remember me, then. That's good. Very good, Symon."

Memories of an old cargo hold smelling of fish, feelings of despair and of light combined together in a kaleidoscope of images. It made my hangover worse.

"You look a little peaked, son. Why don't you sit for a minute?" said the old first mate.

I found myself sitting before I'd made a conscious decision to do so. I rubbed my temples, trying to hide the feeling of helplessness that had come over me.

"Joel," I said. "I'm a little confused."

"Only a little?" He asked with a smile.

"Okay," I admitted, "a lot."

"Ask your questions; I might be able to help," said the old man.

"Why are you here?"

"I'm here to look after Charles, but there are more important matters to discuss."

"The end game. I don't see it." I said slowly.

"You only see the few tasks at hand," said Joel. "At the moment, you are playing checkers. A good game, but a simplistic one. You need to start playing chess."

"What does that mean?" I asked, slightly annoyed.

"Your first real question, then." Joel smiled. "You were taught that light and dark are in a constant tug of war. Good versus evil. White versus black."

I just looked at him.

"You know better than any of your friends that our fight is *not* black and white; it is a swirling kaleidoscope of grays. There are many layers to our campaign, yet you focus on only one. Retrieving the girl. Important, yes. But is it the full picture? And are you seeing the *right* picture?"

"What do you mean?"

Joel smiled. "Let me try something else. You were told that Charles' predicament was over guilt for you. Yet you've convinced yourself that Eve is the real source of guilt. Why?"

"Well, because ... wait. How do you know that?" I stared at the old seaman.

"I listen, Symon," he said simply. "But you really are the source of Charles' recent problem. See the *whole* board."

"Help me," I pleaded, still staring at him.

He shook his head. "That's not the way it works. I can guide and advise only."

"That's convenient," I said, my cynical self finally waking up.

Joel sighed. "Both Belial and Sabnock want you. What does that tell you?"

"They have poor taste in men," I said.

Joel smiled again. "Perhaps. Perhaps not."

I thought it through. "I have something they want."

"Correct. What could that be?"

"I don't know!" I exclaimed.

"Yes, you do. But you won't allow yourself to believe it."

It had been a thought in the back of my mind for a while now, but it seemed too silly to mention. Charles had once told me I was going to be a powerful practitioner. I'd never believed him until I'd leveled the building on Plum Island with barely a thought. That much power had scared the hell out of me.

"They want me," I said quietly.

"Yes. You have a pivotal role to play. You are incredibly gifted, but undisciplined," said Joel.

"I was trained for years..." I began to protest.

"You were. But you have also been away from the battle for just as many years. You are out of practice and vulnerable."

Oh bugger.

"I'm being manipulated," I said. "They want me to play for their team."

"See?" said Joel, sounding a little pleased. "You are beginning to see what's around you. And now that you know, you can prepare yourself for the temptation a bit better."

"But Winnie..." I said.

"Yes, you have to save her. That's important," Joel finished for me. "And you must close the portal."

"So they *are* related," I said.

"Very much so," replied Joel.

"Since they're related, it means one thing." I said, the bottom falling out of my stomach.

Joel nodded. "You have to go back to where this started ten years ago. Bill has some interesting information to help you. He, Father Fine and the Cardinal had a little trouble at the airport. But they will be out and on their way to St. Ignatius by now. Speak to him as soon as you can. Make peace with the Cardinal. He can help in more ways than you can imagine. Then, you must return to Plum Island and finish the job you started so long ago."

****

I exited Charles' room deep in thought, only to be accosted in the hallway by my friends and Assistant Director Palmer.
"What did he say?"
"Is he going to be all right?"
"Did he have anything to say about my daughter's kidnapping?"
Only Eden was quiet, until I held up my hand to silence the onslaught.
"What's our next move?" she asked.
"Well," I said, still thinking furiously. "We head back to St. Ignatius to meet Bill, Peter and the Cardinal. I'm going to need to speak with them. Next, I'm going to have to go visit Eve. And then, assuming I survive Cardinal McGuire's wrath and a detour to Hell, we figure out how to get onto Plum Island to save Winnie."

I looked at the shocked expressions around me, and only then did I realize that the pain and aches that had been plaguing me all morning were suddenly gone.

Chapter Twenty-Nine

Assistant Director Palmer insisted that I ride with him on the way back to the church.

"So, what's the plan?" he asked, as soon as he'd closed the partition between the front and the back of the big SUV. "How do we get my daughter home?"

"I'm still working on that," I said through gritted teeth. I only had a few vague ideas how to proceed; my reunion with Charles had given me very little in the way of information. I'd made a promise to this man to save his daughter and I had every intention of doing just that. The trick was how to do it. And how to avoid whatever temptation I might face.

My gut told me both Charles' and Winnie's kidnappings were related. In both cases demons were directly interacting with humans and not simply using subtle temptation and manipulation from a distance—the usual modus operandi of denizens of the Hell portion of the Shadow-world. First, Belial boldly takes a high-ranking member of the Church, an almost unheard of and very risky act. Then, a woman who'd been held hostage by a demon as a child is directly taken by the same creature years later. And all this happened since the time I arrived back in town just a few days ago. I've never believed in coincidence, and there were too many coincidences to count. Therefore both were connected. But how? And for what purpose?

I rubbed at my temples. My headache was coming back and the near euphoria I had felt when I'd left Charles' bedside was quickly disappearing. I could feel Palmer staring at me, waiting for a more complete answer to his question. I was really beginning to get pissed off with the idea that I was the guy everyone was looking to for answers.

"I need to speak with members of the church and Eve first; then I'll let you know what the plan is." I probably said that a little more harshly than I had intended. Hell, if it were *my* daughter who'd been kidnapped, I'd be carpet-bombing everything in my path to save her.

"Tell me, Bryson, how are you going to speak with a comatose woman?" asked Palmer. It was a fair question, deserving a truthful answer. But I wasn't sure how he'd take it.

With an involuntary shudder at the thought of my first encounter with Eve, I gave him the story straight. I told Palmer about Plum Island, Eve's sacrifice and her life straddling two planes of existence. I told him about my visit with Eve earlier in the week, and how I could, in fact, communicate with a comatose woman, but it had to be on her terms. I'll say this for the man, he took the whole 'Hell is a confirmed place and magic is real' thing pretty well, all things considered.

As we pulled up in front of the church, I tried to prepare myself as best I could for the encounter with Eve. Gambling on getting information from a psychotic demon who used to be my friend didn't seem to be the most prudent course of action, but it was all I had left. My first, unintentional, visit had been a shock; but this time—I reasoned with myself—I'd know what to expect.

"What's the plan?" asked Eden, coming up next to me as I got out of the car.

"You know, I'm getting tired of hearing that question," I sighed. "I don't know," I said for the second time in as many minutes. "But what I *do* know is that I need to get more information from your sister. She knows a lot more of what's happening and maybe—just maybe this time when we chat I'll be able to get enough information to formulate this plan you all seem to want from me. Any pointers before I sit with Eve for a cup of tea?" I asked, with a sideways glance at the non-possessed twin.

"You'll have to move quickly, Symon," she whispered back as we walked up to the entrance. "Learn from your last experience. Remember that whatever you see is an illusion." Then she added, "And try not to throw up this time when you come back to us."

"Thanks," I replied sarcastically. "I'll do my best."

"Symon," said Janice, coming up alongside Eden and me. "Hold on mentally to something from our world. Something important to you. It will help make the transition back to us easier."

"Something important..." I trailed off as we opened the door to the St. Ignatius sanctuary. I'd like to say that the image that popped into my head was a noble one—like one from the movies. You know, like when Superman returned the American flag to the White House at the end of *Superman II*. Or like Charlton Heston when he held up the Ten Commandments. But I'm not that guy. The only thing I could think of right then and there to ground me to our world was the first time Janice and I made love. It was a vivid and powerful memory, so that's what I went with.

"Got it," I said as we all made our way through the recently repaired doors. "Ready."

"Ready for what, Mr. Bryson?"

I was so focused on getting to Eve that I'd practically run into Father Moore, who was standing right inside the vestibule. His arms were crossed, and he had the same evil grin on his face that the Grinch had when he came up with the idea to steal all the Christmas presents from the residents of Whoville. But his eyes said something different. He glared at me as if he'd caught me spiking the holy water in the font. Aaron and I had only done that once. Honest.

Standing behind Father Moore was a contingent of clergymen. The call Father Moore received hadn't been about Charles in the hospital as I'd assumed. He'd obviously been summoned to the airport to fix whatever customs issue had been arranged to stall Cardinal Maguire.

Peter and Bill had bemused looks on their faces. Cardinal Maguire's face was beet-red and he looked fit to be tied. Just like old times. Overnight bags surrounded them.

"Ready for what, Bryson?" Cardinal Maguire asked, repeating his legal lackey's question.

"How was the Vatican, Eminence? Get me anything from the gift shop?" my brain heard my mouth say.

Cardinal Maguire went from beet-red to a shade of purple that wasn't really a natural color for normal folk. I thought he might just kill me on the spot. I needed to learn to use filters when I open my mouth.

"Bryson," he said, "we have rules in this world. You have broken many of them and by all that is Holy I really should have you locked up and the cell bricked over permanently."

"Are we really going to do this dance again, Cardinal Maguire? It's getting boring. You scream at me, I'm snarky to you and nothing gets done. Let's try something different this time, shall we? Besides, enacting a scene from *The Cask of Amontillado* won't help the situation."

"Bryson..." began the fuming Cardinal.

Eden stepped in front of me. "Eminence. Welcome back. As Symon has said, there is a situation we need to make you aware of. Perhaps we could turn the tension here down from a seven to a three for a moment. It's time we filled you in completely."

She is such the kiss-ass politician.

"Eminence," said Palmer calmly, "may I also remind you, respectfully, that Mr. Bryson is still in the Bureau's custody? And as such I cannot allow him to be incarcerated, or thrown behind a brick wall, by anyone other than the Federal Government?"

Oh good. Now they're all fighting for the right to wall me up. Just call me Fortunato.

As Eden, the Cardinal, and Palmer continued to bicker over my fate, a kind of fog seemed to surround me, drowning out all sound. I found myself slowly drawn toward the front of the church, to where a woman in a white nursing outfit stood by a frail figure in a wheelchair near the altar. Even from this distance, I could tell Eve's condition had gotten worse. She looked ... withered.

"Symon," whispered a feminine voice. "Hurry. Come to me."

Dazed, I tried and failed to subtly push past the arguing trio. If I could just get to Eve...

A big, meaty paw clamped onto my shoulder, stopping me dead in my tracks. The argument occurring all around me snapped back into the forefront as if someone had suddenly turned up the volume.

Cardinal Maguire placed just enough pressure on my collarbone to indicate how easily he could snap it in two. The pain is what brought me back from my trance. God, he was strong for an old man.

"You're not going anywhere until we sort this out, Bryson," he snarled. "Oh, how I yearn for the days of the old punishments," the Cardinal said as he squeezed my shoulder a bit harder.

"I'm not going anywhere, Eminence," I replied through clenched teeth, never taking my eyes off Eve twenty-five yards down the aisle from me, "but Eden is right. Let's convene in the Monsignor's office and talk this through. There is information we need to share."

The Cardinal released a little of the pressure on my shoulder. He looked at the Assistant Director of the FBI and Eden both, the latter of whom stood with arms folded, waiting expectantly. The large Holy man took a deep breath.

"Agreed," he said. It sounded like he struggled to get the word out.

"Your Eminence!" protested Father Moore. "This man," he wagged a finger at me, "has violated some of the most sacred rules we have in our Order! I insist—"

"And I insist," interrupted the Cardinal, "that we listen to the whole of Mr. Bryson's tale per Ms. Engel's suggestion. Once we have some answers, then, and only then will I decide the next course of action. Do I make myself clear, Father Moore?"

I was used to screaming from the Cardinal. He hadn't yelled. His reprimand of the Holy Solicitor was said in a low, but calm voice. That scared me more than his shouting ever did.

He practically frog-marched me down the aisle with everyone in tow. We were going to go right past Eve and her nurse. I did my best to angle us closer to the wheelchair.

"Answers?" I said to the Cardinal. "I couldn't agree more, Eminence." Eve was only ten yards away now.

"Symon, don't do it," hissed Eden warningly. "It's a really bad idea."

She was always the bright one. I, not being so bright, chose to ignore her. Five yards now.

"For example," I continued, "how could Charles create a Shadow-world spy without the go-ahead from his superior?"

The Cardinal stopped me right next to Eve.

"What did you say?" boomed Maguire. That was the screaming I was used to.

"You heard me, Eminence. You want some answers and so do I. So let's go get 'em."

"No—!" screamed Father Moore.

With the Cardinal still grasping onto my shoulder, I reached out and touched Eve.

Chapter Thirty

We were standing in the hall of a hospital ward, but not just any hospital. It was a ward from the Plum Island facility I'd been in ten years ago. It was exactly as I'd remembered. But not quite everything was unchanged.

Standing next to me was his Eminence, but he looked younger. A lot younger. His hair was no longer white, but jet black and slicked back in a way I'm sure was fashionable back in the day. He was handsome and seemed to radiate youth and vitality. Instead of wearing the ostentatious garb of his high office, he wore plain monk's robes cinched in the middle with a length of rope. In his hand he held a long, black, lacquered staff.

As disconcerting as this was, the most disturbing thing of all was the large and very warm smile he wore on his face.

"Impressive, Symon," he said in a jocular tone. "Most people would either have died or gone insane if they traveled through someone else's consciousness into the Shadow-world. Perhaps I underestimated you, as Charles has told me time and time again."

"Um, Cardinal…"

"Brother," he corrected. "Or Gene. Whichever you are more comfortable with."

"Gene," I said, recovering a bit from my initial shock, "what's going on?"

"Well, you brought me here, Symon. You tell me," Cardinal, I mean Brother, Maguire said, folding his arms and giving me the same expectant look Charles used to give me. Now I knew where he'd gotten it.

"Well, I came here to get some answers. It's my belief that Eve might be able to put the pieces of this mystery together."

"Uh-huh," nodded Maguire. "And?"

"And, well, Eve called to me while we were in the Church. She told me to hurry."

"So you listened to a woman whose soul has resided in Hell for the last decade and dragged a senior Church official with you," said the young Maguire. "Nicely played. What's next? Are you planning on bringing the Pope to have tea with Satan?"

At the mention of 'Satan,' the hallway in which we were standing rumbled and shook a little. Dust floated down from the drop-ceiling above us.

"Oh hush," said the monk. The rumbling stopped. "Now, Symon, you were saying?" continued the young man as if nothing had just happened.

"Yeah," I said, looking around and trying to pretend I wasn't scared shitless. "I had a feeling. My gut told me Eve has answers that I need."

"Your gut?" asked Maguire. "Look around you, Symon. What does your gut tell you now?"

I looked around the hospital hallway, knowing it was an illusion. Last time I'd been with Eve, we'd been in a burned and ruined version of St. Ignatius. I realized that the imagery had been created for my benefit by Eve. She'd created an environment to frighten and intimidate me. When the setting hadn't affected me, she'd transformed herself into a monster. That's what made me want to go back.

She hadn't wanted me there. Not then. But now...

I looked at Father Gene. "My gut is telling me the same thing: Eve has answers. The illusion is different this time. No fire and brimstone. Just this hallway from our past." A light bulb went off. "It's a clue, isn't it?"

"Very good, Symon," squeaked a high-pitched voice behind me. "I told you he was ready, Gene."

I swung around and saw a little blonde girl of about ten. She looked exactly as I remembered her when we'd first met, down to the pink 'My Little Pony' tee shirt.

"Hello, Eve," I said. "We have to talk."

****

"Hmmm," mused little-girl Eve. "I think it's more likely that you have to listen, Sy."

"Why is that?" I asked.

"Because time is short and you have a lot to do," she said simply.

I looked over toward Brother Gene. He just stood there with his staff cradled against his shoulder looking at me as if to say, "This is your dream. I'm only along for the ride." So be it.

"Okay, Eve, I'll bite. What do I have to do?"

Eve looked over her shoulder, then back at me.

"Save Winnie, of course," she said.

"No shit, Sherlock," I snapped, irritably. "But *how*?"

A gleam of fire appeared in her eyes, and I immediately regretted swearing at the little girl. Mostly because I was afraid that her demon-self would reappear and eat me.

"You *should* be afraid, Sy," she said. Damn it. I forgot she could read my thoughts. I needed to keep it together and focus, or my visit was going to end up a bust.

"Bust," Eve giggled. "Boobies." She giggled some more.

"Eve, stay with us," Brother Maguire said in a soothing tone. "I know it's difficult. But try. Can you do that for me, little one?"

The fire in Eve's eyes winked out as she looked up at the monk. A tear rolled down one cheek.

"I'm trying, Gene. It's so hard ... and I'm so tired."

"Only for a little longer, young one. It's finally coming to an end."

"Promise?" Eve asked, looking up at Brother Maguire with a wide-eyed, child-like innocence.

Brother Maguire got to one knee and looked her straight in the eye. "Promise."

"What about the others?"

"For them too, assuming Symon is up to playing his part."

"What the hell does that mean?" I asked the monk.

"It means you'd better be as powerful as Charles said you are," said Maguire, rising from in front of Eve and patting the young girl's head fondly.

"You know where you are," said Eve, turning to me with a hard stare. It was a statement, not a question.

"Yes. If I remember correctly, this is the hospital level of the old Plum Island building where we found Winnie."

"Correct!" Eve applauded enthusiastically. "But saving Winnie is not the only thing you need to finish, Symon. There is an open portal to the Shadow-world here as well."

"I know. Your sister's developed some sort of technology to block the ... wait. You said 'here as well.' Winnie is on Plum Island then?"

"Yes," Eve said, nodding. "They need her."

"Who's they?"

Eve looked over her shoulder again. "The demons, Sy. Belial and Sabnock."

I knew it. Coincidences are a bunch of crap.

"Why do they need Winnie?" I asked.

"Because I'm dying. They need a life force caught between our two worlds as a power source to keep the portal open."

"Oh God. That means they've used you ... your *soul* to power the portal?"

"For ten years, Sy," she whispered sadly. "Yes. And with my life-energy about gone, they need a new human battery to power the doorway. This time they want a non-practitioner battery."

"Why does that matter?" I asked, horrified.

"Symon," said Monk Maguire, placing a hand on my shoulder. It was a much more gentle touch than when he'd grabbed me back in St. Ignatius. "Eve has been blocking the passageway with her magic. The spells that allowed her to travel between our Earth and the Shadow-world bound her energy to the gate. Her magic has kept the way blocked."

"I thought the devices Eden's company created for the CIA—the beacons kept the portal contained."

"No," said Eve, suddenly sounding more like her sister. "It was me at first. But as I got weaker, creatures and demons from Hell started to get past me and out into our reality. Eden created the beacons to help me block the doorway and minimize damage. She knew the rate at which I was dying and the frequency of the demonic incursions were related. My sister's pretty smart that way."

"But now," explained Maguire, "Eve is too weak to keep the damned in Hell. That's how they've been able to get out. First, due to Charles' feelings of guilt that empowered that foul creature Belial to travel past the beacons..."

"...and second they know I'm dying. My weakness allows them to escape, yet they also know their portal will collapse, when I die. They need someone they know has survived the transition between planes of existence intact to replace me," continued Eve.

"Someone who isn't a practitioner and won't be able to put up a fight," I concluded.

"Exactly," agreed Maguire.

"So we have to go to Plum Island, pull Eve out of the socket and get Winnie before the demons plug her in as their new D-cell," I said. "Okay, how?"

Eve smiled sadly. "It's not like that, Symon. I'm too far gone at this point."

"What do you mean?" I asked, already knowing the answer but refusing to accept it.

"You have to get Winnie, yes," Eve said, "but you are also going to have to kill me at the same time."

****

The scene around us shimmered and suddenly I found myself standing in a large pile of rubble outside, cold sea air whipping around me. I shivered, not entirely due to the weather.

"Where are we now, Symon?" Maguire was standing next to me looking around.

There was a dim light illuminating our surroundings from an unknown source. The pale light was bright enough to see the pit and piles of rubble that lay strewn about our surroundings.

"I'd say we are standing in what was left of the Plum Island facility after I blew it up," I answered. Eve was nowhere in sight.

I was drawn toward the center of the crater and made my way there almost without realizing it. Brother Maguire hesitated a moment, then followed me. Out of the corner of my eye I could see that he was now brandishing his black staff in front of him like a weapon.

I almost made it to the middle of what I assumed was ground zero for the explosion I'd caused, when I was hit by a sudden sense of *wrongness*.

I knew right then and there that I was standing near the portal. Not because there were any visible signs, mind you. Just a strong feeling. So strong, in fact, that I could sense where the tear in the fabric of our world began and ended.

Eve, now appearing as an adult, walked out of the middle of all that wrongness. She was wearing a white, very flimsy, very sheer and very see-through teddy.

"Here is where you have to come, Symon," she said. She walked toward me slowly, sensually. I actually gulped.

The young Maguire hadn't lowered his staff.

"Wh—" My mouth was dry. I cleared my throat and tried again. "Why here?"

"This is where you will find Winnie," she answered, running a seductive finger along my cheek. "This is where you must kill me. To do so means you will have to bring what's left of my body to this place. Only then will I be finally whole. Then can you strike me down and remove Winnie from here. The portal will close when I take my last breath."

There was a whispering sound that came from the portal. It was definitely a voice, although the language was either unknown to me or too low for me to make out. Eve turned her head toward the portal then looked back at me.

"Time grows short, Symon," she said.

"The Portal!" I shouted. The wind had begun to pick up and I could barely hear the sound of my own voice. "Why is it here?"

Eve smiled at me and licked her lips. "Because this is where you created it practitioner-mine," she practically purred. "All that anger. All that power. Released at once. Just to blow up a building."

I fell to my knees as the wind howled even louder. "No," I said. I didn't do this. It couldn't have been me. "You were the one! You were given the spying mission by Charles. You were able to traverse worlds. Not me! It couldn't have been..."

Eve walked behind me and stroked my hair with her hand. She leaned down to me and whispered, "Do you like my outfit, Symon?"

I pulled away from her, horrified.

"What the hell! You tell me I'm responsible for your virtual imprisonment and then come on to me? What is wrong with you?!"

She had a different look on her face now. She almost looked desperate. "Symon. Look at my outfit!" Eve hissed.

"No, you sick bitch! I won't..." My head snapped around by some unseen force and I found myself compelled to stare at Eve. I tried to close my eyes to no avail. I looked.

Eve's body was beautiful. The shape of her breasts was perfect and her light brown skin...

But Eve didn't have light brown skin. She and her sister were Danish and as white as they came. The only person with a shape and coloring like that was Janice...

****

"No—!" screamed Father Moore.

I stumbled away from Eve's wheelchair and practically fell into Janice's arms. Peter and Bill were trying to assist Cardinal Maguire, who motioned them back vehemently.

I stood shakily with Janice's help; then gently pushed her away. I faced the Cardinal.

"Do you have your answers now, Gene?" I asked.

The man's face was unreadable. He walked over to me and clasped my arm. "It wasn't your fault, Symon. You didn't know."

But it was my fault and I should have known. In my anger, I'd used magic to rip a hole in our reality. For the last decade Eve and the Church have been trying to contain the damage. It was all too much.

That's when I turned away from the Cardinal and threw up all over Father Moore. At least this time I had better aim.

Chapter Thirty-One

"You're an idiot," said Janice as she barely caught me when I staggered.

"Yeah," I coughed. "Not really one of my better ideas," I said, wiping bile from my face.

"Did you learn anything?" she asked.

I don't think I'd ever heard the Sanctuary become so quiet so quickly before. And all eyes were on me.

"I think so. I need a minute to sort through it," I lied. I was shaking and needed to regain some control. "Eve is not a straight-answer sort of girl."

"Do you know where my girl is, Bryson?" asked Palmer.

"Yeah," I said. "I think so."

"I wouldn't trust her, Bryson," commented Father Moore in a shaky voice, wiping sick off of himself with a handkerchief Peter had given him.

"I think Mr. Bryson can be trusted to make that determination," said Cardinal Maguire.

The incredulous look Father Moore gave His Eminence was priceless.

To Janice, I whispered, "Can we go someplace a bit more private? I need to sort through the images in my head and I could use some help. And some coffee."

"Yeah ... let's go to the kitchen," she said.

"Palmer," I said, trying to raise my voice but only managing a louder croak, "come with us please. You too, Eden."

"The rest of you in the Monsignor's office with me," barked the Cardinal. "Now."

I gave Maguire a grateful nod and I swear he almost smiled back.

The FBI Assistant Director instructed his men to follow the Cardinal and we split into two groups.

"All right, Bryson, what was that all about?" Palmer said a few minutes later as the four of us sat at the old butcher-block table sipping fresh coffee.

I skipped over some of the more personal bits of my time with Eve and gave Palmer and the women the CliffsNotes version of events.

"So the bottom line is I think Winnie is back on Plum Island," I concluded.

"You're sure?" asked Palmer skeptically.

"Pretty sure," I said feeling the effects of the coffee. Nectar of the gods and all that.

"There is no way we'll be able to get her!" Palmer protested, panic in his voice.

"To be honest, Palmer," said Eden, "Winnie may not even be wholly with us anymore. She was lucky. Winnie'd just been taken when we'd found her ten years ago. The rest of the children on that island were already gone."

"What do you mean 'gone?'" asked Palmer sharply.

Eden was silent. How do you tell a father that his daughter's soul might already be in Hell?

"Should I take your lack of an answer to mean you think my daughter is already dead?" Palmer said, standing.

"No, Assistant Director," Janice said, providing us all with a refill. "Let's be clear. We don't know much at this point. Everything else is speculation. I think what Symon *tried* to say was that Plum Island was the best place to find Winnie..."

"Please call her Elizabeth," Palmer said miserably as he slumped back into his chair.

Janice continued, ignoring the interruption, "...find your daughter. She's near enough to adult age and her soul is that much stronger. We still might be able to get her out."

"There is another problem," I said, sipping coffee from my mug. "The rip between the worlds is on Plum Island as well. If what I saw in my shared vision with Eve is right, it's really large. Eve's very weak now. It wouldn't take a lot of energy to cross from the Shadow-world into our own. There might be thousands of Hell's minions running all over that place by now."

"That explains why the entire place was quarantined. No official explanation was ever given. To this day, nothing is allowed in or out of there," said Palmer. There are even electrical field jamming beacons placed all around the island. We couldn't get a boat or helicopter within a mile of the place."

"The beacons would interfere with magic as well," said Eden quietly.

"How do you know that?" I asked. Eve had already told me, but I wasn't ready to let anyone know that yet.

"My company built them," she said.

"Wow, you're like an arms dealer playing both sides of the war," I pointed out, thoughtfully taking another drink.

"Then how did the demons get off the island in the first place?" asked Aaron. "I mean if these disrupting beacons interfere with magic and all."

"The creatures from the other side must operate on a different frequency," said Eden.

"Hmm. Why don't I believe that?" I asked.

Eden shot me a look. "I don't care if you do or not, Symon. We were asked to develop the technology and test it. When it worked, Eve seemed to get better for a while. So we installed them. That's the truth."

"So you developed these things. How do we shut them down to get on the island?"

"You can't. They are controlled by the people we sold them to. We no longer have access to the devices."

"Bullshit," I said. "You tech weenies always build in a back door or something."

"Not for these guys," said Eden.

"Which guys?"

"Does it matter?" Eden asked.

"Yes," Palmer, Janice, and I said at the same time.

"The Department of Homeland Security," she answered.

****

Eden excused herself to go make a call to her engineering guys to see if there was a way to break into the electrical jamming beacons. At one look from me, Janice nodded slightly and went with her.

Palmer began to ask detailed questions surrounding my vision. The details had faded, but I answered him the best I could. It was pretty frustrating for both of us.

Ten minutes later, Agent Sanchez came into the kitchen.

"Father Moore is gone," he announced.

"Gone?" I asked.

"Yeah," he nodded. "The priest got a call on his cell and he left in a hurry. Thought you should know."

Palmer stood up. "Without more details, Bryson, I have almost no hope of putting together a task force with Ms. Engel to go and get my daughter back, but I'm sure as hell going to try. That's assuming Ms. Engel is willing to help me and can disable her devices. I'll call you in a couple of hours." He began to walk out of the kitchen, then stopped.

"Bryson, I don't know who blew up your apartment in Dublin, but if I were a betting man, I'd place serious money on the clients Ms. Engel sold those jamming beacons to. If that's the case, they know about you, your friends, and probably about all this magic shit. I would be very careful starting now. I don't want you dead before we rescue my little girl." And he left, taking Sanchez with him.

I sat in silence for a moment feeling overwhelmed, when a pair of hands gently fell on my shoulders.

"Close your eyes, Symon," said Janice softly as she began to massage my neck and back. Knots upon knots in my muscles began to soften, and I felt relaxed immediately. Even my headache went away. Janice was a rock star.

"That feels pretty good," I said.

"Shut up and focus on healing, Symon. You are going to need all your strength for what's next," she whispered into my ear.

"Would you both stop that," snapped Aaron, sounding jealous as he, joined by Eden, came back into the room.

"Where's Palmer?" asked Eden.

"Dunno. Said he'd call in a couple of hours," I replied. "Father Moore is gone too. Got a call and high-tailed it out of the church."

"Damn," swore Eden.

"What's wrong?" asked Janice, her magic fingers leaving my shoulder.

"I wanted to speak with Palmer. If we're going to be mounting an assault on Plum Island we will need some heavy government cover," she said.

"I thought your boys could handle everything?" I asked, bemused.

"It's still a government-run facility with a quarantine in place, Symon," Eden explained. "I'll need Federal backup."

"That can wait," said Aaron. "The Cardinal wants to speak with us."

****

When we entered Charles' study, Bill, Peter, and the Cardinal abruptly stopped the quiet conversation they were having. I actually withheld the urge to use a line from that old movie *Animal House*: "Can we dance with your dates?" I know. I was pretty proud of myself too.

The Cardinal stood, smiling. "Come in, Symon. Young William here was just telling us about what he learned during our recent visit to the Vatican. Go ahead, son."

His Eminence was being downright cordial. Although slightly suspicious, I warmed to the change in attitude. I guess if two people share a demonic illusion in Hell, it brings you closer.

I sat and my friends joined me. The FBI agents, Sanchez and Vitale, who'd been with Palmer, must have left with the Assistant Director.

"Right," said Bill, also taken aback by the change in the Cardinal. "As I was telling Father Fine and his Eminence, I wasn't allowed into the Curia offices, the Vatican archive or near the papal chambers, so I sat in a café outside, in Vatican City itself."

"The archives are amazing," said Peter excitedly. "It was only the second time I was allowed..." he stopped, talking at a look from the Cardinal. "Sorry, Father Duncan. Please continue."

"I overheard a few fellow priests chatting," continued Bill. "My German isn't great, but I got the gist of what they were talking about."

"Get on with it, Bill," said Aaron.

"Sorry. Anyway, I got myself invited to their table and they both ended up speaking English. They work for the Pontifical Commission of Sacred Archeology. The two of them had just gotten back from a secret mission in Iraq where they'd found something."

"The Ark of the Covenant?" I asked, with visions of Harrison Ford's whip and fedora in my head.

"Bryson," rumbled the Cardinal. That was more like him.

"No, although that would have been pretty cool, too, since it's supposed to be in Ethiopia," Bill mused. "What they actually found was an ancient, I mean six-thousand-year-old ancient, tablet. From what they told me they deciphered, it was an incantation of sorts. They both laughed at the notion, of course."

"What kind of incantation?" asked Eden, her ancient language interest piqued.

"After chatting for a while, I was able to determine that it was some sort of banishment spell. The kind that would lock demons away in some sort of permanent prison."

"That's not possible," I said. "The best we could do was to send the physical manifestation of a Shadow-world minion back to Hell to lick its wounds for a while."

"Not anymore!" Peter was all smiles.

****

The two priests and Eden went off to translate the ancient incantation to something more useful for us. I only hoped they were right about the permanent banishment part. Something like that could come in pretty damn handy when we finally made it back to Plum Island.

The thought of returning there terrified me, even more so since my second encounter with Eve. It was one of the many reasons I'd hidden in Ireland for so long. But somewhere in the back of my mind, I think I always knew I'd have to return to that Godforsaken island someday. I just thought it would be at some nebulous point called 'later.'

Aaron, Janice, the Cardinal, and I went through our time with Eve in greater detail than I had with Eden and Palmer. I ignored the annoyed looks Janice tossed my way every time I revealed something I hadn't previously. Cardinal Maguire added details in places where my memory faltered.

"So let me get this straight," said Aaron, using that cop voice of his I hated. "You want us to go back to a cursed island, take on a minimum of two demons and probably their minions, rescue a girl before she takes the place of a friend of ours who we have to kill so this portal between Earth and Hell, which you created, can be permanently closed?" He shook his head. "Did I get that right?"

"Yep," I replied. "One point for the Cambridge PD."

"Holy mother of God, Symon," Aaron exclaimed. "And how do you expect us to do all that and survive?"

"Well," I said. "I've given it some thought and here's what we're gonna do..."

****

"You remind me a bit of Charles back in the day, Bryson," said the Cardinal thoughtfully after hearing my plan. "I haven't yet decided if that's a good or bad thing."

Aaron and Janice had left to go brief the rest of the group on our plans. I'd specifically told them not to tell Eden about the part with her sister. I'd figure out a way to do that later.

"I think the tasks at hand will clarify that for you, sir," I said.

"Quite possibly, boy," his Eminence rumbled. "Assuming we survive, of course. Your plan is very risky, but I see it as our only option. I approve, except for one point."

"And that is?"

"Getting onto the island," said the Cardinal. "You seem to be putting a lot of faith in Ms. Engel's engineers' ability to crack into those beacons."

"Actually, Eminence," I said, "I was going to talk to Palmer about that. See, I remembered one of the Monsignor's many history lessons—one he told us before we all visited Plum Island the first time. I was going to ask Palmer for a favor, but it's just occurred to me that the Holy See might have more in the way of... influence."

"Influence over what, Bryson?" asked the Cardinal.

"Well, sir," I began. "I was wondering if there were any high-ranking Catholics you might have sway over? Specifically, high-ranking members of the Coast Guard..."

Chapter Thirty-Two

I found my way back to the kitchen to do what I always did when I felt a little useless: eat some of Peter's leftovers. I found some cold chicken and sandwiches, some of which I polished off as I brought them around to check up on everyone. I'm not totally selfish.

Eden and the two priests continued to work a translation to our traditional spell casting language of Latin (after all, no one knew how to *speak* Sumerian anymore, as Eden had explained to me) of the incantation Bill had discovered in Rome. Somehow, Eden had already gotten photographs of the actual tablets the Germans had discovered. I didn't ask and she didn't tell.

She'd also instructed the engineers at her company to try and crack into the beacons surrounding Plum Island. Eden was more hopeful that she, Peter, and Bill could have a workable spell in time for our sojourn back to Plum Island than in the ability of her engineers to crack a highly complex security key. She used phrases like 'symmetric-key algorithms' and 'block ciphers.' After about two minutes, my eyes glazed over and she gave up on trying to explain it to me. She grabbed a few of the sandwiches I'd brought and went back to work on the permanent banishing spell. I noticed that Eve was in her chair near where the three spell casters were working. I walked over to her and knelt down beside her, taking care not to touch her.

"Eve," I spoke softly, "we're coming. Hang in there a little longer." It might have been my imagination, but I thought I saw her mouth twitch a little in an attempt at a smile.

Aaron had gone off to Boston to meet up with Flint and the other heavies in Eden's security team. He'd protested my crazy plan more than the rest; however, I had no doubt he'd play his part, maybe even coming back with a tank or something.

I found Janice by herself in the Sanctuary. Her eyes were closed and she was either meditating or in silent prayer. I turned to leave her be when she called out to me.

"Symon, I wanted to talk to you."

I walked over to her and offered up a chicken leg.

She accepted with a look of gratitude and said, "You know Peter'd be annoyed to catch us eating in here."

"Hey, I finished eating back in the kitchen. From my perspective, you'd be in trouble, not me," I protested.

I slid into the pew next to her and we sat in silence for a moment.

"Symon, this plan of yours is risky. I'm frightened for you."

"Frightened for me?" I asked.

"For all of us," she hastened to add.

I smiled a little. "I'm frightened for me—for all of us, too."

She punched my shoulder lightly. "Don't make fun. I'm serious!"

"I know, and I'm open to a better plan if you have one. But time is short and I don't know how long Winnie or Eve can hold out."

"I know, I know. It's just..."

"Spill it," I said.

"Most of us have kept our skills current, Symon. When was the last time you used magic?" she asked tentatively.

"Just the other night when we located the Monsignor," I said.

"Symon, that was mostly Bill and Aaron. *When?*"

I thought about that. I'd sworn off magic a decade ago. I never used any of my talent in Ireland. But I had to have used something in this last crazy week...

Janice saw the look on my face. "Exactly," she said.

"I've gotten done what needed to be done without it," I said.

"Symon, you left us completely disillusioned," Janice sighed. "What did Charles tell us the basic foundation for all magic was?"

"Faith," I replied automatically. "Belief in oneself and a higher power. From that, anything is possible."

"Right. What do you believe, Symon?" Janice asked.

"I'm not sure," I answered finally. "I haven't thought about it much, to be honest. I've just been reacting since I landed."

"I'm not sure if you know this or not, but Charles' program here at St. Ignatius was an experiment," she said looking away from me.

"What do you mean—experiment?"

"For two thousand years, the Pontification Order of the Magi taught only Catholics. Hardcore, papal-adoring Catholics who had the gift. They ignored anyone outside the faith." She paused for a moment. "And I heard stories that anyone with talent who refused the Church's teachings ... disappeared."

"Why are you telling me this now?" I asked. "Is the Cardinal going to make me disappear?" I tried to joke, but she turned again to look at me all serious-like.

"No. I'm not explaining what I want to say," Janice shook her head. "Look, Peter and Bill's magic is based on the traditional Church doctrine. Eve's magic was emotion-based and her sister's is the polar opposite—fact or scientifically based. My magic comes from deep traditions of my Shaman ancestors and the natural elements."

"What's your point?"

"You have always been our leader, even when you didn't want to be. According to Charles, it's the role you were born for. What we are about to do will stretch all of our talents as practitioners to the limit."

"Okay. I'll say it again. What's your bloody point, Janice?" I was beginning to get angry.

She looked away from me again. "My point is this, Sy. Your plan involves some serious and complex stuff. You haven't used magic in a decade. I—*we*—want to know if you still can."

****

Janice led me by the hand to the old school gym. As we walked in silence, I finally realized the last time I really had used magic was when I destroyed the Plum Island facility and created the portal that had been Eve's virtual prison. Neither one of those were highlights for a resume.

The gym was empty, dark, and musty. Just like it had been a few nights (a few lifetimes?) ago when we'd used the large silver circle and me as just the catalyst.

We walked to the center of the court, and I could immediately feel a buzz of power as we passed over the edge of the silver circle.

"Sit," Janice commanded.

I looked at her and barked like a dog.

"Sit and center yourself, funny man. This is important."

I did as I was told. My knees creaked a little when I sat, Indian-style in the middle of the circle. Crap, I was getting old.

Janice stood over me and placed her hands on my head. "Close your eyes, Symon. Feel the energy swirl around you. Let your body reconnect with the Earth. I'll be back in a moment."

I closed my eyes and felt the gentle brush of her fingers through my hair as she left. This was one of the first exercises Charles taught us. Center and focus.

I felt the connection to the Earth, and the energy that flowed through my body, but it seemed muted somehow. Different from when we'd used the tracking spell, and very different from when I'd called this church my home.

Janice came back a few minutes later carrying an old, dusty box. She opened it and pulled out a dozen or so large candles, which she laid in a circular pattern around me about twice the diameter of the silver circle. This, too, was an old exercise.

"Do you remember this one, Symon?" Janice asked quietly.

"Yes," I replied. "Light the candles, levitate the candles. The more that can be lit and lifted at one time, the better your focus and magical connection."

"Good. Let's see what you've got," she said.

I closed my eyes again. Using the connection with the Earth, I reached out to the candles.

"You're trying too hard, trying to force it. Let the energy flow through you. Then you can control it," Janice whispered.

"Can I get the X-wing out of the swamp instead?" I asked.

"Focus, Symon," Janice chided.

I tried again. The connection was there. The energy was there. I could *feel* it. But I couldn't bring them together. Sweat beaded on my forehead. I exhaled loudly from effort and frustration.

"I can't do it. Damn it. Something is wrong." I swore again.

Janice came into the circle and sat in front of me.

"Give me your hands, Symon."

I placed mine in hers. Her touch was warm and the energy of the Earth flowed through both of us. I took a slow, deep breath, held it for a moment, then released it.

"Okay," I said. "Let's try this again."

I focused my will, not on the candles, but on the energy around us. After about a minute, I let go of Janice and stood up, frustrated as hell.

"This is a total waste of time!" I exploded. "We need to get to Plum Island. Now. Why aren't we moving?"

Janice stood a second later. "Everyone is doing what they need to. We are preparing. Calm down, Symon. We'll be into the fire soon enough."

"Calm down!" I spat. "Preparing. What, exactly, are *you* doing to prepare?"

Janice is not pleasant when her fuse has been lit. And my little tantrum apparently not only lit the fuse, but threw gasoline on the fire.

"I don't *need* to prepare, you whiney little bastard," she said, her voice echoing in fury. She barely moved one arm. A dozen of the candles immediately levitated about three feet off the ground and ignited, casting an eerie light around the old gym.

Janice glared at me for about a minute. Suddenly, she shuddered and closed her eyes. The candles slowly dropped to the ground and the flames dimmed until all that remained were tiny glowing embers on each wick. "You were the best of us, Symon. What happened to you?"

"I quit," I whispered.

"I know," said Janice. "But why? Was it really because Charles lied about Eve's mission, or was it something else?"

I was quiet for a moment. Yes, I blamed Charles. But looking at the situation ten years on, were my feelings and decision to leave really because of what the Monsignor did? Or was it something else entirely?

Maybe fear?

"You saw what happened before we evacuated the island," I said. Janice nodded.

"That was pure anger," I said. "You have no idea what that felt like."

"Explain it to me."

"I was furious. We'd lost the captain, Eve, and dozens of children that night."

"And?" Janice prompted.

"And I wanted to wipe the whole situation away. I let my anger flow through me and I destroyed an entire building. It was wrath-of-God type of stuff. And I felt like..."

"God?"

"No," I shook my head, "but I did feel, in that tiniest of moments, like the world was mine to do with as I pleased. And destroying that place pleased me."

"But you also created the portal at the same time," Janice said.

"I didn't know that!"

Janice looked up at me. A single tear slowly ran down one cheek.

"You know you were the one who was supposed to walk between the two worlds, Symon, don't you? It was never meant to be Eve."

"I ... what the fuck are you talking about?"

"You are stronger. Your center for magic is emotion-based, like Eve. You could have handled being Charles' spy."

"Then ... why wasn't it me?"

"The Monsignor wasn't sure it would work. He didn't want risk losing you to his desperate plan. You were his pride and joy. The student he thought of as a son."

The bitterness in her voice was unmistakable.

"You knew. You knew and never told me," I said through gritted teeth. Fury. Disbelief.

"Yes,"

"*Why?*" I shouted. My anger made the silver circle in the floor of the gym crackle with electricity.

"Because if I told you, you would've gone to Charles and demanded to be his spy," she said.

"Of course I would have! If I'd gone instead of Eve, maybe none of this would ever have happened! Maybe I—"

"Maybe you would have died," she said, tears now streaming from her face.

"But, *Eve—*"

"What's done is done, Sy," she said, wiping the tears from her face. "Now we need to fix what's broken and repair the damage that's been done. To do that, you need to be able to use magic again."

"I can't, Janice. I can't even light the fucking candles..."

"But you can, my old love. Look around you."

I looked. My mouth opened in shock.

Not only were the twenty or so candles Janice had set out burning brightly and dancing high overhead, but it looked like every other candle stored in the church had joined them. There were now hundreds, all burning brightly above us.

"Did I...?"

"Yes," Janice said, "it is all you. Remember how you feel right now, because tonight, you'll need it."

Chapter Thirty-Three

"You know," said a voice from the darkness, "the Hennessey's are going to be pretty upset when I tell them the custom-made candles for their wedding next week have been used."

The many dozens of candles floating above Janice and me suddenly dropped to the ground, their flames extinguishing at the same time.

Peter walked into the gym. "There were a few people lighting prayer candles in the Sanctuary as well. Scared the living heck out of them. Bill's smoothing things over with them now." But the old priest was smiling, so I figured I wasn't in too much trouble.

"I guess I overdid it a bit. Sorry," I said, shrugging my shoulders.

"No you're not and you shouldn't be!" Janice exclaimed.

"Come, both of you," said Peter. "I think we've unlocked the banishment incantation. We just need to test it."

We walked into the choir practice room where Eden and the clergymen had been working on the banishment spell. Only Eden was there, so I assumed Bill was still calming the parishioners who witnessed their candles floating away from them. I could only imagine how that conversation was going.

"I heard you did well, Symon," Eden said with her back to us.

"Thanks, Teach," I replied. "Do I have to write an essay too?"

She turned and looked at me in that annoyed way women usually look at me. After living on this earth for thirty years, I was used to it.

"Come take a look at what we found," Eden replied, ignoring my wit.

On a series of tables, Eden, Bill, and Peter had already compiled copious amount of notes to accompany the photographs of the ancient tablets. I glanced down at the notes, written in at least three languages and looked back at her.

"Small words and pictures, please," I pleaded.

That made her smile a bit.

"Okay. What we have here is actually an ancient Sumerian tablet written in code. Sumerian hasn't been translated by the scholars consistently to date," she said with a slight look of disdain. "But what we figure is that banishing a demon permanently is not so much about locking them back in Hell, but actually sending them into a third plane of existence."

"A third plane?" Janice asked. "We were only taught about two: our universe and the combination of Heaven and Hell—the Shadow-world."

"Yes," said Eden with that professorial tone I so hated, "but physicists have extrapolated that there could be as many as eleven dimensions surrounding us. Actually, the theory is over a hundred years old. American philosopher William James theorized about the multiverse..."

"Me stupid," I grunted in my best caveman-speak. "You speak tiny words."

"Right," said Eden. "We've developed a pretty complex spell that we think will get the job done."

That was better.

"You think?" I asked. "How do we confirm it? If our plan works, we are going to piss off some pretty bad monsters. I'd hate for them to show up in a decade or two looking for revenge."

"Oh, finding out if it's permanent will take some time, of course. But we'll deal with that part. Testing the banishing piece should be easy," Eden said. "We just have to summon up a minor demon and try to banish it. That'll be your job, Cro-Magnon man."

Swell.

****

My Latin has always been less than perfect. One might say 'piss-poor' in fact.

While Eden, Janice and Peter set up space to trap some minor evil entity (they still hadn't decided what creature to conjure up), Bill walked me through what he felt was the closest translation to the tongue of ancient Sumerian magi.

Now, Bill is one of the nicest and calmest people I know. I, on the other hand, could be construed as one of the more frustrating individuals known to mankind.

"Okay, Symon," he said, letting out a large sigh. "Let's try it again. It's not that tough. *Exsilium, Malum unus est vestri fortuna ut pacis populus mos vos reperio cruciatus eternus.*"

"Exilum..." I said.

"EXSILIUM!" Bill shouted.

"Oh yeah," I said. "Exsilium Malum unus est... uh... est... what was that middle thing?"

"How in all that is Holy did you pass Latin?" the poor exasperated priest sputtered.

"Sister Lorraine was sweet on me," I said.

Twenty minutes later, I had the incantation down pat. Bill muttered something about a stiff drink afterwards.

Eden and the gang had decided on summoning a little fiend by the name of Surgat.

"Symon," said Janice, "we've placed protective sigils around this room, so if the incantation doesn't work the creature will be trapped in here. All you will need to do is to smudge the chalk summoning circle we've drawn on the floor: the connection from Surgat to Hell will be broken. The earthly body of the creature should disintegrate shortly thereafter."

"Using the words 'if' and 'should' with something like this isn't inspiring much confidence, Janice," I said. "And why are you telling me all this? It's like you won't be here when we do the experiment."

"We won't. The spell needs to be focused and from a single source. That's you."

"Hey, Peter," I called over my shoulder. "Isn't there an issue from the Church's perspective, summoning up a demon? And shouldn't we do this someplace else, like the sandwich shop across the street?"

"Oh, we'll be fine, Symon," the older priest said. "This is all for God's work. Besides, the power of this place will help contain the creature should it happen to kill you and break through our sigils."

Oh, *come on*. I thought. Really, really loud.

"One more thing, Symon," said Eden, walking over to me with a piece of wood about the size of a drumstick. "This is a focused spell.

You'll need to say the incantation while pointing this at the creature's heart..."

"I swear to God," I said looking disgustedly at the little stick: "If you say 'magic wand,' my rule against hitting women goes out the window."

"Symon," Eden said, "your magic is broad and untamed. This ... wand ... will help you focus your energy and the spell."

"Bang, zoom Alice," I said in my best Jackie Gleeson voice. "Why do I have to be the one to test this?"

"Because when we get to Plum Island," replied Bill, "you are the one who will probably be able to get the closest to the demons. They still want you for some reason," he finished by shaking his head.

"So, we are all clear," said Eden, a little louder. "You all should take up positions outside this room to reinforce the protective sigils. I will summon Surgat, exit the space and magically seal the door behind me. Then it's up to you, Symon."

"Don't screw up," they all said at once.

Nice.

I was pretty sure that this was another test, so I nodded once and turned to face the chalk sigil. If this was really a test, I planned on passing it with flying colors so we could get on with our rescue mission. The clock was ticking and I hoped this would be the last big hurdle to jump over before we headed out. Winnie and Eve wouldn't last much longer.

"Ready," I said, and pointed the stupid magic wand at the center of the circle.

The rest of the team trooped out of the practice room, leaving Eden and me alone.

There was a little 'pop' sound and a tiny winged creature appeared in the middle of the chalk circle.

"It's all yours, Symon," Eden said. I heard the door close behind me and felt the energy of a magical lock being engaged.

The creature was staring wide-eyed at me. It wasn't more than two feet tall. It was covered in brown fur and had the face of a rodent. Its wide, yellow, snake-like eyes looked at me in surprise and blinked.

For a demon, the little guy was kind of cute.

It fluttered its wings and poked a long, bony finger at me. There was a brief blue glow and I heard what sounded like the clicking of a lock.

The damn thing stepped out of the circle.

"You dare summon me, mortal?" it said, in a high-pitched, birdlike voice. "What is it you want with Surgat, one who unlocks locks?"

Good job, Eden. You conjured up Hell's miniature locksmith.

I pointed the wand at the creature and began the incantation.

It flew at me so fast I didn't have time to raise a shield. Or even duck. All I saw was a blur of motion, then numerous claws in my face.

Dropping to one knee, I swatted at the creature. It flew off to my right and I heard it hit the wall of the practice room. There was a low sounding gong and another 'click' sound.

That's when I noticed that I was no longer holding my magic freakin' wand. The creature had broken the stick in half and the pieces were lying on the floor next to me.

Ignoring me now, the little winged nightmare crawled on the ceiling and the wall. It was systematically trying to unlock the sigils surrounding the room.

I darted over the chalk circle and smeared the edge, breaking the creature's connection to Hell. Or so I thought.

It tittered. Demons shouldn't titter.

"Oh, I'm here now, mortal. Can't get rid of me *that* easily. Why don't you sit there like a good ape and just bleed."

I wiped my hand across my brow and saw blood. The little fiend had done a number on my face. The little cuts began to sting as blood mixed with sweat.

I heard another click and a birdlike exclamation of glee.

"I don't think so you little ferret," I snarled, and stood up, pointing a finger at the thing. "*Vegrandis flamma.*"

A small, blue fireball flew from my fingers and hit the creature right in the small of its back. With a little squeal, it fell to the ground in a smoldering mess.

It flopped around on the floor, trying to put out the fire, when I shouted, "*Exsilium, Malum unus est vestri fortuna ut pacis populus mos vos reperio cruciatus eternus!*"

The creature let out a loud scream as it lifted off the ground and began to spin wildly in the air. Its body fell in on itself and it just disappeared, as if it had been sucked into a drain.

The room was instantly silent. Only the acrid smell of burning fur remained to indicate anything had been here with me at all.

"Y'all can come back in now," I called to the team. "The flying rat is gone."

****

"Can't you do anything without leaving a mess, Sy?" asked Peter, clicking his tongue in disapproval when he saw the state of the practice room. I watched my friends clean up, not even remotely interested in helping. When asked why, I just replied: "I cook, you clean. Them's the rules."

Janice attended to the little scratches on my face, and quietly explained that it was indeed a 'last test' and that Eden specifically picked the little rat-faced demon for its uncanny ability to blow through magical snares. What a bitch.

As the cleanup was finishing, Cardinal Maguire came into the room. He took one look around the place and said, "This looks like Bryson's handiwork."

"Yes, but it worked," I replied, a little hurt.

"Well then, we are all set," his Eminence said. "I just received a call from the Commandant of the United States Coast Guard. He's not happy, but pressure from both the Vatican and the President persuaded him to make the loan."

"Excellent!" I said, standing. "It's about time. When can we leave?"

"Immediately," Maguire said. "We can be on Plum Island by midnight. We'll just need to ask Ms. Engel's security team to meet us there with Mr. North. I believe he's secured what you requested, Symon."

"My people are still working on shutting down the beacons, Eminence," said Eden. "There is no way to get on the island."

"No way a *powered* vehicle can get us there," I corrected her. "The Cardinal and some good Catholics in the Coast Guard have provided us with alternate transportation."

"And what's that?" Eden asked.

"The only still-commissioned sailing vessel in the U.S. fleet: The USCG *Eagle*. See?" I said smugly to Eden. "Sometimes I actually listened to Charles' tall tales."

Chapter Thirty-Four

By now, the spring day had turned to a cool twilight. However, the chill that permeated the church had nothing to do with the weather.

"There is an Amtrak leaving Back Bay Station in about an hour," I said, as I rushed from the practice room. "If we blow through a few red lights, we can make it."

I stopped. No one was following me.

"Let's go, people!" I shouted, annoyed.

"Eden, would you go and get your sister and bring her here, please," said Cardinal Maguire calmly. "The rest of you, get your travel gear. Five minutes. Go."

Everyone left in a quick yet orderly manner, leaving me alone with the Cardinal. I looked at him rather nastily.

"Aaron and Ms. Engel's security team are on their way to St. Ignatius, as is Mr. Palmer and his two agents. We'll meet here and then head out."

"By the time we assemble at St. Ignatius, we'll have missed the train, Eminence," I said, trying to stay as calm as possible.

"Patience, Bryson. We'll move when we are ready," said the Cardinal, smugly. Then he cocked his head slightly to one side. "Help Aaron and the security team bring in their gear. Bring them to the gymnasium. They're out by the back loading dock."

"But..."

"Now, Symon. *Please.*"

Since our encounter with Eve, Maguire had been a very different man, at least toward me. I'd never actually heard him say 'please' before. It was ... off-putting. I looked at him for a moment, a bit confused and fuming at the same time; then took off at a sprint for the loading area without another word.

****

The big aluminum garage door was up already and no fewer than twenty men and women were unloading a white, unmarked truck.

I recognized Flint who was moving in as much gear as anyone else, despite only being able to use one arm. I felt a bit guilty about that. Kowalski was with him, as was the redhead I'd met at Janice's home. To my surprise, both agents Vitale and Sanchez were lifting equipment in harmony with the rest of the security team. I saw Palmer speaking with Aaron quietly off to the side.

I headed toward my best friend and the Associate Director and caught them in the middle of a hushed conversation.

"...don't know," Aaron was saying. "If he passes the test then..."

"I passed the test, thanks," I said. "In fact I passed *both* of them with flying colors."

Aaron glanced my way with a crooked smile on his face. "Full mayhem included, I presume."

"Always," I replied with my stock answer to our old mantra. I matched his smile. Just like old times.

He clapped his hand on my back. "Good, Symon. We were all a bit worried that the rust wouldn't come off."

"Palmer, I thought you were going to call us," I said. "Wasn't expecting to see you here."

Palmer laughed. It was one of those laughs dripping with sarcasm.

"The Bureau doesn't release resources easily even with the best of evidence," he said. "And they certainly won't release them to a victim's father working from a hunch. They suggested rather strongly I take a 'leave of absence' until the matter with my daughter could be handled 'objectively.'"

"That's when he got my call," chimed in Aaron.

"Yeah," nodded Palmer. "Detective North provided me with the incentive I needed to take management up on their leave offer. Sanchez and Vitale volunteered to come with me. We are all officially off duty."

I looked over at the hard-at-work agents.

"Good men are hard to find," I said.

"Aaron mentioned you have a plan. Let's hear it."

I quickly outlined the plan for Palmer, including my frustration that we weren't in route already, when a booming voice shouted, "Bryson! More lifting, less yapping!"

That was better. The 'nice' Cardinal Maguire had been making me feel very uncomfortable.

Aaron, Palmer, and I hurried to the truck and helped Eden's security team unload the rest of the gear. I saw crates marked in three or four languages. The English labels said things like "Rocket Propelled Grenades - Do Not Drop" and "M16 Assault Rifles."

I looked at my watch. Only five minutes until the Amtrak was scheduled to leave. There was no way we'd make it. I clicked my tongue in disapproval.

"Train's leaving in five," I said disgustedly to Aaron. "I guess they probably wouldn't have let us on with grenades and stuff anyway."

"Ya think?" he snorted.

I was still trying to figure out how the hell we were going to get all the people and gear to Connecticut as we brought the last of the equipment through the kitchen and into the old gym. Candles still littered the floor, and I noticed that Janice and Bill were putting the final touches on an extremely large circle they'd constructed on the floor using some reddish-colored powder. When the last of the gear was stacked, they closed the circle. Curiosity now began to overtake impatience.

Janice walked over to me, and before I could ask her what was going on, she said, "Here, I thought you might need this." She held out her hand.

Balanced delicately in her palm were my old silver circle and a delicate thread that was about two feet long. It was made of multiple strands of silver interwoven with...

"Feathers?" I asked.

"I made it for you. For luck," she added.

"Thank you, Janice. For everything. Not just..." Bugger. I was never good at this.

She put her finger to my lips. "Hush. Don't ruin the moment," Janice said with a twinkle in her eye.

She wrapped the silver circle five times with the thread, then, standing on her toes, she reached around my neck. With a word I didn't recognize, Janice closed the necklace around me. I could feel the silver threads bond to one another. I sensed the low hum of magic running the length of the necklace.

"This will hold your circle right near your heart," she said and kissed me gently on the lips, "where your passion is greatest."

My face suddenly felt warm. The sensation lasted for only a few seconds then faded. I brought up one hand to my cheek and could feel that the scratches rat-faced demon-boy had etched into my face were gone. The feathers were obviously woven into the necklace for more than luck.

"People, I assume we are ready?" bellowed Cardinal Maguire from somewhere near center court. There was a murmur of agreement around me. I stood on the tips of my toes and could see the Cardinal standing with one arm stretched above his head. There was a loud "pop" and a familiar black staff appeared in his hands.

"He's gonna show off, isn't he?" I whispered to Janice.

"Hush," she whispered back.

Maguire looked around the room and caught my eye and smiled. "*Punctum!*" he shouted.

There was a large flash of light and a loud clap of thunder. My nostrils suddenly filled with the scent of damp, salty sea air. I looked around in confusion for a moment until I recognized where I was.

Dozens of people and a couple of tons of equipment were sitting on a pier in Connecticut, not more than twenty feet away from the docked USCG *Eagle*.

"And you wanted to take the train, Bryson," the Cardinal said.

****

We loaded the ship as the Cardinal shook hands and spoke with a very official-looking man wearing a very expensive suit—so not your typical bureaucrat. He seemed to be the only one in the area when we arrived. I guess the Cardinal arranged for the lack of prying eyes too.

"That was a helluva spell," I said to Aaron as we humped equipment up the gangway.

"The Cardinal is one helluva mage, Sy," Aaron responded. "We're still young, from a practitioner perspective, and have loads to learn."

I wasn't feeling young at the moment.

"If we weren't about to embark on a life-or-death mission, I'd seriously consider a nap. I don't know how the old man does it." Aaron laughed.

"What's so funny?" I asked.

"Symon, do you know how old the Cardinal is?"

"I dunno. Mid-sixties?" I guessed.

"No, Symon. Cardinal Maguire has been in charge of our order since it was created."

"Eighty?" I said, tentatively.

Aaron laughed again. "You never did pay attention."

"What?" I said.

"The Pontifical Order of the Magi was formed during the time when the Holy See resided in France. The Avignon Papacy?"

I gave him a blank stare.

"Pope John the Twenty Second," he said.

"So?"

"Pope John ran the Catholic Church in the 1300s," Aaron said as he lifted another crate.

"Wait," I said. "You're saying…"

"Cardinal Maguire is over seven hundred years old," Aaron said matter-of-factly.

"Holy shit," I swore, as I dropped my end of the crate on my foot.

****

We loaded the ship quickly and set sail posthaste. Twilight had given way to night and the air turned very cold. I couldn't help but be reminded of the last time I'd taken this voyage.

The old ship was at full sail and cut through the waves with ease. The *Eagle* was a fast ship and it seemed like the perimeter of beacons Eden's company had placed around Plum Island were reached in no time. I was standing alone at the bow of the ship when I heard someone call out, "Here we go!"

Two minutes later I felt it as the ship sailed right past the beacons. I suddenly felt more tired than I already was and my senses seemed to be duller. The sounds of the waves slapping the hull were less thunderous and colors were less bright.

"It's nighttime, Symon," I told myself. "Colors are less bright because it's *dark*."

One phase of the mission was down. Of course the next bit would be the hardest part. But if we hadn't gotten past Eden's beacons, this little mission would have come to a grinding halt fast. And Winnie would never be rescued.

Aaron, the FBI guys, and the security team had spent the entire trip readying the large weapons cache. When I'd offered to help earlier,

Aaron shoved an assault shotgun in my hands, similar to the one I'd used when we'd rescued Charles. As he tossed two bandoliers of ammo at me, he said, "This is your favorite. Go make sure you have that banishing spell right."

The Cardinal and the rest of the clergy had sequestered themselves in an officer's cabin aft; presumably to prepare themselves for the tasks ahead. I probably should've taken Aaron's advice and found some solitude to practice; however, nervous energy made me wander the ship.

I came across Eden and Janice, who were sitting with Eve on the main deck. Janice was singing in a low, soothing voice, while Eden sat quietly adjusting her sister's blankets to protect her against the cold air. Both women wore latex gloves—an obvious precaution against an unscheduled visit with Eve in the Shadow-world.

As I approached, Eden looked up at me and smiled. It was the first genuine, uncalculating look I'd gotten from her since I'd arrived back in the States.

"I think Janice's singing is helping Eve," she said. "Don't you think she looks better, Sy?"

Initially I thought it was wishful thinking on Eden's part, but then I took a closer look. Eve's skin color had changed from her normal grayish pallor to a fuller, almost rosy shade. Her sunken features had filled out as well. The dark, almost black circles under her eyes had all but disappeared.

"Actually, I think she does look better," I said thoughtfully. "Her soul is holding the portal open on Plum Island. Do you think the closer we get...?"

"Before I forget," interrupted Eden. She reached down into the bag next to her and pulled out one of those bulky mobiles I'd seen her people use.

"A cell phone?" I looked at her quizzically. "They won't work on the island."

"I haven't given up on my engineers yet, Sy," she replied, handing me the device. "I have some pretty good geeks working for me. If they do their job, the phone might come in handy."

"Land ho!" called out a disembodied voice from above. I had to step hard on the urge to reply back with a loud, pirate-esque "Aarg!" Nervous energy, like I said.

It was the first time I'd heard from a member of the supposedly hand-picked crew sailing the *Eagle*.

The Cardinal's use of serious magic in front of a large number of non-practitioners and his liberal use of his obviously significant political clout to arrange our journey went against everything I knew about His Eminence. His almost cowboy-like practitioner antics were disturbing, to say the least. Even more, his change in demeanor and reckless behavior started right after he and I visited Eve. Don't get me wrong; the shift in the man to a more action-oriented position was one I appreciated. It had given us a fighting chance to save Winnie and to sort out the mistakes—my mistakes—of the past.

The ship pulled up to the same pier where we'd docked the *Katie Mae* ten years ago. I shivered a bit at the memory as I refocused my thoughts on the mission ahead.

"Right. Save the girl, banish the demons, get out alive. No problem," I muttered aloud.

The pier had partially collapsed in the ten years since we'd been here, and we barely had enough water between the bottom of the hull and the silt to get us to a point where we all could safely disembark.

"Okay," I called over the wind, "I'm pretty sure Winnie is being held near the portal at the center of the island." Where I'd blown up a building and created it, I thought darkly.

The portal and, I guessed, Winnie were a couple of miles from the dock. And, as I was pretty sure we wouldn't find a working truck like last time, it was going to take a lot more work to get everyone and our gear to the right positions. Not to mention doing it all before someone or something, noticed.

"Let's get moving before the bad guys know we're here," I called out. "Everybody ready?"

Silence.

"Hey, are you guys listening...?"

"They can't hear you, Symon."

A woman joined me at the rail. At first, I thought it was Eden. But my blood turned cold as I realized that it wasn't Eden. It just looked like her.

Eve turned and looked at me, a tear in her eye. "I'm sorry. We have to do this alone."

I looked around the deck and saw Eden, Janice, and some of the security men who had begun to spill onto the deck, ready for action. They all seemed frozen in place.

"What have you done, Eve?" I asked quietly.

"I'm sorry, Symon," Eve said again, beginning to sob. "It's the deal I had with them."

"What deal!" I shouted.

"If I bring you to them, they won't harm me. Or the children," Eve said, sounding miserable. "Forgive me."

"A deal with who? What children?" I shouted, trying to be heard over the wind that had suddenly picked up.

"Belial. Sabnock," Eve said. "They are both here."

Laughter rang out all around us. I realized then that Belial's "banishment" from the Blue Hill Avenue church had been nothing more than an act. I suddenly saw stars as I felt a heavy blow to the back of my head. I stumbled forward and fell into nothingness.

Chapter Thirty-Five

I came to my senses slowly. The first thing I realized was the fact that I probably wasn't dead. This little fun-fact was explained to me by the series of aches and pains that made themselves known to me in shocking detail.

There was the excruciating pain that came from the back of my head. Somewhere in the pea soup of my memory, I remembered being cold-cocked.

Then there was a burning sensation over my entire body and I seemed to be in a standing position against what felt like a wooden post.

I opened my eyes. Fear suddenly eclipsed the pain.

I was tied to a wooden post, all right. Not surprisingly, my shotgun was nowhere to be found.

"Oh good," said a hissing, very recognizable voice. "Symon Bryson awakens."

From behind me, a winged demon lazily hopped over my stake and landed in a squatting position. The creature turned to me with a big gloating smile on its face.

"Belial," I spat.

"Yes indeed, Symon Bryson," it said gleefully. "Our plan is working perfectly, Sabnock, do you not agree?"

The creature with the body of an ancient Roman warrior and the head of lion appeared next to Belial.

"My plan, you mean, oh great one," said Sabnock.

"Of course, master of disease and pestilence," hissed Belial, sounding annoyed. There seemed to be a pecking order. I filed that away as I tried to shake away the cobwebs in my head.

"Where's the girl?" I growled.

"Which one, Symon Bryson," asked Sabnock, in an almost bored tone. "Winnie Palmer or the demon-witch?"

My head felt like lead as I did my best to look around from my unique vantage point. To my right stood another stake. Tied to it was a young woman with red hair.

Through the bruises and caked blood on her face, I recognized her. It was Winnie, all grown up. Her head lolled to one side and she had the appearance of death about her.

"You fucking pricks," I said, turning to the demons, my head screaming in pain from the quick motion. I ignored it. "What have you done to her?"

Both demons laughed. It was a cruel and disgusting sound.

"She had to be prepared, Symon Bryson," hissed the bat-like Belial. "The demon-witch needs to be replaced," it said, while motioning with one hand.

A group of Belial's skratta minions—the goblin-like creatures we'd fought at the Blue Hill Avenue church—appeared, dragging Eve with them. She, too, was a bloody mess.

I probably would have been more horrified than I already was at the sight of Eve, if it weren't for the fact that she'd freakin' betrayed me.

The little goblins dumped Eve unceremoniously at the base of Winnie's upside-down cross, and chattered excitedly to themselves as they faded away into the murk that surrounded us.

"We had a deal," I heard Eve mumble. "We brought him to you."

Belial kicked her.

"Stupid witch," it said. "Your soul has been in Hell for ten years. Have you learned nothing about our kind in that time?"

Eve sobbed as she tried to rise from the ground. "You promised the children would be safe!" she cried. There was a sickly wet sound as she sat up. It appeared as though someone had carved runes into her body with a knife. I looked away.

"Those souls you have been protecting were *mine* to barter with," snarled Sabnock. "Soon they will be mine again. Souls of the innocent rarely enter our domain. They will be put to good use."

Children, I thought.

I had a flashback to ten years prior. Sabnock, surrounded by children brought for sacrifice to the fiend. Their bodies had disintegrated as Sabnock had been banished back to Hell. For a decade, Eve must have been watching over the innocent souls of the children.

"He is slow to catch on," hissed Belial to Sabnock as if the demon had read my thoughts. "Are you sure he is the one?"

"Yes," said Sabnock. "Could you not feel the power when he arrived back on this continent? He is the one of the prophecy, Belial. You shall soon see."

"Why is there always some sort of prophecy?" I muttered.

Eve coughed and I looked at her mutilated body with a mixture of pity and anger welling up inside me. She caught my gaze and then did something completely unexpected.

She winked.

Belial and Sabnock continued their debate, but I wasn't listening. Eve stared at me with an intensity that I couldn't turn away from. That's when I felt it. The odd wind-talking sensation I hadn't felt for a very long time.

Play for time, said a small voice in my head.

And just like that, Eve had gone back to sobbing and the link between us was gone.

"...he will serve his purpose and I will, through him, control all of Hell," Sabnock was saying.

"*We* will, you mean!" shouted Belial.

That gave me an idea. The two demons obviously didn't trust each other. Maybe if I could buy some time, I'd stand a better the chance of figuring a way to get us out of this. And while I'm at it, I might as well wish for a pony.

What was it Charles used to say? If you fall off a cliff, you might as well try to fly. I had nothing to lose. And souls to try and save. I looked over again at Winnie's unconscious form.

"Hey!" I shouted. "You boys mind explaining to me what this prophesy is all about?" And for the first time in many years, I prayed. "Please, Lord let this work."

"Only the most cunning of plans, Symon Bryson," said Belial in his scratchy, snake-like voice.

"Since my master first ordered me captured decades ago," said Sabnock with a sideways look at Belial, "we have been planning and manipulating toward this day."

"Your master?" I asked.

"The Morningstar," replied Belial. "Our Emperor and King."

"The Morningstar. Lucifer," I said, and spat. Belial immediately hopped over to me and hit me hard enough to loosen a few teeth. I could feel blood trickle from my mouth.

"You do *not* insult the Morningstar!" shouted Belial.

"Why not?" asked Sabnock, nonchalantly. Belial spun around to stare at Sabnock in shock.

"Blasphemy! You dare to..."

"Our King left *us*, Belial. Remember that." Turning its feline face to me, Sabnock said, "That is why we are here, Symon Bryson. You see, we achieved our Master's goal of opening up a portal between our planes of existence. No longer are we limited by short, power-draining incursions into your world. Even the weakest creature of Hell can now walk the Earth with impunity."

"Why didn't you take over the Earth, then?" I asked.

"Because the Morningstar was cunning and had plans of his own," said Belial bitterly.

"We found the unique creature whose soul we needed to open the portal in Winnie Palmer," continued Sabnock. "Millennia in planning, centuries of searching and decades of execution came down to one evening, just like tonight."

"Then we showed up to spoil the party ten years ago," I said.

Belial punched me again and I almost blacked out for the umpteenth time in a week.

"Yes," Belial said. "We thought all was lost, until you opened the portal yourself. Unfortunately, you used the soul of the demon-witch to do it."

"Her soul was significantly less pure than the child's had been," said Sabnock. "Your enormous power created a temporary opening. Much weaker and unstable, of course."

"But it served a purpose. It let the Morningstar leave," hissed Belial.

"I don't understand,"

"We didn't invade your world, Symon Bryson, because Hell was thrown into turmoil. Our King abandoned us."

I thought that through for a moment. Then began to laugh. I couldn't help it.

"So what you are saying, boys," I said, chortling to myself, "is that Lucifer himself went out for a pack of cigarettes and never came back?"

"Crudely put, but essentially correct," said Sabnock.

"Many demons wanted control," hissed Belial. "Battles rage on still. Sabnock and I do not fight because it is futile."

"You're cowards, you mean."

I grunted as Belial hit me again.

"No, Symon Bryson," said Sabnock. "There are ancient texts that foretell a time when the Fallen One would leave Hell. A new ruler would then be found. A mortal ruler of great power. I remembered this prophesy."

"We remembered!" shouted Belial.

Sabnock nodded to the winged demon with a sigh. "Of course, Lord Belial. We."

"Unfortunately before we could search for the one, we found mechanical devices that the demon-witch's sister had placed around this island," hissed Belial, eying Sabnock dangerously. "We had a portal, but our movement was severely limited. We couldn't leave the island for more than short periods."

The creatures had been very forthcoming, but I knew it couldn't last for long. My mind raced, trying to figure out a way to free Winnie and get out of there, but I was coming up with nothing.

"Which is why we cleverly arranged for your return, Symon Bryson," said Sabnock.

My attention came back to the demons.

"Why is that?" I asked.

"Have you not noticed where you are?" mocked Sabnock. "We are in the center of the crater you made when you destroyed the building I was a prisoner in. Your magic still radiates in this place."

As my bloodied and bruised head panned around drunkenly, I realized it was indeed the crater I'd seen in my vision with Eve.

I realized I was staked directly at the entrance to the portal I'd unwittingly created all those years ago. I couldn't see it, but I could feel the evil of Hell seeping from the invisible maw I'd made.

"My handiwork," I said through gritted teeth. "So?"

"We can use your power to replace the demon-witch's soul with that of Winnie Palmer," said Belial. "All we need is your blood to power the spell."

"Why don't you just kill me, then, and take it?" I asked.

"He really is stupid," said Belial, its voice full of disdain.

"No, Belial," replied Sabnock. "Symon Bryson only requires teaching. And we are meant to teach him. He *is* the one."

"Okay, so you can't or won't kill me," I said. "So what?"

"Symon Bryson," said Sabnock, speaking in cold condescension. "Your heart must beat still if your blood is to have the power we need. First, you will replace the tainted soul of the demon-witch with the still-pure soul of Winnie Palmer. Once the portal is stable, you will then disable the limiting devices around this island. Once these tasks are done," The creature licked its lips, "then you will complete your destiny."

"What destiny?" I shouted.

"The prophecy says that the one to take the Morningstar's place as ruler of Hell will be a mortal mage who can live in both realms. With our guidance, this will be you."

****

There are many ways to get blood for a spell. The quickest and cleanest is to use a silver knife, like I had done when we'd tracked down Charles a few nights ago.

The way Sabnock and Belial chose to obtain my blood wasn't so clean. To Belial's delight, Sabnock suggested that the winged demon extract my blood "any way he saw fit, as long as I lived long enough to replace the witch and could be installed as king."

They untied me from the stake and Belial clawed at my face. Deep cuts spilled blood down the front of my shirt and onto the ground. I screamed in pain and fury, trying to use my magic to kill the creature.

Nothing happened, of course. Thank you, Eden.

"The devices put around this island interfere completely with human magic, Symon Bryson," chuckled Belial. "Our magic on the other hand..." The creature raised one hand.

Rocks pelted at me from every direction, sending me to my knees and drawing even more blood. I tried to shield my body as best as I could. More sharp stones struck me.

I heard a familiar chittering and when I looked up, saw that a large number of skratta had formed a circle around Belial and me. They were joined by half a dozen black beasts that resembled panthers, but as large as sedans. I'd never seen their like before. Their fur was made of fire and each cat had a set of grotesque horns rising from flaming heads. Sabnock's minions, I guessed.

More of my blood spilled as Belial hit me again. I scrambled to try and get away from it, trying a second spell out of desperation.

Nothing.

"Stupid monkey," sputtered Belial as it hit me again. "You have much to learn before becoming our king!"

It was then I noticed that the demon had been beating me around the portal entrance. It was trying to get me to spill blood in a rough circle.

A loud moan distracted the beast and it turned toward the sound. Winnie was waking up.

With the creature's attention momentarily off me, I scrambled to move away from the blood circle I'd been inadvertently making. I'd be damned if I was going to make the coming of Armageddon easy for them.

Two of the huge flaming cats leapt in front of me. They both let out menacing growls. The message was clear—get back to the circle. Well, to hell with that. I'll be damned if I was going to let these demons win.

I staggered to my feet in front of the beasts. The loss of blood had made me woozy and I stumbled. Steadying myself I made ready to toss myself at the animals.

"Here kitties," I slurred drunkenly. "I have a snack for you!"

Both animals licked their lips with their flaming tongues.

"Enough!" shouted Sabnock. "You have had your fun, Belial. Hold Symon Bryson down and collect his blood so we can close the circle and be done with this."

Suddenly, a dozen skratta were on top of me, holding me down. I tried to struggle, but in my weakened state I was no match for the ugly little goblins.

Belial appeared, standing above me. He was holding a black stone dagger in one hand and an equally black bowl in the other.

"Time to bleed, Symon Bryson," said the demon.

I'd failed. Again. My first time on this cursed island had been a disaster. The rescuing of Charles had been sloppy and had almost killed the Monsignor. And now, the clincher—I was going to finish the job and help usher in destruction on an epic scale.

I looked at the creature with total hatred. It came at me with the knife, slowly turning it over in its hand to prolong my torture. I refused to be frightened. I refused to give the beast the satisfaction of seeing me look at it with anything but defiance.

"God," I thought. "We have never seen eye to eye, and I've never been one of your biggest supporters. But now would be a really good time for us to make up before it all literally goes to hell."

Time gave all appearances that it had slowed down to a crawl. Four things happened simultaneously.

I felt the sensation of my body connecting to the earth magically.

The necklace Janice had given me glowed with a light so bright that the skratta released me and scampered away with squeals of terror.

The wounds on my body instantly healed.

Oh, and the fourth thing? The cell phone Eden had given me, rang.

"What was that?" Belial asked in a mild panic, stepping away from me and watching his minions scatter. The phone rang again.

"That, bitches," I said rising to my feet, my power rising proportionally with my anger, "was the bell for round two. Now we do it my way."

Chapter Thirty-Six

I spent ten years learning about magic at St. Ignatius. Most of that time was (in my opinion) wasted on "history" and "theory." It was only in my late teens when we learned real spell-casting and combat. Our first real mission had been on Plum Island. It was to have been a test of our skills and our power. My emotions had gotten the better of me then and anger had fueled my destruction of the building.

I was far angrier now, and Janice had told to use my emotions to fuel my magic.

I raised both my hands and blasted Belial with twin red beams of fire. The creature incinerated without uttering a single sound.

"That's what I think of your job offer," I snarled.

There was screaming from Sabnock in a language I didn't recognize, and hundreds of skratta and those flaming panthers closed ranks around me. I swept one arm and a legion of the little goblins turned to ash. The remaining skratta scattered, screaming in fear. I then proceeded to blast the three nearest big cats as they pounced past the retreating goblins. Red fire streamed from my fingertips and the demon animals fell about my feet, twitching, their demonic lives snuffed out with ease.

Somewhere in the back of my mind, I realized that I was doing advanced magic. Wordlessly and effortlessly. But instead of being frightened or shocked at that fact, I reveled in it. I tasted power and ordered a second helping.

I laid waste to an army of creatures that Sabnock and Belial had brought with them. It seemed to take only seconds.

"Symon, stop. Please."

The voice was in my head. Breathing heavily, I lowered my arms and realized I'd been about to strike down Eve. Her broken and beaten form was lying by Winnie, who still hung on the stake. I suddenly felt drained. And ashamed.

"You were wise to listen to the demon-witch, Symon Bryson," said a furious voice.

I looked past the stake that bound Winnie and the sickly Eve to see Sabnock. The demon was standing in a fire, holding its old spear. And just like old times, the demon had surrounded itself with children.

Very familiar-looking children.

"You are everything I thought you would be, mage. And more. You have done me a favor by removing that vile creature Belial, so I will not kill you for destroying my beloved Menhiti."

Still breathing heavily, I said, "That's awfully nice of you. I see you are still hiding behind children, Sabnock. You're nothing more than a coward."

The demon tilted its head to me. "Perhaps, Symon Bryson. However, I find, once again, that these children prove useful to me."

"How's that?" I asked, suddenly feeling exhausted.

"As leverage, of course," said Sabnock simply. "You will close the circle of blood voluntarily, or I will kill each one of these pathetic sprogs."

I heard a whimper from Eve and saw her raise her head slightly.

"They're dead already, Sabnock," I pointed out to the demon. "They died over a decade ago."

"True and untrue, Symon Bryson," said Sabnock. "These little ones lost their original bodies in our first encounter. But their souls were the first carried to Hell by your portal."

I winced at the reference to 'my portal.'

"The demon-witch soon followed and gathered up the innocent souls you condemned that day. She has been protecting them ever since." Out of the corner of my eye I saw Eve move almost imperceptibly.

"As approaching death weakened her, I was able to find those whom she protected for so long and create earthly bodies for them to use in my service. An even better investment for me, rather than just trading their souls for favors."

"Earthly bodies?" said Eve. "You have brought them all back?"

"Yes, demon-witch. And you can watch them all die once again should Symon Bryson not complete the blood circle."

"You always were an idiot, Sabnock," Eve snarled and jumped to her feet. "*Calx permoveo!*"

Instantly, four pillars of light shimmered around us. Cardinal Maguire, Bill, Peter and one other person I didn't immediately recognize, appeared.

"About time Ms. Engel," said the Cardinal. "We were beginning to worry."

"The children," Eve croaked, slowly sinking to the ground.

It suddenly hit me who the old man who'd arrived with the clergymen was. It was that old sea dog, Joel. But he looked very different than when I'd first met him on the *Katie Mae* or in Charles' hospital room the other night.

For starters, he had a set of freakin' *wings*.

"I will protect the innocent," said Joel. Turning to me, he said, "You must close the portal and end this now, Symon. Finish what you started." And with that, both the angel and the children were just gone.

Sabnock roared with fury and charged at us. The Cardinal held up his hand and his black staff appeared once again. This time, the weapon glowed with white-hot ancient runes. "I've got this creature. Bryson! Go get Miss Palmer and close the portal!"

I raced over to Winnie, who was now fully awake, her eyes wide with terror.

"S'okay, Winnie," I said, "we'll get you out of here." I looked around wildly and spotted Belial's black knife lying a couple yards away.

Sabnock and the Cardinal were having the mother of all battles behind me. No, I didn't stop to watch, but any practitioner for miles could feel the power being thrown around. I grabbed the knife and went back to Winnie and noticed that both Peter and Bill were with Eve. His Eminence was fighting the demon alone.

Quickly, I cut Winnie down. The young woman fell into my arms.

"Bill!" I shouted, "come take her!" I waited just long enough for Father Duncan to get to Winnie's side, then turned to face the battle.

"Symon! The Banishing Spell!" said Bill.

Oh bugger. I'd forgotten all about that. In my anger I'd blasted Belial into the middle of next week. The creature was hurt, but would eventually be back. I'd have to deal with that later.

But Sabnock. I was going to send it where no demon had gone before. Phasers set to annihilate, Mr. Sulu.

Sabnock and his Eminence were using magic and fighting—staff verses spear—at an incredible speed. The two of them were little more than blurs, punctuated by the occasional light of a cast spell.

Sabnock's spear blocked a sweeping attack from the Cardinal. A fireball thrown by the demon was deflected harmlessly by the shield Maguire had in place. Then the old man stumbled.

I raised my own hands, shouting, *"Vis pulsus!"* A pulse of wind gouged into the surface of the crater and slammed full-force into Sabnock, throwing the creature off balance and allowing the Cardinal to regain his footing.

"Bryson! What are you doing! You need to close the portal!" the holy man shouted.

Sabnock turned on me before I could answer. *"So will I send upon you famine and evil beasts, and they shall bereave thee: and pestilence and blood shall pass through thee; and I will bring the sword upon thee."* The demon pointed its spear at me. I raised my hands, knowing full well that I'd never be able to block it in time.

"No!" screamed Cardinal Maguire and shoved me out of the way. The big man took the full blast from Sabnock's spear. I watched in horror as his Eminence fell to his knees and large pustules appeared on his face.

"This day may not have been the victory I had hoped for," said Sabnock triumphantly, "But the death of the Hunter will do nicely."

The demon was hit by two white-hot fireballs and fell back from me and the Cardinal. Peter and Bill had joined the fight.

I stumbled over to the Cardinal, who was still on his knees, almost as if in silent prayer. I touched his shoulders and the Cardinal shivered a little.

Opening his eyes, the man looked at me and smiled.

The disease was ravaging his body. I could see the Cardinal's skin beginning to blacken and peel away in places. Yet he was still smiling.

"Symon," he said with difficulty. "You must get the Palmer girl out of here and complete your mission. You must finish what you started ten years ago."

"Eminence, I..."

The Cardinal coughed. Dark blood dribbled out of the side of his mouth.

"Take my staff, banish that son of a bitch, and close that portal. For once in your life, take an order. Can you do that, boy?"

"Yes, Eminence."

"Now, I'm ready," the Cardinal said, but he didn't seem to be speaking to me.

The light disappeared from Cardinal Eugene Maguire's eyes.

"Symon, we really could use your help!" Peter called out.

I laid the Cardinal's body gently on the ground. Next to his Eminence's lifeless body was his black staff.

I picked it up. It felt a lot heavier than it looked. The runes I'd seen glowing a bright white during the battle, now shone a deep fiery red.

"Any time you are ready, master," said a voice in my head. It had a very sarcastic Irish accent.

I tried to drop the staff, but my fingers wouldn't let go of it. The damn stick had spoken to me!

"Symon!" shouted Bill.

I turned to see my two priestly friends being pinned down by Sabnock. The creature raised its deadly spear at them.

I pointed the talking staff at Sabnock.

"*Exsilium, Malum unus est vestri fortuna ut pacis populus mos vos reperio cruciatus eternus!*"

A beam of red fire shot out from the end of the black staff and hit Sabnock squarely in the center of its chest.

The creature let out the type of scream you'd hear from pigs in a slaughterhouse. The demon dropped its spear, rose up from the ground, and began to spin.

With a sickening wet sound, Sabnock folded in on itself, just like that little demon had back at St. Ignatius. The lion-headed creature was gone.

I dropped to the ground, exhausted. Seeing Belial's dropped knife, I crawled over to it. There was still one more thing I needed to do.

Bill and Peter rushed over to me.

"Help me up," I said to them.

The holy men hauled me to my feet.

"Can you get Winnie and make your way back to the others?" I asked.

"Yes," they both replied together.

"What are you going to do, Symon?" asked Peter.

"I'm going to finish this mess once and for all."

****

The priests left with Winnie. Neither one of them could teleport, so they had to make the trek back to the *Eagle* the old fashioned way.

I was all alone with Eve.

She coughed and a trickle of blood ran from her mouth. Time was very short.

"Eve," I said, "can you hear me?"

Her eyes fluttered open. She smiled.

"Not bad, Symon," she said.

"Tell that to the Cardinal," I muttered bitterly.

"Is there any other way to close this portal down?" I asked gently, already knowing the answer. "Too many people have died today already."

"You saved forty children, Symon," said Eve. "That counts for something."

"Maybe," I replied. Somehow, I knew there would be some sort of accounting for my actions at a later date. For what I'd done, and for what I was about to do.

"No, Symon. It's the only way."

"Is Winnie far enough away? I don't want this to start all over again."

"Almost. She is far enough away that her soul is safe. Once I'm gone, the portal should collapse on itself."

"I'm staying with you," I said.

"You can't, Symon!" Eve tried to sit up in protest but failed. She fell back hard and I barely caught her.

"You will either die, or become the next soul to power the portal. You have to kill me from outside the crater."

"No," I said. "You won't die alone."

"Don't be stupid," Eve said.

"Why change now?"

A flicker of a smile appeared on her face. Then she looked at me, eyes wide and brimming with tears.

"Tell my sister I love her and forgive her, okay?"

"I will." Tears formed in my eyes too.

I plunged Belial's knife into Eve's chest.

****

"Symon."

I opened my eyes, but there was nothing but blackness all around me.

"Symon," came the same voice again.

"What?" I said, rather annoyed.

A figure suddenly appeared in front of me. It was a large man wearing a grey cloak.

"Cardinal Maguire, you're alive!" I said joyfully.

"No, son," the big man said. "I'm still dead."

"So I guess that means I'm dead too, huh. I guess it's better than being a battery powering a portal to Hell."

The big man laughed. "No, you're not dead. Not yet anyway. You've closed the portal my son. Well done."

I knew the Cardinal was right. I'd felt the portal close.

I looked around for a moment. "Where am I?" I finally asked.

"That place between wakefulness and sleep where you have unbelievably vivid dreams only to lose them when your eyes finally open. You know what I'm talking about?"

"Yeah."

"It's the closest analogy I could think of," explained Maguire.

"Come, Eugene, we have a long life to review," said another voice. And just as suddenly as Maguire had appeared, a being of pure white light appeared next to the former Cardinal. The creature was tall, about six foot ten. The light made it almost impossible to see its features.

Except for the wings.

"The boy needs to know," said Maguire.

"He'll find out for himself in time," answered the creature bathed in light, in a voice I thought I recognized.

"Joel?" I asked.

"Sometimes," said the being. "For right now you can call me Jeremiel."

"Why am I here?" I asked.

"Good question, Symon," said Jeremiel. "Keep asking it throughout your life and you might actually head in the right direction this time."

"When we spoke ten years ago, you said the choice about the future was mine to make." I remembered clearly now the conversation I'd had with 'Joel' before leaving for Ireland.

"Free will must be allowed at all times," the light-being nodded. "And you chose."

"It's all my fault, isn't it? I chose to leave, stranding a friend between life and Hell for ten years. I watched that same friend die just now."

My voice seemed to echo around me. Both Maguire and Jeremiel stood silently.

"How do I ever atone for that?" I asked.

"Symon, the situation isn't black and white as you would so love to believe," said Maguire. "You do what you can and pray it's right. You made a mistake ten years ago. You have corrected that mistake. You stopped the suffering of a woman trapped in a Hellish existence and saved many children."

"But Eve was tortured because of..."

"No, Symon," said Jeremiel. "You freed her. Others will pay for what was done to her. And I look forward to their life reviews when the time comes."

"But..."

"Be at peace, Symon. This day has brought you heartbreak and pain. But it has also released burdens that have been weighing on your soul for a decade," said the angel. "Celebrate the lives of those who died serving our cause. What's important is that you've come back to us. Rest now. Tomorrow will bring clarity of spirit."

With that, Jeremiel put his hand on my forehead. I felt the anguish and pain leave me. "Come, Eugene," I heard the angel as I drifted toward sleep. "We have a long life to review together."

Chapter Thirty-Seven

I awoke feeling refreshed, as if I'd slept for a week. From the gentle rocking of my bed, I gathered I was on a boat. It all came rushing back. The *Eagle*. Cardinal Maguire. Demons.

And the death of a friend.

I sat up quickly, only to notice the silhouette of a woman standing over me.

"Janice?" I asked.

"No, Mr. Bryson. I'm Elizabeth." The room was suddenly bathed in a bright flickering light. A red-headed woman placed an old oil lantern on the weathered table next to my bed. I had to blink away a few tears that had little to do with the quick transition from dark to light.

"Hm," I grunted, wiping away the dampness on my cheeks. "You'll always be Winnie to me."

She wrinkled up her nose. "You sound like my dad," she said.

"He's a good man. I take that as a compliment."

A silence draped over us then like a heavy shroud.

"So, uh, where am I?" I asked.

"Well," Winnie said, "we are currently onboard a big Coast Guard ship apparently heading to Connecticut, I think."

"Are you okay?" I asked.

"I will be," she smiled a little. "That woman, Janice, helped me. The memories..."

"They'll fade in time," I lied.

"Thank you, Symon," said Winnie, looking away from me. I could tell she didn't believe me. I never could lie to women very well.

"My father," she said after taking a moment to compose herself, "he told me this is the second time you have saved me. Is that true?"

"Yes," I said simply.

"I don't remember the first time," she said.

"Good."

There was another uncomfortable silence. "My father and the others are with the children. I don't know where they all came from, but they are being looked after. I...," she hesitated for a second. "I just wanted to stay here and make sure you weren't, you know."

"Dead?"

She shook her head. "No. Alone." She started to cry.

I never knew what a crying woman wanted to hear. "It will be okay, Winnie. You're safe now. I promise." Ugh. I needed a scriptwriter.

I put my hand on her shoulder, and she leaned into me and sobbed. I held her like that for a long time. Maybe it wasn't words she needed after all.

****

Winnie and I left the stateroom once she'd composed herself. We arrived on the deck of the *Eagle* to find utter chaos: the good kind caused by dozens of children running around squealing in delight. Members of the clergy, Eden's security team, and a couple of FBI guys were trying to corral them, or at least shepherd them from (too much) trouble.

I spotted Peter sitting on a hatch near the main mast. He was wiping sweat from his brow and had an exasperated, yet happy, look on his face that I hadn't seen in a long time.

I gave Winnie a quick hug and walked over to sit with the old priest.

"Remind you of anything?" I asked.

"Good Lord, I've missed the school," he said. He put away his white handkerchief. "You had us worried, Sy."

"I was a bit worried myself, Peter," I said. "Me, Eve, Winnie, two demons, and a bunch of flaming cats and Munchkin rejects. It was a helluva party. You guys almost missed it."

Peter looked up at me with a pained expression on his face.

"It was the Cardinal's idea. Apparently he experienced a vision with Eve that was a little different from yours. Or he saw more. He never did tell us which."

"Then why all the men and the hardware?" I asked. "Why the show of force if he knew it wasn't going to be used?"

The old priest looked at his feet for a moment, then glanced at me with a hard look. "They weren't to assault Plum Island, Symon: not in the way you were led to believe."

"Then what was all the heavy artillery for?"

"The Cardinal told us you would be tempted," Peter said quietly. "If you succumbed to temptation, he told us we'd only get one shot at you."

We sat in silence for a moment as I let that sink in.

"Well," I said. "I'll bet Flint would've loved that."

"He didn't know," replied Peter quickly. "No one but members of the Church knew what the Cardinal had planned."

"And the angel."

"Who?" said Peter, looking at me confused.

"Jeremiel," I said. "The angel who saved the kids."

"What are you talking about, Symon?" asked Peter. "You brought the children to the ship. Bill and I had just arrived with Ms. Palmer when it happened. You transported them all here yourself. I wanted to ask you how you did that."

I studied my old friend for a moment and realized he believed exactly what he'd said. Interesting.

"We thought it was his Eminence returning, but before you collapsed, you told us that he and Eve were dead and that we needed to leave immediately. What happened, Symon?"

I told Peter most of the story, leaving out anything to do with Jeremiel for the time being. Somehow the omission seemed ... prudent.

"Mary, mother of God," he finally uttered. "The Monsignor knew it was bad but ... Lucifer? Walking the Earth? Sweet Jesus..."

I thought my being made into the new ruler of Hell was more important. Apparently, Peter felt that the epitome of evil wandering the Earth had priority. Priests.

"Symon, look at what's happened in the world just in the past few years... wars... famine... plagues. The global economic collapse. Billions of people have been suffering."

"I was working in a pub for ten years, Father," I said honestly. "I didn't pay much attention to anything outside of Dublin. You think Lucifer is behind all of the world's current woes?"

"I don't know, my son," said Peter, deep in thought. "Human beings have a great propensity to cause evil all on their own. But the footsteps of the Fallen One now fall in our realm. It's very troubling to say the least. Let's go find Eden. Then I have to call the Vatican."

****

We found Eden in the radio room of the old sailing vessel. Kowalski was with her trying to juggle a couple of open cell phone calls while she barked orders to both him and the radioman.

"That's right, a bus," she snapped into one phone. "I have forty children to transport to Cambridge, Massachusetts. Make sure it's stocked with plenty of food and water. I dunno! Whatever kids eat these days." She looked at Peter and me and held up a finger. Not *that* finger.

To the radio man, she said, "Send my thanks to the Commandant and tell him I will brief him personally in the morning."

Into another phone, she said, "Flint will be sending pictures of them as soon as he can chase them all down. I want to find their families as soon as we can." Nodding at Kowalski who closed both cell phones, Eden motioned us outside the radio room.

"As you can see, gentlemen, I'm extraordinarily busy. What can I do for you?"

"Eden," I said, "I'm so sorry about Eve."

Eden looked at me, her face unreadable. "Me too, Symon, but I can't deal with that now. If that's all..."

"Christ, Eden. You just lost your sister!" I shouted. "It's okay to be a little human about that—"

SLAP.

I staggered back a step. My face stung, but more from shame than the impact.

"Don't you *dare*—" Eden started then stopped herself.

She closed her eyes and began again. "I lost her ten years ago, Symon," her voice broke as she struggling to maintain a calm tone. "It's just taken a decade for her to finally rest in peace. How I deal with this is absolutely none of your concern. Now. What do you want?"

"Um," said Peter looking nervously between Eden and me. "Charles was right. The situation is far worse than the Church believed."

As I rubbed my jaw, Peter quickly told Eden about Sabnock's declaration that Satan had left Hell and was somewhere walking the Earth. Thankfully, he left out the part about the demon's career plans for me.

When he finished, Eden just nodded. "Okay. Now we at least know what we are up against. Thank you, Peter."

To me, she said, "Symon, we need to get the current situation stabilized. Then you and I will have a very long talk. But for now, I really need you to get out of my sight."

****

Peter and I hurried away from the radio room and headed back to the main deck where some semblance of calm had been restored. The lights from the Connecticut shore were growing brighter as we approached and by the time the *Eagle* reached the dock, the children had tired themselves out.

"Bryson," said a voice behind me.

A tearful Assistant Director stood there, holding his daughter's hand.

"I ... wanted to say ... thank you. For saving my daughter."

He held out his hand. I shook it.

"If there is anything I can ever do to repay you—"

"Seeing the two of you together is a start," I said, smiling.

Winnie—Elizabeth, leaned toward me and kissed me on the cheek.

"Thank you, Symon," she whispered.

Father and daughter turned and walked away together. I watched them go, thankful to be left to my thoughts for the remainder of the return trip.

****

Lining the dock were a series of black Town Cars, a large box truck, and one of those nice buses used for cross-country trips and rock band tours. I offered to help with the unloading, but Aaron and Bill said they could coordinate that. Appreciation wouldn't even begin to describe what I felt for my friends.

"We'll talk later," Aaron said. There were a lot of people who wanted to talk later. I was too tired to worry about that.

Elizabeth came up to me, taking both my hands in hers.

"Ms. Engel asked me to accompany the children back to Cambridge," she said. "We are bringing them all back to St. Ignatius for now. She feels that's the best place for them until we locate all the families."

I nodded. It was about all I could do.

"I... Thank you, Symon," she stuttered.

"I think you've said thank you more than enough times, Elizabeth," I muttered softly.

"I'll see you in Cambridge?" she asked.

"Probably," I replied.

One of Eden's security men called out to the young woman.

"I have to go. Elizabeth gave me a quick peck on the cheek and dashed off toward the bus.

As I watched her get on board, I noticed Eden speaking with the same suited gentlemen I'd noticed before our departure. Standing next to the man was a dour-looking Father Moore. The Holy Solicitor gave me a dark look, then turned his back dismissively toward me to focus on what looked like a very heated discussion between the Mystery Suit-Man and Eden.

I debated walking over to see what it was all about, when a gentle hand touched my shoulder.

"Come, Symon," said Janice. "Let's get you home. You must be absolutely exhausted.

She led me toward one of the Town Cars that sat, engine idling, ready to depart. She opened the back door for me and I got in. The seats of a car never felt so good.

Janice got in after me and shut the door.

"Let's go," she said to the driver.

The car moved away from the activity at the pier and I sank further into the seat, closing my eyes.

"You're just awesome," I said. "Have I told you that lately?"

"You're sweet," she said distractedly. "We have a long drive ahead and I have a lot of questions, Symon. We all do, but I thought you could use a little rest first."

"See?" I mumbled. "Awesome."

"Did you see how happy Peter was with all those kids running around?"

"Mm-hmmm," I mumbled.

The car accelerated onto a highway and began its long trek to Massachusetts.

"I can't believe the Cardinal and Eve are gone," Janice said.

So rest wasn't the real reason Janice had put me in a car. She wanted to talk. The awesomeness faded a little.

"As Charles always told us, there would be casualties in our war against evil," I answered.

"That's a bit callous, Sy," scolded Janice.

"I'm sorry," I said. "I'm shattered, Janice. My kindness filter is turned off at the moment. I watched them die. I'm still kind of processing the whole thing."

Janice was silent for a moment apparently deciding on a new tack to take with me.

"You said 'our war.' Are you coming back?"

God, what a question, I thought. Too much had happened in the last week. Everything was pretty confusing and I needed time to sort it all out.

"I don't know," was all I could respond. It was honest at least. "I'm physically and emotionally not with it right now, Janice. I promise we'll talk about this ... just not now, Okay?"

Another moment of silence.

"Can I ask you one more thing though?" she said, followed quickly by, "Just one. I promise."

"Sure," I said, sighing.

"What are you doing wearing Cardinal Maguire's ring?" she asked.

Chapter Thirty-Eight

I spent the next month helping out at St. Ignatius. Utilizing all the assets of both the Church and Eden's company to find the families of the children we'd rescued from Plum Island turned up nothing. Not even a decade-old photo on a milk carton. Even the FBI struck out on that score—saying they must have all been runaways. Yeah, I didn't believe it either. I'd do my own checking, but for now—they seemed to be very happy at the church.

With no one to look after them, Peter cut a deal with Eden to fund the rebuilding of the old school that had been such a big part of my childhood. As Charles was still undergoing rehab and staying at Mass General, I'd been allowed to stay in his suite on campus. My rent, as Peter told me, was to help in the reconstruction of the school.

The work was hard, but satisfying. It had given me an excuse to focus on things other than demons, Hell and dead friends.

My evenings were spent trying to figure out what the ring I'd apparently inherited from the late Cardinal Maguire was. I hadn't had much luck on that score, and Peter, being the only person I really spoke to during that month, couldn't offer any clues other than that the markings were old and Celtic. Having lived in Dublin for a decade, I'd already figured that bit out for myself. The words were mostly unknown to me, but I did understand one word—*Aspatria*—Ash of Patrick. I probably could have used resources at Eden's company to further my investigation, but that would have meant speaking with her, something I was keen to avoid.

The other project I'd worked on with Charles came to fruition one drizzly May morning. I met my old mentor at the hospital. It was hard seeing him in a wheelchair—even Janice hadn't been able to restore the use of his legs—but he looked very impressive in his new vestments. He'd been promoted to Bishop the week before.

"I don't know how you convinced them, Symon," he said upon seeing me enter his ward, "but I'm very impressed."

I helped my old mentor down to the waiting car provided by Eden's company (at Charles' request) and we sped off.

We arrived at the old Blue Hill Avenue church. The crowd that had gathered on this overcast day was impressive, as were the number of construction vehicles around the remains of the once grand structure.

The Governor of Massachusetts and the Mayor of Boston were both on hand and all smiles. To be honest, I never liked ceremonies of any sort, so my mind wandered during the myriad of speeches about urban renewal and hope for the future that the politicians doled out that morning. I thought about both Cardinal Maguire's sacrifice and Eve's choice. There was a smattering of applause as Bishop DuBarry was introduced. Charles rolled up to the microphone to speak.

"This site, once a great center of learning and worship, has been neither for far too long. On behalf of the Holy See and the Arch Dioceses of Boston, it is my great honor to consecrate this long overdue renewal project. As we endeavor to bring the light of Jesus Christ back to this dark place, I ask all of you to remember that in the darkest of times, it is those who work for the light who will win in the end."

There was a smattering of additional applause. But I knew Charles' speech hadn't just been for the rebuilding of the church.

The ceremonial ribbon was cut and a final prayer was offered up. Then it was done.

Belial had said, back when we'd rescued Charles, that places of despair allowed the demonic influence to grow and flourish. Well, strike one dark place off the list.

Many well-wishers shook Charles' hand as I wheeled him toward the waiting sedan that would take him to the airport. The Holy Father had requested his presence in Rome, and my old mentor was about to embark on his next role in the world of two thousand year old Papal politics.

Flint was standing by the town car, with the back door already open. With a gentleness I never expected from the big man, he carefully picked Charles up and placed him in the car. We proceeded to fold up the Cardinal's chair and place it in the trunk of the vehicle.

"Symon," said Charles, "have you decided what you are going to do?"

That was a question I'd been asking myself for the better part of the last month. I'd sequestered myself in St. Ignatius and hadn't spoken with most of my old friends. I wasn't any closer to an answer to that question and told Charles as much.

"Go talk to them," Charles prodded, nodding over his shoulder. Aaron, Janice, Eden, Bill, and Peter were standing across the street, watching me with worried expressions on their faces. "They're your friends and can help you."

"Perhaps, Excellency." I said, noncommittally. "Safe flight, Charles." Smiling, I said, "Tell the Pope I said 'Hi.'"

I closed the car door. The sedan began to pull away but the vehicle suddenly stopped. Charles' window slid down.

"Symon," he called. "A word of advice."

"Sir?"

"Don't piss the ring off."

The car drove off.

The very light rain had stopped and the clouds were already beginning to break up. I could see patches of blue sky and I sighed, taking a deep breath. It smelled like spring.

I looked over at my old friends. It was time.

Their conversation stopped as soon as they saw me approaching. They all looked at me with a guarded sense of anticipation.

"It was a nice ceremony," commented Janice. "I don't know how you persuaded the Church to renovate this place, Symon, but it was a good thing."

I shrugged. "I think Charles had more to do with convincing the Vatican to open up their wallet than I did. I just agreed with what he said to them."

"Well," said Eden, "it showed you can maneuver through politics if you really want to, Symon. Maybe you have grown up. A little." She looked haggard—the loss of her sister etched on her face. I wanted to say something—anything—to offer her some small comfort. But I really didn't know how to start. Fortunately, Aaron came to my rescue.

"Hey," said Aaron, "remember that place near MIT that has their menu formatted like the Periodic table? They still do a mean breakfast. Why don't we all go eat? That way Peter doesn't have to cook for a change."

"Yeah," I sighed. "Okay. Let's go."

****

Surrounded by a veritable cornucopia of breakfast burritos, fresh pastries, and plates of eggs and apple-turkey sausage (not to mention a never ending supply of hot coffee), we talked.

Not about demons, death, and magic. Just about old times, school antics, and the shared crazy adventures we all had as teenagers. We all laughed, even Eden. It was a good morning for the soul.

Wiping tears from his eyes, Peter said. "I didn't know half of what you clowns got up to. I swear if I did, I would have shackled you all to your beds."

"I don't believe that for a minute, Father," said Bill. "I think you lived vicariously through the rest of us back then."

We all laughed again at the well-remembered look of stern disapproval Peter bestowed upon his young protégé.

"Well," said Aaron, pushing his chair back and standing, "I have to go collect a few things from the precinct house. No time like the present as the weekend shift will be a bit lighter."

"What do you mean?" I asked.

"I resigned last week," he replied. "I got a better offer. After what just happened, the tame world of police reports just doesn't do it for me anymore."

"Yeah," said Janice, also standing. "I have to head back to Maine. God knows what condition my house is in. I'll walk you out, Aaron."

Both tried to leave cash on the table, but Eden wouldn't hear of it. "What's the use in having an expense account, if you can't spend it?" she said.

Aaron and Janice left together, and I watched them go with a twinge of jealousy.

"William and I have to head out as well. The school still needs some work, and although Ms. Palmer is fantastic with the children, I think our newest teacher might have her hands full. Thank you, Eden, for a lovely meal," said Peter.

"I guess we also should prepare Mass for tonight," said Bill. "Any idea what the sermon will be about, Father?"

Peter looked at me and smiled. "I've always liked the story about the Prodigal Son. Good day, all." And with that, the two clergymen exited.

"Symon, do you have a few minutes?" asked Eden softly. "I'd like to speak with you for a bit. I know you've been avoiding me, but it's time to talk. Come with me to my office?"

She was right. I'd been avoiding a conversation with her for far too long.

"Yeah, okay, Eden," I sighed. We left the restaurant and I was surprised to see Aaron lurking near the door.

"You okay?" I asked. But he didn't answer me.

"Eden, can I speak to Symon for a few minutes?" asked Aaron.

Eden looked at her watch, then at me. "I'll be in the car. Take your time," she said.

One of her Town Cars was idling across the street. I waited until she got in.

"What's up?" I asked.

Aaron didn't meet my eyes. "I want to clear up a couple of things. Can we walk for a few minutes?"

"Um, sure," I said. I mean, really. What *could* I say?

I waved Eden on. The car sat for a moment or two, then pulled away from the curb.

Aaron and I walked in silence for a few minutes. We passed the old Kodak building that had been abandoned for years and cut through the parking lot of a pharmaceutical company. We walked up Mass Ave. to the Harvard Bridge. Foot traffic was very light and we stopped halfway across the bridge, admiring the view of Boston over the Charles River.

"We gonna talk or walk?" I said finally.

Aaron sighed and turned his back to the view to face me.

"Janice," he began.

"Look, Aaron," I cut him off, "you guys got married and divorced: end of story. It's in the past. I'm sorry for that, but you guys seem to get along great, so…"

"I'm gay," said Aaron. "Wow. That was not the way I wanted to tell you, but it was the only way I could think of to shut you the hell up." He turned away from me and leaned against the rail watching the boaters glide along the river.

"No you're not," I said. He's not gay. I mean we used to party with girls all the time. I would have known if my best friend was gay. I looked at Aaron, back turned to me, and realized that he wasn't pulling my leg.

I felt like a fucking idiot.

"How long have you… I didn't know, man," I said. God, I'm an asshole.

"Do you remember that little blonde at MIT?" asked Aaron.

"Yeah. I thought you were never gonna get laid." I said. "What was her name? Mary-something?"

"Yeah," nodded Aaron. "That's her. Funny, I didn't remember her name until you mentioned it. Anyway, that's when I knew."

"How come? I don't understand." God, I was making a mess of this.

"When you left, we were all devastated," said Aaron. "Janice fell apart. I'm not entirely sure she didn't have a nervous breakdown. Between what happened to Eve and you leaving, she…" He shook his head at the memory. "It was a bad scene, Sy."

"But married?" was all my brain was able to make my mouth say.

"She was my friend, too. We both felt alone. I was selfish and I wanted to hurt you. I screwed up." He turned to face me and sighed. "Ten years ago our world fell apart. Janice needed me. And to be honest, I needed her. We'd both lost the same things. The church, our home, our purpose, and the man we loved."

"I … wait. The man we…? What the fuck, Aaron!"

He continued as if he hadn't heard me, like he'd been practicing this for a while. "In a fit of stupidity, I convinced her to marry me. Neither one of us wanted to go through life alone with what we'd experienced. Please tell me you understand, at least a little."

"No. I don't."

"I really didn't expect you would, man," his voice returned to that icy cop tone I always hated. "But I thought you should know. Anyway, Eden is waiting for you. It's only about two miles from here to the Hancock building."

He turned and began to walk back toward Cambridge.

"Aaron, wait!" I shouted.

He stopped, but kept his back to me.

"How did you expect me to react?" I shouted at him. "First you tell me you're gay, which I really don't have a problem with. But then you tell me you're in love with me *and* used Janice to get back at me?"

He turned to me and said, "You gonna hit me again?"

To be honest, I almost did. Instead, I turned my back to him and walked away as quickly as I could toward Boston.

****

The last time I'd entered the Hancock tower, I'd been basically under arrest and spent my time between a locked cell and an interrogation room. This time I was whisked upstairs in a private executive elevator to the top floor of the building. When the door opened, I found myself standing in a wide-open executive suite with a three hundred and sixty degree view of Boston. It took my breath away.

"Come sit, Symon," Eden said, and steered me toward a massive glass conference table to the left of what looked like a computer data center she'd set up. A group of people staring at monitors and speaking quietly into headsets turned and looked at us.

"Try not to destroy my new command center, Symon," Eden said with a wry smile. "I just got it up and running."

Other than the dozen or so leather chairs surrounding the large table, and a similarly built desk and chair by the north-facing window bank, the space was sterile. Not a book, piece of paper, or pen to be found anywhere.

"Great view, but a little cold, don't you think?"

Eden smiled.

"What did Aaron want?"

"To clear the air," I replied. I hoped that Eden would take the hint and let it drop.

Nodding to me, Eden said, "Please bring up the offer for Mr. Bryson, and we need the room."

The people manning the computers and phones put down their headsets and left quietly.

"Only a couple people I trust work in here. And until I wall off the conference room and my office, they'll just have to deal with the occasional interruption," Eden said as she waived her hand nonchalantly.

Immediately, the windows changed color to black, obscuring the outside world from view as subtle lighting snapped on, bathing the entire floor in a warm light. A miniature projector popped out of the ceiling and began to hum slightly. Cast on the dark spaces that had only moments before been a panoramic view of the city, now were stunning reproductions of artwork from around the world. What I assumed to be holographic sculptures appeared around the room as well, and a Bach concerto began to play lightly from hidden speakers.

"Are you trying to seduce me or did you want to talk?" I asked.

"Sit," Eden replied.

I did as I was told. The image of a wide-screen monitor appeared, curving around me only a few feet from my face. On the holographic display was a picture of me. Digital text appeared next to my photo. It was a journal of my entire life.

I turned my head toward Eden and the false image turned with me, blocking my view. Unthinking, I swiped at the image with my hand, and it slid away from me a few feet as if I'd physically pushed it. That's when I totally lied.

"I'm not impressed with your toys, Eden. What's this all about?"

"It's about finding the most evil being ever created and who now walks our world, Symon. It's about making sure my sister's sacrifice wasn't in vain. And I need your help."

"Thanks, but I think I've had enough of this weirdness. The quiet life I had in Dublin really appeals to me at the moment." I said, trying not to let images of Eve's death cloud my judgment. "You have plenty of people and power, Eden. I'm sure you and your resources are capable of finding Lucifer yourselves."

Eden reached into her suit jacket, pulled out a piece of paper and tossed it on the conference table. "First class ticket back to Ireland. One way."

I hesitated a moment, then picked it up. "What's the catch?" I asked.

"No catch," she said. "But I will tell you we haven't figured out exactly who used your motorcycle as a bomb to blow up your apartment building in Dublin. So I've arranged for a place for you to stay for a while and for some protection, should you choose to go."

"Uh-huh. Or?"

"Or," Eden said, "you could come back into the fold and help us like you were meant to."

She stood and began to pace, slowly walking around her giant Star Trek holosuite. "Look, Sy," she sounded exasperated now. "Organized religion has controlled the world of magic and knowledge of the Shadow-world for millennia. They dictated to the people for many generations. With the dawning of the mega-corporations and the information age, everything has changed. Even the Church knows that. Why do you think Charles was allowed to train non-Catholics in the art?" Eden asked, turning toward me. "You are the most powerful of all of us. We need you."

"I really don't have a choice, do I?" I said, heavily.

"You do, Symon. You can go back to Europe and try to live a quiet life. We might be able to protect you there. But I ask you to think about a couple of things. Yes, we closed the portal to the Shadow-world, but Lucifer himself is walking in our world. Your failure to banish Belial to the unknown plane surely has warned the residents of Hell that a new power is rising." I opened my mouth to protest the word "failure," but Eden cut me off.

"Symon, Lucifer and his ilk want nothing less than ownership of Earth and its people." she said. "The large-scale war between Heaven and Hell—the Shadow-world war—historically has been in balance, with our world the ultimate prize. That's why it's been more of a 'cold' war then a 'hot' one in the past. But not anymore. If you could poison the world slowly, weaken it, the ultimate result could be changed with very little effort. That is Lucifer's ultimate goal, I'm sure of it."

I just looked at her. "He's been here for ten years poisoning the well."

"Exactly. And look at the results. Economic distress, massive natural disasters, more wars than I can count, Eden sighed. "I can't make you stay. But we sure as hell could use your help. If things continue to go the way they have been..."

She didn't need to finish the sentence. The world would be lost.

No pressure.

"What are you offering?" I asked quietly.

She tossed a thick envelope at me. "It's all there."

I took it without opening it.

"I'll think about it," I said, and walked out.

Chapter Thirty-Nine

I stayed in my room at St. Ignatius that evening, in self-imposed exile. As I stared at the still unopened envelope Eden had given me, I listened to Peter's passionate sermon over the loudspeaker system: the tale of the Prodigal Son in all its glory. I'd forgotten that he could captivate an audience almost as well as Charles could with his sermons.

Much like the younger son of the parable, I'd gone to a distant land, partied my ass off, and returned an empty shell. I'd left for a reason, of course. My own fear of the power I could use. Perhaps even more frightening was the way I could wield it.

"But we had to celebrate and be glad, because this brother of yours was dead and is alive again; he was lost and is found," Peter said, ending the sermon with a final quote from Luke.

Lost and is found, indeed.

I closed my eyes, but sleep never came. All I could see was the devastation brought by two minor demons, the loss of friends, and the mistakes that I'd already made. Around three in the morning I finally got up, showered and got dressed.

I found myself where I'd always ended up during troubling times while living at the parish. The kitchen. It was dark, of course. But I had no difficulty finding my way to the coffee pot and made a cup for myself. I sat at the old butcher block table, switched on the light, and finally opened the envelope. Inside was an employment contract outlining job responsibilities, with a very generous pay and benefits offer. It included the use of a corporate apartment located in a Brownstone on Commonwealth Avenue in Boston. A new home, should I want it.

I found a TV remote and flicked on the small set mounted in the upper corner over the table. The early morning news was the only thing I could find, so I sat with my cuppa and watched the talking heads for a while.

News of famine, rescue efforts in the aftermath of an earthquake in Indonesia, economic disasters, and projections of a devastating hurricane season cycled around twice before I finally turned off the set. Eden was right. The world was on the edge. But could I really help to tip the scales away from the darkness? And what did a contract with Eden's company really mean?

I walked over to the massive stainless steel fridge and opened it. I didn't really feel like eating, but I didn't know what else to do.

I was scrounging around the fridge, contemplating a platter of deviled eggs, when I noticed a large Tupperware bowl with a note on it.

I took both the bowl (which was filled with chicken salad) and the note out, and opened the latter.

Thought you'd be sneaking around in the middle of the night so I left this for you. The rest is for our students, so don't touch! -Peter

He knew me so well.

There was also, I noticed, a postscript—

PS - Eden came by after Mass and left something for you. It's in the vestibule.

I grabbed a fork with my chicken salad and ate while I made my way to see what Eden had left. I still had my Dublin ticket upstairs, so I had no idea what it could be.

Despite the fact that I didn't think I was hungry, I demolished the entire salad during my walk through the dimly lit sanctuary. I mean it was Peter's chicken salad, how could I not eat it?

Anyway, I almost dropped the empty bowl when I got to the vestibule. Sitting there in the corner was a brand new, black Yamaha Super Sport motorbike.

"Wow," I said running my hand over the frame. There was a helmet sitting on the floor next to the bike and I picked it up. Another note was inside.

Thought you could use a little fresh air to think about the offer. -E

As far as bribes went, I had to admit this was a doozey. I mean, she obviously heard me lament the loss of my bike in Dublin when the apartment went ka-blewie. But right now I didn't care. A long bike ride was exactly what I needed.

I hurried back to drop off my used dishes and to leave a quick note of thanks for Peter, grabbed my leather jacket from upstairs and quietly wheeled the bike out front. I noticed the gas tank had already been topped up.

I swung my leg over the saddle and started the motorcycle. The powerful machine purred to life. Putting on my helmet, I popped the clutch and gave it some gas. Like a thoroughbred leaping out of the starting gate, the bike and I, as one, shot down the road.

Eden had been right. A long ride would give me time to think. And I knew exactly where the journey would take me.

Chapter Forty

I got to Maine a few hours later as the sun was beginning to rise. It had been a long ride and I was tired but exhilarated at the same time. Realizing how early it was, I slowed the bike down with the intention of shutting it down before I got within earshot of Janice's house. But she was standing on her front stoop, two mugs of coffee in hand.

I turned off the bike and took off my helmet in astonishment. "How did you know?" I asked.

Just then a hawk swooped down past me and flew into the open front window of Janice's place. I swear that damn bird winked at me.

"A little birdie told me you might be heading this way," she said, handing me a mug. It was steaming hot and most welcome after the chilly ride.

"Give me your jacket and I'll clean it off. It's covered in bug guts," she said, and turned to walk into the house. She paused in the entranceway. "You coming?" she called over her shoulder.

"You're not going to just hose me down in the yard this time?" I asked, following her inside.

"Behave," she said.

"What? What did I do?" I asked, stopping just at the entranceway.

"I wasn't talking to you," she said enigmatically. "I'll be back in a moment. I assume we'll be having a lively discussion about whether or not you'll be staying. Since I already know you will be, your side of the discussion should be fun."

Janice headed into her kitchen, leaving me gob-smacked. "Well if you already know the outcome, why didn't you tell me so I could have gotten some sleep?" I muttered to myself.

"Because you needed the ride up here to clear your head, Symon."

I nearly jumped out of my skin as I turned around and saw an old woman with skin weathered the color of bronze and shockingly white hair pulled back into a ponytail. She was sitting at Janice's dining room table playing with a deck of cards. I hadn't seen this woman in a long time. It was Janice's grandmother.

"I'm sorry, I didn't see you there, Miranda," I said. She hadn't changed a bit since I'd last seen her over ten years before. Down to the clothes she was wearing, she was exactly as I remembered her when she'd beaten me with a broom after catching me and her granddaughter, um, enjoying nature.

"Humph," she snorted. "Never in the moment, are you Symon?" she said, with a twinkle in her eyes.

"No, ma'am. Sorry, ma'am," I said.

"Come here, Symon. I want to show you something."

Hesitantly, and sneaking a quick glance to see if there were any brooms within the old woman's reach, I approached the table. I noticed the cards she was playing with weren't your normal deck. They looked more like tarot cards.

"Sit down, young man," she said, flipping the cards down as she spoke. "You have questions, and the cards can answer them. Shall we see what the cards hold for you?"

Miranda, quite frankly, had always been a little crazy. But if one didn't humor her, one did so at one's own peril. I speak from experience. I sat down. Besides, if I were very lucky, I'd get one of her pumpkin spice muffins. I found myself suddenly craving one. The last time I'd had one was right after my broom beating. But she was like that. Crazy.

Miranda flipped over a card. "This represents the questioner, that's you, boy," She said. "The Foole. It figures."

"Hold on—" I protested.

"Don't be offended." She waved her hand dismissively. "It means that you are about to begin a new journey, one that will overturn the status quo. You have an important decision to make today, young man."

"I know that, that's why I've come to see your granddaughter."

"Even as a little girl, she could always calm the minds of others," said the old medicine woman. "Gifted, my granddaughter is." The old woman looked me in the eye, a slight frown on her brow.

"You broke her heart, Symon. Be very careful what you do from here. She still loves you, although wild buffalo couldn't *drag* an admission out of her. Your decision will affect many, but I ask that you think not only of yourself. Can you do that?"

I stared straight back into her eyes. "Yeah, I think so."

She squinted for a moment, "You'd better be sure, boy. You will have many decisions to make, each one more difficult than the last. You will only get through what's ahead by being the man you were meant to be and controlling your power. Remember the vision I gave you."

"That was *you* on the plane?" I asked.

"What plane, Symon?" asked Janice, as she came into the room. She handed me my jacket. It looked almost new.

"I was just asking your—" I turned to look at Miranda, but she was gone. And so were the tarot cards. The only thing left on the table was a single muffin. Pumpkin spice.

Janice looked at me curiously. "I was just talking to myself. Sorry." I reached over and picked up the muffin and as I did so, I caught movement out of the corner of my eye. A hawk was standing on a wooden perch inside the living room, preening itself.

"So I wanted to talk to you about Eden and what she'd offered," I said, taking a bite out of the muffin. It tasted like heaven.

"I can't make up your mind for you, Symon."

"I understand that," I replied. "But my head and my heart are telling me two different things."

"Oh?" she said, with a knowing look.

"My head is telling me to run as far away from all of this as quickly as possible."

"And your heart?"

I got up from the table and began to pace. "My heart is telling me to grow up. To stay and fight."

"Hmmm," Janice said. "Well, your heart and mind have been in conflict in the past. How did it work out for you?"

"Shitty."

Janice walked over to me and placed a hand on my heart. The silver circle underneath my shirt warmed to her touch.

"Passion is your greatest strength, Symon. I'd listen to your heart."

Her hand remained over my heart. I suddenly knew exactly how it felt to be Daniel before his stint in the lion's den.

"I'll need help," I said.

Janice laughed. "Yeah, because we all were going to make popcorn, sit back with a beer, and watch you take on the world."

"What do you mean?" I asked.

"Come with me, my old love," Janice said, and slipped her hand into mine. She led me toward the back of her home, toward her bedroom.

"Um, Janice?" I asked nervously.

"Don't be a pig," she said, laughter in her voice.

We went through her bedroom and out the double French doors to her back yard. I let go of her hand in surprise.

The back garden of Janice's home was beautiful. Spring flowers bloomed everywhere. Two dear grazed lazily in the sun and there were birds everywhere.

A large patch of perfectly manicured lawn lay off to our left. Sitting on chairs, loungers and the lawn itself were Aaron, Bill, Peter, Eden, Elizabeth, and a few others from Eden's company I recognized from the recent adventure we'd shared. All but Aaron looked up at me.

"He's in," said Janice.

Everyone broke out in applause, even Aaron. As my face turned red with embarrassment, Janice leaned in and whispered, "You have ten years' worth of magic to catch up on, Sy. Time to get started."

THE END

Coming Soon From Pfoxchase

THE YOUNG PRACTITIONER

BOOK TWO

OF

THE ARCANA CHRONICLES

By

R.B. WOOD

Turn the Page for an Exciting Look at
The Young Practitioner

Prologue

North Africa, November, 1942 - 45km west of Tunis

The M4 Sherman tank ground to a halt with a sick sputter from its Continental R975 C1 engine.

"C'mon baby!" begged Captain Ronald "Deuce" Norton as he caressed the turret of the metal beast from his lookout position atop the war machine.

The sputtering continued for another thirty seconds or so, then stopped with a metallic grinding. The beast was dead. Again.

"FUBAR!" drawled a southern voice below the captain from the belly of the beast.

"J.T., it's the second time that damn engine has died in the last hour. Can you fix it or not, Sergeant?"

"Ain't been a machine I couldn't fix, Deuce. You have yourself a genuine Kansas farm boy here! We kin fix anythin' that runs!" replied the happy-go-lucky Sergeant, Jonathan "J.T." Tompkins. Captain Norton rolled his eyes. Would he ever get used to the eternal optimism of this boy?

It was over a hundred degrees already and it was only eight o'clock in the morning. The tank had been a part of a larger American First Armored Division racing Eastbound to join Montgomery and the British for a push toward Tunis. The five-man crew had been told to leave their tank when the engine faltered due to the desert sand, but the crew stubbornly refused to give up their metallic beast.

Now they were on their own, at least an hour behind the rest of the convoy.

"Damn it," muttered Norton, as he wiped the sweat that poured into his eyes. The General was gonna have his ass and he knew it.

He opened his canteen and took a long swig. The water was hot, but at least it was wet. After Pearl Harbor, he'd known the country was going to be at war. He wanted a shot at the Japanese for what they did in Hawaii. Instead he'd been shipped to North Africa and been put in command of a metal hotbox in the middle of the desert.

"Damn it all to hell," he said.

He sighed and climbed out of his command seat lifting his binoculars to his eyes. He took a quick look around. Nothing but a series of dunes in front of them.

"All right boys," he called back into the tank. "Might as well get out of there while the sergeant works his miracle to get us running again."

The Captain climbed the rest of the way out and jumped to the ground. A loud scrambling was heard as the two drivers and gunner tried to climb over each other to reach the hatch first.

Corporal David Bernstein was first. The kid from Brooklyn hopped out with ease and practically had his Lucky Strike lit before he reached the ground. Privates Remco Engel from Massachusetts and Frank Wilson from California were next. All boys around the age of eighteen.

"J.T., you better get us movin' again or we're gonna thump ya," said Bernstein.

"Yeah!" said Wilson, pounding his fist on the outside of the tank.

"Which one of you rubes has the radio?" asked the Captain. The three men all looked at each other sheepishly.

"Engel, go get it will you? Jesus H. Christ, boy!"

Norton didn't like the kid from Massachusetts under his command. His accent sounded German, and he hated Germans almost as much as the Japanese.

"Yessir!" said the Private and hopped back into the Sherman without another word.

"Cap't, can we have him dig a latrine for us when he gets back?" asked Wilson. "K-ration's doin' things to my gut you wouldn't believe."

Before Norton could answer, he felt a sharp pain in his chest. Both Wilson and Bernstein were staring at him wide-eyed.

Norton tried to say 'what are you two assholes lookin' at?' but all that came out was a gurgling sound.

The Captain looked down and saw a red stain on his chest. It was the last thing he would ever see. He was dead before he hit the ground.

"Snipers!" screamed Bernstein in his thick Brooklyn accent. "Take cover behind…"

A red spray flew from the man's head and a bloody, still-lit cigarette bounced off Wilson's shoulder.

"Holy shit!" Wilson said, diving to his right just as a ricochet sounded behind him.

Crawling on the ground, he made his way to the back of the tank. Dirt kicked up around him as sniper fire continued to track his movements.

"You okay Captain?" called Engel from inside the tank.

"Cap's dead and so's Bernstein!" Wilson screamed back.

"Where's the bastard shooting from?" Engel called back.

"Hundred yards, behind a dune off to the right, I think!"

Another shot kicked up sand near Wilson's boot. He drew his legs in close.

"Do something!" he shouted.

The big tank shuddered as the turret spun in the direction Wilson thought the shots had come from.

There was a couple of clicking sounds, then nothing.

"Damn you Engel...!" began Wilson.

The 75mm canon roared and a second or two later there was a muffled explosion. Wilson put his hands over his ears and closed his eyes.

****

Twenty minutes later, Engel and J.T. emerged from their steel foxhole. They found Wilson shaking and lying in the fetal position at the back of the tank. The man had pissed himself.

Engel had put a couple more shells into the various dunes around them, but no additional shots came from the hills.

While J.T. checked on Wilson, Engel went over to the two bodies lying next to the tank. Captain Norton and Corporal Bernstein were both very dead.

"J.T.," said Engel. "Get on the radio and get us some help. I'll get Wilson back into the tank, ok?"

After a fleeting look of annoyance, J.T. nodded and said, "You got it Engel."

Engel heard J.T. on the handset. The Dutchman from Massachusetts knelt by Wilson.

"J.T." Engel shouted a moment later. The Kansas native went to the back of the tank to find Engel kneeling over a dead man in a pool of blood. It was only the two of them now.

"He ... must have been hit," said Engel, his voice shaking.

"Jesus, Engel," said J.T. "That leaves just you and me, man." Looking around, squinting, J.T. continued. "Wish we could see if we got them Huns. Command is sending someone, but it might be a day or two 'til they get here."

"The Captain had a pair of glasses. I'll go find them and take a look around. It would be nice to be able to dig in until help arrives."

Engel found the late captain's binoculars about three yards from the dead man. After wiping off a bit of the commander's blood, he scoped out the sand dunes ahead.

As he slowly panned around him, Engel's eyes picked up something unusual near where he'd planted the first shell. A reflection-like metal of some sort imbedded in the sand.

"Hey J.T.," he called out. "I am going to go scout up ahead. Keep your head down, ok?"

"You too Engel. Put your helmet on!" the Kansas man called back.

Despite the heat, and with a glance at what was left of Bernstein's head, Engel slapped on his helmet.

Cautiously, and using whatever cover he could find, it took all of twenty minutes for the soldier to make it to the dune blown apart by the tank's main gun.

The crater he'd blown into the dune was about twenty feet long and five feet high. When he got closer he saw that it was about five feet deep as well.

Scattered behind the crater he saw what was left of two dead men. It wasn't until he found half of a German helmet with the stylized eagle on it that he confirmed who'd been killed.

"Serves you guys right," he spat.

Engel took out the glasses again and swept the area. There was nothing else to see.

With a sigh of relief, he started to make his way back to the Sherman tank, when he caught sight of the metal piece that had brought him out here in the first place.

Sticking out of the dune was a heavy plate of lead. It was roughly two feet square and showed blast damage where the 75mm shell had dislodged it.

"What the hell is that?" he mumbled to himself. The sweat was pouring off him like a river and he'd long since drunk the contents of his canteen.

The impact crater was deep—deeper than Engel had originally thought. He stumbled through the sand toward the gaping hole.

The shell had torn a gash in what looked like a large lead box running the length of the sand dune. Curiosity overriding dehydration, Engel poked his head into the box.

He recoiled in disbelief.

Half running, half stumbling through the sand, he made his way back to the tank, laughing to himself.

J.T., who'd had enough of the stench inside the Sherman, had poked his head out of the turret hatch. He watched as Engel made a beeline toward him.

"What is it Engel? More Nazis?" he yelled.

Engel clambered onto the tank, completely out of breath.

"Here, hold on a minute," said J.T. He reached down into the tank and brought out a canteen.

Engel gulped down the contents.

"Jesus Private, you're white as a ghost," J.T. said nervously. "What's wrong with you?"

"My ... my shot killed the snipers," Engel stuttered. "But it blew a hole in this big metal box."

"Yeah, so?"

"There's a body in it," said Engel, still breathing heavy.

"It's war, Rem," said J.T. as he pointed to the late Captain still lying where he fell.

"No, you do not understand," Engel said. "It looks like a man, but cannot be. It would be a man about twenty feet tall!"

"Heat's got to you boy," said J.T. shaking his head.

"Come see for yourself," Engel said, nervously laughing to himself.

"What, and get shot? No thanks," said J.T.

"I got the Germans with the first shot. Come see for yourself, or are you chicken?" said Engel.

The jibe worked. Without another word, J.T. jumped down from the turret and marched purposely toward the dune. Engel hurried to catch up.

"It's gotta be fake!" J.T. exclaimed a few minutes later.

"It's not. It is some sort of monster," Engel said. "And it has been buried here a long time."

"How the hell do you know that?" J.T. said dubiously.

"Look at the bandages," Engel replied. "It is like an Egyptian mummy. Like I've seen in the movies."

"What is it doing out here all by itself?" J.T. asked.

"It is not alone, J.T." said Engel quietly, pointing. "Look."

J.T. stood and looked where Rem indicated. There were hundreds of mounds exactly the same size and shape of the giant's tomb.

"Jesus H. Christ, Rem," said J.T. "It's a Goddamn grave yard."

"Yes," said Engel. "It is. I cannot believe I actually found it." In one fluid, rapid motion, Engel grabbed his side arm, put it to J.T.'s temple and pulled the trigger.

The young man from Kansas fell over, dead long before his body stopped twitching. Engel reached down and picked up the bloodied radio his victim had dropped. He switched it to a channel he knew to be monitored.

Looking at the open giant's tomb, he clicked a button on the handset.

"Betrieb erfüllt," he said. *"Sagen Sie dem Führer fand ich die alte Begräbnisstätte."*

CHAPTER ONE

I was startled awake by the sound of bullets ricocheting off the armor plating of the big black sedan that was taking me to my old parish church; St. Ignatius. It was three in the morning.

"Ah, for fuck sake! What the hell, Crystal?"

Crystal McIntyre, my driver and personal assistant to Eden Engel, the CEO of my current employer, Engel Associates, glanced at me via the review mirror.

"Thought you could use the adrenaline rush, Mr. Bryson, so I arranged to have us shot at."

"Funny girl. Where are they?"

"On a motorcycle to our left. Two riders, the one in the back has an Uzi."

As if on cue, bullets again raked the Towncar. Crystal jerked the wheel hard to the left, pushing the would-be assassins into on-coming traffic. Horns blared and there was a screeching of tires. Even at three in the morning, there was traffic on the Mass Avenue Bridge connecting Boston to Cambridge.

I'd received a call twenty minutes ago from Father Peter Fine, parish priest at St. Ignatius, asking for my immediate presence at the church. After that cryptic request, the line had gone dead.

The guys on the bike avoided becoming road pizza and were back on our heels.

"This is the third time in as many months. I thought your boss ran a security company," I muttered under my breath.

"It's your company too, Mr. Bryson. There's a MAC10 under your seat if you feel like helping out while I drive." Crystal slammed on the brakes and yanked the wheel to the right. The car spun sideway and bounced over the curb onto Memorial Drive.

"Spraying bullets all over the place is messy. I've a better idea."

As the car roared down Memorial Drive with the Evel Knievel twins in pursuit, I closed my eyes. The last two hit teams had been killed before I could find out who the hell they were. This time, I wanted someone alive to question.

I calmed my mind. Time seemed to slow and my senses sharpened. I could smell Crystal's perfume, mixing with the leather scent of the seats. I could feel the tires of the Towncar spinning on the pavement, and I knew the left front tire was slowly losing air. I could sense the desperation and the determination of the assassins behind us.

I could feel the magic flowing through me.

"Stop the car," I said slowly. "Now."

The black sedan squealed to a sliding halt. Before the car came to a stop, I was out the back and standing in the middle of the road facing my adversaries.

An electric sensation coursed through my veins, the ring finger of my right hand began to heat up, and a voice in my head said, "*Wait...*"

I felt the vibration of the motorbike as at roared toward me. My focus was solely on the bike, the riders and the gun spitting fire from its muzzle.

"*Sinum,*" I thought.

Little sparks jumped all around me as bullets harmlessly disintegrated as they came into contact with my shield spell.

"*Now!*" said the voice in my head.

What was once a silver ring on my right hand transformed into a six-foot black staff. In one fluid motion, I sidestepped the motorcycle and used the staff to clothesline both of the riders.

The bike careened wildly and momentum carried it into the side of the Towncar where it shattered upon impact. The two assassins hit the pavement and slid across the road, slamming into the wreckage of their bike and the sedan. The back of the big black car was destroyed.

I just know I'm gonna have to pay for that.

The ring was once again on my finger as I turned toward our injured assailants. One was sprawled in the middle of the wreckage and lay motionless. The other, the one who'd been shooting at us, was moving feebly, trying to crawl over to where his gun had dropped on the road.

"*Aduro*," I said, pointing a finger at the weapon. The metal immediately turned white hot and melted into the blacktop.

I slowly walked over to the crawling man—who was still trying to reach for the molten remains of his weapon—and squat down next to him.

He was dressed in a heavy, expensive-looking black leather jump suit, wearing a custom-made French Ruby helmet that had cracked like an egg when his head had bounced off the pavement.

I ripped off the pieces of the helmet and was surprised to see the bleeding face of a woman. She had long black hair, dark eyes and what would have been a beautifully sculpted face had she not broken her nose and split her lip in the crash.

Those dark eyes looked up at me.

"Who are you?" I asked.

She coughed. More blood dribbled from her mouth.

"Who I am does not matter, Symon," she said with a slight accent. "What matters is you grow more powerful by the day and that you must be stopped. I have failed in this, but more will come."

"More of who?" I asked, firmer now.

"Is she alive? Who is she?" asked Crystal who had appeared at my side.

The woman's eyes went wide. She said something in a language that was vaguely familiar to me, and then her body went slack.

"Yes, and I don't know," I answered Crystal. "She's gonna need an ambulance. I'm no good at healing magic."

"I've already called for one and for backup," the redhead said. "The police will be here shortly. I'll stay and take care of this mess. The Church is only a mile from here and another car will pick you up across the park. Go."

"What about the other rider?"

"Dead. Go, Mr. Bryson. Ms. Engel will be pissed if she has to bail you out of jail again."

****

A second Towncar was already waiting for me when I crossed through the park. I could hear sirens in the background and was relieved to see a big brute of a man standing by the idling vehicle.

"Evening Flint," I said.

"Three AM and you're already causing problems, Bryson. Get in."

The bald man opened the back door and I was thankful to climb into the warm interior of the sedan. The early morning fall air was chilly, but expending power had dropped my body temperature a few degrees. Between the cold, and the after-effect of the spellcasting, I was shaking like a leaf. What was supposed to have been a twenty-minute car ride from my brownstone in Boston to St. Ignatius in Cambridge had turned ... complicated.

"It wasn't my fault this time Flint," I said as the man squeezed himself behind the wheel. "People just keep shooting at me."

"I don't blame them," said Flint.

Ever since we'd met earlier this year, a grudging respect had grown between us. We still hated each other, mind you. But it was a respectful hatred. Even though the man hadn't an ounce of magical ability, he could still handle himself in situations that would send normal people to the loony bin. Or the morgue.

We drove the last few minutes in silence. When we finally arrived in the old Cambridge neighborhood that was the home of my former school, we immediately knew something was wrong.

St. Ignatius was lit up like Christmas Eve mass. Even the newly refurbished dormitories were ablaze with light, which meant all the young students rescued last spring were up and about.

"This doesn't look good," I muttered. "Flint, any idea what's going on?"

"Just that the Father wanted to see you right away, Bryson. He didn't use the distress-word nor did any alarms go off, so we didn't call in the cavalry. Just you."

I got out of the car, told Flint to wait, and hurried up the steps. I opened the large oak doors into the cathedral and was almost run over by a tall black man wearing all black vestments with a white collar—Father William Duncan—an old friend and fellow practitioner.

"Bill!" I said, startled at his appearance. He looked disheveled and was extremely pale.

"Oh thank God you're finally here, Symon," said Bill.

"What's going on?"

"It's Jasmine. She's back."

When Bill and I, along with a few others, had been living at St. Ignatius as orphaned kids with special talents the Church wanted to exploit, Bill had had a serious relationship with a college girl two years older than he from the neighborhood. A brilliant science major named

Jasmine DuPre. We'd all thought he's end up marrying her, but God apparently had other plans for the now ordained priest.

"How is she? Is everything okay?"

"She's ... fine," Bill said hesitantly. "She's asked for sanctuary for her ... and her son, Isaac."

"Why?"

"She hasn't said yet," Bill said. "All Jasmine's said is that she wants protection and that she needs to speak directly to you. That's when Peter called."

"Where are they?"

"In the nave ... but Symon," Bill said grabbing my arm. "There is something about her son ... he has power."

"Our kind of power?" I asked.

"Yes, and no," said mysteriously. "Come see for yourself."

I walked with Bill through the foyer into the nave and stopped dead in my tracks.

The pews were filled with students from the school. I could see Peter, along with Aaron North, former detective of the Cambridge PD, and Janice Williams; my former lover, Narragansett shaman and all around pain-in-the ass, as well. They were all silent and pointing at the east wall behind the altar.

Floating in front of a statue of Christ on the Cross, suspended thirty feet off the ground was a child of about ten, completely engulfed in flame. Seemingly unbothered by the fire, he hung in front of the image of Christ, studying the statue.

"Mommie," said the miniature human torch. "Why is Jesus so dusty?"

"That's Isaac," said Bill quietly. "He's—he's my son."

ABOUT THE AUTHOR

R.B. Wood is a technology consultant and a writer of Urban Fantasy, Science Fiction and quite frankly anything else that strikes his fancy. He is working on the follow up to The Prodigal's Foole, as well as a Science Fiction trilogy and a collaborative comic book project. He is also host of The Word Count podcast.

R.B. currently lives in Boston with his partner, Tina, his dog Jack, three cats and various other critters that visit from time to time.

Feel free to contact him at:

WEB: http://www.rbwood.com

FACEBOOK: http://www.facebook.com/rbwoodwriter

The Word Count Podcast:
http://itunes.apple.com/podcast/the-word-count/id392550989

Made in the USA
Charleston, SC
15 October 2011